Readers love ARIEL TACHNA's
Partnership in Blood novels

I0614017

"I absolutely love this series."
—Romance Junkies

"I've thoroughly enjoyed the premise for these books and the characters, and recommend them to any reader who enjoys paranormal fantasy; especially those involving vampires, wizards and magic."
— Literary Nymphs Reviews

"…an amazingly well written series that I know that paranormal romantics will enjoy."
—Night Owl Reviews

"[Reparation in Blood] is action packed and full of fascinating and amazing characters. A worthwhile read and fitting end to the series."
—Bitten by Books

"This series is definitely for anyone looking for a new twist on Vampires, and who likes a bit of angst and a bit of adventure mixed into their romance."
—Dark Diva Reviews

"Ariel Tachna has created a truly original version of the vampire archetype…"
—Steve Williams, Suite 101

http://www.dreamspinnerpress.com

By Ariel Tachna

All For One (with Nicki Bennett)
Best Ideas
Château d'Eternité
Checkmate (with Nicki Bennett)
Fallout
Her Two Dads
Highland Lover
In Search of Fireworks
The Inventor's Companion
The Matelot
Music of the Heart
Once in a Lifetime
Out of the Fire
Overdrive
The Path
Rediscovery
Revelations in the Dark
Riding Double (Dreamspinner Anthology)
Rose Among the Ruins
Seducing C.C.
Stolen Moments
A Summer Place
Sutcliffe Cove (with Madeleine Urban)
Testament to Love
Under the Skin (with Nicki Bennett)
Why Nileas Loved the Sea

THE EXPLORING LIMITS SERIES (WITH NICKI BENNETT)
Exploring Limits • Stretching Limits • Refining Limits
Breaking Limits • Transcending Limits • No Limits

GAMES LOVERS PLAY
Amorous Liaison • Best Behavior • Ride 'em Cowboy

HOT CARGO
Hot Cargo (with Nicki Bennett) • Something About Harry (with Nicki Bennett)
Healing in His Wings

LANG DOWNS
Inherit the Sky • Chase the Stars • Outlast the Night • Conquer the Flames

PARTNERSHIP IN BLOOD
Alliance in Blood • Covenant in Blood • Conflict in Blood • Reparation in Blood
Perilous Partnership • Reluctant Partnerships • Lycan Partnership • Partnership Reborn

AVAILABLE AT DREAMSPINNER PRESS
http://www.dreamspinnerpress.com

Reparation in Blood

ARIEL TACHNA

Partnership in Blood:
Volume Four

Dreamspinner Press

Published by
DREAMSPINNER PRESS

5032 Capital Circle SW, Suite 2, PMB# 279, Tallahassee, FL 32305-7886 USA
http://www.dreamspinnerpress.com/

Reparation in Blood
© 2014 Ariel Tachna.

ISBN: 978-1-63216-666-1
Digital ISBN: 978-1-63216-667-8
Library of Congress Control Number: 2014950196
Second Edition October 2014
First Edition published by Dreamspinner Press, October 2009

Printed in the United States of America
∞
This paper meets the requirements of
ANSI/NISO Z39.48-1992 (Permanence of Paper).

To my adopted sisters, Nancy, Holly, Connie, Cat, Carol, Madeleine, Gwen, and Julianne, who read and reread and edit and encourage. Without you, this dream would never have come to pass.

Chapter 1

THIERRY FROWNED as he sat at the kitchen table watching Alain. It had not even been twenty-four hours since Orlando was captured and already his best friend looked haggard, physical and emotional exhaustion wreaking havoc on him. Thierry feared what would happen if those hours stretched into days. He was even more afraid of them stretching into weeks—weeks Orlando did not have, since he could only feed from Alain.

His mind raced with possibilities for finding the missing vampire. Night patrols were searching every location Monique Leclerc, the defector wizard, could identify as a place Serrier had used in the hopes of catching a break and finding Orlando that way, but she had been very honest about the fact that the dark leader deliberately kept his forces fragmented so that anyone captured could only reveal a portion of his plans and hideouts. Thierry was not completely sure how he felt about placing so much importance on her information, but it was the best lead they had at the moment since the wizards they captured during the battle at place Pigalle either knew nothing of value or feared Serrier's retribution should they talk more than they feared going to jail. Thierry was not sure he blamed them. With the exception of Raymond, every wizard who had talked in exchange for a lighter sentence had met a nasty end in prison, despite the best efforts of the wardens.

He watched helplessly as Alain pushed the chair back, the legs scraping harshly across the white tiles on the kitchen floor. His face contorted, he began pacing, a caged lion with no way to escape the confines of its cell. "You're going to wear yourself out and then you'll be no good to Orlando when we do find him," Thierry scolded, though he knew his admonishment would meet with scorn.

He was right.

"Like you'd be sitting here calmly if Sebastien were the one in their hands," Alain snarled.

"No, I wouldn't be," Thierry agreed, "and you'd be sitting where I am, reminding me to take care of myself."

"I should be out searching for him," Alain protested. "I have the best chance of sensing him if they've got him hidden!"

"Maybe," Thierry allowed, "but you can't go with every patrol—that would take too long. It's faster to let them do their jobs while you rest. We aren't sending inexperienced people into the sites. They know Serrier's tricks."

Alain shook his head, but Thierry ignored him. "You've barely slept since he was taken, except for the few hours I knocked you out. You can't go on like that and expect to be able to feed Orlando when he *is* rescued." He emphasized the word *is*, absolutely refusing to consider what might happen to both Alain and Orlando if they could not find the vampire in time.

Alain's face crumpled. "You don't understand," he insisted. "He can't feed from anyone else but me, so he's going to be slower to recover from whatever they do to him." He struggled to explain thoughts and feelings that defied rationality. "He's the other half of me, Thierry. It feels like my soul's being torn in two, just being apart from him. And when I can feel him hurting, it's even worse. I can't rest because he can't."

Thierry did not ask how that had happened in less than a month. He did not have to. He had a partner of his own, albeit without the added depth of the brand on Alain's neck. He could not sense Sebastien's emotions the way Alain could sense Orlando's, but he knew he would be just as frantic, just as far beyond reason, if Sebastien were missing instead of simply out on his way to get Alain's clothes from Orlando's apartment.

"I do understand," Thierry replied softly. A slight blush stained his cheeks as he thought about everything that had transpired between Sebastien and himself since their first meeting, culminating in their lovemaking the night before.

The look on Thierry's face was so at odds with his usual demeanor that it roused Alain from his self-absorption. Not even Thierry's blush was enough to supplant Orlando in his thoughts, but Thierry had been his best friend for thirty years. He would not be much of a friend if he could not acknowledge the change in the other man's life, despite the turmoil in his own. "Being with Sebastien seems to agree with you. You look happy again in a way you haven't in a long time."

Thierry's blush deepened. "I knew from watching you and Orlando together that making love with a vampire would be even more amazing than just having one feed from me, but I hadn't even come close to imagining what it felt like to have his fangs in my neck when we.... Sorry," he broke off, seeing the odd look on Alain's face, "too much information."

"It's not that," Alain replied, his voice tight with suppressed emotion. "It's just that we never... Orlando never fed from me while we made love. He was afraid he'd hurt me."

"Merde," Thierry cursed under his breath. "I'm sorry, Alain. I can't seem to say anything right tonight."

"There isn't anything to say," Alain said hoarsely. "He had his reasons and I have to respect that." He turned away, not wanting Thierry to see the depth of his pain, made worse by the accidental comment. He should have known he could not hide from Thierry, though. A comforting hand settled on his shoulder.

"We'll get him back," Thierry promised, "and when we do, you can change his mind."

"That's the worst part," Alain rasped. "I think he *had* changed his mind, but there wasn't time. We got the news of the attack at place Pigalle and spent the evening focused on that. And then he was captured."

"Then in the office before we left, you weren't...?" Thierry began.

"He jerked me off as he fed, but that's hardly making love," Alain explained. "You arrived right at the end."

"I'm sorry. If I'd known, I wouldn't have interrupted," Thierry apologized.

Alain shrugged, but his emotions were raw in his voice. "You couldn't have known, but even if you had, there wasn't time. I wouldn't have wanted to share something that intimate for the first time in the office anyway. I just wish we'd had more time."

"You'll have the time," Thierry promised. "We'll get him back and end this war and you'll have the rest of your life to discover everything about each other. You have to believe that."

"You tell me that, and then you won't let me do anything to find him!" Alain shouted.

"What would you do that we aren't already doing?" Thierry demanded. "Tell me one thing you can do right now that no one else can do just as well and I'll stop hassling you to rest and let you go do it. One thing, Alain."

Alain opened his mouth to reply, only to shut it again, frustration easily visible on his face. "Damn it, Thierry, I can't just sit here and do nothing!"

"You aren't going to sit anywhere," Thierry replied firmly. "As soon as Sebastien gets back, you're going to take a shower, change clothes, and go to sleep, if I have to knock you out myself. On second thought, the shower can wait for tomorrow. You have to sleep or you won't be able to search tomorrow either. Orlando needs you strong, not on the verge of collapse."

"Fuck you," Alain snarled angrily, pulling away from Thierry and stalking toward the door. "I don't know why you think you know what's best for me, but you don't. Not this time. I'm not going to stay here and listen to your platitudes and condescending attitude. If you won't help me find him, then I'll do it on my own."

The words hurt, even knowing the irrationality that motivated them. They hurt enough that Thierry did not react immediately, biting back his own temper as he tried to keep the shouting match from escalating. Alain apparently did not need any input from Thierry to keep the argument going, though.

"Are you jealous?" Alain snapped, turning back when he reached the door. "Is that why you won't help me? Or are you just too interested in dragging Sebastien back into bed when he gets here to give a shit about what they're doing to Orlando?"

"Don't even go there," Thierry growled back, his temper getting the better of him. "You know I busted my balls last night and all day today trying to find him, but I'm exhausted, you're exhausted, and the only reason Sebastien isn't is because he's a vampire. There isn't any more we can do tonight."

"What's going on?" Sebastien asked, walking into the tense situation.

Alain's head turned, his glare transferring to the vampire, but whatever words sprang to his lips never passed them. Thierry hit him in the side with a sleeping spell before they could. Sebastien's quick reflexes kept the unconscious wizard from hitting the floor.

"You should have let him fall," Thierry muttered. "Ungrateful bastard."

Sebastien's eyebrows shot up. "What in the world happened?" he asked again, hefting Alain over his shoulder and starting toward the bedroom. "I've never seen you act that way toward Alain."

"Dump him in bed and I'll tell you," Thierry answered, the sting of Alain's accusations still strong.

Sebastien carried the other wizard into the guest room and settled him on the bed, pulling off his shoes so he could sleep more comfortably. He set down the bag of Alain's things he was carrying where the wizard would see it when he awoke and returned to the kitchen. "Okay, what's going on?"

Thierry sighed. "I haven't a fucking clue. We were talking—of course, he wants to keep searching for Orlando even though he's completely strung out—and then he asked about you... about us. I answered his question honestly because I've never had any secrets from him, and it hit a nerve. And the next thing I know, he's shouting at me, accusing me of keeping him from going after Orlando because I'm jealous of their bond or because I just want to get you in bed again. How can he think that?"

"He doesn't think it," Sebastien insisted. "He isn't thinking at all. He's absolutely out of his mind with worry and fear. Imagine what it would feel like to be forced to sit and watch Serrier torture Alain. You're in the room, but you can't say anything, can't do anything to stop it. All you can do is suffer with him. That's what Alain's going through with Orlando. He can't see it, but he can feel Orlando's pain, and he's helpless. And it's driving him to say and do things he doesn't mean and would never normally do. But he can't stop himself because he's hurting and so he lashes out at the people around him. He knows, on some level, that nothing he does would be enough to break your friendship and so he's letting all the filth inside him out at you."

"It wasn't even the things he said," Thierry mused softly, Sebastien's presence calming him. "It was the hateful way he said them, like he wanted to hurt me."

"He probably did," Sebastien admitted. "In some twisted way, it probably made him feel less alone to know you were miserable too." He took a deep breath and forced himself to remember the darkest days of his life.

"When Thibaut died, I was angry at the universe. The cruel irony of the Aveu de Sang is that the Avoué can't be turned because his partner can't drain him or her, but in the first flush of love, I didn't consider that. He was young. I didn't think about what would happen when he was old. So there I was, holding the body of my Avoué, alone for the first time in almost sixty years. Vampires came to hold vigil with me, but I didn't want company. I wanted to be alone to grieve. The anger was eating me up inside so I lashed out at everyone, trying to drive them away. Some of them went, but one woman stayed and let me pour out all that ugliness until I was exhausted and had nothing else to give. I asked her finally why she put up with that, and she told me I had to get it out or go insane with it—and she refused to see another vampire perish from bottled-up grief. I never saw her again after that night. She came to comfort me and left again, taking my pain with her."

"So what will happen now?"

"I don't know," Sebastien admitted. "Alain's the human half of the Aveu de Sang, not the vampire half, and I don't know of any cases where the human lost the vampire rather than the other way around. I'm sure it's happened. I just don't know of any instances. And Orlando isn't lost. Missing, yes, but not lost, at least not yet, so Alain has hope to hold onto. Of course, that could complicate things, even make them worse as his grief wars with that hope. I just don't know."

"Can you think of any other way to find Orlando that we haven't already tried?" Thierry asked instead. "Alain can sense him. Can we use that?"

"Maybe," Sebastien replied. "I could always tell if Thibaut was home when I got there if I'd been out at night, could always tell when he came home even before I heard him moving around. Alain says it isn't directional, but he might be able to narrow down where to search by the strength of the feelings. We'll just have to experiment and see."

"It would be easy enough to create a grid in the city and check each one to see if the feeling got stronger or weaker," Thierry mused aloud. "The more areas we eliminate, the more we'd be able to concentrate our forces."

"And because Alain would have to be involved, it would ease some of his frustration at doing nothing."

"Not to mention giving him a reason not to block the bond the way Marcel wants him to do while he's on duty," Thierry added. "If that helps ease a little of his guilt, maybe he'll be able to focus more clearly on using the bond to tell us something useful in the search."

Sebastien nodded. "You should sleep, too, while he's out. If this morning was any indication, once your spell wears off, he'll be fighting to go again."

Thierry smiled sadly. "I used a stronger spell this time than last night. Hopefully that'll buy us a little more time, but you're right." He offered the vampire his hand. "I can't even imagine what torture he's going through." He shuddered. "I'm not jealous of their bond and I'm not unaware of how much Alain's hurting, but if he'd accused me of being glad it wasn't you, he'd have been right."

Sebastien took the outstretched hand, walking at Thierry's side toward their bedroom. "That's a perfectly normal reaction. I felt the same way when Laurent was killed. I wouldn't wish that pain on anyone, but I was ridiculously thankful it wasn't you."

Crossing the threshold, Thierry pulled the vampire's slighter form against his, holding on. Sebastien returned the embrace, their bodies resting together, each drawing strength and solace from the other's presence. With unspoken agreement, they undressed each other and climbed into bed, lying face to face, arms around each other in silent support until Thierry's eyes finally closed in sleep.

THE WAVE of anger Orlando felt from Alain surprised him. He understood the frustration, the fear, the grief, but this was a new emotion. The vampire felt his fangs begin to elongate, his hackles rising at the thought of someone upsetting his wizard.

He tried to project back calming thoughts, assuring Alain of his relative safety and of the depth of his love, but the emotions did not seem to penetrate. Concern growing, Orlando rose to pace the room. He did not know what had happened to work Alain up into the frenzy that came through their bond, but not being able to go to his lover, to soothe him, was a physical ache in Orlando's chest. Angrily, he rattled the door to his prison cell, but the lock was as secure as the first time he had tried.

As suddenly as the anger had begun, it ended, sending a jolt of panic through Orlando. It took a moment to realize that Alain was asleep. He frowned, the contrast between the vibrancy of the anger and the calm of Alain's sleeping mind striking him as odd, until he remembered that his lover was a wizard, undoubtedly surrounded by other wizards. He would not put it past Thierry or Marcel to put Alain to sleep, if that was what it took to calm him down.

Relaxing a little, he returned to the narrow cot that was the only furniture in the room, the springs poking him through the thin mattress. Still, Orlando thought, it could be worse. He could have nowhere to lie but on the stone floor.

The rattle of a key in the lock drew his attention. He rose to his feet, preferring to face whoever came through the door from a position of relative power. If he had the chance to fight, he intended to take it. The wizards could overpower him with their magic, but physically they were no match for his preternatural strength.

The big wizard, the one who used to be Alain's friend, stood at the door, wand in hand. "You're Eric Simonet, aren't you?" Orlando asked before the wizard could bind him.

The question took Eric completely off guard. "Why do you want to know?" he demanded.

"Alain told me about you," Orlando replied simply. "He misses you."

Eric frowned, not wanting to hear such things. They made his job so much more difficult. Especially now. "That's in the past," he ground out.

"For you, maybe, but not for him."

"You know him well?" Eric asked, remembering that he had seen this vampire fighting at Magnier's side during the battle where he was taken.

Orlando did not answer, unable to force himself to deny it, yet not willing to give the dark wizards any information that might help them.

Eric took the silence as an affirmation. "I have only one regret," he told the vampire. "That he and Thierry hate me now."

"They don't!" Orlando protested. "They would welcome you back with open arms."

"It's too late for that. Serrier's waiting for you."

Chapter 2

DAVID TOLD himself he was a fool for coming to Sang Froid uninvited, especially after the way he and Angélique had argued the last time they were alone together. He had fought at her side during the battle at place Pigalle, determined not to leave her unprotected regardless of the personal tension between them—but he didn't have the excuse of Milice business, the alliance, or her protection now. He only had the inexplicable gut feeling that she needed him.

Her manager showed him in silently, not asking questions, simply guiding him to the door of her private quarters and leaving him there. He raised his hand to knock, knuckles hovering an inch from the door. He realized with a twinge he had absolutely no idea how she would react to his arrival. He was her partner, but she considered him neither friend nor lover, despite the fact he would have liked to be both.

His hand fell to the doorknob, turning it and walking inside. Angélique stood by the open window, wrapped tightly in a thick shawl, her arms wrapped around her waist as she stared blindly at the starry sky. He wanted to go to her and offer comfort, but he was afraid she would take it the wrong way. She had already accused him of thinking she was weak because of her past. Implying now that she was not independent enough to deal with whatever was bothering her would only make matters worse. He knew that, and yet he felt compelled to check on her.

She turned at the sound of his footsteps, dark eyes luminous as she stared at him for a moment. He opened his mouth to speak, to ask what was wrong, but before he could say anything, she was moving toward him, reaching for him, inviting the embrace he had wanted to offer. His arms closed tightly around her, feeling the slight shivers that wracked her body. He crooned to her softly, his hands stroking up and down her back in silent comfort.

Angélique shuddered more strongly as she let down her guard, now that she did not have to face the memory of Karine's broken body alone. She did not know what had brought David to her, but she did not care. She needed him and he was here. Nothing else mattered at the moment. One large hand moved up to cradle the back of her head, holding her against his shoulder, sliding through her long hair with soothing repetitiveness. Slowly, she felt herself relax.

Her body went limp in his arms, but he could feel the underlying unease that remained. He kneaded gently at the stiff muscles of her back, a frown forming as he realized how upset she truly was. Glancing around the living room, he saw a doorway leading to a hall. "You need to relax. Come with me."

He led her down the corridor, opening doors until he found the bathroom, pleased to see a large claw-foot tub against the wall. He opened the taps and poured in a generous measure of bath salts he saw on the shelf above the tub, then he turned back to Angélique, loosening the brocade shawl from around her shoulders. Keeping his touch as impersonal as possible, he unbuttoned her blouse, eyes drawn inevitably to the fading henna marks on her breasts and belly. He resisted the urge to trace them again as he had done when they were fresh, setting her shirt aside neatly and unfastening her skirt.

She stood unmoving as he undressed her, making him wonder if she was in shock. He studied her eyes, the pupils dilated, though that could be as much from the dim light in the room as from shock. He folded her skirt and put it on top of her blouse. A glance at her feet revealed soft slippers so he unsnapped the clasp on her bra, pointedly ignoring his body's reaction to her full breasts, and slid off the matching underwear. He piled her hair messily on top of her head, securing it with a clip and trying not to think how it highlighted the tempting curve of her neck. Testing the temperature of the water, he urged her to step out of her slippers and into the tub.

She moved mechanically, sitting down in the chest-deep water, the bubbles hiding her from his gaze again. Seeing her settled, he started toward the door, intending to find her a brandy or something, anything to help restore her to herself. The touch of her hand on his startled him. "Don't go," she whispered, her voice barely audible. "Don't leave me alone."

He turned back immediately, the quiet pleading in her voice so different from her usual, assertive tone that it overcame any hesitation he had about watching her in her bath. "Do you want to tell me what happened?"

"No," she answered honestly, her eyes closing as the words conjured up images she would rather forget. She knew they would never completely leave her, one more set of nightmares to haunt her resting mind.

David accepted the demurral, sitting on the rug next to the tub. He folded her hand between his, thumb stroking her wrist gently, comfortingly, as he traced the lines of henna on her skin.

Eyes closed, the sight of the blood on Karine's body haunted her, bringing back memories she tried to suppress. Most of the sultan's guests had been well mannered, not wanting to lose her master's favor, but the slave master who had first trained her had not been so kind. She knew all too well the terror of being forced onto her back, onto her knees, body used with no concern for her pain. He had been careful not to mark her, but he had been determined to break her, to turn her into a slave with no thought other than her master's pleasure. "They raped that poor girl before they killed her," she said hoarsely, a shudder going through her as she remembered the fear of those early days, never knowing when her body would be used, or by whom. She had put that experience behind her once she was in the harem. At least there, she was always given time to prepare herself for her lovers, allowed the freedom of movement to guide their interactions in ways that brought her pleasure as well. She rarely thought of the slave master now, but finding Karine had brought it all back.

"What girl?" David asked softly, unaware of the situation.

"Jean's… friend, Karine," Angélique said, realizing she did not know what other title to give the young woman. "Her body was dumped on my doorstep this morning. She'd been tortured horribly and brutally raped before…." Her voice broke on the words, unable to finish her sentence.

"Don't think about it anymore," David instructed, though he knew that was easier said than done. "Concentrate on what you're feeling now. The hot water relaxing you, the sandalwood bath salts soaking into your skin, the scent filling your nose. Let everything else go."

None of those things provided sufficient distraction, but the touch of his hand did. Turning her hand so their fingers entwined, she pulled him toward her, bringing his palm to her cheek and resting against it. His fingers stroked the smooth skin of her cheek, one digit sliding lower, behind her ear, sending a shiver of a very different sort through her. Rising to her feet, the water sluicing down her skin, she reached for a towel, pressing it into his hands invitingly.

David took the towel, desire kicking him hard in the gut as she bent to let the water out of the tub, then straightened again, body on full display. He pushed that emotion aside, though. She did not need a slavering madman. She needed to be held, cosseted, comforted, even if she would disagree. Shaking open the towel, he wrapped it around her as she stepped from the tub into his arms. Tendrils of her hair tickled his chin, curling damply from the steam of the bath. He brushed his lips across them as his hands rubbed briskly over the cloth. She leaned into the touch of his hands, her body undulating gracefully as he dried her.

"Take me to bed," she murmured, her lips moving against his neck as she spoke.

David froze, aching to take what she was offering. He tipped her head up toward his, kissing her sweetly, tenderly. Her body arched against his, the thick nap of the towel not shielding her eagerness in any way as she responded to the kiss, licking at his lips in invitation.

He allowed himself one long, lingering kiss, plundering her mouth with all the passion she incited before he lifted his head and tucked her face against his shoulder, his chin resting on the crown of her head. She squirmed in his arms, but he held her tightly, stroking her back soothingly. "You need to rest," he insisted. "Have you slept at all since we fought off Serrier's wizards?"

Angélique's head snapped up, eyes flashing. "Don't tell me what I need!"

David hushed her softly, urging her head back to his shoulder. "I'm not being condescending," he promised, "but I saw you when I came in. You were barely reacting to anything around you, including me. You're exhausted and probably in shock, and I wouldn't be doing either of us any favors by having sex with you tonight. It would only make things more complicated than they already are. Just let me hold you tonight."

Stepping away from him, she reached up to unclasp her hair, deliberately putting herself on display for him. It was a gesture she had learned to use to great effect in the harem, the angle of her arms lifting her breasts as if in offering. The dark locks tumbled free, falling in disarray around her shoulders, down her back and over her chest, hiding her partially from his view. Holding his gaze, she slowly brushed her tresses back over her shoulders, revealing her bosom again.

He tore his eyes away, turning his back on her and walking the rest of the way down the hall to the bedroom. He had offered to stay. Now he would have to find the fortitude to resist the bounty on display until he knew for sure it was what she wanted—not because she needed comfort but because she wanted him.

Perturbed, she tossed the towel over the rack and, nude, followed him down the hall. He was not supposed to be able to resist her charms, not when she finally decided to offer herself to him. Still, he had walked toward her room, not toward the door, which meant she would have another opportunity. Once she got him naked and in bed, she would overcome his scruples.

She walked into the bedroom to find him picking through her underwear drawer, in search of what, she had no idea. The scowl on his face each time he pulled out another sheer negligee made her smile. "If you're looking for something to make it easier to resist me, you're out of luck," she informed him drolly. "All my nightwear is intended to entice, not to hide."

His scowl deepened, but he did not give voice to his dour thoughts. Had the situation been different, he would not have been complaining about enticement on her part, but tonight, he needed to stay in control. Pulling his sweater and T-shirt off, he tossed the soft cotton garment in her direction. "Put that on. It should cover you some."

Angélique raised the garment to her face, inhaling deeply of David's strong, masculine scent. She considered refusing on principle, but the thought of sleeping surrounded by his shirt was its own turn-on. She slipped it over her head, smiling when the hem only brushed the top of her buttocks, leaving them and her nest of curls still bare to his view.

David sighed as he realized his mistake. While his shirt covered her breasts and most of the henna tattoos, it focused his gaze lower, on her long legs and curl-covered mound. There was nothing to be done about it now, though. He gestured toward the bed. "Go on, lie down."

"Don't even think you're getting in my bed with your jeans on," she warned while she did as he directed, slipping under the duvet and watching him expectantly.

David's lips tightened, but he stripped down to his dark briefs, knowing the tight fit of the clingy fabric would reveal his half-swollen state, but Angélique had been a courtesan. She knew the effect she had on men. She was not at all above exploiting it either, if her actions tonight were any indication. Setting his jeans aside, he climbed in bed with her, rolling her to her side so he could spoon up behind her, his body surrounding hers. His hands settled, one on her hip, the other on her stomach, holding her firmly against him but limiting her range of movement.

Angélique let him move her as he pleased, enjoying the feeling of his hands on her body, even for something as utilitarian as finding a comfortable position. When he had them settled and made no move to do anything else, she squirmed back against him, rubbing her bottom against his swiftly growing shaft, a thrill of pleasure going through her at the idea that he was not completely immune to her charms.

"Hold still," he growled in her ear, the desire to abandon his scruples making it hard to lie still himself. "You're supposed to be relaxing."

"That's easier said than done with you poking me in the back," she teased huskily, hoping it would not be long before he was poking her in other places. "There's a quick solution to our restlessness."

David pushed up on one elbow and looked down at her seriously. "You really have no idea how confusing you are, do you? One minute, you tell me not to treat you like a concubine, and the next, you're inciting me like a cock tease and I don't know how I'm supposed to react to that. If I give in, you accuse me of treating you like everyone else, but you do your best to taunt me into treating you that way anyway, even when I'm trying to be a gentleman. Is that really what you want, Angélique? Do you really want me to roll you beneath me and use you for an empty physical release? If that's really what you want, I'll give it to you—hell, I'm only a man and you'd tempt a saint—but I'd rather comfort you."

Angélique looked up at him in surprise. "You would lie here next to me, as we are, and be content with nothing more than holding me while we slept?"

David snorted. "You haven't heard a word I've said since I walked in the door, have you? Yes, Angélique, I would be content with that because it's what you need right now. I'm not a martyr. I'm sure, if we sleep like this enough nights, I'll end up giving in to your temptation, but I'd rather do it on a night when we both want it rather than on a night so fraught with high emotion." He settled back on the bed and adjusted her in his embrace, one hand slipping beneath his shirt to rest on the skin of her abdomen. He nuzzled her neck softly. "Some night when you've painted yourself for me. For now, sleep. There's time enough for the rest later."

She shivered at the touch of his hand on bare skin, at the thought of decorating her body for his pleasure. It would be hers as well. He would be a considerate lover, she was sure, taking the time to ensure her pleasure before finding his own. His insistence on caring for her tonight was proof of that.

She snuggled deeper into his embrace, letting his warmth seep into her very bones, chasing away the chill of the night and the horror of the morning. She did not expect to sleep, certainly not quickly. Between the events of the morning and the desire his presence inspired, she was wound too tightly to even think of resting. The slow stroke of his thumb on her skin was soothing, though, his breathing low and even, barely ruffling the hair by her ear. Her last thought before she drifted off into reverie was that she could get used to this.

If someone had told David after the battle outside Sang Froid he would spend the following night in Angélique's bed, he would have laughed in their face—yet here he was, exactly where a part of him had wanted to be from the very beginning. She was two completely different women, he mused as her body relaxed slowly in his arms. Strong, determined, capable, independent—the side she showed the world—and then there was this sudden, unexpected vulnerability.

She would hate him for being glad to see that softness beneath the world-wise exterior, but it appealed to him, to his better side. If he had not seen it, he would never have had the strength to resist her tonight, and he was glad he had, glad to simply hold her and offer comfort that way. He suspected she had not had a lot of nonsexual comfort in her life. His breath caught on the sudden realization that he wanted to be the one to provide it, to show her all the things she had missed in life.

He suppressed a chuckle. If that did not earn him a glare and probably a thump, he did not know what would. He did not have to tell her. He would simply show her. Arms tightening a little, he was surprised to see she had closed her eyes and relaxed into his embrace. With a smile, he closed his eyes and fell asleep.

Chapter 3

"HE'S GOING to pitch a fit when he finally wakes up," Sebastien told Thierry as they looked at Alain, still sound asleep in Thierry's guest bedroom.

"If he's strong enough to pitch a proper fit, I'll let him," Thierry replied honestly. "Your idea is a good one, but he was too exhausted last night to be able to spend the day crisscrossing the city. When he wakes up from the second spell, maybe he'll be rested enough not to keel over in the middle of the day."

"He's still not going to like it. It was bad enough catching him off guard with the first spell. Your sneaking into his room in the middle of the night to cast another one is going to make him furious."

Thierry shrugged. "He'll get over it. I did what was best for him."

Sebastien was not sure Thierry was right, but he had not felt his lover slip from his arms, coming back to consciousness only when Thierry came back to bed, the spell already cast. The vampire understood what was driving Alain, not only his love for Orlando but also the Aveu de Sang, a powerful, magical force that defied explanation but that bound a vampire and his Avoué too tightly to separate. Alain would be livid when he awoke. Sebastien was not looking forward to that conversation.

"Let's go see what happened overnight," the vampire said simply. The rest could wait until Alain came to.

"ANY LUCK?" Thierry asked when he and Sebastien joined Jean, Raymond and Marcel in the Salle des Cartes. He was afraid he already knew the answer. If they had found anything, Alain would have been the first one they notified.

Marcel shook his head glumly. "Every place we've searched has been as empty as the place you and Alain first went to."

"We knew it was a long shot from the first," Raymond reminded them. "Serrier did the same thing after I defected, and we've seen it on the few occasions when we've managed to convince captured wizards to turn state's evidence in exchange for lighter sentences. He slips away before we can get there, leaving the buildings abandoned."

"So what do we do now?" Jean demanded. "We can't just leave Orlando in their hands. It's already been more than thirty hours since he was taken, and we don't know when he last fed."

"Right before the battle," Thierry interrupted. "I don't know how much more time that buys us, but he and Alain managed a few minutes alone before we went to place Pigalle, long enough for him to feed." Thierry's heart clenched when he thought of Alain's revelations from the night before and his confession of what they had not had time to do.

"How long does he have?" Raymond inquired. "Before it becomes critical."

Jean looked at Sebastien, the question as clear on his face as it had been in Raymond's words. He hated the fact that he had to rely on the other vampire to answer the question, but in this area, Sebastien was the best source of information they had, and Jean could not justify squandering it just because he didn't like how the other man had come by that information. Not when Orlando's safety hung in the balance.

"Less than a month after their Aveu de Sang?" Sebastien mused, trying to take into consideration all the factors that had not affected him and Thibaut. He was surprised Jean had even asked him, given the tension that still reigned between them. It had gotten a little better since the alliance formed, but they were hardly friends. "I don't know how much Alain being a wizard will change things, but my best guess would be four days, five at the most, only a little longer than if he didn't have the bond at all. But, well, there are other extenuating circumstances too." He would not break Orlando's confidence, but the knowledge that the bond had only been partially consummated worried him. "That might make it no more than an unbonded vampire."

"Putain de merde," Jean cursed. "It's already been half that and we don't have a single idea where to look now."

"Actually, Sebastien had an idea last night," Thierry interjected. "We just have to wait for Alain so we can carry it out. We're hoping he can use their bond to narrow down an area to search."

"He said it was directionless," Jean protested.

"Yes, but we're hoping it will vary in strength as he moves closer to or farther from Orlando's location," Sebastien explained. "It won't lead us to Orlando, but it might let us focus our search on a particular part of the city. The less area we have to search, the more likely we are to stumble across him."

Jean scowled. "There has to be a better way."

"Then find it," Marcel declared. "Raymond's a researcher. You're the chef de la Cour of Paris. Surely you have resources that might lead to ideas we haven't explored yet."

"I asked Jean-Paul, the bouquiniste, to hold any books with references to vampires for me," Raymond told them, "but I haven't had time to go back and see what he found. It's a shot in the dark, but there might be something. Would monsieur Lombard let us search his library?"

"For Orlando, he might," Jean answered, remembering their first meeting and how impressed Lombard had been when he heard Orlando had taken an Avoué. "He seemed to take a liking to Orlando. We could go ask, although he won't answer the door in the daylight. Maybe Mireille will let us in."

"What are you waiting for?" Marcel prompted. "You have my cell number. I'll keep it with me. Call if you learn anything that might help us."

"Jean, see if you can find Mireille," Raymond suggested as the two of them left the Salle des Cartes. "I'll go by the bouquinistes and see if Jean-Paul or any of the others have anything we could use. I'll meet you back here in fifteen minutes."

At Jean's nod, Raymond disappeared, rematerializing a few seconds later on the banks of the Seine. At that hour, only a few of the stalls were open yet, but Raymond was relieved to see Jean-Paul at his post.

"Ah, Raymond, I wondered how long it would be before you came back to see me," the bouquiniste said with a smile. "I have some books for you."

"I'm glad to hear that," Raymond replied with an answering smile. His eyes widened as Jean-Paul began setting book after book on the table he used for purchases. By the time he was done, twenty books sat on the table. Raymond boggled. "You've been busy."

Jean-Paul shrugged. "After the news of the alliance hit, the other bouquinistes started bringing me things, saying you might find them useful. I figured anything to help win this war." His face tightened. "It's not just wizards and vampires being affected. My brother-in-law's cousin was injured by a dark wizard's spell. He's going to recover, they think, but they're not sure if he'll ever regain use of his left arm."

"I'm sorry to hear that," Raymond apologized sincerely. "We're doing the best we can."

"I know that," Jean-Paul assured him. "Nobody blames the Milice for what was clearly dark magic. We want to see the war over as fast as may be, like everyone else, and if that means gathering information, well, that's what we bouquinistes are best at."

Raymond nodded. "How much do I owe you?"

"A victory, once and for all," Jean-Paul declared firmly. "You take these and you use them and you win this war and we'll be even."

"I can't do that!" Raymond protested. "That's hundreds of euros worth of books. This is your livelihood. You can't throw away that kind of money."

"Only one of these books was mine," Jean-Paul said. "One came from Philippe, two stalls down. Another from Hugo, another from Pauline. We can all stand to lose the price of a single book. We can't stand to lose this war. Consider it our contribution to the cause."

"Thank you," Raymond said sincerely, still shaking his head at their generosity. "We will win this war. It may not be this week or this month, but we will win it. The tide's turning and there's nothing Serrier can do about it now. We just have to keep harrying him until we can bring him down once and for all."

"Good. Now, off to your research, since I'm sure it was a pressing question that brought you here."

Raymond repeated his thanks and, gathering the books with a spell, returned to Milice headquarters.

As soon as Raymond was gone, Jean went to see if Caroline and Mireille were on duty that morning. If not, he would have to see if someone could tell him where Caroline lived because he suspected that was where he would find Mireille. As sensitive as the redheaded vampire was, she would have wanted her partner's company and comfort with all that had transpired.

He found her moments later as she and Caroline reported for duty, but Mireille's face fell when she heard Jean's request. "He's left town on his yearly pilgrimage," she explained. "He locks the house when he's gone. I don't even have a key. Usually I stay in a hotel, but this time I stayed with Caroline."

Jean's cursing grew more vile. He prayed Raymond had better luck than he did or their research would be unproductive indeed.

"I really am sorry, Jean," Mireille apologized. "I'd help if I could."

"When do you expect him back?"

Mireille paused to think. "No later than two more nights. Maybe even tomorrow night. It depends on train schedules and when he can travel after dark."

"Let me know as soon as he's back, please," he requested. "Orlando doesn't have a lot of time and we're running out of ideas."

Mireille nodded immediately, hating the thought of what Orlando must surely be enduring. She only hoped they found a way to rescue him in time.

Pacing restlessly, Jean waited for Raymond to return. The wizard reappeared a few minutes later, arms full of books. "It seems Jean-Paul had more books on vampires than he realized," Raymond commented with a smile. When it was not returned, he set them down and turned to Jean. "What's wrong?"

"We can't access monsieur Lombard's library until at least tomorrow night. He's out of town and Mireille doesn't have a key," Jean explained. "We can look through my books, but he has a much more extensive library than I have."

"All right," Raymond declared. "Let's tell Marcel about the change in plans and we'll take these back to your apartment and get started there. If I need anything from my place, I can get it at some point. This is a setback, but that doesn't mean we don't still have places to look."

Jean took a deep breath, consciously willing away the negativity. He had to keep believing they could save Orlando. "Let's go. We're wasting time Orlando doesn't have."

They arrived back in the Salle des Cartes at the same time as one of the newest patrol leaders, Jérôme Sabatie. The younger wizard had a face like a thunderstorm, every line of his body screaming his anger and frustration.

Before Raymond and Jean could tell Marcel of their change of plans, Jérôme had whirled on Monique Leclerc, the turncoat wizard. She had joined the others assembled in the war room in the short time Raymond and Jean had been away.

"Salope!" he shouted, lunging in her direction, only to be intercepted by the big vampire at her side. "Why did you do it? Why'd you send us into a trap?"

"Back off," Antonio growled, the words rumbling from deep in his chest. "Monique didn't send anyone into a trap."

"Then why the hell is one of my people lying in the infirmary in critical condition?" Jérôme yelled. "They were waiting for us!"

"Maybe they were," Raymond agreed calmly, "but not because she sent you there knowing that. Serrier has his organization set up so that if something like this happens, or someone squeals, he can pull out of a few hideouts. And since he has to know we're searching for Orlando since we took Monique in on that information, it would make sense for him to leave traps behind. In some places, it's just spells, but that doesn't mean he hasn't left patrols in others."

"Or she gave us a bunch of old, abandoned locations to lull us into complacency and then sprung the real trap," Jérôme contended.

"Blood doesn't lie," Antonio insisted.

"Maybe not, but people do," Jérôme snapped. "She's your partner. Of course you'd want her on our side. You'd say whatever it took to get Marcel to accept her."

"Jérôme, that's enough," Thierry intervened, pulling the patrol leader away from both Monique and her partner. "I understand you're upset—that's perfectly normal when one of your people gets hurt—but your accusations aren't helping. Antonio isn't the only vampire who's vouched for Monique's sincerity. And the other vampire has a partner in the Milice and so every reason to tell us if Monique was in any way complicit in Serrier's continuing plots."

"People do change sides," Raymond said quietly from his place at Jean's side. "It happens sometimes that people make bad choices and then realize the error of their ways and find a way to get out. A month ago, you looked at me exactly the same way you're looking at her, accusing me of the same kind of duplicity. Do you still think it now?"

Jérôme had to admit he did not. "Then give Monique the same benefit of the doubt," Raymond suggested. "Your energy would be much better spent giving Marcel a coherent report and then checking on your wounded friend than it would be in attacking the only lead we have at this point."

Shamefaced, Jérôme turned to Marcel and began his report of how they had gone to search a location near Montparnasse, one of the few places Monique had identified on the Rive Gauche. As in the other locations so far, they had found empty rooms, wards still up but no one to defend them. They had gotten inside with relatively little trouble and started a methodical search of the building. Jérôme assured Marcel repeatedly that they had checked for auras before they went in and found none, but even so, as they started back down from the upper floors, they had been met by a group of dark wizards who attacked immediately and viciously, using dangerous, painful spells, but no *Abbattoires*.

"He must have figured that one out," Raymond mused softly. He did not add that Serrier was undoubtedly testing spells on Orlando to see which ones would in fact work on the vampires. Jean was worried enough as it was. If he had not already reached that conclusion on his own, Raymond did not want to add it to his current concerns.

They managed to fight their way free, Jérôme reported, but not before Mathieu Gastineau took a spell in the back that severed his spine and nearly overloaded his heart. "The medics are guardedly hopeful they can keep him alive," the patrol leader finished, "but they aren't sure he'll ever walk again."

"Does he have a partner?" Monique interrupted softly.

"Why do you care?" Jérôme spat.

"Because when Serrier tortured me, thinking I was a spy, Antonio feeding from me eased the pain of his magic. Maybe your friend's partner can help him now since there's a magical cause to his injuries," Monique explained with quiet dignity.

"It helped me, too, after the Rite d'équilibrage," Thierry commented, hoping to diffuse the remaining tension in the room. "It's worth a try, Jérôme. Even if it doesn't cure him completely, if it eases his pain, that's still helpful. Why don't you go see if you can find Mathieu's partner—she's probably glued to his side—and suggest she try it?"

Marcel shook his head in amazement as Jérôme left to take the message. "There's still so much we don't know about these partnerships we've created," he mused. "So far, everything's worked to our advantage, but I wonder how long that will be true."

"If monsieur Lombard is right, it will stay true," Jean replied. "A vampire's nature generally keeps him from hurting those who have become important to him. I don't see our magical natures being pulled into a bond that would force us to go against that very nature."

"Let's hope you're right," Marcel agreed. "Now, what are you still doing here? I thought you were going to talk to monsieur Lombard."

Raymond quickly explained what had happened and where they would be. "If someone would oblige and send Jean to me?"

Thierry offered and Raymond winked out, his name appearing on the locator map on the rue d'Anjou. At Jean's nod of permission, he sent the chef de la Cour to join his partner.

"I can't give you an exact location because I don't know it," Monique said softly as quiet fell over the room again, "but I overheard Serrier talking to Simonet and Jonnet about a place north of St-Denis. The only wizards he trusts as much as he trusts them are Aguiraud and that bastard, Blanchet. It's still a huge area to search, but if he really has abandoned all the hideouts I knew about, he might have retreated there."

"When Alain gets here, we'll start downtown and work our way north, then," Thierry decided. "If Sebastien's idea works, at least knowing he's likely in the north narrows down the portion of the city Alain has to check on his own."

"Thierry, you fucking bastard! Where are you?"

Sebastien arched an eyebrow. "Alain's here."

Chapter 4

SEBASTIEN LET Alain take a swing, Thierry dodging it at the last second, before he wrapped strong arms around the furious wizard. "That's enough," he said calmly as Alain continued to struggle against an embrace he would not be able to break except by magical means. "Focus your anger where it belongs, not on Thierry."

"Did you find something?" Alain asked immediately, his voice so hopeful it broke Sebastien's heart.

"Not yet, but now it's your turn to search, and you can't do that until you're calm enough to control your magic," Thierry replied firmly. "You needed the sleep. I made sure you got it. End of story."

It was not the end as far as Alain was concerned, but there were more pressing matters to deal with first. He shook off Sebastien's arms. "I won't hit him again, even if he does deserve it."

Sebastien shot Thierry a look that said "I told you so" so clearly the words were not necessary. Thierry shrugged and led Alain to the map. With a tap of his wand, he drew up the map that showed the locations Monique had identified. "We know he isn't in any of these precise locations, but that doesn't mean he isn't close by. Monique also told us that she heard Serrier talking about a hideout north of St-Denis, but we don't have any more information than that. My suggestion would be to start at avenue de la République and work north from there, to see if the sense of the bond gets stronger. If it does, we'll keep working north. If it doesn't, we'll try the Rive Gauche and see if that leads anywhere."

"You can stay here and mark the grid," Alain told Thierry coolly.

"You aren't going alone," Thierry protested.

"I wasn't planning on it," Alain replied. "I'm sure there's someone on duty who won't knock me unconscious when I turn my head."

"That's enough," Marcel interrupted. "Neither of you are hotheaded teenagers anymore. Act like adults or you're both off duty. Alain, if you'd rather not take Thierry with you, Caroline's on duty. I'm sure she and Mireille would go with you."

"Take Sebastien with you as well," Thierry suggested, trying to hide the hurt at Alain's words. "He didn't have anything to do with my spells and I'd feel better knowing you had more eyes to watch your back while you search."

Alain wanted to snap again, but Thierry's suggestion was a good one, and however angry he was about the lost hours he could have used to search for Orlando, he knew Thierry's decision had not been made maliciously. It was not the choice Alain would have made and he did not appreciate having the choice taken from him, but Thierry had not intended any harm. "That's up to him."

"Let's find Caroline and Mireille and get started then," Sebastien declared. "Time's passing."

They found Caroline and Mireille getting ready to leave on patrol. As soon as they heard what Alain needed, they agreed to join him instead. Alain grabbed the two vampires and cast the displacement spell, and the four of them reappeared at the place de la République. Finding a relatively quiet doorway, Alain closed his eyes, shielded behind his three companions from curious gazes and unfriendly magic, and focused on the bond with Orlando.

To his relief, his lover's mind was calm. Alain concentrated, projecting all his love and strength in the vampire's direction, trying to sense anything he could in return, anything that would give him an idea of how to help Orlando, but nothing flowed back to him. He told himself that was because Orlando was resting, not because he could not feel Alain's touch anymore.

"Where now?" he asked Sebastien.

"North. Let's try place Pigalle and see if it's any stronger."

Alain nodded and they made the jump, Alain displacing both vampires while Caroline followed.

"Try again," Sebastien prompted when they arrived back at the site of Orlando's disappearance.

Alain did as the vampire instructed, pushing aside the pain in his chest at being in the spot where he had failed his lover. Eyes closing, he let the bond fill his mind, trying to see if he could detect any difference in its strength here as opposed to in the place de la République. He thought it felt richer here than before, but he could not tell if that was the location or the fact that Orlando was beginning to respond to him, waking perhaps, to return the love and longing Alain projected.

"Is it any stronger?" Sebastien asked when Alain opened his eyes.

"Maybe," Alain replied. "I can't tell for sure, though."

"Let's move further north, then. We can try the porte de la Chapelle, and then head into St-Denis if it still feels stronger."

Again, they made the jump and again Alain concentrated on the bond. It was definitely stronger this time, Orlando's emotions coming through clearly enough that Alain could even tell his lover was hiding something from him, though he could not tell what. He frowned at the thought, knowing Serrier's ways all too well. At least he could still feel his vampire, though, which meant that he was not hurt too badly. "Let's try St-Denis. It definitely feels stronger."

On Alain's mark, they winked out to the place Pierre de Montreuil in front of the Tribunal d'Instance in St-Denis. When Alain focused on the bond this time, he could sense no difference from the feelings at porte de la Chapelle. Frowning, he looked at Sebastien. "It feels the same."

Sebastien nodded and considered. "It could mean we didn't move any closer. We can try backtracking a little."

They spent the next three hours crisscrossing the north side of the city, bouncing back and forth across the boulevard périphérique in the hopes of narrowing down their search, but the only change Alain felt as the day wore on was in Orlando's emotions, which ebbed and flowed, probably in response to Alain's own frustrations. Both wizards were flagging by the time Alain had to admit defeat. Then a burst of fear and pain came through the bond, sending him to his knees as he fought down nausea.

JEAN SLAMMED the book shut in frustration. "Even the ones that have accurate information don't have anything to help us," he ranted.

Raymond looked up from his notes. "There has to be something. We simply have to find it."

"I don't even know where else to look!"

"Then let's think instead of searching randomly. Search spells focus on something unique to a person: their auras, their hair or skin or blood, though most wizards won't use the last except under extreme circumstances," Raymond explained.

Jean looked at the clock. "This qualifies as extreme circumstances. We have less than thirty-six hours to find him if Sebastien's right about how long he can go without feeding."

"I'm also not most wizards," Raymond reminded him with a smile. "We've already established that vampires don't have auras. My guess is that the seeking spell would work best with blood, but I don't know if we could find anything with Orlando's blood on it. Hair would be easiest—from a shirt or his pillow or the shower drain."

"Hair didn't work for the repères," Jean reminded Raymond. "Do you think it would work for this?"

"It's a different kind of spell—like seeking like, instead of trying to imprint one person's identity on a disparate object. It's worth a try. And if it doesn't work with hair, we'll try with blood."

"Will it work if you try it on me, though?" Jean asked. "Or do we need to go back to Milice headquarters?"

"It'll be faster to have someone come here, if you don't mind," Raymond suggested. "Rather than having to go back, send someone here to get you, and then bring you back."

"That's fine," Jean agreed, admitting the logic of Raymond's argument.

Raymond dialed Marcel's number, explaining the situation quickly when the Milice general answered. Marcel promised to send Catherine right away since Thierry wanted to stay and keep track of Alain's progress.

A few minutes later, she appeared outside Jean's door, knocking lightly.

Jean let her in and shared a secret smile with Raymond as she marveled at the furnishings and decorations. After a couple of moments, she flushed and apologized, only increasing the two men's amusement.

"If it makes you feel any better, Catherine, I reacted the same way when I first saw it," Raymond assured her. "It looks like a museum and feels like a home."

The sentiment surprised Jean enough that it showed on his face for a moment. Raymond did not elaborate with Catherine there, but he resolved to find time—soon—to make sure the chef de la Cour understood how much more than that he had become to his partner in the past few days.

"So what do you need me to do?" Catherine asked, her manner becoming all business again once she mastered her amazement.

Jean plucked a strand of hair from his head and set it on the table. "See if you can find me using my hair."

"Just a regular seeking spell?" Catherine verified.

Raymond nodded. "We've got to find a way to locate Orlando and this is the only idea we have at the moment."

Catherine nodded, shuddering at the thought of what Alain had to be suffering, knowing his partner was in Serrier's hands. She knew she would be beside herself with worry if it were Justin instead of Orlando. "Go in one of the other rooms, if you would," she requested.

Jean disappeared into the kitchen, not wanting to go into the bedroom in case the spell worked and she followed him in there. He had the only wizard he wanted in his bedroom there already. Catherine did not need to see it.

As soon as he was out of the room, Catherine cast the spell. For a moment, nothing happened. Raymond was ready to give up and call Jean back into the room to try it with blood when Catherine suddenly took a step toward the kitchen. "It's working," she declared. "I can feel a definite tug toward the other room."

"End the spell," Raymond said. "Let's try it again with him farther away. It doesn't do us any good if it only works in the next room."

Calling Jean back into the room, he relayed the good news. Jean's sigh of relief was audibly heartfelt.

"Can you go outside somewhere so we can try it again?" Raymond requested. "We need to see if the range is beyond that of the next room. Sometimes spells are limited by distance."

"How far should I go?"

"Start with the end of the block. If that works, we'll try farther afield."

Jean nodded and left. Catherine waited about five minutes, then cast the spell a second time. Once again, there was a delay, as if the magic could not quite decide what to make of the vampire's magical nature, but eventually, it tugged her toward the door and down the steps.

"One more test," Raymond proposed, "so we don't get Alain's hopes up until we're sure it can work. Catherine, can you go home and try it from there? That should be enough distance to compare to anywhere in the city Serrier's likely to have stashed Orlando."

"Here," Jean said, tugging another hair free. "So you don't have to go back inside."

Catherine took it and disappeared. "Trying to get rid of her?" Raymond teased lightly.

Jean shrugged. "The faster we figure out if this works, the faster we can rescue Orlando or move on to some other option. I don't like that Serrier's forces almost took out a patrol last night. I agree with you that Monique probably didn't send them into a trap, but they were ready to fight vampires, not just wizards. And that means Serrier's getting information. I doubt he's experimenting on the rogue, so that means he's experimenting on Orlando. That boy's suffered enough since he was turned. He doesn't need to suffer anymore."

"I don't know what we can do that we aren't already doing," Raymond admitted, "but if he can be found, we'll find him. The best minds we have are working on it from as many angles as we can come up with."

It took long enough for Catherine to arrive back at Jean's apartment that the vampire was ready to give up, pacing restlessly as he wracked his brain for another way to find Orlando. When she finally knocked on the door, he jerked it open. "What took so long?"

"I came back on foot so I'd know the spell was actually guiding me, not my memory of where you lived," she explained, feeling a little defensive. "I wanted to make absolutely sure it worked."

"Let's go find Alain," Raymond declared.

ORLANDO STUMBLED when Vincent pushed him back into his cell. He hurt all over, but he had the grim satisfaction of knowing he had not let his torturers hear him beg. He had not been able to stop himself from grimacing, from bending double as the pain ate at his insides, but he had not uttered a sound. They could do what they wanted to his body. He would not let them touch his mind.

"Get some rest," the big wizard ordered. "You'll need it."

Orlando glared at him silently, refusing to acknowledge the advice, however wise it might be.

Vincent shrugged and left him alone. Free from prying eyes, Orlando curled up on the cot, feeling his body struggling to repair the damage done to it today. Most of it had been magical, not physical. He had only a few cuts and bruises from what Serrier had done, but he felt like his guts were twisting and his skin burning all over. He could feel his hunger growing, not urgent yet, but slowly demanding attention. If the torture turned from magical to physical, he would need it even more, his body requiring sustenance to heal itself.

He wondered as he lay there how long he had until his reserves were exhausted. He had no idea what would happen then. He could only pray Alain got there in time.

The door opened again and Serrier walked in with a woman Orlando had never seen before. She glanced at the dark wizard once before approaching Orlando. He sat up, face stoic as he waited to see what new torture they had planned, but she simply held out her arm, her movements stiff, as if compelled by magic. Orlando glanced up at her face, seeing hints of panic in her eyes, and realized she was as much a victim in this situation as he was.

Confused, Orlando glanced back and forth between her and Serrier. "Go on," Serrier prompted. "You need blood because we're not done with you yet, and I have no intention of losing you until I've learned everything I need to know."

Orlando did not move. Her blood would only weaken him further and he surely did not want that. Serrier, it seemed, had other ideas, because a binding spell hit Orlando a moment later. The dark wizard pulled out a knife and sliced open her wrist, ordering her to lift it to the vampire's mouth. Her arm moved, though clearly not of her own volition, pressing the bleeding cut over Orlando's lips.

The taste of foreign blood gagged Orlando immediately, his stomach heaving in protest. The binding spell kept him from pulling away, blood pooling in his mouth as he tried not to swallow. Eventually, though, it was swallow or choke. His reflexes took over, the poison—for any blood but Alain's was poison to him—running down into his stomach. Bile rose, spewing out as his system rejected the toxin.

"What the hell?" Serrier demanded. "Edouard, get in here! You said he'd need to feed. What is this?"

Edouard strode in lazily, followed by Eric and Vincent. "What happened?"

"He refused to eat. When I tried to force him, he threw up everywhere."

Edouard's eyebrows lifted, a mingling of respect and scorn on his face. "So the boy thinks he's a man?"

Personally, Eric thought Edouard was one to talk. He appeared as young as or younger than the vampire seated on the bed, who was looking more than a little peaked.

"What's that supposed to mean?" Serrier demanded. "I don't have time for riddles."

"It means he's got a lover stashed somewhere, one foolish enough to bind himself to a vampire for life. Anyone else's blood will make him sick," Edouard explained. "Weakling…. He's just assured his own destruction."

"Why didn't you tell me sooner? I still need him a little longer!"

"Because you can't tell by looking at the vampire," Edouard replied, his tone one of a teacher talking to a difficult child. "You can only tell by looking at the mortal. Whatever spineless creature bound himself to this child bears a brand of some sort on his neck to mark him." He turned to Orlando, a sneer on his face. "Is it one of your puny allies? I'll make sure to keep an eye out for her. When I find her, I'll bring her back so you can watch me taste my fill before I kill her."

Orlando snorted at the thought. Alain would make mincemeat of the pathetic pretender.

"Enough," Serrier declared. "I have other business to attend to. While the Milice is distracted trying to rescue their ally, I intend to take advantage of what we've learned today. Let's go."

The woman, Edouard, and Vincent followed Serrier out immediately, but Eric lingered at the door, looking at Orlando appraisingly. He had been at Alain's side during the battle, never more than a few feet from his side until Lapeyre's spell hit the wizard. The vampire had used the word "partner" when he referred to Alain, but now Eric wondered if it could be more.

"Eric!"

The sound of his name drew him from his thoughts and he shut the door behind him, whispering a spell to release the bonds on Orlando as he did.

Still heaving, Orlando bent double as soon as he was free from the spell, gasping for breath as his system purged itself of the woman's blood. When he could, he lay back on the bed again. "Hurry, Alain," he whispered to the empty darkness.

Chapter 5

"THEY'RE RUNNING around like fools chasing their tails," Serrier gloated when Eric and Vincent joined him and Simon. "We have to press our advantage while they're distracted by our success in capturing a vampire."

"What about the traitor?" Simon asked.

Serrier's face tightened, fists clenching where they sat on the table. "She's a dead woman. I've given the order. If anyone sees her, I want her taken down, no questions asked. We lost safe houses we couldn't stand to lose because of her treachery."

The other three wizards nodded. "So what happens now?" Eric inquired.

"Now we attack. The spy's dead so we don't have to worry about him passing information. We lay our plans carefully, using what we've learned today, and we show Chavinier that we're still a force to be reckoned with."

"So what's our target?" Simon asked.

"Notre-Dame," Serrier declared, his face twisting into a sardonic grin. "The very heart of the city, the cathedral, the seat of religious fervor in the country. We'll show them that their Lady, their patron saint, their god and their wizards can't keep them safe any longer."

Vincent winced inwardly, the rhetoric he had once found so rousing now sounding like empty platitudes in his head. He had seen enough in the past few weeks to make him realize that the kind of world Serrier envisioned would have no place for any but those as twisted as he was. Somewhere in the past two years, Vincent had changed, and he'd had enough. He needed out, and soon. Destroying national treasures for no reason, experimenting on another person, vampire or not, letting Blanchet's tortures go unchecked… were not things Vincent could accept any longer. He had to find a way to convince Eric to come with him, because the thought of leaving his lover behind was as unacceptable as Serrier's behavior.

"Is there a reason not to choose a more strategic location?" Eric interjected. "Once Chavinier realizes we've taken the vampires into account in our plans, he won't be caught off guard a second time. Why not attack l'Élysée or Matignon?"

"Why not commit suicide?" Simon countered. "They're so heavily warded we won't get in there until the Milice is defeated. At least at Notre-Dame, we have the opportunity to remind the entire city that we're here and we're a serious threat. It wasn't warded at all the last time I was there. Unless

Chavinier has ordered them put up in the past week, he'll have no way of even knowing we're there ahead of time."

"So when do we attack?" Vincent asked, dreading the answer.

"After dark," Serrier replied. "We want the vampires to come to our little party so Chavinier sees the folly of trusting them. They might be impervious to some spells, but not to all of them, as our poor unfortunate guinea pig proved for us today. And once they're down, we can take out the wizards and then bring the vampires back and make sure they get a good glimpse of daylight tomorrow morning."

Simon's laugh was nearly as cruel as Serrier's expression. "That's one way to reduce their numbers."

"It might be worth keeping a few others just to make sure the one we have isn't an oddity when it comes to his resistance to pain," Eric commented, his voice determinedly neutral. "He seemed remarkably undisturbed despite his body's apparent distress."

Vincent frowned, surprised Eric would make such a suggestion. He had thought the other wizard was as bothered by the cruelty as he was.

Serrier considered the idea for a moment. "You might be right," he agreed. "We'll see how many we bring down tonight. The one we have won't be any good to us much longer if he can't even eat."

"You don't think we've learned all we can from him?" Vincent asked cautiously, his stomach turning at the thought of having to watch another vampire suffer the way the one had today.

"Of course not," Serrier replied with a dismissive wave of his hand. "I'm sure there are still spells we haven't tried on him."

Vincent started to protest again when Eric's hand landed on his knee beneath the table, squeezing tightly. The gesture startled the bald wizard enough that he did not give voice to his thoughts, looking at Eric instead. The other wizard shook his head slightly, a quelling look on his face. Vincent subsided unhappily, more determined than ever to have a long talk with Eric at the first possible opportunity.

"So what's the plan for tonight, then?" Eric asked, drawing attention back to the matter at hand.

"If there still aren't any wards—and why would there be?—then a simple frontal assault should be sufficient," Serrier declared. "Arrive on the parvis, bring the building down, and leave. A patrol of twenty ought to be able to handle that expeditiously."

"I'll lead them," Simon offered. "It's been awhile since I've been out with a patrol. It'll do them good to see I'm still capable of command. And I'll get a chance to see if any of my new spells work as well in battle as they do in the quiet of my library."

Serrier nodded his agreement. "Eric, you and Vincent see if you can learn anything else from the vampire. They're searching hard for him, which makes me wonder why he's special. Chavinier's never put this effort into rescuing anyone else before."

Privately, Vincent figured that was because they were usually dead within hours of being taken, before Chavinier had a chance to mount any kind of rescue attempt, but he kept silent, not wanting to draw any more attention to himself. To his relief, Eric, too, remained silent, simply acknowledging the order with a nod.

"Do you mind if we get something to eat before we get started?" Vincent asked Pascal when he did not immediately give more directions. "I haven't eaten since breakfast."

Serrier waved a hand absentmindedly in their direction, his attention focused entirely on Simon and their plans for the night.

"The crêperie?" Eric asked as they walked outside.

"No," Vincent said with a shake of his head. "Let's go to my apartment. I want to talk to you."

Eric started to cast a displacement spell, but Vincent stopped him with a shake of his head. "I'd rather walk."

Eric was surprised, but he had no reason to argue, falling into step beside Vincent as they walked toward the nearest subway stop. The train ride into town passed in silence, each man lost in his own thoughts.

Vincent spent the ride trying to decide how to broach his twin concerns with Eric. Before this evening, he would not have hesitated, but the comments his lover had made during the meeting left him unnerved. Had he trusted unwisely when he asked Eric about the possibility of getting out? The thought of being the next one on Serrier's torture list twisted his stomach in knots— but Eric had not revealed him at the meeting, as he surely would have done if he had betrayal in mind.

Eric's thoughts still centered around the revelation the vampire had made before the meeting began. If he believed what the creature said, Alain and Thierry missed him. He had convinced himself they were done with him. That was what had allowed him to do what he needed to do. He had pushed the thought aside during the meeting with Serrier, forcing himself to act as he had soon after his arrival, to be the wizard Serrier believed he was. It was that or endanger himself and probably Vincent as well. A week ago, he had not cared about his own fate, truly expecting to give his life for the cause—but things had changed since then, another path presenting itself, and now he wondered at the wisdom of his previous choices.

"What's up?" Eric asked when they arrived in the privacy of Vincent's apartment.

"I think I need to be asking you that question," Vincent replied, pulling off his jacket and hanging it on the coat stand by the door. "What was with you today? Since when do you advocate cruelty?"

Eric's brow furrowed as he followed suit. "What are you talking about?"

"'It might be worth keeping a few others just to make sure the one we have isn't an oddity when it comes to his resistance to pain'," Vincent quoted, his face twisting bitterly as the words struck at his heart again. "What the hell is that about?"

Eric's face cleared. "If Pascal brings them back and stakes them out in the sun, they'll die for sure," he explained, sitting down on the couch and patting the space beside him. "At least if he's experimenting on them, there's a chance they might escape or be rescued. I don't want him to torture them, but I want him to kill them even less. My preference would be not to capture anyone."

"You could've fooled me," Vincent muttered. He was being unfair, but Eric had planned and executed the vampire's kidnapping with apparent ease, seemingly untroubled by the creature's fate. And to hear him suggesting it again with such casualness left Vincent incredibly uncomfortable.

"I had to fool Pascal," Eric reminded him. "He's already looking for ulterior motives in everything, especially after the spy, so I can't suggest that such cruelty is unnecessary. He doesn't understand that concept."

"We've got to get out," Vincent repeated, finally sitting down next to Eric. "I don't know how much longer I can do this."

"How?" Eric challenged as he had the first time.

"Monique got out," Vincent replied, his voice soft as he contemplated the magnitude of what he was about to suggest.

"But at what price?" Eric inquired, turning to face Vincent. He wanted there to be a way, but he would not take an even greater risk until he knew they could make it work for sure. "We know she's giving them information because of where they've turned up, but we don't know what she's getting in return."

"Protection at least," Vincent pointed out. "She hasn't been home since the last time she left Pascal's, which means they've got her stashed somewhere."

"So what do you suggest? You know if we try the same, Pascal'll just disappear again, with the vampire, and Chavinier won't be as trusting a second time. He'll actually want results, not just guesses."

"So we take the vampire with us."

"We'd never get out alive!" Eric protested. He could just imagine them trying to smuggle the vampire out of Serrier's base, even if the vampire cooperated. It was a recipe for disaster unless they timed it exactly right.

"Not right now," Vincent agreed, "but Pascal has to sleep sometime. It doesn't have to be tonight. We can wait and watch and plan a little. Not for weeks, obviously, but tonight and tomorrow, surely."

"I don't know," Eric hesitated. "It's a huge risk."

"Riskier than going into battle? Riskier than facing trial and prison time if we're captured instead of killed? You told me to find a way out and you'd think about it. I've found one, so think fast."

"Promise me you won't do anything rash," Eric pleaded, mind racing with plans and backup plans and contingencies. "Give me some time to think about it, to figure out how it could work."

"We'll have a better chance of success together than if I tried it alone," Vincent agreed. "We'd have to make sure Pascal—or Claude—doesn't kill him before we can save him. I don't think a dead body will earn us nearly as many points as a live one."

"No, probably not," Eric admitted with a chuckle, his stomach churning nervously at the thought of what Vincent was proposing. He said he had no intention of going back, but seeing Alain and Thierry, having the vampire say they missed him, reminded him of how good things had been before Danielle died. He had a hole in his heart where his wife had once dwelled, but it wasn't the only hole. His friendship—relationship—with Vincent notwithstanding, there were two other holes that Alain and Thierry once filled. The thought of being able to go back honorably, to prove to them that he was not all they surely believed he had become, was tempting. "Let's see what tonight brings. We'll have to have everything in place if we're going to get out alive. I'm not sure even together we'd be a match for Serrier if he finds out, and I know we wouldn't be if he has Simon with him."

Vincent nodded slowly, still wanting to act now that his own mind was made up, but he saw the sense in Eric's words. Eric reached for him, enfolding his arms around his lover's waist. "We don't have to go straight back. Pascal's so lost in his planning, he won't miss us for a couple of hours at least."

Vincent let himself be persuaded when Eric nudged him gently in the direction of the bedroom.

"HELLO, PUSSY."

Adèle spun around at the sound of Jude's insolent drawl. "About damn time you got here," she snapped. "Where have you been the past two days?"

"Did you miss me?"

"Hell, no," she retorted, "but you've missed two days of duty."

"We weren't on the schedule," Jude protested.

"We got put on the schedule," Adèle informed him. "And you weren't there."

"Nobody told me."

"Nobody could reach you to tell you," Adèle replied. "So you're derelict and I'm getting the blame, too, because I got stuck with a partner whose only care is fucking me over."

"Not fucking you over," Jude drawled, advancing on her and reaching for her waist, "just fucking you."

"Don't even think about it!" Adèle snarled, batting his hands away as he crowded her. "I let it happen last time—hell, I even got off despite your pathetic attempts—but I'm not about to let it happen again, not when people are already looking at me askance because of your actions."

"You certainly moaned and squirmed like a two-bit whore," Jude agreed, catching her hands. "A dirty slut who even likes it up the ass. I should've known the moment I laid eyes on you."

"Maybe you'd have kept your distance if you had," she retorted, snatching her hands free and moving so the table was between them. "We'd both have been a hell of a lot happier."

"Oh, I don't know about that," Jude disagreed, vaulting the table lightly to corner her. "I've rather enjoyed our little... interludes. You purr so nicely beneath my touch."

She wanted to snap back at him, to slap him down, but she could hardly deny her body's reaction to him, not when she had come explosively at his hands three times in the past week. "I like it better when you purr beneath mine," she retorted, palms itching to touch him again. She knew it was stupid, knew she would regret it, but she was, in many ways, as much a creature of impulse as the vampires. Giving in to her desire, she caught his arm in a martial arts hold, flipping him to the floor, coming down to straddle him, one hand moving between his legs to squeeze his balls tightly. "You had your way with me last time. It's my turn."

"You aren't strong enough to take it," Jude goaded, though he made no move to throw her off. He could do it, but given where her hands were, she could well inflict more damage than he was willing to accept in the process. She would have to move her hand eventually, though, and when she did, he would be ready.

"Oh, really?" she challenged, squeezing his sac roughly as she spoke. "Which of us is on his back at the moment?"

"I don't need you on your back to fuck you," Jude reminded her. "Or have you forgotten already?"

Adèle's grip tightened until she won a grimace from his face. "I haven't forgotten anything," she snapped, "including what gets you off, and that's my orgasm, so maybe you ought to think twice about antagonizing me."

"You think I need you to get off?" Jude scoffed. "All I need is a willing body."

"Really?" Adèle sneered, pushing away and standing up. "Then go find one. I'm sure someone out there can get past your attitude and Neanderthal technique."

Jude was on his feet in a second, pinning her to the wall. "What do I need with someone else when I have a willing body right here?" he demanded, thigh pushing hers apart as his hand closed roughly over her breast, kneading it almost hard enough to hurt. She gasped in surprise, though she should have expected the move, her body melting into his touch even as her mind protested that she should fight him rather than giving in like the wanton he accused her of being.

Her head thumped against the wall as she sagged in his arms. "Purr for me, pretty pussy," he husked, tweaking the nipple that stabbed his palm even through her clothes. She glared at him, but her back arched anyway, pressing her flesh more firmly against his hand. With a grin, he pulled her sweater up, baring her stomach and bra. He popped the clasp, pulling the cups away, his eager hands taking the place of the scraps of silk. Her moan was music to his ears. He leaned forward, pressing against the full length of her body, his breath tickling her ear. "Are you wet for me, pussy? Hollow and aching and desperate to be filled?"

"Not by you," she spat, her eyes flashing with the mixture of lust and hatred that only he could inspire.

"Really?" he challenged, taking a step back.

A part of Adèle wanted to grab him and pull him back against her, but she could not let him win. Pushing away from the wall, she sent him one last venomous glare and headed toward the door to her office. Her fingers had just closed around the doorknob when hard hands wrenched her backward, against a firm body, his erection nudging her buttocks in a way that could not be misunderstood. "Prick," she spat as he unbuttoned her slacks and shoved them down, hand sliding between her legs to finger her sopping slit.

"Mine," he growled in her ear, his fangs grazing the pierced lobe. "Nobody's going to fuck you but me."

She relaxed against him, letting him have his way, her body thrumming with unchecked desire. After a moment, she turned in his arms, his grip loosening to let her move. She draped her arms welcomingly around his neck. When he bent to bite her neck, she made her move, her knee rising sharply to connect with his groin. He gasped and bent double, releasing her completely. "I decide who fucks me," she told him coldly, "not you."

With a last, satisfied glare, she stormed out of the room, slamming the door behind her and locking it with a spell guaranteed to keep him inside until she was ready to deal with him again.

Chapter 6

"THE TRACKING spell worked?" Alain asked, eyes lighting with hope at Raymond's news.

Jean, Raymond, and Catherine all nodded. "So we just need one of Orlando's hairs so we can find him," Raymond added. "I figured you could get into his apartment to get one."

"Of course," Alain replied. "I'll be right back." Before the other wizards could say anything else, he had disappeared. Orlando's apartment—their apartment—was cold and dark. Alain refused to dwell on it, reminding himself that they would be back soon, bringing light and warmth and love to the empty rooms.

He felt a pang as he walked into their bedroom to find Orlando's hairbrush. The sheets were mussed from their last lovemaking here in their room before Orlando left to talk to Sebastien. Alain had not asked the other vampire what they talked about. He wanted to hear it, whatever it was, from Orlando himself.

He knew he needed to hurry, but he took a moment anyway to sit on the edge of the bed, his hand running over the indention left from Orlando's head on the pillow. He lifted it to his face, inhaling his lover's scent from the cotton of the pillowcase. Tears threatened again, as they had frequently since Orlando's disappearance. This time, he let them fall. He needed to let out all the fear and worry before he was reunited with his vampire so he could focus on whatever Orlando needed once he was rescued.

His mind tossed up images of Orlando bloody and broken by whatever torture Serrier visited upon him. He had seen bodies before, when Serrier was done with them, and knew the depth of cruelty the dark wizard and his henchmen were capable of. He did not know what his blood and his love could heal, but he prayed they would be enough. Silently, he railed at the heavens for taking Orlando from him just when they were finally starting to make progress in their relationship, when Orlando was truly beginning to heal from the abuse he had suffered at his maker's hands. And now this....

No one should have to suffer as Orlando had done before or as he was doing now. The shield Marcel had insisted that Alain erect kept him from feeling what Serrier was doing to his lover at this exact moment, but he had felt the bursts of pain and the deep, lingering ache, and knew Orlando was suffering again. He started to lower his shields, wanting to know, but he stopped himself. This was their bed, their haven against the rest of the world. He wanted to be able to bring Orlando here free of the pain he was feeling now rather than have the memory of this time haunting them even here. Orlando would surely taste it every time they were together here if he tainted their bed with such awful emotions.

Alain ached to the core of his being with Orlando's absence. He had mourned when Henri was killed, but this was a loss of a completely different magnitude. He felt as if his soul had been rent in two, a portion of him sundered from his body, as tangible a loss as the loss of a limb. Without Orlando at his side, he was a shadow of the man he had been, a mere wraith rather than a vibrant human being.

It would be so easy to drown in his grief, in the overwhelming sense of loss he felt at being alone in a room he had shared with his lover for far too brief a time, but he reminded himself firmly why he was here. They had a plan finally, a tested way to find Orlando, and he was wasting time.

Setting aside the pillow with one last caress, as if he could somehow touch Orlando by touching his belongings, Alain rose to search for his lover's hairbrush. Finding it in the bathroom in the drawer beneath the sink, he carefully untangled a handful of strands, tucking them in his pocket. He started to put the brush away but then changed his mind. The more hair they had, the better the chance of the spell working. He cast the displacement spell to return to Milice headquarters, Orlando's brush in hand.

"They went to the general's office," the wizard on duty in the Salle des Cartes informed Alain when he reappeared. "They said for you to meet them there."

Alain nodded, hurrying through the corridors to Marcel's office. It rankled that he would not be the one to do the spell that would lead to Orlando's rescue, but getting Orlando back was far more important than his pride.

"Did you find something?" Jean asked as soon as Alain walked through the door.

Alain held up the brush. "I figured the more hair we had, the easier it would be to find him," he explained, setting it on Marcel's desk.

"It certainly can't hurt," Marcel agreed. "Thierry and Sebastien led a patrol out when we got a report of an attack. You can wait for him if you want, or Raymond can do the spell. I've been summoned to Parlement or I'd stay and help."

Alain looked over at the dark-haired wizard, flanked protectively by the chef de la Cour. Orlando was as important to Jean as he was to Alain, albeit in a very different way, and if he read the other pairing's body language correctly, Raymond would no more disappoint Jean than Alain would willingly disappoint Orlando. "There's no reason to wait," he said. "I trust Raymond to do the spell."

They were words Raymond had never expected to hear.

"Good," Marcel declared with a smile. "I can't wait any longer, but let me know how he is when you get him home."

"I will," Alain promised as Marcel winked out.

"Let's find him and bring him home," Raymond proposed, still marveling inwardly at Alain's show of trust. He resisted the urge to glance at Jean for reassurance or confirmation. How things had changed in the month since the alliance formed!

"Yes," Alain agreed, "it's past time."

Raymond concentrated on the brush in front of him, casting the tracking spell. He could feel his magic spreading out, searching for Orlando. He turned, keeping an eye on Marcel's smaller version of the locator map to gauge as best he could how far afield his senses stretched. Occasionally, he would feel an empty pocket, and he made note of those for future reference as they could well be additional strongholds for the dark wizards. The familiar tug toward the object of the search did not materialize, though. With a frown, he cast the spell again, investing more power into it so it would search a wider area. To his delight, the stronger spell penetrated some of the dead zones from the first spell, but a minute passed with no location for Orlando.

"I need more power," he muttered. "Wherever he is, Serrier's got him warded and I can't get my magic through all of them."

"I don't think it'll work for me to add to the spell," Alain replied in frustration. "I can see who else is around."

"Or I can bite you," Jean offered. "It worked during the Piège-Pouvoir. There's no reason it shouldn't work now, too."

Alain did not say anything, not wanting to put pressure on either of the other men, but he remembered the incredible surge of power he had felt when Orlando fed from him during the Piège-Pouvoir, far more powerful than the combined magic of two wizards on their own.

"It's worth a try," Raymond agreed.

"Do you want me to leave?" Alain volunteered, not wanting to impose on the intimate moment. Yes, they had been in the same room during the Piège-Pouvoir, but on the other side of the lake, far enough he could barely see the other pairs. Marcel's office was nowhere near as spacious as the underground cavern.

Raymond wanted to say yes, given the incredible intimacy that had so recently developed between Jean and himself, but he could hardly ask the other wizard to be absent while they searched for his missing lover. "It's all right, you can stay."

He did not miss Alain's sigh of relief at his answer. Turning to Jean, he hesitated, his sense of decorum pushing him to offer his wrist while the rest of him wanted to offer his neck. Jean took the decision from him, stepping behind him and urging him to face the desk again. Raymond's eyes closed instinctively as he leaned into Jean's touch, his lover's fangs on his neck sending a surge of lust and power through him. Forcing himself to concentrate, he channeled all the summoned strength into the tracking spell. It washed out of him, obliterating the few remaining pockets of Serrier's wards within the city, but as his magic spread out into the banlieues, dead zones began appearing again. Not many—and Raymond took careful note of each one—but either the distance or the strength of the wards kept him from penetrating, even with Jean's assistance.

And still, he felt no resonance with Orlando.

He forced his senses to stretch as far as they would go, reaching the edges of l'Ile-de-France and going beyond, into Bourgogne, Picardie, Normandie, Champagne, and toward Tours, but eventually he reached the limits of even his augmented strength. Collapsing in Jean's arms, he ended the spell. "I'm sorry. I can't find him."

Alain's face fell, disappointment visible in every line of his body. "What happened?"

"I got through the wards within the city, but there were some places farther away that I couldn't breach. Either the distance played a role or they're far more heavily protected than anywhere inside the périphérique," Raymond explained. "I could feel the magical vacuum, but I couldn't break through."

"But that still tells us where to search," Alain exclaimed, eyes losing some of their haunted look. "If we search where you couldn't sense anything, we'll find him eventually." He lowered the shields he had kept in place since coming on duty, making sure he could still sense Orlando's presence. As always, his lover's emotions washed into his, the force and depth of his love a balm to Alain's soul and a prod to his guilt.

"I'll mark the places," Raymond agreed, "but if they're that heavily warded, this isn't going to be a short, simple task. There were about a dozen of them, and that assumes he hasn't gone farther afield than I searched. I reached the limits of my power in the tracking spell at about two hundred kilometers."

"That's still more than we could ever have searched without the spell," Jean reminded him. "And it narrows our search down. Now we have to follow up on the locations you identified."

"Didn't Mireille say monsieur Lombard might be back tonight?" Raymond asked, changing the subject slightly as he began pinpointing locations on the map. "It might be worth going by his house to see if he has any other ideas, something that might speed up the search even more."

Jean nodded. "We can certainly do that. Even if he doesn't have any suggestions, he'll still want to know what's going on. Alain, can you start searching with your patrol while Raymond and I do that? We can join you when we get back, or try other locations at the same time to speed up the process."

"That works," Alain agreed, looking at the map and mentally charting where to begin. "I'll mark places off the map as we clear them and you can see where I am from my repère."

"That's all of them," Raymond declared, stepping away from the map. "Let's go, Jean. The sooner we get to monsieur Lombard's, the sooner we'll be able to help, one way or another."

The two men left Alain alone with his plans and were walking down the corridor toward the exit when an angry Adèle stormed out of her office, slamming the door behind her. "Fucking bastard!" she spat as she locked the door. "Thinking he's God's gift to women and we should all just spread our legs for him whenever he wants. Stupid prick!"

"You'd eat a less irascible man alive, darling," Jean commented, drawing her attention and her ire.

"You probably agree with him," she snarled. "I should just let him do whatever he wants, treat me like a whore, fuck me without regard for my pleasure just because he's a man and I'm not, is that it?"

"I didn't say that at all," Jean replied coolly, "but I'm not blind either. Say what you like, but I seriously doubt all the color in your cheeks is from anger or even from righteous indignation." He caught her arm, pinning her against the wall with his body. "You may hate him—you may even have reason to hate him—but he's exactly the kind of man it takes to turn you on." His hands moved roughly over her body, surprising a moan from her lips. Stepping back, he dropped them to his side. "As I was saying."

Adèle's jaw dropped in surprise before her eyes narrowed and her wand lifted, the spell coming unbidden to her lips. Raymond blocked it with a wave of his hand. "He's right, Adèle, and you know it. We all know it." He suppressed the surge of jealousy at the sight of Jean's hands on someone else, especially Adèle, since she had been a bone of contention between them early in the alliance. His partner was proving a point, nothing more.

"That doesn't give Jude the right to accost me any time he chooses," she pressed.

"No, it doesn't," Jean agreed. "He's in your office, I presume." She nodded. "Leave him there for now. We'll deal with this once and for all when Marcel gets back. In the meantime, stay out and away from him. You won't help your case otherwise."

Adèle started to protest that she could fight her own battles, but she bit back the words. The matter had come to the attention of the alliance leaders now. It was out of her hands. She deliberately ignored the little voice that whispered she would miss the thrill of the fight.

Putting Adèle and her troubles from his mind, Jean led the way out of Milice headquarters into the darkening evening. "It'll be winter before long," he mused aloud as the last of the autumn leaves rattled around their feet. "I wonder if it'll snow this year."

"If it doesn't, we'll just have to go somewhere that does have some," Raymond answered impulsively. "Now that you aren't limited by daylight, and with a little bit of magic, we can do things like that."

Jean's expression softened. "I'd like that," he replied, forbearing to reach for the wizard's hand. He did not want to scare the other man off with more seriousness than he was ready for.

Side by side, they navigated the Métro to île St-Louis. By the time they reached monsieur Lombard's house, full darkness had fallen. Jean rang the bell and waited, but the house remained silent.

He rang a second time, fingers tapping impatiently against his thigh as the seconds passed. Raymond caught the nervous digits, stilling them gently in his. "Mireille said it might be tomorrow night," he reminded Jean. "By then, we'll probably have found him and it won't matter anyway. Let's head back."

"Do you mind if we go by Notre-Dame on the way?" Jean asked softly. "I… I'd like to take a minute to pray."

"Of course I don't mind," Raymond exclaimed. "I forget at times that you were a seminarian. Just keep reminding me."

"My lack of daily devotion would appall my mentors," Jean replied with a chuckle as they crossed the Pont Saint-Louis to the île de la Cité and walked up the rue du Cloître Notre-Dame to the entrance of the cathedral. "But I still find comfort in prayer during times of stress, and this definitely qualifies."

"Take the time you need," Raymond insisted, standing respectfully in the back of the church whose faith he did not share. He did not need it, though, to appreciate the majesty of the building or to sense the sacred well of power upon which the chapel was built. With a smile, he thought again, as he often had, that every faith drew upon the same mystic energy, each giving its own spin to a truth that defied expression.

Jean genuflected and walked down the central aisle to the altar rail, kneeling down, rosary in hand as he prayed for Orlando's safety and quick rescue. His lips moved in silent supplication as he sent his petition winging heavenward on the scent of incense and the smoke of votives offered as proof of faith. Images of his friend as he had first seen him, broken, bleeding, teetering on the edge of self-destruction, rose up to haunt him. Orlando knew the depths of human—or vampiric—cruelty in a way few others had experienced. On more than one occasion, he had heard the younger vampire swear he would walk out into the sunlight rather than be subject to such tortures again. The thought that Orlando might reach that stage again before they could get there to rescue him scared Jean as nothing in his long existence had ever done.

That had been before Alain, though. Surely the arrival of the wizard in Orlando's purview, the Aveu de Sang that bound them together in this world and some said in the next, would give Orlando the hope he needed to hold out against the kind of desolation he had known in his previous captivity. Alain said he could sense Orlando still, could feel his emotions, and while the wizard was concerned about Orlando's physical condition, he had not voiced any worry over his emotional state. Orlando did not have a deceptive bone in his body. If he was that desperate again, Alain would surely know it, no matter how hard the vampire tried to hide it.

Jean held on to those thoughts as he continued to pray, counting them the partial answer to his prayers. Orlando's return would answer the rest.

Chapter 7

RAYMOND STOOD patiently at the back of the church, his eyes darting around nervously. Too much had happened in the past few days for him to be completely comfortable out in the relative open like this. Catching sight of the font of holy water, he crossed to it with a sigh of relief. At least with water beneath his fingers, he would have some warning of any magical approach. The pooled liquid channeled the power inherent in the cathedral, even more powerful to him for being on an island in the middle of the river. The feeling lulled him into a light trance as he communed with the elemental magic, letting the tension of the past few days ease and the connection restore his strength.

A sudden ripple, an exterior disturbance, broke him out of his meditative trance. Frowning, he focused on the water in the basin, consciously using the power of the location to stretch his senses much as he had done with the tracking spell, but with a broader focus.

He bit back a curse, conscious of standing on hallowed ground, and reached for his cell phone, calling Milice headquarters for backup. He had just started down the aisle to get Jean and try to leave by one of the side doors when the first spell rocked the roof above them.

"We've got to get out of here," he shouted to Jean, no longer worrying about respecting the sanctity of the church. Their safety came first. "Dark wizards—they're on the parvis and to the north, but they haven't made it around to the south door yet."

"No," Jean protested immediately, the thought of anything threatening any church, but this church in particular, tearing at his soul. "If we leave, they'll destroy the cathedral for sure."

"If we stay, they may well destroy us," Raymond reminded him. "I'm good, but I'm only one wizard against at least twenty. I've called for help. A patrol will be here as soon as they can."

"Then we have to hold out until they get here." He would not let Serrier's evil desecrate holy ground.

"No," Raymond contradicted. "We have to get out of here. They'll deal with it when they get here."

"Go on," Jean said, eyes already darting into the shadows as he planned how he could get behind the wizards and take them down one at a time. He hated the thought of perpetrating violence here, but the other option was even more unthinkable. "I know they have a price on your head. I'll do what damage I can until the patrol gets here."

"Like hell I'm leaving you to face them alone," Raymond cried. "If you won't come with me, I'll stay with you and hope reinforcements get here in a hurry. Come on."

He pulled Jean toward the south transept. At least there they would have walls on three sides, limiting the direction their attackers could come at them. When the first wizard appeared through the north portal, he cast an *Abbatoire*. He would only get one chance at each of them, and with no one else to rely on, he would have to take them down right away or he would be turning his magic on himself. Death at his own hand was preferable to the tortures Serrier would make him suffer. Immediately, a warning shout rang out. "They know we're here," he warned Jean. "Do your best to block the door behind us. That way I only have to worry about the ones in front of us."

Jean started toward the door as more wizards streamed in across from them. He turned back, torn between doing as Raymond asked and staying at his partner's side to protect him as best he could. His protective instincts won out. Just as he reached Raymond again, two wizards cast at him simultaneously. Raymond blocked the first spell, but could not stop the second one. He braced himself for the pain that would wrack his body, but it never came.

Contorting his body into a tight flip that ended with him directly beside Raymond, Jean knocked him to the side before the spell could. The magic intended for Raymond hit the vampire instead, sending him to his knees, retching as his stomach tied itself in knots. "Merde," Raymond cursed, heaving Jean over his shoulder and retreating to the corner. Depositing Jean at his feet, he ducked behind the statue of Jeanne d'Arc, letting the spells bounce harmlessly off the stone as he did his best to soothe Jean. The spell would wear off in a few minutes, but the magical antidote would be useless coming from Raymond's wand.

"It's not real, right?" Jean gasped through the pain in his abdomen.

"It's just pain, not real damage," Raymond confirmed.

"Then stop them."

Anger growing as he watched Jean struggle through the pain, Raymond focused beyond the statue again, waiting patiently for the chance to strike at whoever had dared to attack his partner. He crept forward slowly, clinging to the shadows in the hopes of escaping detection a little longer. They knew he was there, of course, and unless the wizard who had cast the spell that hit Jean had not bothered to watch it hit, they knew he was not the one hurt, but he could hope his lack of immediate retaliation had convinced them he had given up.

Turning the corner to the bas-côté, he ducked into the first chapel, using the altar as cover while he searched for a target. Movement drew his eyes to the other side of the nave and he shot off a spell, the other wizard having barely enough time to turn before he went down.

Raymond resisted the urge to glance at his watch, to calculate how long it would take reinforcements to arrive. He could not count on that. He had to rely on his own wits, and maybe Jean's, if the vampire recovered quickly enough from the pain spell.

Hearing footsteps nearing his hiding place, he whispered a displacement spell, reappearing in the back of the déambulatoire. Wishing Thierry was there to reinforce the stones, he nonetheless cast a strengthening spell, hoping to keep the building intact a little longer since it was of such vital importance to Jean. Even with his assistance, though, the cathedral shuddered around him as if the stones themselves were crying out in protest at the violation of holy ground.

He was ready to abandon the fight, for even as sacred a location as this one was not worth their lives, when he heard the shouts of Milice wizards calling for the dark wizards to drop their wands and surrender. Heaving a sigh of relief, he started working his way back toward where he had left Jean, hoping his partner had the good sense to keep his head down until the spell lost its grip on him.

To his relief, he found Jean exactly where he had left him behind the statue of Jeanne d'Arc. The vampire had pushed himself up to sitting, his trunk protected by the stone base, only his feet sticking out. "Come on," he said, reaching for Jean's arm. "The cavalry's here. We can get you to the infirmary."

Jean shook his head. "It isn't magical medicine I need. I need to know the cathedral is safe, and then I need to feed."

"Can you stand?" Raymond asked. Jean nodded and rose painfully to his feet, leaning heavily on Raymond's arm as he experimentally took a few steps forward. Shouts still rang out all through the church, spells of all kinds flying, chipping stone and scattering furniture, but it sounded to Raymond like the Milice was slowly gaining the upper hand.

Senses on high alert, Raymond helped Jean slowly toward the nave. Not seeing any more dark wizards, he returned one of the straight-backed chairs to standing and eased Jean into it. "Stay here while I see what's going on. If more fighting breaks out, get down. Don't take any chances."

Jean nodded his agreement, though his instincts protested at the thought of hiding helplessly while others fought. He overruled them, knowing the fading pain in his belly would keep him from being effective and possibly cause him to get hurt far worse. He refused to consider that Serrier's wizards knew to use pain spells rather than killing spells because they had tested them on Orlando. He had enough worries at the moment without adding to them.

He kept a close eye on Raymond, though, as he walked down the nave toward the main entrance, occasionally stopping to move a chair or a kneeler out of his path. Jean had no idea what he would be able to do if someone attacked, but he knew he would try. Fortunately, no attack materialized.

Moments later, Thierry and Sebastien came into view, checking with Raymond and then glancing toward Jean.

The vampire rose painfully to his feet, joining them halfway down the long nave.

"They're gone," Thierry told Jean, "but the church is pretty badly damaged. I could see cracks in the flying buttresses and the walls. We need to get everyone out so I can try to repair it at least enough that we don't have to worry about it collapsing until stone masons can come and shore it up properly."

Jean frowned, glancing around at the size of the church. "That's a pretty large job for one wizard, especially if it's as damaged as you say."

"It is," Thierry agreed, "but I'm the only one here with an affinity to earth. I'll do what I can and hope it's enough."

"Let Sebastien bite you as you cast the spells," Raymond suggested. "When Jean fed from me while I searched for Orlando, I was able to expand the search to cover easily four times the area without a loss of clarity. If Sebastien can boost your strength even a fraction of that, you'll be able to do your work more safely and effectively."

Thierry nodded. "That's a good idea. Assuming Sebastien's willing." The teasing light in his eyes brought a smile to Sebastien's face as well, his willingness clear.

"Just be careful," Jean warned. "This will be a lot more taxing than searching for Orlando was. You wouldn't want...." He trailed off as he remembered his agreement not to tell Sebastien about what had almost happened in the parc de la Courneuve.

"Wouldn't want what?" Sebastien asked sharply. "Is there a danger I need to know about?"

"Sorry," Jean apologized to Thierry. "It slipped out."

Thierry shrugged. "There's always a danger when dealing with the element we resonate with. If we're not careful, we can get drawn into the element just like I did into the elemental magic during the Rite d'équilibrage."

"Except that if you get drawn too far into your element, you blend with it," Raymond added, wanting to make sure Sebastien understood the danger. "In Thierry's case, he could turn into stone if he got too deep in without someone to pull him back."

"How do you know about it, Jean?" Sebastien asked, ignoring Thierry for a moment. "Did something happen to Raymond?"

Jean looked to Thierry for help, but the blond wizard would not meet his gaze. "Not to Raymond. To Thierry. When we were searching for Orlando, he tried to use his connection to find where they'd taken Orlando. It looked like he was changing...."

"And you didn't tell me?" Sebastien roared. Both Thierry and Jean flinched, though it was not clear which of them the angry vampire was addressing.

"It was over and he was fine," Jean replied, feeling like nothing more than a schoolboy called on the carpet by the headmaster.

"And if it had been Raymond who almost melted into a puddle, wouldn't you have wanted to know?" Sebastien challenged.

"Well, yes, but—"

"No buts," Sebastien interrupted coldly. "Thierry said to empty the cathedral so he could work. I want this done so we aren't going to talk about this now, but I won't forget it, rest assured."

Jean's face tightened. "You forget yourself, Noyer."

"I asked him not to tell you," Thierry interrupted, trying to head off the confrontation between the two vampires. "I knew you'd worry, and I didn't see any reason for it when it was a stupid mistake I haven't made since I first realized my connection with the earth—and one I won't make again. If you're going to be angry, be angry with me, not with Jean."

"We'll discuss this later," Sebastien promised. "For now, get the cathedral stabilized. I'd rather not have it come down around my ears."

"I tried to shore it up a little back in the déambulatoire," Raymond told Thierry. "Just so you know. And I don't know if you can tap into it, but there's a well of elemental magic here. I wonder if the church wasn't built on the site of an old grove; this is sacred space from far before the spread of Christianity. If you can reach it, that'll help boost your power, too. Jean got hit with a spell, so I'm going to get him taken care of. Let us know when everything's stabilized here."

"We will," Thierry promised, dismissing them from his mind as he considered where to begin casting his spell. After a few moments' internal debate, he decided on the pillar closest to where the nave and transept met. It was near the center of the church, which would allow his spell to radiate outward. Resting his hands against the stone, he felt the resonance Raymond had described and the outrage of sacred space violated by magic with foul intent. He had already started radiating healing energy into the living force that invested the building when Sebastien stepped up behind him, arms coming around him to rest his hands against the stone as well. His lover's fangs brushed his neck before piercing deeply. Thierry's head fell back against the vampire's shoulder, letting Sebastien take his weight.

Even warned, Thierry was caught off guard by the magnitude of the power that suddenly flowed through him from both directions. With his magic boosted by Sebastien's fangs, he connected with the stones in a way he had never done before, going beyond the surface to the very core of their being. They rejoiced in his presence, in the touch of a mind and hands that could understand them, pouring out their story in a rush of images that stole

Thierry's breath as he struggled to assimilate them all and still provide the stabilization the building needed.

After a moment, he let the images flow over him and simply listened. The situation was not so critical that he had to start the spells immediately. He saw the stones awakened, quarried from their resting place up the river and ferried to their current location, shaped to fit perfectly one against the other. He felt them come to life as they drew in the inherent magic of the location. To his surprise, as they showed him how they were set one upon another, they revealed the secret of one of the foremen, a wizard in a time of persecution. He had lingered every evening with the excuse of getting things ready for the next day, waiting until he was alone to channel his magic into the building, using his misunderstood gift in his own quiet way to add to the glory of the God he worshipped with all his heart, even knowing he would be excommunicated or worse if he was discovered.

The stones' amusement at the coronation of Henry V of England, who thought to claim the French throne by taking the crown in Paris, not realizing that the French would never recognize a king crowned anywhere but in Reims, brought a smile to Thierry's face as well.

The amusement changed to fear as they recounted the horrors they had seen during the Nazi occupation, executions on the parvis in violation of the sanctity of the church, a sanctity the Nazis never acknowledged. They showed him images of people huddled in fear at the foot of the altar or praying fervently at the statue of Jeanne d'Arc, begging for salvation from the monsters who had taken over their lives. Thierry projected reassurance back, reminding the stones that those times had passed, that democracy had returned once again.

They replied with images of the battle tonight, directed not at other people, but at them. It was the opening Thierry needed to bring up his purpose in being there. He sent out tendrils of healing magic, offering them to the aging, aching building. The stones accepted his offer immediately, cracks and weakness mending, repairing damage from the most recent battle and then going deeper, to the very foundation of the church, renewing the magical bonds from the early foreman until the church stood as solidly as the day it was built.

Gasping, Thierry broke free of the spell, collapsing in Sebastien's arms, his head spinning with everything he had seen and felt.

"Are you all right?" Sebastien asked immediately.

Thierry took a moment to reply, taking stock of himself. To his surprise, he felt no magical drain. Either Sebastien had strengthened him even more than Raymond had suggested was possible or else Notre-Dame itself had restored him as he restored it. "I'm fine," he said finally, wonder imbuing his voice. "I don't know why I'm fine, but I really am."

"Are you sure?" Sebastien pressed. "I could feel the drain on you."

Thierry nodded even as he repeated his self-inventory. Glancing around the church he saw now with new eyes, he mused aloud, "I think we've made a mistake all these years. We should have been doing the Rites d'équilibrage here. Earth, water, wind, fire… they're all here and at a crossroads of magical power the likes of which I've rarely felt. Marcel needs to know about this."

"Later," Sebastien growled. The combination of the desire he felt for his partner, which bubbled constantly just below the surface, and the fear that still rode him at the thought of nearly losing his lover without even knowing it, was enough to put all other considerations from his mind. "We have other things to discuss first, like the fact that you didn't tell me about what happened while you were searching for Orlando that first night."

Chapter 8

"REPORT?" SERRIER asked as soon as Simon and his patrol reappeared.

"Payet was there for some reason when we arrived," Simon spat, "with a vampire, maybe even Bellaiche, although it was hard to tell in the dimness. The spells worked, but he managed to get a call out for help and so we had to pull back before we brought the cathedral down. It was odd, though. It felt like the building itself was resisting our magic."

"That isn't possible," Serrier exclaimed, rising from his feet at the unprecedented news. "It's a building, inanimate stone. Only a locus should be able to resist that kind of magic, and we would have known if there was one here in Paris."

"I have no idea, but it didn't crumble the way it should have," Simon replied defensively. "I just know what I saw, so unless I've lost all capacity to judge the strength of my spells, something strange went on tonight."

"I need to think about this," Serrier declared, beginning to pace agitatedly, his mind racing with possibilities. "If there's a locus right here in Paris, that changes our plans. In the meantime, you said the spells worked on the vampires?"

Simon nodded. "Bellaiche, or whoever the vampire was, went down immediately and stayed down the whole time we were fighting. And I'm pretty sure I saw other vampires go down once the Milice reinforcements got there. Either that or Chavinier's got new recruits I don't know."

"What spells did you use?"

"Pain spells," Simon replied. "We might not be able to kill them, but we can definitely incapacitate them, and it has the advantage of working on wizard and vampire alike."

"Good. Then it's time to press our advantage. They won't be expecting us to attack again so soon when we've been regrouping after each attack. Get your patrol ready to go back out. Hit randomly. It doesn't have to be anything 'important'. The important thing is to show we're as strong as their alliance," Serrier sneered.

"And the locus, if it is one?"

"I'll send someone back to check, discreetly, and if it is, we'll make our plans accordingly," Serrier declared, "but until then, let's remind Paris we're here. Strike and leave. Don't engage the Milice, just create chaos."

Simon grinned. He might not have Claude's obsession with torture, but he was not at all opposed to striking fear into the hearts of the city's denizens. They needed to understand how helpless the Milice ultimately was against the power of the dark wizards. "We can do that." He shouted for his patrol to regroup and led them back out into the night.

In the shadows, Eric frowned. This was not a complication he needed. Shrugging since there was nothing he could do about Simon and his goons, he retreated back to the basement. And the vampire. He had invented an errand to send Vincent on, giving him a chance to talk with the man alone.

"What would your life be worth to the Milice?" he asked, stepping through the door.

Orlando roused from the near-slumber he tried to escape to whenever his captors left him alone long enough. His entire body hurt, but not as badly as before. Apparently, the rest had allowed him to heal at least some. "What does it matter?" he asked dully. He clung to hope as much as he could, but he was aware of the passage of time. He could feel his body weakening, the time without food combining with the torture inflicted on him to drain his strength even more quickly than normal. "You're not about to let me go and endanger your place here, and I'm not stupid. I know Serrier will find a way to destroy me once he's done experimenting on me."

"You're undoubtedly right," Eric agreed, stomach churning as he considered the possible repercussions of what he was about to do. If the vampire betrayed him, he would be dead, but almost certainly not as swiftly or mercifully as Serrier had dealt with Dominique. No, if Serrier found out about this conversation, he would be Claude's next plaything. Still, he had to try. He had promised Vincent he would consider their options. "At least about Serrier, but you told me Alain and Thierry would welcome me back if I changed sides again. Was it the truth? Or were you just trying to gain some sympathy?"

"You must really think I'm a fool," Orlando cried, sitting up slowly, his body protesting even that much unnecessary movement. "You can't trust any answer I give to that question because I'm hardly about to admit to the latter, so even if I say the former, you'd have to fear I was lying."

"Are you?" Eric pressed.

"What does it matter?" the vampire repeated, hopelessness creeping over him as he faced the big wizard. He knew Alain was still searching for him, but he could also feel his lover's increasing desperation. He had survived torture and imprisonment once, but that was before Alain, before the Aveu de Sang. That promise gave him the hope of rescue he had not had the last time, but it also limited his time starkly. He had until his last feeding ran out, and then his time was up, his magical life force spent.

"Because, according to Serrier's pet vampire, somewhere out there is a person bearing your mark," Eric replied honestly. He took a deep breath, memories assailing him. "I know what it's like to lose everyone dear to you in one fell blow. You'd appeal to Alain, and you were fighting at his side when we took you. You talked about him like you know him well. Maybe I'd like a chance to do right by an old friend."

"Maybe you'd like a chance to hurt me worse because you blame Alain for what happened to your family," Orlando retorted blandly, seeing the trap for what it was. "You wizards think you're subtle, but vampires have had centuries to perfect that art. You won't trap me into saying something I don't want to reveal."

Eric was sure Alain would not simply have mentioned his role in the deaths of Eric's family to a casual acquaintance. Even blinded by anger and grief, he had seen how remorseful Alain was. It had not changed anything, but he had known it. He would not brag about it now. "He wouldn't have told you about that unless you meant something to him," he concluded aloud. "I'm no Morgana, whatever he may think."

Orlando frowned, confused for a moment by the apparent non sequitur. Then the coin dropped and he remembered a conversation he and Alain had when his lover had finally told him everything that had happened with Eric, about the code they and Thierry had developed using the names of great wizards from the past. If he remembered correctly, Morgana was the name of the betrayer. And if so, that meant.... "Merlin knows what else you might be," he replied tentatively, not entirely sure he had all the details straight. If he was right, though, he might have just found an ally. And if he was not, he might still turn it to his advantage.

"Thank all the gods!" Eric breathed, even the inaccurate response— since everything was far from well—enough to assure him the vampire was well in Alain's or Thierry's confidence. "I wasn't sure he'd have told you, even with all the rest. Why would he, after all? I changed sides."

"You took a hell of a chance," Orlando commented, stomach still roiling at the thought of everything he had just learned. If, in fact, the wizard was telling him the truth. "So what happens now?"

"Now I figure out how to get you free," Eric answered honestly, "but it isn't going to happen tonight, I'm afraid. Serrier's determined to remind the world he's here and powerful. There will be wizards coming and going all night long. There's no way I'd be able to smuggle you out. Which means waiting until tomorrow night at least."

"I can hold out until tomorrow night," Orlando assured him, taking stock of his physical state one more time now that he had a true hope of escape. "I'm not sure how much longer beyond that." He saw no harm in revealing that when the rogue had already told them as much. The instincts bred by le jeu des Cours warned him that this was too simple, though, so he put his alternate plan in motion as well. "If you can't get me out, though, if Serrier finds a way to destroy me, will you take this to Alain?" He reached in his pocket and pulled out his signet ring. "Give him that much peace at least." His hand trembled as he passed the only physical link to Alain over to a stranger. His heart protested the loss, but if the wizard took the ring with him when he left to go home, it would appear on the locator map, assuming someone was there to see it. And if they saw it, someone would come and either capture Simonet or follow him back here, either of which would tell the Milice where to find him.

Eric took the gold band and examined it closely. "This isn't any ordinary ring," he commented.

"No, it isn't," Orlando agreed, thinking of everything that simple ornament had meant over the time since he was made. It had been a symbol of his torture, then his liberation, and finally, now, of his love. He had not been without it since the day Thurloe was destroyed. He only hoped he would see it again some day. "It's the ring we used to bind ourselves to one another. If anything happens to me, I want him to have it."

"If it comes to that, I'll make sure he gets it," Eric promised, mind racing with details now that he had committed himself to this path, "but I'd much rather deliver you to him than the ring."

Orlando smiled. With his repère in hand, Eric was likely to do both.

THE WARDS around the seemingly abandoned building were the most complex Alain had ever seen outside of Milice headquarters. Even with the advice Raymond had given him, it took him an alarmingly long time to dismantle them. He hoped that meant they were protecting something important, but this was the third dead zone he and his patrol had investigated without any luck so far. They had encountered plenty of resistance, but no sign of Orlando—and each time it became clear they were getting the upper hand, the dark wizards simply vanished, leaving them to deal with booby traps and magical land mines. They had not dared to leave a building unsearched, though, in case there was some indication of where the dark wizards had gone or where they held Orlando captive.

The wards fell finally beneath Alain's determination. The patrol braced for the expected counterattack, but none came. "Wait," Alain said when one of his wizards started forward, everything about the situation striking him as wrong.

"What is it, Alain?" Lt. Fouquet asked, having long ago come to trust his captain's instincts where danger was concerned.

"I don't know," Alain replied honestly, "but it doesn't feel right. If they're there, why aren't they attacking? And if they aren't, why was it so heavily warded? It's not like our presence has gone unnoticed tonight." Glancing around, he found a large pebble and tossed it toward the building.

Nothing happened.

To his left, Maurice Quenaud rolled his eyes. He did not know why they were doing this. It was all a wild goose chase anyway. They were wasting time and resources on one vampire when they could be out engaging Serrier directly. When the pebble did not result in any great cataclysm, he shook his head and urged, "Let's go. Time's passing." He took two steps forward, ignoring Alain's shouted warning.

It was the last sound he ever heard as the warehouse exploded in flames.

"What the hell?" Lt. Fouquet exclaimed as they all jumped back, throwing up arms to cover their faces against the conflagration.

Alain did not reply right away, a stream of curses coming out of his mouth instead. He had not known the dead wizard well, but he seemed to remember Marcel saying something about him having a young family. Why the general had let the kid fight was beyond Alain, but that was relatively normal where Marcel was concerned. Alain rarely understood more than half of what the wily old fox did.

"Put it out," he barked, focusing on containing the damage first. He would worry about the rest later, including having to tell Marcel about Maurice's death.

His patrol spread out, casting dampening spells on the flames and repellent spells on the surrounding buildings to keep the fire from spreading.

Alain was torn as he worked alongside his patrol. He knew they needed to stay and get the fire under control, but he chafed at the restriction. Thankfully, Orlando had not been in the blaze—he could still feel the touch of his lover's mind—which meant he was somewhere else, somewhere where Alain was not. He silently regretted Maurice's impetuousness. With a little more time, Alain would have discovered the spell and they could have either nullified it or warded around it so no one else would stumble into it instead of spending time dealing with the aftermath.

Time they should have been spending searching for Orlando.

With a frustrated groan, he pulled his cell phone off his belt when it started vibrating. "Magnier," he snapped.

"Alain, you need to bring your patrol back in. There have been reports of attacks all over the city. We need everyone who isn't completely exhausted here," Marcel told him sadly. "I'm sorry."

"Putain!" Alain cursed. "We've got a problem here, but I'll send them back in as soon as we've dealt with it."

"Alain," Marcel warned.

"Don't order me to come with them," Alain interrupted. "I'd hate to have to disobey a direct order."

"You won't help him by getting yourself killed," Marcel reminded the younger wizard.

"I won't get myself killed," Alain promised, "but I have to do this. Even with the shields up, I can feel him hurting now. I won't leave him in their hands a moment longer than I have to. If that means facing dereliction of duty charges, so be it."

Marcel sighed. "You know me better than that, my boy. Go on. Do what you have to do, but I have to have your patrol back."

"Let us get these fires out and I'll send them," Alain agreed.

Anger bubbled up within him as he ended the call. Frustration, helplessness, guilt and grief blended together in a foul brew that choked him with its strength. He wanted to rage against the night, to curse and shout and rant and rampage, but none of that would help Orlando. Nor would it make him feel any better. He remembered all too well the last time he lost control that way, taking his rage out on the wizard who had killed his wife and son. And killing Eric's family in the process.

He needed to be in control, to focus everything he was on finding Orlando. Once his lover was safe, he could release his emotions and the magical firestorm it would surely provoke. Or he could let Orlando fuck it out of him. He bit back a half sob, half chuckle at the thought. Silently, he beseeched all the gods and goddesses, from the Ancients through modern Christianity, to allow him to find his lover before it was too late.

He had never been an especially pious man, but for Orlando's safety, he would make any vow, any offering. Even his own life, though he imagined his lover would not appreciate that particular gesture. Regardless, he would consider it a small price to pay for knowing Orlando was free from Serrier's tortures.

It took another fifteen minutes to get the fires out, fifteen minutes that seemed like an age to Alain, chafing as he was at anything that kept him from moving on to the next possible site where Orlando could be held. When the blaze was finally contained, he called to Lt. Fouquet, explaining Marcel's orders.

"Do you think this explosion is part of that?" Lt. Fouquet asked. "Or do you think he's figured out what we're doing?"

Alain shrugged. "It could be either. Or both. It doesn't matter. You have to take the patrol back to headquarters and help Marcel in any way you can."

"You're not coming with us?"

Alain shook his head. "I can't abandon Orlando. And if Serrier has realized we're searching actively, he'll pull back and back as far as he can. The longer I delay, the less likely we'll find Orlando at all, much less before they kill him."

Lt. Fouquet nodded. "I haven't always agreed with you, but I didn't want command of a patrol this way. I don't want to see anything happen to you. Are you sure you won't take someone else with you?"

Alain's lips quirked in a half smile. "Thanks, but Marcel made it pretty clear that while he'd accept me doing what I need to do, he needed everyone else on other things. I don't want to get anyone else in trouble."

Lt. Fouquet's eyebrows twitched in amusement. "Every man and woman in this patrol would choose to help you regardless of 'trouble' if you asked."

"Which is why I'm not asking."

Fouquet shook his head. "You're a better man than I am, then. Good luck, and don't hesitate to call for backup if you get in over your head. We'll come even if the general won't send anyone else."

Alain watched as his patrol gathered. He let Lt. Fouquet give them their orders, making his own position clear by his silence. To his surprise, each member saluted him before returning to Milice headquarters, leaving him alone on the empty street.

Chapter 9

ON THE parvis outside, Jean looked back at the cathedral once more. "Are you sure we should leave?"

"I can't help Thierry with what he's doing," Raymond replied, "not really, and Sebastien will be much more comfortable without us there. Besides, we need to get somewhere private so you can feed. I know how much that spell hurts."

"It isn't as bad now," Jean insisted. "Your magic in my blood is already fighting it. We've got to deal with Adèle and Jude. I won't have one of my Cour abusing his position within the alliance."

"I seriously doubt he was the only one out of line," Raymond commented, walking toward the subway stop so they could return to Milice headquarters. "I'd be willing to bet Adèle did her share of it, too."

Jean shrugged. "She may have, but I don't think she started it. Remember the way she acted the morning after the Rite d'équilibrage, when the wild magic was still loose? She didn't want what happened between them, however much it might have turned her on, and that's the ultimate issue. And even if she does at some level, the rancor between them is bad for the alliance. We have to deal with it before it spreads."

Raymond could hardly argue with that. "Just tell me if the pain gets worse," he requested. "We can go to my office if you need to feed before we get back to your apartment."

"I will," Jean agreed as they descended into the subway. There were only a few other passengers waiting for the late train, but Jean and Raymond let the conversation between them cease for the moment, not wanting to risk anyone overhearing anything important. As the subway rattled into the station, Raymond let his hand settle on Jean's back, needing that much connection to his lover. Once again, they had faced down Serrier's forces and escaped—but they were not completely unscathed, and that bothered Raymond immensely. He should have protected Jean. That spell should have hit him, not the vampire. He knew his partner would protest that statement, and in all actuality, he would be right to do so. With Raymond down, Jean would have been defenseless against the attacking wizards, whereas Raymond had been able to pick a few of them off and keep the cathedral from falling before reinforcements arrived. That knowledge did not make his failure to protect his partner any easier to bear.

"Stop brooding," Jean murmured, his lips against Raymond's ear. "I'm feeling better all the time, a fact I attribute directly to feeding before we went to the church."

Raymond shivered at the brush of Jean's breath against his skin, ruffling the ends of his short, dark hair. He was still getting used to the idea that Jean was actually his lover, not just his partner—a new enough concept already. The unexpected reminder sent lust thrilling along his nerves. They had not made love in several days, the demands of the war, Jean's fear for Orlando, and his grief over the woman's—Karine's, he remembered—death keeping them from stealing more than snatches of sleep here and there. Raymond resolved that tonight would be different. He could feel his own reserves nearing depletion and he would need all his strength to feed Jean as well as fight if Alain's patrol succeeded in locating Orlando.

Arriving at their stop, they exited the Métro and returned to Milice headquarters. Jean's hand found Raymond's as they walked, fingers entwining in silent promise.

They entered the building to find total chaos.

"What's going on?" Raymond asked the first wizard they passed.

"Serrier is creating calamities all over the city," was the answer, thrown over a shoulder as the other wizard ran down the hall toward the Salle des Cartes.

"Merde," Raymond cursed. "I was hoping the attack at Notre-Dame was it."

"Let's find Marcel," Jean suggested. "He'll know what's going on and what we can do to help."

Raymond shook his head. "What we're doing to help is taking you home and making sure you're healed. And don't argue. If you weren't the chef de la Cour it might not matter as much, but you have to be strong and visible at Marcel's side when he deals with the fallout from this. You can't do that if you're still hurting from the spell that hit you."

The words were far too heated to be simply the sentiments of an ally, bringing a smile to Jean's face. He had hoped to win Raymond's affection, but he had not expected it to happen any time soon. Perhaps he had been overly cautious in his estimates. "All right," he agreed, though in truth, the pain was nearly gone. "Let's just check in with Marcel first."

Mollified, Raymond accepted the compromise and followed Jean to Marcel's office. Marcel, though, was on the phone, white head nodding occasionally in response to whatever the person on the other end was saying. He looked up when Raymond and Jean came in, but shook his head, gesturing to the phone and waving them away.

Raymond scribbled a note saying Jean was hurt and that they would be in his office. Marcel glanced up at Jean who quirked an eyebrow to assure the general he was not seriously injured. Marcel nodded again and turned his attention back to the conversation and the smaller locator map on the wall behind his desk.

"He knows where we're going," Raymond told Jean as they started down to the basement where Raymond's office was located. "He'll call if he needs us."

Jean followed along willingly. They still had to deal with Adèle and Jude, but that required both him and Marcel, and the general was clearly occupied with other matters—probably related to Serrier's sudden rash of attacks, if the worried look on his face and the scattering of names across the map were any indication.

Knowing he could do nothing at the moment about any of the concerns on his mind, he relaxed into the certainty of what would happen once they were alone in Raymond's office. His partner would insist he feed, although it was no longer as urgent as it had been at the cathedral, Raymond's blood having worked its magic quite effectively even without a boost. And when the feeding evoked the same, uninhibited lust it always did, the vampire rather hoped his partner would prove willing to assuage that need as well.

Raymond unlocked his office, his hand on Jean's lower back urging him through the door into the tiny space. The vampire stepped inside and smiled as he always did at the clutter of books and papers all over the desk and floor. Deciding to encourage the proceedings along a little, he pretended to stagger forward two steps, Raymond's hand coming to his elbow to steady him. "I think I ought to sit down," he told his lover.

Immediately, Raymond changed a pile of books into a couch as he had done once before, helping Jean over to it with careful hands and easing him down onto the soft surface. He stripped off his coat and unbuttoned the top couple of buttons on his shirt swiftly, offering Jean his neck. Jean shook his head and undid several more buttons, lowering his head to the curve of Raymond's chest, a few inches above his nipple. "Your neck is already so torn up," he said by way of explanation, though the thought of his claim being so visible for all to see was an incredible aphrodisiac. It gave him an excuse, though, to get Raymond that much more undressed.

"I don't have anything to hide," Raymond insisted, but that was the extent of his protests as his body arched without his volition into the seductive pull of Jean's fangs.

Jean smiled as the hot blood hit his mouth, both from Raymond's comment and from the conspicuously absent taste of fear. Apparently, all it took to keep his lover from fearing his bite was to scare him with something else first. Pushing that thought aside, he concentrated on the wizard, feeling his fatigue. The last thing he wanted was to drain him dangerously, so he sipped delicately, keeping the contact light as he leaned across the other man's body.

Jean's fangs had their usual effect on Raymond, his cock swelling in his pants. All the fear of the previous hours came rushing back, reminding him how close he had come to losing his partner. His hands tangled in Jean's dark hair, holding him tightly. He tried to restrain himself, knowing Jean was still injured, still grieving, but each pull of his lover's fangs weakened his resistance.

Lifting his head momentarily, Jean met Raymond's eyes, the desire he tasted in his lover's blood, that he saw on Raymond's face, washing over him and healing the ragged edges of his heart. "I want you, too," he husked. "It's okay to be grateful we both survived. It's okay to celebrate it."

A part of Raymond wanted to take Jean's words at face value, but he kept remembering the look on the vampire's face as they laid Karine to rest, and that held him back. "What about Karine?"

"She didn't deserve what was done to her because of me, but I've said my good-byes already," Jean replied honestly. "She was my past, even before she died. You're my present and my future."

The words were enough to ease the foremost of Raymond's concerns. "I don't keep lube here," he murmured, voicing the other one.

"Then I guess you'll have to top," Jean answered with a grin. If he cared to press it, he was sure Raymond could change something consumable into lube, but that would mean stopping to search, and neither of them had that much patience at the moment. "I'll recover far faster than you would, especially since I've just fed."

"I'm not going to hurt you!" Raymond protested.

"With just spit for lube, it's going to hurt a little, no matter how careful you are," Jean reminded him, "but it'll be worth it." He pushed back to his knees and started undressing. "Come on, Raymond," he urged. "I could taste the desperation in your blood. Stop being so noble and fuck me already."

Raymond's control snapped.

He tackled Jean to the couch, bearing his lover down onto the soft cushions, attacking the vampire's mouth with his own and sucking on the lower lip heedless of the sharp fangs. His hands finished the task Jean's had begun, stripping him bare. Lifting his own hand to his mouth, Raymond sucked on two fingers until they were glistening with saliva. He lowered them between Jean's legs, reminding himself to stay in control—an attempt that was doomed to failure from the moment his lover pressed back against him, taking both fingers in without so much as a grimace of pain. He shunted his fingers in and out of the tight portal, stretching it as much as his patience would allow.

He had never known this kind of insane, possessive need, this fierce desire to claim. Sex was supposed to be fun. Intense fun, but fun. This was something different, something dark and heady and wild and far too unfettered to be "fun." For a crazy moment, he wished for fangs like Jean's so he could pierce his lover the same way he had been marked, leaving a sign for all to see that Jean was *his*! He settled for sucking hard on the pale flesh of his vampire's neck, raising a lover's mark almost as telling as the bite marks adorning his own skin. His digits continued their work, preparing Jean for him, but it took only moments before his control failed and his body's—and Jean's—demands took over. He reared back long enough to tear his pants open and spit in his palm, slicking his cock as best he could before covering the vampire again, the tip of his erection finding his lover's eager entrance.

"Mine," he growled in Jean's ear, despite expecting the other man to refute his claim. He had watched the vampire take a spell for him tonight, had felt the bone-deep fear of losing a lover he was only coming to appreciate, and his entire being had screamed in protest. Instincts he had not known he possessed reared their heads, demanding to be acknowledged and assuaged in the most primal of ways.

Jean squirmed beneath him but made no effort to push him away, tipping his head back in a gesture of submission that caught Raymond off guard even as it fired his blood. His mouth returned to the livid mark, sucking on it harder, darkening it more. The vampire pushed up into his mouth, giving Raymond a feeling of power unlike anything he had ever known. He wondered if this was what Jean felt each time he fed. If so, it was a miracle the vampire was not constantly at someone's throat. That thought triggered such an upswell of jealousy that Raymond bit harder, thrusting almost roughly into his lover's body. Jean was *his,* not anyone else's!

Jean moaned beneath the sudden onslaught, hoping this was what Raymond had felt the other night when he lost control, his dominant instincts taking over after the failed search for Edouard. "Yours," he agreed softly as Raymond pushed deeper and deeper into him. The dearth of lubrication only heightened the experience, somehow, adding to the desperation he had tasted in his lover's blood and which governed his own actions now. He needed this as much as Raymond did, and the slight bite of pain only fueled his desire.

His hands scrabbled at the wizard's back, seeking purchase on cloth-covered shoulders. The barrier between them suddenly intolerable, he tore at the fabric, ripping it away so he could reach sweat-slick skin. Raymond did not even pause in his rapacious plundering, the fate of his shirt of no consequence next to the fierce, almost painful need to leave his mark so deep on Jean's body and soul that the vampire would never consider looking elsewhere while he lived.

Finding bare skin, Jean bit down again, no longer worrying about such niceties as when he had last fed or how much he had already taken from the man above him. He had started to wonder if the same magical resonance that allowed Raymond's magic to protect him from sunlight would also keep Jean's feeding from hurting Raymond, but he had not found time to discuss it with his partner. Now was certainly not the time, but the vigor he felt in his lover's blood, the complete lack of any of the fading he usually tasted as he drained someone dry to turn them, certainly appeared to corroborate his theory. His lips picked up the rhythm of Raymond's hips, sucking in time to his lover's thrusts, joining them as completely as he knew how. The sense of rightness, of destiny bringing them to this moment was so potent it made Jean's head spin.

Then his climax hit him and his head spun for an entirely different reason, his cock spurting untouched between their bodies as Raymond continued to pummel him. The arm of the couch bit into his back, a sudden draft of cold air nipped at his sticky flesh, and the muscle in his thigh threatened to cramp. But Jean ignored all the tender indignities inherent in making love. He reveled instead in the connection with his lover, in the lust-darkened gaze that met his, in the mask of ecstasy that contorted Raymond's face, in the gasps and grunts and groans of passion that fell from the wizard's lips as he lost himself in Jean's body.

He thumbed Raymond's peaked nipples, wanting to see to his lover's pleasure as Raymond had seen to his. At the tender gesture, his wizard's hips stuttered against his, a deeper, longer groan escaping. Jean released one tender bud, pulling Raymond's head down to his for a kiss. Just before their lips connected, he whispered, "Yours."

The single, simple word catapulted Raymond into rapturous release, his body spasming violently against the vampire's, his cock disgorging its creamy homage deep inside Jean's body, the sudden slickness easing the way for the continued thrusts as Raymond chased every last sensation for both himself and his lover.

"Jean, I...."

The vampire stopped the words, whatever they might have been, with a kiss. "Don't say anything. We're both run ragged, overworked, strained to our last ounce of strength. We've been thrown together so often, so completely, that neither of us knows what we're really thinking or feeling. When the war is over, when Orlando is safe and Serrier in chains, then we'll have time to examine what lies between us and decide together where we go from here."

"And if that day doesn't come, for one or both of us?" Raymond pressed.

"Then we'll comfort ourselves with knowing we took care of each other as best we could in the time we had," Jean promised.

"Cold comfort," the wizard snorted.

"Better than none at all," Jean reminded him.

"Would it be better if I returned to my own apartment until the war is over?" Raymond did not want to make the offer, did not want to return to the cold garret he called home, not when his other option was Jean's lush rooms, but the vampire's words shook his confidence.

"No!" Jean exclaimed. "Seigneur Jésus, no!" His arms tightened as if to keep his lover from fleeing. "That's not what I meant. I just don't want us to say things we'll regret later. I want you at my side, in battle, in briefings, and most definitely in bed, but everything is too fraught now for us to make decisions beyond the next battle or the next move in Parlement. Our time will come."

"I'm going to hold you to that," Raymond declared.

"Please do," Jean replied, mating his lips to his lover's again to seal their promise.

Chapter 10

ADÈLE SHIFTED from one foot to another as she tried to work up the nerve to knock on the door to Marcel's office. She had received a summons, and she was not looking forward to the coming interview. Finally deciding nothing could be gained by delaying, she knocked and waited for him to acknowledge her presence.

Marcel's smile was warm when she entered, leaving her even more off balance than before. If he had not called her because of Jude, then she had no idea what he wanted.

"How are you this evening, Adèle?" the general asked.

"Well enough," she replied.

"Your partner hasn't arrived yet?"

"He's here. He's in my office," she answered.

"Why didn't you have him come with you?" Marcel asked, surprised.

Adèle hesitated, debating how much to say. Apparently, Jean had not talked to Marcel yet, giving her the opportunity to tell her side of the story first—not that it made the situation any less than totally fucked up. "He isn't just in my office," she began. "He's *locked* in my office."

Marcel frowned. "Sit down," he directed. "I have a feeling this is going to be a long conversation."

Obediently, Adèle sank into one of the chairs across the desk from him, her stomach churning nervously as she considered how to explain. "He's very much a product of his time," she started diplomatically, "as am I, and our ideas about women and their... place in life conflict strongly."

Marcel nodded sympathetically. "I can see that being a problem. Even more so for someone as independent as you."

"He thinks that because I do my job, because I'm not some shy, retiring thing, that I must be some sort of harlot," she blurted out, "and therefore he can treat me any way he wants."

"Has he hurt you?" Marcel asked sharply.

"He takes great pleasure in it," Adèle replied immediately. "Every chance he gets."

"Why didn't you say something?" Marcel exclaimed. "I could have said something to him. Or Jean could have. Just because he's your partner is no reason for him to abuse you in any way!"

Adèle blushed. "It isn't that simple."

Marcel raised an eyebrow in surprise, wondering what was complicated about being hurt. "So what are we going to do about it?" he asked.

"What do you mean?" she replied.

"I mean I can't very well have one member of the Milice deliberately hurting another one. How long has this been going on? Surely not from the beginning."

"Not quite that long," Adèle agreed. "Since the Rite d'équilibrage went wrong. You know the wild magic caught us. Ever since, we can't be together alone without sex rearing its head, and between us, that can't be anything but ugly."

Marcel frowned. "You should have said something."

Adèle flushed, thinking about the fireworks between herself and Jude. "I thought I could handle him. I thought I could separate the sex and everything else."

Marcel shook his head. "It's not a weakness to ask for help when you need it, my dear," he reminded her. "If anything, it's a sign of weakness not to ask."

She bowed her head, ashamed beneath the gentle scolding as no amount of shouted recriminations or accusations could ever have made her feel. "I need help."

"This isn't something I can handle alone, since Jude is a vampire, not a wizard. We'll have to wait for Jean and Raymond to come back. Jean was wounded at the battle at Notre-Dame and Raymond went to make sure he was seen to properly."

Adèle wondered what the medics would be able to do for a vampire, but before she could ask, a knock on the door interrupted them. "Entrez," Marcel called.

Jean and Raymond walked in, the vampire looking much better than the last time Marcel had seen him, but it was the smug look on Raymond's face that drew Marcel's attention. It seemed he had paid too little attention to the partnership in front of him. With the issues Adèle had raised, he thought perhaps another conversation with the two new arrivals might be in order as well. First, though, they had to deal with Jude. "Adèle has requested help in dealing with her partner," he told Jean.

The chef de la Cour eyed Adèle curiously, wondering exactly what she had told the general. "Yes, I thought she might," was all he said, though. "I saw her earlier, after their latest run-in, and told her we'd take care of it when you got back from your meeting."

"Do you have a suggestion?" Marcel asked, not wanting to trespass in Cour business if Jean had a way of reining in the other vampire.

"Unfortunately, vampire law doesn't consider what he's doing wrong," Jean apologized. "Immoral, maybe, but not illegal. Because we've been shunned for so long, our laws tend to govern only our interactions with each other, not with those outside our community. I can make threats, but most of them would be hollow."

Marcel hummed softly. "We've predicated the alliance on the bonds that form between partners and the fact that a wizard can cast a spell around his partner without hurting him, but in truth, while that gives us a flexibility we wouldn't otherwise have, we still saw advantages in working together before we knew about the protective effects of our blood," he mused aloud. "The rest of the structure of the alliance, with the partners patrolling together, has stemmed from the desire of most vampires and wizards to be near their partners, not from any actual, strategic necessity."

"In some respects, having partners patrolling together actually complicates matters," Raymond pointed out. "Since our magic doesn't affect our vampires, we have to rely on another wizard for any kind of magical displacement, a consideration that occasionally slows us down in a fight."

"So is there any reason why Adèle and Jude have to work together at all?" Marcel asked the room in general.

"My only concern is what would happen if he got caught outside after daybreak during a battle," Jean said.

Marcel nodded. "There exist spells, usually only used in the legal system, that make it impossible for one person to get within a certain distance of another. I could probably tailor one of those in such a way that Jude could still feed, in supervised circumstances, but otherwise couldn't approach Adèle."

"Does that spell work both ways?" Jean asked. He could easily guess what had transpired between the two after the Piège-Pouvoir, given his own feelings at the time.

"It doesn't usually need to," Marcel replied. "It's used as a restraining order, where one party usually wants nothing to do with the other, but the second party won't leave the first alone. There's no reason I can't cast it twice, though."

"I don't need a spell to keep away from him," Adèle spoke up. "I don't want anything to do with the bastard."

Jean did not reply, just cocked an eyebrow at her. Raymond, though, broke in. "You say that, and right now you even believe it, but what about when the partnership bond starts kicking in and the elemental magic starts pushing you toward him? Yes, you always have a choice. Even with the wild magic after the Rite d'équilibrage, it was possible to resist, but Jean was right earlier. You may hate Jude for the way he treats you, but he matches you perfectly on a certain level. You'd eat a gentle man alive."

Adèle bit back the retort that sprang to her lips. This was not a conversation she cared to have with Marcel present, especially not when Jean had already shown himself willing to prove his point physically. "Fine, cast the spell twice if that'll make you happy."

"Adèle," Marcel said with mild reproof, "none of this makes us happy, but it seems to have become necessary. We can't afford to have tension in the

Milice. There's enough pressure on us from the outside without creating it on the inside, particularly tonight with Serrier on a rampage for some reason."

"There's more," Raymond interjected, "but we can deal with that when we're done here. Shall I go get Jude?"

Marcel nodded.

"I'll come with you," Jean said, his own protective instincts kicking in at the thought of Raymond facing an angry Jude alone. He knew intellectually that his partner's magic would be sufficient defense, but rationality had nothing to do with his reaction.

The other vampire's shouts were audible all the way down the hall to Adèle's office as Jean and Raymond approached, the variety of insults he heaped upon her head enough to surprise even the world-weary chef de la Cour. As soon as Raymond released the spell sealing the door, Jude barged out, screaming invectives.

"Enough!" Jean roared, the volume surprising Raymond, who had grown used to his partner's affable persona. The sound was enough to startle Jude into silence for a moment as well. "I don't know what you thought you were doing," the chef de la Cour went on, the mantle of authority palpable about him though he wore none of the emblems of his rank, "but it ends now. You will not threaten the stability of this alliance nor our chance to have true equality for the first time because you don't have enough good sense to keep your pants zipped. And don't say a word about her provocative ways. This isn't the sixteenth century and you aren't in Elizabethan England anymore. Get over it. We're going to go back upstairs, and you're going to keep your mouth shut and accept the consequences of your actions."

"Or what?" Jude said sullenly.

"Or you'll be out of the alliance," Jean replied. "As it is, you'll still be able to feed from Adèle so you have the protection of her blood, but if you fight it, I'll see even that taken away before I'll see you endanger us all."

"I ought to just leave now," Jude muttered.

"Be my guest," Jean retorted. "You've caused more problems than you're worth. The only reason I spoke up for you at all is I know Adèle's kind just as well as I know yours. She gets off on the power struggle between you just like you do. Unfortunately, there's a war going on and your behavior— the behavior of both of you—compromises the integrity of this alliance. That is not permissible."

"You've been out to get me ever since I arrived from England," Jude accused.

Jean snorted. "If that were true, I'd have cut you loose a long time ago, Jude. I don't like you much, but that doesn't change the fact that you're a vampire in my Cour. I'll do what I can to protect you, but you've crossed a line this time that I can't alter. If it makes you feel any better—not that you deserve to feel any better—Adèle's facing the same consequences that you are. Let's go. Marcel's waiting."

With Jean and Raymond on either side, they marched Jude back to Marcel's office. The vampire remained silent, even when they entered the room and he faced Adèle again, but his expression hardened with a mixture of anger and lust that no one in the room had any trouble reading. Marcel's lips thinned as he came to understand the true depths of animosity between the partners. He had let the easy camaraderie of the teams he dealt with more frequently lull him into believing all the partnerships were working equally as well. He knew Raymond and Jean had gotten off to a rough start, but they had worked through it fairly quickly and moved on to what was clearly a positive relationship now. He would talk to Raymond and Jean after this and see if they thought a closer review of the other pairings was appropriate. He could not afford to have tension festering unaddressed within the alliance, especially not now.

"It's come to our attention that you and Adèle have trouble interacting appropriately," Marcel began.

Jude snorted, but held his tongue at Jean's sharp look.

"To ensure no further problems," Marcel continued, "Jean and I have agreed that you will not be allowed in the same room together except when supervised, and then only when you need to feed in order to be protected on duty."

"That might be a little hard to enforce," Jude commented drolly.

Marcel laughed humorlessly. "You forget who you're talking to, boy." Jude's hackles rose at the affront, but Jean's hand tightened on his shoulder, restraining him. He could perhaps have thrown the other vampire off, but he was not quite at the point of that kind of open rebellion. "Who are you calling 'boy'?" he challenged nonetheless. "I've been around for centuries."

"When you stop acting like a spoiled child deprived of a favorite toy, I'll stop calling you one," Marcel replied with great dignity. "A modified Ordre de restriction will make it possible for you to feed from Adèle in my presence or Jean's, but otherwise you won't be able to remain in the same room with each other or work on the same patrol. I'll make sure she's aware of your patrol schedule so she's available should you need to feed. Outside of that situation, though, neither of you will make any attempt to see or contact the other. Is that clear?"

Adèle nodded immediately, wanting nothing more than for this meeting to be over so she could return to her duties. She could feel Jude's stare on her like a lead weight. She knew he blamed her for this, and she was willing to admit some degree of responsibility, but some of it was his as well and she refused to shoulder the blame alone.

Jude glared a moment longer, uncomfortably aware of being faced with an authority he could not ignore or overrule. He placed the blame for this ignominy squarely on Adèle's fair shoulders and resolved to find a way around the magical restrictions—but he would do so quietly, when there were not as many people around. For now, he nodded slowly, letting his gaze rake Adèle's body familiarly one more time. He might not be allowed to touch for now, but he would know the pleasure of her writhing beneath him again eventually. He simply had to figure out how.

"Jean, Raymond, you've witnessed their agreement to the spell," Marcel said formally. Both men nodded as well. "Very well, let's begin." Marcel cast the initial spell, its strength enough to have both Jude and Adèle struggling to stay where they were as it tried to force them apart. Marcel quickly added the modification so they could be in the same room when supervised by either himself or Jean. The pressure to separate eased as the second part of the spell took effect. "When did you last feed?" Marcel asked when he was done.

"A couple of days ago," the vampire replied.

Inwardly, Adèle quailed. She could not do this with the others watching. She was still too on edge from their earlier confrontation. If Jude fed from her now, she was likely to come from his fangs alone, like the harlot he accused her of being. "Our duty ends well before sunrise," she protested. "He doesn't need to feed tonight."

Jude's smile turned predatory as he looked at her. "Why not, pussy? Afraid you'll like it and show the old man you aren't the sweet innocent angel he thinks you are?"

"Prick," she retorted, forgetting her audience in her anger at her partner. "The only part of you I like seeing is your backside as you're falling on it because you're thinking with your dick, not your brain."

Marcel sighed. "Children," he interrupted, "if we can forget about your pettiness for a few moments, the rest of us have work to do. Adèle, give him your wrist and let him feed. We'll turn our heads if you'd like."

It would not make any difference, Adèle thought resignedly. She had never been able to be quiet as she climaxed. Holding out her hand, she turned her head, focusing on Marcel's fatherly face as Jude turned her wrist over and bit her quickly. She was silently grateful he seemed as interested as she was in getting this over quickly. The other three men averted their gazes respectfully, giving the illusion of what privacy they could. Adèle did not know whether to be grateful or not. To her surprise, she did not feel the same rush of passion that she usually did when Jude bit her—but whether it was because of her humiliation, the presence of others in the room, or something in the spell itself, she did not know.

Jude fed swiftly, knowing Jean in particular would know exactly how long it should take. When the others looked away, he saw his chance to test the limits of this new spell. With one hand still holding his partner's wrist, he let the other wander up her arm toward her breast. He got as far as her elbow but could not go any farther. His eyes flew immediately to Marcel's face, glaring as he caught the knowing twinkle in the old man's eyes.

Adèle felt the intrusive touch, felt it halt and looked down to Jude, catching his expression and realizing what Marcel must have done. Honesty compelled her to admit to herself that she did not know if she was relieved or disappointed. Were the war not going on.... She squashed that train of thought before it could blossom. The war *was* going on, and everything else took second place to that.

It had to.

Chapter 11

WHEN JUDE had finished and the recalcitrant partners were ordered to separate patrols, Marcel slumped into his chair, running his hands through his white hair in a rare show of desperation. "Have we made a mistake in encouraging the partnerships?" he asked Jean and Raymond.

"No!" they both replied immediately. "The 'mistake', if it is one, was in underestimating how far-reaching the effects would be," Raymond added.

"I should have anticipated it when I saw how Orlando reacted to Alain," Jean admitted. "He's never taken to someone the way he did to his Avoué, but I was so happy to see him finally shaking off his past that I didn't question it beyond verifying his well-being."

"Monsieur Lombard posited that however odd the pairings seemed, they were right at some level," Raymond continued. "Our problem is that it isn't always the level that makes for good partners in a military situation. Adèle can rant and rave all she wants about the way Jude treats her—and he's a real bastard to her—but she'd walk all over a different kind of man. She may hate him, but she's also attracted to him. On a sexual level, he's exactly what she needs."

"Unfortunately, that's not the level we need people to connect on," Marcel replied drolly.

"At least not the only level we need people to connect on," Raymond amended. "Sex magic is like blood magic in that a lot of wizards aren't comfortable with it, but it's also incredibly powerful. The bonds we're creating have incredible potential for beyond the war, on a magical level as well as a personal one."

Marcel sighed. "This isn't a can of worms I want to open right now. Serrier's attacking all over the city tonight, and we nearly lost Notre-Dame to him. Not to mention Alain essentially defecting to continue searching for Orlando. Yes, I know," he added, forestalling Jean's protest, "we need to find him, and Alain has the best chance of being successful, but it's one more thing the Conseil des Ministres isn't going to understand."

"Fuck the Conseil des Ministres," Jean spat.

"I'd rather not," Marcel replied sardonically. "They're so not my type."

The response was so out of character for the Milice general that it surprised a laugh from Jean. Raymond did not seem at all surprised, though, making Jean wonder how much more the older man hid beneath his controlled, affable façade.

"What is your type?" Jean asked daringly.

"Ah, if only I were twenty years younger," Marcel quipped, "I'd give Raymond a run for your attention, young man."

Jean laughed even harder. "If one of us is old, it's me, Général," he teased back. "So watch who you're calling young."

Marcel chuckled, the tension coiling his gut easing slightly. "I have to report to l'Elysée in about an hour," he told them. "The President wants a report of what's going on and why the scales suddenly seem to be tipping against us."

"They aren't!" Raymond protested. "This is a sign of Serrier's desperation, not his victory. Even now, with them beginning to figure out what spells to use against vampires, we still beat them easily at Notre-Dame. And with Monique's defection, we've narrowed down even more the places where he can hide. It's just a matter of time before his rebellion collapses."

"Time Orlando doesn't have," Jean muttered.

"I know he's your friend," Marcel apologized, "and I know what he is to Alain. I like the boy myself, but he's still only one person. I'm tasked with the protection of the entire city, the entire country. I'm sorry I can't commit more resources to finding him."

"I know," Jean replied bitterly. "The good of the many must outweigh the good of the one. It doesn't mean I have to like it."

"*I* don't like it," Marcel assured him, "but it's the choice I have to make."

Resolutely changing the subject, Jean asked, "Do you want me to come with you tonight? Will it help your case for the President and whoever else is there to see a united front?"

"It certainly can't hurt," Marcel replied gratefully. "The last thing we want is for the President to start questioning the alliance."

"Vampires keep their word, but it's gone far beyond that now," Jean replied insistently. "Serrier's made it personal now, a fact we aren't likely to forget any time soon."

"If he were smart, he wouldn't have targeted the vampires," Raymond agreed, "but then again, if he were smart, he'd have found a different way to bring about the change he desires."

"If he desired true change, we could have discussed it," Marcel concurred, "but there's no place in our society for his kind of intolerance or oligarchic control. The fact that wizards can do magic doesn't—shouldn't— grant us extra rights. Extra responsibilities, perhaps, but not extra rights."

"Just as being vampires should not deny us," Jean agreed.

"You two are preaching to the choir," Raymond laughed. "Save those arguments for the doubters who need to be convinced, not for me. I'm already on your side."

"Raymond mentioned you were hurt, Jean," Marcel commented. "Did the medics get you taken care of?"

Jean smiled, glancing at Raymond, the warmth of his memories momentarily visible in his eyes. "They wouldn't have been able to do anything for me, but Raymond made sure I got everything I needed. I'm fine now."

Raymond flushed slightly at the subtle reminder of all that had passed between them in his office, but hearing that Jean had needed their interlude as badly as he did warmed his heart. "It was the least I could do," he demurred.

"There's one other thing we need to think about, though I hesitate to bring it up," Marcel said slowly. "Are there other partners out there having problems like Adèle and Jude? And if so, is there a way to head it off before it gets completely out of control like it did between them?"

Jean and Raymond eyed one another for a moment before Raymond replied, weighing his words carefully as he spoke. "We didn't know what we were getting into when we started the partnerships. I know I keep saying that, but the fact is that everyone's gotten more than they signed up for. If we'd known, if we'd realized Alain's and Orlando's relationship was a herald of things to come rather than the fluke we painted it to be, we could have warned people to be on their guard. The magical impulse can be resisted, but it has to be consciously resisted. And very few of us actively did that when the alliance first formed."

"And now?" Marcel asked. "Do we tell people now?"

"I don't think so," Jean replied. "I know that's different from my earlier opinion, but with the exception of Adèle, and possibly Angélique, I haven't seen any signs that the vampires are unhappy with their new relationships. And a lot of them are happier than I've ever seen them. Orlando, certainly, but he's not the only one. And Angélique, at least, seems to be dealing with her partner in a civilized fashion, even if there is some tension there."

"Besides Adèle, have you heard any of the wizards complaining?" Raymond asked.

"No, but I don't know that they'd say anything to me. Even Adèle didn't until forced into it," Marcel pointed out.

"So maybe the thing to do is talk to the various captains and see if any of them are aware of problems in their companies," Raymond suggested. "Even if no one's said anything directly, they'd see the kind of destructive behavior we noticed between Adèle and Jude. I don't want to create problems where there aren't any, but I know how the kind of poison those two were spewing can fester. We need to be united."

Marcel laughed softly, though there was no humor in the sound. "I'll speak to them as they come in. It just feels like everything's spinning out of control suddenly. Alain's gone off on his own because his partner's missing. Adèle and her partner can't be in the same room together anymore. I haven't seen Thierry since I sent him as backup to Notre-Dame."

"He and Sebastien stayed to stabilize the cathedral," Raymond reminded Marcel. "I did what I could, but without Thierry's affinity, that was limited."

"After all you did earlier with searching for Orlando and then holding off the attack until Thierry's patrol could arrive, I think you can be excused for not singlehandedly stopping the cathedral from collapsing," Jean protested hotly.

"Nobody's criticizing him," Marcel pacified. "I'm well aware of Raymond's contributions to the war effort."

"Sorry," Jean apologized. "I just get tired of everyone putting him down, himself included." He glared at his lover for a moment.

"We'll have to break him of that habit," Marcel agreed with a paternal smile. "But I'm due at l'Élysée, so it'll have to wait until we return. Raymond, are you coming with us?"

The dark-haired wizard started to shake his head until he caught the expression on Jean's face. He settled for answering, "If you want me to."

ALONE WITH Thierry at last, having reported back in at the Salle des Cartes and hearing that Marcel was already gone, Sebastien spun his lover against a wall with a low growl. "What were you thinking, not telling me what happened, what *could* have happened?" he demanded roughly. "I could have lost you before I ever had you, and I didn't even know it!"

"What purpose would it have served after the fact?" Thierry countered, keeping a tight rein on his temper. "It was over, a beginner's mistake I wouldn't have made except for the desperation of the situation."

"And the situation is less desperate now?" Sebastien inquired, his voice still hard. "The risk is somehow less than it was then?"

"No," Thierry admitted, "but it reminded me to be careful, to keep an eye on how fully I'm investing myself any time I commune with the elements. Although, if the feat we managed at Notre-Dame tonight is any indication, as long as you feed from me, I won't have to worry about it. The connection tonight was far deeper than I've ever gone before—and there was no trouble at all, any sense of weakening."

"That's good, I suppose," Sebastien allowed, "but that still doesn't change the fact that you hid it from me when it happened before."

"I didn't want to worry you," Thierry insisted. "I knew you'd react this way and it wouldn't serve any purpose except to start an argument."

Sebastien sighed and ran a hand through his long hair. "I care what happens to you. Isn't that reason enough to tell me?"

Thierry shrugged. "It's just been so long since I've had anyone to care about me on that level. I was only thinking about avoiding an argument. I won't do it again, I promise."

"See that you don't," Sebastien admonished, lowering his head and kissing Thierry gently. The kiss grew heated quickly, though, the stress of the night and the desperation that seemed to rule everyone's lives at the moment adding to the intensity of their interaction.

"Need you," Thierry gasped, his head falling back against the wall, his neck on silent offer.

Sebastien lowered his head, sucking on the bruised skin of Thierry's neck but not biting down. The blood he had taken at the cathedral would hold him for some time, and he did not want to weaken Thierry unnecessarily—not when they did not know what the next hours and days would bring. Instead, he lapped at the healing wounds, letting his saliva work its restorative magic on the scabbed skin. His lover shifted against him, drawing Sebastien's attention to other appetites. His hands slid around Thierry's hips, fingers spreading wide across the globes of the blond's ass, squeezing gently at first, then with more force when Thierry moaned and pressed more tightly against him.

One hand continuing its exploration, Sebastien used the other to open Thierry's pants, pushing them down to the tops of his thighs and reaching inside his boxers to draw out the already hard cock. He wondered if Thierry had been hard since they left Notre-Dame. The thought amused him enough to raise his head and ask.

Red stained Thierry's cheeks at the question. "All you have to do is touch me and I get hard," he admitted.

"That's not an answer," Sebastien teased, stroking the firm flesh. He doubted Thierry had thought to stock the office with lube, which meant improvising. The fluid beginning to leak from the blond's cock would suffice nicely. Now he just had to get enough of it to do the job. Somehow he thought Thierry would not complain.

Whatever Thierry might have answered was lost in Sebastien's mouth as he kissed his wizard again, hand shuttling up and down the hard length, coaxing more and more semen from its tip. Thierry's hips picked up the rhythm, fucking Sebastien's fist urgently, the tension of the day stealing his control.

"Can't…." Thierry gasped, tearing his lips from Sebastien's.

"Don't hold back," Sebastien urged, grip tightening as he worked to bring the other man joy.

Still feeling selfish despite Sebastien's words, Thierry tried to reach for his vampire, to return some of the pleasure he was feeling, but Sebastien stilled his hands. "Come for me," he whispered, his breath tickling Thierry's ear.

The sound of that voice, deep and husky purring in his ear, sent Thierry over the edge, his release spurting out into Sebastien's waiting hand. His breath rasped in and out as his lungs threatened to stop working, all thought, all energy sapped from him along with his seed.

Sebastien supported Thierry's weight with his leg, using his clean hand to open his own trousers. "Can you get your pants off or do you want to turn around?" he asked, squeezing Thierry's buttocks again. "I need to be inside you."

Hands still trembling, Thierry pushed on his jeans, toeing off one shoe and pulling his foot free, leaving the fabric piled around his other foot. He hooked his ankle around the back of Sebastien's knees, opening himself to the vampire's touch. He supposed he could have spelled his clothes off, but he did not need to be completely naked—only bare enough for Sebastien to fuck him. There was something unspeakably erotic about this half-clothed fumbling, as if their need to be joined was so great they could not even take the time to fully undress. "Take me."

"Oh, I will," Sebastien promised, hitching Thierry's ankle higher on his leg, "but not just yet. I want you hard and aching for me again first."

It would not take much, Thierry realized, his cock already filling again. "Just touch me," he pleaded.

Sebastien obliged, smearing the cooling cream on his fingers before sliding them between Thierry's parted legs to find the tight opening that still clenched automatically against his intrusion. "Relax, Thierry, let me in," the vampire urged, his fingers rubbing back and forth over the little rosette.

Consciously, Thierry relaxed the tense muscle, opening himself to Sebastien's caress. A thick finger worked its way inside, the burn greater this time without real lube, but Thierry forced himself not to clench around it. With each tantalizing swipe, it grew easier to accept. Then Sebastien's fingertip found his prostate, massaging it deliberately, and Thierry's whole body jerked forward, his cock swelling at the persistent stimulation. "Putain," he groaned.

Sebastien took the curse as an invitation to add a second finger, stretching Thierry as swiftly as he dared, his own control precarious after the frustration of the day and the thrill of watching his wizard come undone at his touch.

"Now," Thierry begged, starting to lower his leg so he could turn around, but Sebastien stopped him, catching his hips and lifting him so Thierry's legs could wrap around his waist.

"I want to see your face when I claim you," Sebastien insisted, smearing his own fluid over his shaft before positioning the tip at Thierry's entrance. "I want to know it feels as good to you as it does to me."

Thierry moaned as the hard shaft made its way inside him, forced deeper by his own weight, until he could sink no farther. His head fell back against the wall with a loud thump as Sebastien started to move within him, hot, strong hands supporting him so all he had to do was feel.

"Touch yourself," Sebastien ordered, his own hands occupied with holding his wizard in place. "Make yourself come for me."

Thierry obeyed swiftly, his hand mimicking the gestures Sebastien had used earlier, slipping up and down his sticky cock in time with the movements of Sebastien's hips. He could feel the vampire's thrusts growing erratic. "Let go," he pleaded hoarsely. "I'm right with you."

Sebastien captured Thierry's lips in a passionate kiss, linking them in every way possible, his climax blindsiding him suddenly. He thrust one last time, legs trembling with his release. He slid slowly to his knees, taking Thierry with him so they knelt on the carpeted floor, mostly still dressed, covered in sweat and semen. "Nobody's made me feel like you do since Thibaut died," Sebastien whispered against Thierry's lips.

SHIVERING, ALAIN pulled his cloak tighter around him, wishing he had thought to grab his gloves. His fingers were numb, making it nearly impossible to hold his wand. He could cast without it, but as exhausted as he was, having it as a focus was growing more and more necessary. He glanced down at the map Raymond had given him with the warded zones marked. He was making progress, but too slowly. He had only marked off two since Marcel had called his patrol in, and there were still eight to go. Huddling in a doorway to get out of the wind for a few minutes, he closed his eyes and concentrated on feeling Orlando. He needed the reassurance that touch would bring, but while he could sense his lover still, he received no answering wave of love and longing. He told himself the vampire was simply resting while he could, but not even that insistence could completely erase the doubts that assailed him. Had Orlando given up on him? Had he lost hope? Sinking to his knees, he tried to summon the strength for the next displacement, the next search, hoping against hope it would be the right one, the one that would unite him with Orlando.

Chapter 12

WHEN THIERRY and Sebastien had recovered and readjusted their clothing, Sebastien brought back up the topic that had started their fight, and the resulting lovemaking. "How do I know if you're connecting too deeply with the stones, and how do I pull you back if you do?"

Thierry shook his head. "You have a one-track mind."

Sebastien shrugged. "I just don't want anything to happen to you. In the time I've known you, I've almost lost you to the elemental magic twice. I'd rather know what to do to help than be caught unprepared if it happens again."

"Jean slapped me when calling my name didn't work," Thierry admitted. "With the wild magic during the Rite d'équilibrage, Alain and Raymond cast a spell to break the connection. I don't know if there's anything you could have done in that situation. But given what happened at the cathedral tonight, if that wasn't a fluke of the location, biting me would do it. That boosts my power to the point that I'm far less likely to be drawn in. It also gives me a connection with this world rather than the magical one."

"That's certainly no hardship," Sebastien smirked.

Thierry rolled his eyes. "We should go see if Marcel's back. I need to tell him what happened. I don't know why we didn't know there was a locus here in Paris, unless it's because we've historically avoided anything to do with the Church because of their intolerance of us, but even if we can't use it to our advantage, we've got to make sure Serrier doesn't take possession of it. We'd never unseat him if he did."

"It's that powerful?"

"The only place I've felt its like is Stonehenge," Thierry replied. "And they say that was the seat of Merlin's power."

"So whose seat of power was this?"

"I have no idea," Thierry replied. "I don't know whether the wizard makes the place or the place makes the wizard. I don't know that it matters either. What matters is what we do with this new knowledge."

"Let's go see if Marcel's around to tell, then," Sebastien agreed. "Did you leave any wards in place to protect the church?"

Thierry shook his head. "I tried, but it resisted, like its magic was too big to be contained by my puny strength."

Sebastien cocked an eyebrow. "Puny?"

"Maybe not in comparison to other wizards, and with your help, I was far stronger than usual—but compared to the well of power contained in the church, yes, puny," Thierry repeated, starting down the hall toward Marcel's office. "I told you I'd never felt anything like it."

"So how do we keep Serrier from getting to it, then?" Sebastien asked.

"I don't know," Thierry replied. "A coalition, maybe. Or maybe we don't ward it but simply keep a sentry stationed there constantly to warn of any attacks. We were fortunate Jean and Raymond were there tonight, but we can't count on those kinds of coincidences. Strategy, not luck, is how we'll win this war."

They met Marcel, Jean, and Raymond in the hallway outside Marcel's office. The fatigue on Marcel's face shocked Thierry to the core. In all the time since the war started, he had never seen the older man looking so worn. His eyes lit up a little at seeing Thierry and Sebastien, though. "Tell me you have good news," Marcel asked. "Any kind of good news."

Thierry smiled. "I might have something for you. Let's go in your office. Actually, I imagine Raymond's already told you."

"About the cathedral?" Raymond verified as the door to Marcel's office shut behind the five of them. "No, we had other things to deal with first. I take it you think it's a locus, too."

"A locus?" Marcel asked, eyes growing wide. "Here in Paris?"

"Yes," Raymond and Thierry confirmed. "I was going to tell you earlier," Raymond added, "but with Adèle and Jude to deal with and then the meeting with the President, it got pushed aside. Notre-Dame is almost certainly a locus."

"Not almost," Thierry corrected. "It *is* a locus. So powerful, in fact, that the stones were… sentient, I guess is the word. I saw the entire history of the cathedral from their perspective."

"That must have been quite an experience," Marcel commented drolly.

"You'd be amazed," Thierry agreed. "One of the foremen was a wizard, but I don't think that's where the power comes from. I think it's far older than that."

"There was probably a grove there before the church built," Raymond added. "It had the same feeling of ancient power that I've felt at Stonehenge or the Pyramids or Machu Picchu. I always posited there ought to be a fourth, for the four elements, but I'd never found any reference to another."

"So how did we not know it was here?" Marcel asked rhetorically. "There have been wizards in Paris for thousands of years."

"The ancient ones probably did know, although they might not have realized it was a locus," Raymond answered. "But the early Christians made a habit of building their churches on sites sacred to the locals, so I'm sure that's why it was lost."

"There was a cathedral there before Notre-Dame," Jean commented, "dedicated to Saint-Etienne. Before that, I don't know. The old cathedral was already there when I was born. Monsieur Lombard might know what was there before it. He's almost a thousand years older than I am."

"It doesn't matter," Marcel decided. "We just need to make sure Serrier doesn't figure it out."

"His wizards were there tonight, Aguiraud included," Raymond warned. "I doubt he missed it."

"Particularly since some of those spells would have brought down a lesser building," Thierry agreed. "And I couldn't ward the cathedral. I tried, but it was too strong."

Marcel frowned. "That complicates matters. I barely have enough wizards to go around, what with Serrier using this hit and run technique, and now I'm going to have to station a patrol at the cathedral, too."

"Not necessarily a whole patrol," Thierry disagreed. "A sentry or two, enough to hold off any attackers until help can arrive."

"I wonder if we could use the inherent magic to create a ward," Raymond mused aloud. "To convince the locus itself to side with us."

Marcel pursed his lips. "Thierry, you had the most contact with it. What do you think?"

Thierry considered the question for a moment before replying slowly. "It's possible," he mused. "The stones were horrified with the Nazi brutality they witnessed and with the violence at the church tonight. The question is whether they can distinguish dark intent. We know because we know who sided with whom, but this is elemental magic. Can it make that distinction?"

"Do we have anything to lose by trying?" Sebastien asked. "Even if all we succeed in doing is convincing the locus to ward itself against all magic, we're no worse off than we were when we didn't know it was there and far better off than we'd be if Serrier got control of it."

"The only way to tell is to try," Marcel said quietly. "But I think we should keep this to ourselves for the moment. Between the three of us here, with the help of your partners, we ought to be strong enough to do whatever can be done. I know we're all exhausted, but we can't afford to wait. Thierry, Raymond, are you willing to try?"

Both wizards nodded.

"I can't feed again tonight," Jean warned them. "Even if Raymond could stand it, I'm already glutted. Any more, and I'll be sick."

"The same for me," Sebastien admitted.

"Merde," Marcel cursed softly. "Well, we'll have to do it the old-fashioned way then, just us wizards."

"Jean and Sebastien should still come with us," Raymond insisted. "They can stand watch, both in case Serrier arrives again and to make sure we don't get drawn in too deeply."

"That's a good idea," Marcel agreed. "Although I think since we won't have the vampires' help, it might be a good idea to have all four elements represented. We have earth and water, but we need fire and air."

"Alain won't come," Thierry said immediately. "I don't know where he is, but I do know he won't abandon the search for Orlando, not even for this."

"I know," Marcel replied sadly. "I was thinking Caroline would be a good choice for air and David for fire."

"Not Adèle?" Thierry asked, surprised.

"Adèle and her partner are no longer on speaking terms," Marcel answered shortly. "They'll patrol separately, but they won't be available for anything that requires a partnership. If we're lucky, Caroline's and David's partners won't have fed recently and we'll have at least some vampire involvement. I think that's important, and not just for the strength it adds to our magic."

Thierry and Sebastien exchanged surprised looks at the comment about Adèle and Jude, but they did not pursue it at the moment. "Let's get them to the cathedral as quickly as possible," Thierry said instead. "I can't shake the feeling of urgency."

Marcel nodded. "I'll call them and have them meet us there. If you four would like to go ahead, I'll join you as soon as I've spoken with Caroline and David."

"I'll bring Jean if you'll bring Sebastien," Thierry offered, his instincts screaming at him to return to the cathedral as quickly as possible.

Raymond signaled his agreement with a wave of his hand. Thierry took Jean's arm and winked them out, reappearing outside the cathedral. A moment later, Sebastien and Raymond appeared next to them. Sinking to his knees, Thierry connected with the stone, seeking any change since he had left a few hours earlier. Everything was just as he had left it, much to his relief. Breaking the connection, he rose to his feet again, rubbing his hands together. "Let's go inside. It's cold out here." He spared a thought for Alain, out in the night alone. He only hoped it netted them something, because he did not know how much longer his friend could go on like this.

"So what's the story with Adèle?" Thierry asked when they were inside.

Jean and Raymond exchanged a frustrated glance. Raymond gestured for Jean to go ahead. Quickly, he laid out the situation with a shake of his head as he finished by explaining about the restraining order.

Thierry rolled his eyes. "I love the woman, I really do. She's a damn fine wizard and doesn't know the meaning of the word fear in a fight, but sometimes she can be so fucking juvenile."

"Jude wasn't any better, I assure you," Jean said sadly. "He's nearly five hundred years old and he still behaves like he did the day he was turned. He always stays just this side of vampire law, so we never have any reason to discipline him, but he's still the kind that gives the rest of us a bad name."

"The worst of it is that it's made Marcel question the mechanics of the alliance," Raymond added. "Not its existence, but whether we've made a mistake in structuring it the way we have."

Thierry and Sebastien exchanged resigned glances. "Don't condemn the entire alliance because two people aren't mature enough to handle it."

"That's what we told him," Raymond assured them. "Fortunately, there are far more successful partnerships than dysfunctional ones."

Marcel arrived at that moment, interrupting their conversation. He looked around the building as if he had never seen it before. "I've been here more times than I can count, on school trips as a child, for state funerals as the president of l'ANS, with friends visiting from other places who wanted to do all the touristy things in Paris, but it was always just a building, just another church. An impressive one, admittedly, but just a church."

"Touch the stone," Thierry said softly. "Did you ever do that? I never did before, not with any intent anyway. I wouldn't have even today, if Raymond hadn't told me the building was damaged. I just figured I'd shore up the walls a bit until the stone masons could come fix it."

Marcel set his hand on the column nearest him, his eyes closing as he connected with the magic inherent in the place. A moment later, he opened them again, the blue depths blazing with power. Thierry took an instinctive step back, though he knew Marcel would never be a threat to him. Even so, the flush of power made the usually affable face downright intimidating.

"He really is the most powerful wizard alive, isn't he?" Jean murmured at Raymond's elbow.

"Oh, by far," Raymond agreed. "We should be grateful he's on our side or we'd have no hope of winning this war. If we can corner Serrier long enough for it to come to a fight, Marcel will take him out. It's pinning him down that's the problem. Every time we think we know where he is, he disappears just like he's done with Orlando."

"I'm not even sure why the rest of us are here," Thierry added softly. "He's more powerful alone than the four other wizards combined."

"Imagine what he'd be like with a partner to add to his strength."

Thierry's eyes grew wide. "I can't even fathom it."

"I can," Raymond said softly. "He'd light up the night. He already glows with it."

Caroline and Mireille arrived, followed almost immediately by Angélique and David, breaking Marcel's concentration. He released the connection, but the afterglow of power remained in his eyes.

"What's going on?" David asked.

"Connect with the fire in the candles," Marcel directed simply, "and tell me what you feel."

David did as directed, jerking back as if burned almost immediately. "My God," he breathed reverently, "so much power."

The expression on David's face, the tone of his voice, intrigued Caroline. Casting her eyes heavenward, she summoned a breeze through the lofty arches, catching her breath when her small spell came back to her magnified a hundred times or more. "This is amazing!"

"Yes, it is," Marcel agreed, "and now we're going to try to convince this font of magical power that it wants to side with us or, at the very least, stay out of the war entirely."

Caroline's and David's eyes grew wide. "What do you want us to do?" Caroline asked after a moment.

"Channel your strength into Thierry, much like we would do for a Rite d'équilibrage," Marcel instructed. "He'll guide us from there. And if your partners would oblige and bite you while you're working, it will increase our magical output significantly."

Angélique and Mireille both looked at Jean in shock and surprise. It took the chef de la Cour a moment to realize neither of these sets of partners had been present at any of the discussions about the ability of vampires to increase their partners' magical ability. He explained quickly, assuring them no one would view them askance for feeding from their partners in public.

Awkwardly, Mireille stepped to Caroline's side. She was not used to feeding in a standing position or in public, but she wanted to help and Jean said it was all right. "How do we do this?" she asked Caroline softly.

"Stand behind me so I have my hands free," the blonde wizard suggested. "Can you bite me at that angle?"

Mireille shook her head, frustrated by her lack of height. "I'm too short."

Hearing the self-deprecation in the vampire's voice, Caroline turned and captured her lover's face in her hands. "You're perfect. We'll just have to try something else."

"Stand on a kneeler," Sebastien suggested, pulling one of the low wicker kneelers from in front of the reliquary. "That should give you the extra few inches you need."

Stepping up, Mireille realized Sebastien was right. She flashed him a grateful smile as she wrapped her arms around Caroline, pulling her wizard into a tender embrace, her lips lowering to the elegant curve of her lover's neck. The other vampire's assistance and casual acceptance did more than any words could have to erase Mireille's lingering hesitations. However much what they were doing went against the taboos she had lived with as a vampire, she was doing the right thing by participating in this alliance, this ritual, and this relationship. She belonged here, now, in this place.

As she nuzzled the smooth skin, she watched the others, curious to see how they would arrange themselves. To her surprise, neither Sebastien nor Jean approached his partner. Her eyebrows knitted into a frown at the same time Angélique asked the question.

"Sebastien and I have both fed already today in the aid of the alliance," Jean explained. "We dare not overtax our partners or ourselves."

Accepting that answer, Mireille waited for Angélique to decide where to stand before she bit Caroline. This was not simply feeding, but part of a larger ritual, and it seemed fitting to wait for it to begin.

Not bothering to even try a kneeler, Angélique moved to David's side, slipping beneath his arm and pulling aside the open collar of his button-down shirt to reveal a patch of smooth skin just below his collarbone. Mireille envied the other vampire her audacity, but she did not have the courage to imitate her. "You're perfect just the way you are," Caroline whispered again as if she could sense Mireille's thoughts. "I have no desire to make a public spectacle of our relationship. You can bite me anywhere you want later, when we're alone."

"Promise?" Mireille asked huskily.

"Absolutely," Caroline replied, squeezing the hands that encircled her waist. She left one hand entwined with Mireille's as she waited for Marcel to give the signal to begin. When he did, she closed her eyes, concentrating on channeling her magic into Thierry.

Hearing the chanting begin, Mireille sealed her lips over the spot she had chosen on Caroline's neck, biting down daintily as she savored the rich spice of her lover's blood. The sense of Caroline's magic was far stronger than it had ever been before, soaking Mireille with its power. Her grip tightened on the hand still holding hers, grounding her as she felt Caroline's mind soaring with the breeze that swirled through the church at her command.

Thierry braced himself for the influx of magic from the other wizards. He had been the focus of rituals before, but the amount of power from the four wizards far outstripped what he had channeled from larger numbers on previous occasions. He could only imagine what it would be like if Sebastien and Jean were involved. He doubted any of them could imagine what it would be like if Marcel had found a partner as well.

When he felt he could control the magic coursing through him, Thierry stretched his senses out to the stones of the church again, feeling the connection that had so impressed him earlier. With the additional magic at his command, he felt more in control this time, guiding the communion with the stones rather than being controlled by it. Indeed, with the other elements represented, he felt the full magnitude of the locus's power. Summoning his memory of the earlier battle, he projected it outward along with his—their— horror at the thought of such violence being perpetrated on sacred ground. The locus responded, the elemental magic resonating with fury at the disrespect. Thierry added another image, this time of Serrier's forces attacking the vampires at place Pigalle, then others of the carnage the dark wizards were wreaking on the city and the Milice's efforts to curtail those depredations. Finally, he drew one more picture, of Serrier returning to the cathedral, trying to bend the locus to his will. The resulting backlash from the church was so powerful it nearly knocked Thierry to his knees. Only Sebastien's arms kept him from falling.

At Marcel's prompting, Thierry sent one more image, of a Milice wizard standing guard, protecting the locus from such misuse. This time, the surge he felt was one of approval. Releasing his focus, Thierry separated his mind from the elements and then from the other wizards. "I don't think we have to worry about Serrier taking control of the locus," he said slowly, when everyone's eyes had regained their usual focus and the vampires had relinquished their holds on their partners. "In fact, I hope he tries. If I'm reading the situation right, the magical repercussions could seriously weaken him."

"It worked, then?" Raymond asked.

"You couldn't tell?"

Raymond shook his head. "My element is the weakest here, the river outside my only real connection. I could tell you made a connection, but I couldn't read it."

"I could," Marcel interjected, "and I would say Thierry's assessment is accurate. We'll leave a sentry on guard here to be safe, but I don't think we have anything to worry about. Everyone get some rest. You've gone far beyond the call of duty tonight. I'll see you at base tomorrow."

Gratefully, Thierry and Raymond sagged against their partners. "If you'd oblige, Marcel?" Raymond asked, exhaustion clear in his voice.

"Us as well," three more voices echoed.

Marcel smiled and sent each of the pairs back to their respective homes.

"Not quite where I'd intended us to end up," Raymond said with a tired smile as he looked around his cluttered garret.

"We're together," Jean said. "That's all that matters. You should get some sleep. You're asleep on your feet."

Raymond's eyes twinkled despite his fatigue. "You just want to get me in bed, that's all."

Jean's grin turned rakish. "If I wanted that, I'd have you there already, but I'll be a little sore to take you again for a day or two. You loved me too well earlier tonight."

"I'm...."

"If you say you're sorry, I'll give you something to be sorry about," Jean warned. "I wasn't complaining earlier and I'm not complaining now. I wanted you to take me and I'll be fine in a day or two. Get in bed and let me hold you while you sleep."

Across town, Angélique took advantage of Marcel's magic to get her first look at David's apartment. It was a bachelor pad, to be sure, but a nice one, with a living room and dining room separate from the kitchen and from the bedroom. "I should have known you had an affinity to fire, with that hair," she said, still pondering all she had seen and felt that night as well as David's tender care for her the night before.

David flushed and ran his hand self-consciously through his strawberry blond hair. "The bane of my existence," he admitted. "All through school, I wanted to either be a sexy blond or a dashing brunet and instead I was this comical redhead with pale skin and freckles."

"You might not be a blond or a brunet," Angélique countered, "but you have the sexy, dashing part down pat."

"You don't have to humor me. I know how women see me."

Angélique cocked an eyebrow at him. "Mon œil!" she retorted. "Or if you're right, then they're blind and you've been meeting the wrong women. Maybe you aren't the best looking man in the alliance, but you are surely the most honorable. Most men would have been all over me last night like flies on honey. I wouldn't have said no, but I also wouldn't have felt about them in the morning the way I felt about you. You could have taken advantage of me last night, but you didn't, and that makes you far more attractive than any color hair or skin could ever do."

David understood just what it must have cost Angélique to make that admission. Quietly, he gathered her in his arms, resting his chin on the top of her head, enjoying the undemanding closeness. "When the moment's right, we'll both know it. Until then…."

"Until then, we'll enjoy the anticipation," Angélique finished, leading David to the bedroom and lying down beside him. She smiled when his arms closed around her, pulling her close and settling her against him. Perhaps they could make this work after all.

Chapter 13

"CAPTAIN DUMONT! Captain Dumont!"

Thierry's shoulders drooped. He was so close to being off duty and out of here for the day. And now this, whatever this was. He could feel Sebastien bristle protectively next to him, the vampire as aware as he was of how much energy he had expended in the last twelve hours.

"Yes?"

"Orlando's repère… it showed up on the locator map in the Salle des Cartes!"

All fatigue forgotten, Thierry turned. "Well, what are you waiting for? Note the location so we can get there!"

The lieutenant handed Thierry a slip of paper with an address written on it. "I was going to tell the general, but then I saw you."

"I'll take care of it," Thierry promised, pulling his cell phone from his pocket and calling Alain. He hoped his friend was not in the middle of a fight, but even if he was, this would be welcome news.

"Thierry?"

Thierry winced at the despair and desperation he heard in Alain's voice when he answered on the first ring. "Where are you?"

"Somewhere north of the city."

"Never mind," Thierry decided. "Meet me at—" he paused and looked at the paper, "—the corner of rue du Hameau and rue de Cadix. Orlando's repère showed up on the map."

The pause on the other end of the line was palpable. "Thierry, that's…."

"Yeah, I know," Thierry replied. "Not a thing we can do about it except go see what's happening."

"I'll meet you there."

"Give me five minutes so I can find someone to bring Sebastien with me. Wait for me, Alain. Don't face him alone."

Silence was the only reply as the line went dead. "Putain de merde," Thierry cursed. "If he gets himself killed, I'll haunt his grave, I swear I will."

"What's going on?" Sebastien asked as he followed Thierry back into the depths of Milice headquarters. "What's so special about that address?"

Thierry shook his head as he picked up his pace with each step. "I'll explain later. We've got to get there immediately, because Alain won't wait for me and he's even more exhausted than I am. He can't face Simonet alone."

Sebastien filed the name away for later with every intention of getting an explanation at a more opportune moment. For now, though, he simply followed Thierry's lead.

"Is the repère still on the map?" he asked when they reached the Salle des Cartes.

"Yes, sir," the lieutenant replied.

"Good. Send my partner there, please."

As soon as the young man nodded, Thierry cast his own spell, arriving on the lightening street corner that had once been as familiar as the streets around his house. Sebastien appeared next to him a moment later.

"Where's Alain?"

"Probably already inside," Thierry fumed, "although I don't hear shouting."

Alain appeared just then, stumbling to his knees as he lost his balance. Thierry stifled another curse at the sight of his friend's face. Red-rimmed eyes underscored by dark, bruise-like circles topped sunken, grayish cheeks. Even more than that, though, was the haunted, almost dead look in the usually sparkling blue orbs. Thierry realized just how used to seeing Alain smile he had become in the past few weeks, despite the challenges of the war and the alliance. No smile graced the other wizard's face now, no light shone from his eyes. Only the movement of his limbs still gave any indication of life. Alain pushed to his feet slowly, painfully, but he brushed aside Thierry's helping hand. "I'm fine."

"Like hell you are," Thierry muttered, but he let it go. "How do you want to do this?"

Alain simply stared at him like he was speaking gibberish and started toward the apartments, running his wand between his fingers. He did not even look back over his shoulder to see if Thierry and Sebastien followed. He knew and cared about only one thing: Orlando was inside that building.

"He's going to get us all killed going in there like this," Sebastien warned, his voice low as he stalked alongside his wizard.

"Not if I can help it," Thierry assured his partner as he drew his own wand, though the sight of Alain so lost in depression and exhaustion that he could hardly even speak worried him more than he cared to think about. As Alain stormed the door to the building, Thierry cast a sealing spell to keep any dark wizards from arriving to help Simonet. They had enough to worry about without adding anyone else to the mix.

Alain climbed the stairs two at a time, the thought that each step brought him that much closer to his lover enough to have him all but running by the time he reached the landing. Peripherally he was aware of Thierry and Sebastien only a step behind him, but his concentration was fixed entirely on the apartment above, one where he had once been a welcome guest. His face tightened as he played out scenarios for facing Eric again. He wanted to believe some portion of his old friend remained buried beneath the hardened façade, some half-forgotten side he could appeal to for Orlando's release, but he also knew as surely as he knew his own name that he would kill Eric if that was the only way to rescue Orlando. He would not leave his lover in the dark wizards' hands even a moment longer, no matter what it took.

"He hasn't changed the wards," Thierry marveled as they passed right through Eric's outer layer of defense. "Why hasn't he changed the wards? Alain, wait!"

Alain did not even pause, though, too intent on reaching Orlando to care about anything else.

"I don't like this," Thierry muttered, beginning to chant softly to raise his magic to the fore, ready for any unexpected attack. "He should've changed the wards the moment he switched sides so we couldn't come after him."

"Maybe he wanted you to come after him," Sebastien murmured at Thierry's elbow, the second layer of wards catching him. "But he obviously didn't want me coming after him," he added drolly as he waited for Thierry to cast the spell that would let him pass.

Those few precious seconds were enough for Alain to reach the door, unlocking it with a flick of his wand and shoving his way into the apartment. "Orlando!"

Silence.

"Orlando!" Alain shouted again. "Where are you?"

Cursing enough to have his magic sparking around him, Thierry ran after Alain, wand at the ready as he searched for Eric or any other threat. The entire situation made him nervous. It was too easy, and that made him suspect a trap, but no attack materialized.

"Orlando!" Alain's voice grew more frantic with each repeated shout of his lover's name. He tore through the apartment, searching the rooms with ever increasing desperation. Kitchen, bathroom, bedrooms, closets... but no Orlando. Reaching the end of the hall and the master bedroom, he slammed the door open, sure Simonet was holding Orlando captive there, but it, too, was empty. His legs gave out beneath him as the hope that had buoyed him to that point dissipated like fog in sunlight. A muffled sob escaped his lips. "I don't understand," he said hoarsely.

"What the hell?" Thierry muttered, flipping open his cell and calling Milice headquarters. "How long ago did the repère disappear?" he demanded when the officer on duty answered.

"It's still there, sir," the wizard replied. "We were ready to start celebrating. It shows you right next to him."

"The room's empty! How is the repère still visible?" Thierry demanded.

"His repère is tied to his ring, not to him," Alain said dully. "If Simonet took the ring and brought it here, it would show up, even without Orlando." He forced himself to his feet again and began searching the room. It only took a moment. There, on the top of Eric's dresser, was the ring that perfectly matched the imprint on his neck. Eyes closing, Alain lifted the gold band to his lips as if in kissing it, he could transfer that touch to Orlando himself.

"What could possibly have separated him from this?" he asked, not wanting to contemplate the answer. "He wouldn't have given it up willingly. Not just because it's his repère, but because he used it to make our Aveu de Sang." His voice grew more panicked as he spoke, his mind conjuring up images of Orlando's lifeless body, the ring torn from his finger by his murderer and kept as some sort of sick trophy.

"Alain, stop," Sebastien said, grabbing the wizard's shoulders and giving him a firm shake. "You don't need the repère to tell you Orlando's alive. All you have to do is close your eyes and feel him. Maybe he didn't give it up willingly, but that doesn't mean he's gone."

Alain struggled to focus on the bond between Orlando and himself, a wave of love swamping him as soon as he relaxed enough to let it through. The surge of emotion proved Sebastien's words, but it did little to ease Alain's desolation. "But now we don't even have this much link to his whereabouts."

"We didn't have it before either," Thierry reminded him. "Serrier obviously figured out how to ward against the repères. We already knew he was trying, so it shouldn't come as a surprise that he succeeded. We just have to keep looking. We'll find him. Come on, let's get out of here so you can get some rest."

"Time's running out," Alain insisted with a shake of his head. "It's already been almost three days, and he can't go much longer than that without feeding. I can feel him getting weaker, Thierry, and that's only going to get worse. I'll rest when he's safe again."

Thierry seriously considered another sleeping spell, but he had already abused Alain's trust once. His friend had forgiven him the last time, but Thierry did not hope to be so lucky again. "Let's go then," he said. "Where are we going next?"

Alain shook his head. "You can't go with me. Marcel called everyone back in."

"I'm off duty as of half an hour ago," Thierry informed him, looking at his watch. "What I do in my off time is up to me."

"Unless it affects your ability to do your job when you go back on duty," Alain retorted. Face sobering, he looked at Sebastien. "I'm not sure I'm strong enough to displace Sebastien and myself."

"So we'll go the old-fashioned way," Thierry said with a shrug. "It's slower, but it's better than you going alone. You're so pale you look like a ghost."

Sebastien agreed with that assessment, but he was not sure Thierry was all that much stronger, after the battle at Notre-Dame and then the ritual to shore up the building. At least if they took the Métro to get from place to place, they would not be expending what magical energy remained to them, except in the actual search and rescue for Orlando. Resolving to keep a close eye on his partner—he knew better than to think either of them would have any influence on Alain—he tilted his head toward the door. "Let's go then, before the occupant comes home. Presumably he has wards that would let him know someone's been here."

"You'd think," Thierry agreed as they left Eric's apartment, "but then again, you'd think he'd have changed the wards when he changed sides."

"So tell me what happened," Sebastien requested as they followed Alain back to the street and toward the nearest Métro stop. Alarmingly, Alain's movements seemed more fitting for an automaton than for a living, breathing man. He walked as if in a daze, his eyes fixed on the sidewalk in front of him without ever looking up or down, left or right. "There's obviously a lot more to this story than just a wizard who changed sides."

"Simonet—Eric—was like our kid brother," Thierry said softly, not wanting to upset Alain with those memories. "When we really were kids, he was mostly annoying, the way tagalongs always are, but as we grew up, the three of us became inseparable. The three musketeers. That's how people referred to us."

"So what happened?"

"The war started and there was an attack at Alain's house. His ex-wife and son were killed. Eric's wife and kids were hiding in the closet. Edwige managed to get them hidden before the dark wizards broke in. Anyway, we didn't know they were there and one of Alain's spells went wild as we were trying to defend ourselves and take out the wizard who'd killed Edwige and Henri," Thierry explained. "We didn't even know they were there until we found them dead. Alain's magic killed them, and Eric couldn't forgive him for it. That was already bad enough, but Eric was one of the two wizards who captured Orlando at place Pigalle."

"And he's done God only knows what to him since then," Alain spat as they stood on the subway platform waiting for the train to arrive.

"You don't know that he's been responsible for a single thing that's been done to Orlando," Thierry insisted.

"You don't know that he hasn't been," Alain retorted. "He's just as bad as the rest of them. I wish he weren't, but I don't see how we can deny it any longer. He cast the spell that took Orlando prisoner and he had Orlando's ring. That means he was close enough to get it from him, and I can't imagine Orlando giving it up willingly, which means he took it by force."

"It's awfully hard to take anything from a vampire by force," Sebastien observed mildly, not wanting to get between the two friends, but feeling the need to defend Thierry as well. "Orlando's smart. He may have given it to the wizard hoping it would lead you to him."

"Even if that was the case," Alain replied coldly, though hope leapt in his heart at the idea that Orlando might have tried such a trick, "it still means Simonet was close enough for Orlando to give it to him, and I know how much pain I've felt from him. Simonet's a dead man if he crosses my path."

Thierry's eyes widened. They had known it might come to that if they ended up facing Eric in battle, but somehow they had always avoided that eventuality. Alain was not talking about a chance meeting now, though. Thierry recognized the tone of his friend's voice, and it boded ill for everyone involved. "Alain," Thierry chided. "You know we can't do that."

"He knows nothing of the sort," Sebastien interrupted as the train arrived. They got on, the conversation continuing unabated. "Nor would Orlando if the situation were reversed. There's nothing rational about what he's feeling, Thierry, nor will there be until Orlando's safe in his arms again. The Aveu de Sang doesn't leave room for rational thought when your Avoué is in danger."

Gratitude flared for a moment in Alain's eyes before dying out again, leaving nothing but the flat chill of icy rage, the expression even more cruel for the light of humanity that had shown momentarily through the grief and anger. It made Thierry realize once again just how much Orlando's absence was tearing Alain apart. "So where do we go next?" he asked, changing the subject.

"North," Alain replied tiredly. "All the remaining sites Raymond couldn't penetrate with his seeking spell were to the north of the city. St-Denis and farther out."

"How many do you have left?" Thierry asked.

"Three," Alain said, his voice rough. "I just hope he's in one of them, because I don't know where else to look if he's not."

"If he's not, we'll try the seeking spell again, with more of us this time, so we can search farther afield," Thierry assured him. "We aren't giving up, I promise."

Alain tried to summon a smile, but a jolt of pain from Orlando stopped the expression before it could form. "We have to hurry." His eyes grew wild with desperation as he felt another wave of pain. "They're hurting him."

"Go," Sebastien directed, though he hated the thought of Thierry going into danger without him. "Use your magic and go. I'll head back to Milice headquarters and wait for you there."

"Are you sure?" Thierry checked.

"Go, or he's going to go without you," Sebastien insisted. "Just be careful."

Thierry searched Sebastien's face a second longer, then turned back to Alain. "Give me the next address."

Alain repeated it from memory, casting the displacement spell almost before he had said the last words. A second later, Thierry followed, leaving

Sebastien alone in the subway car to examine the map and figure out how to get back to Milice headquarters.

Arriving at their destination, Alain did not even wait long enough to make sure Thierry was at his side. He trusted the other wizard to be there, but even more than that, he could not leave Orlando in the dark wizards' grasp any longer. Praying this was the right location, he stormed forward, heedless of anything now except finding Orlando. Behind him, he could hear Thierry cursing his foolhardiness, but even his friend's warnings could no longer hold him back. He stumbled as he ran forward, going to his hands and knees, exhaustion dragging him down, but he pulled himself upright again, forging ahead as Thierry caught up with him.

"You're going to get us killed," Thierry warned, grabbing his arm and slowing him down. He could not help but be amazed at the renewed vigor in Alain's movements. He was still obviously exhausted, but at the same time, he seemed to have lost the automaton mindset that had so disturbed Thierry when they first met at Eric's apartment. Perhaps it was having someone at his side. Perhaps it was knowing Eric had been close enough to Orlando to take the ring. Either way, Thierry hoped the emotional lift could overcome the physical exhaustion for a few more hours. "And that won't do Orlando any good at all."

"Fuck that!" Alain spat. "If we give them a chance to recover from our initial attack, we'll never get inside."

Thierry sighed. "All right, let's go. I just hope we survive."

Chapter 14

"I DON'T know that there's anything else he can tell us," Eric told Serrier seriously. "We can keep trying different spells, but we've already gotten to the point where we can predict which ones will work and which ones won't, so that's really just a waste of time at this point. Not to mention that he's in so much pain that it's hard to gauge the effectiveness of any new spells. If we could let him recover for a few days, it might be different, but that isn't an option either."

"So what do you suggest?" Serrier asked.

"Let me dispose of him," Eric offered, stomach roiling as he tried his first tactic. "He's worthless to us now, just taking up space. I'll dump him somewhere in the sun so he won't be found. Then tonight, Vincent and I can try to get another vampire, hopefully one we can keep around a little longer this time."

"And deprive us all of the pleasure of watching him turn to ash?" Serrier shook his head. "I don't think so. We'll stake him out tomorrow if Claude tires of him between now and then."

"If you want the 'pleasure' of watching him burn, don't give him to Claude," Eric warned. "I doubt he's strong enough to withstand that kind of torture, even overnight."

"And since when are you an expert on vampires?" Serrier challenged.

"I'm not," Eric replied, well aware of the minefield he was navigating, "but a blind man could see how his reactions have changed over the past day since we tried to force feed him. He's stopped fighting the way he was before, stopped attempting to escape every time one of us turns our back. He's given up, and that tells me he's too weak to withstand Claude's torture."

Serrier's eyes narrowed. "I'm not so sure. He hasn't cried out once since the first night. That doesn't sound to me like someone who's weak with pain. Yes, we can make his body react, but we haven't broken him."

"Do we need to?" Eric asked.

Serrier laughed, the cruel sound grating on Eric's nerves. "You're getting soft on me, Simonet," he scolded. "Watch yourself, or I might start wondering where your true loyalties lie."

"Where they always have," Eric assured the dark wizard, "but that doesn't mean I condone cruelty for cruelty's sake. If I thought we could still learn something from the vampire, that would be different, but giving him to Claude is pointless."

"You didn't complain with the woman," Serrier remarked. "Or with any of the girls we gave to our pet vampire. So what makes this vampire different?"

"Nothing," Eric hastened to reply. "I just thought—"

"You thought now might be a good time to test my resolve?" Serrier demanded. "There's never a good time for that."

Before Eric could do more than brace himself, the pain spell hit his side, bending him double. He bit back a cry, determined to show no more reaction than Orlando had done. Calling on a trick he had learned years ago, he closed his eyes, conjuring up a vision of his first night with Vincent. At the memory, both powerful and cherished, his endorphins kicked in, driving back the pain without having to use any outward magic that Serrier might sense.

The second spell to hit him hurt worse and required greater concentration to throw off, but he managed after a few painful seconds. The third one, though, broke his trance, sending him writhing onto the floor. How long he stayed there, he could not say, but strong hands lifting his head and a glass of water against his lips eventually roused him from his stupor.

"It didn't go well, I take it," Vincent observed softly as he helped Eric sit up.

Eric shook his head, wincing when the movement started his nerves jangling again. The fact that Vincent had even mentioned their plan let him know his lover had taken measures to assure they would not be overheard. "I think he was more angry than suspicious, though, because he didn't kill me outright. He just tortured me a bit. If he'd really suspected something, I'd be dead."

"That isn't particularly reassuring."

Eric shrugged. "It was a calculated risk. They're going to kill Orlando in the morning. We've got to get him out of here now."

"No can do," Vincent replied. "Claude's already working on him—and while I wouldn't mind killing the bastard, you aren't in any shape to help in a fight yet, and I can't do this alone. He'll be all right for a few more hours while you recover."

Eric wanted to argue. The thought that the man suffering Claude's spells was Alain's lover was enough to make him push his limits. When he could not even stand without Vincent's assistance, though, he had to admit defeat. "I hope you're right."

"Serrier won't let Blanchet kill him. He wants to watch him burn in the sunlight," Vincent said in disgust. "We'll come back before nightfall and see how things look. Let's get you out of here so you can rest."

Eric nodded gingerly. "You'll have to help me. I don't think I can get there by myself right now."

"He hurt you that bad?" Vincent queried.

"Yeah, it hurts enough that I'm not sure I could concentrate on casting a spell with any accuracy. I'd rather not try." He caught the concern on Vincent's face. "Yes, it's a risk, but not as much as staying here. Take me home."

Vincent's face tightened as he cast the displacement spell that transported them both to his apartment.

Easing Eric down onto the bed, he ran his hands over the long limbs. "What hurts?"

"Everything," Eric gasped, "but I don't think it's anything tangible. Everything I heard him cast was just pain spells."

"Lie down and let me check anyway," Vincent insisted.

Eric subsided on the bed. It felt too good to lie down for him to protest with any real force. He ignored the twitching of stressed muscles and abused nerves and waited for the spasms to pass. Vincent manhandled him gently out of his clothes, examining his body carefully, but Eric knew already what the other man would find.

"Nothing bleeding, nothing broken," Vincent reported, relief clear in his voice. "We just have to ride out the lingering effects." He pushed on Eric's hip. "Scoot over so I can lie down with you. You need to sleep, but I imagine it'll be awhile before you can. Maybe we can figure out how to get our vampire free while we wait for the pain to lessen enough for you to rest."

Eric moved as requested, curling into Vincent's arms as much as his aching limbs would allow. They lay that way for a few moments, Eric's trembling continuing as the magic wracked his body. "I can try a counter spell," Vincent offered after another tremor shook Eric. "I'm not all that good at them, but it might help a little."

"It's worth a try," Eric agreed. Vincent reached for his wand on the bedside table, casting a healing spell on his lover's twitching form. The pain did not disappear completely, but it did decrease enough that Eric could lie mostly still. "Thank you," he murmured, eyes beginning to close now that he did not hurt quite so badly.

Relieved he could help, Vincent let Eric sleep. He kept his own wand firmly in his grasp, though. He had no idea if anyone would come looking for them, but he intended to be ready if they did. His mind raced as he lay there next to his lover, turning over scenario after scenario, trying to decide which would be the most likely to result in saving the vampire and in escaping unscathed themselves.

When Eric finally stirred again some hours later, Vincent had come to one nerve-wracking conclusion. Alone, they had very little chance for success.

"Feeling better?" he asked, forcing his voice to stay level.

"Somewhat," Eric affirmed. "Thanks."

Vincent shrugged. "You'd have done the same for me."

Eric smiled and kissed the other wizard lightly. "What time is it?"

"Nearly dusk," Vincent replied. "I've been thinking, and I don't like the conclusion I came to."

"What's that?" Eric asked, pushing up on one elbow so he could see Vincent's face.

"I don't think we can do this alone, but I have no idea who else to trust."

Eric's eyes widened, wondering if this was the opening he had been waiting for. Taking a deep breath, he considered his options, took another deep breath, and rolled the dice. "I do."

Vincent blinked in surprise, his eyebrows arching up in silent question.

"The Milice."

"Are you out of your fucking mind?" Vincent demanded, sitting up and grabbing Eric by the shoulders. "Why would they believe us? Even if the vampire means as much to them as you think he does, why would they help us? If we give them the information they need, they'll just rescue him themselves and leave us high and dry."

"That might be true, if you called," Eric admitted, though he hoped Marcel would listen regardless, "but they'll believe me. I've been feeding them information from the moment I switched sides."

"You're the spy?" Vincent could not quite take in the magnitude of the revelation. He knew the other wizard had once fought with Chavinier, but in all the time they had been friends, he had never gotten the slightest hint of conflicted loyalties until very recently—and only then after Vincent brought up the idea of switching sides. His stomach churned as he wondered how much information he had inadvertently provided over the last two years.

"One of them, anyway," Eric admitted. "I don't know if Monique or Dominique were or not, but I know Marcel has multiple sources of information."

"So we do what? Pick up the phone and call them?"

"Pretty much," Eric replied. "I have a number that rings in Marcel's office. When I have information, I call him there. If he answers, I pass it on. If he doesn't, I call back later. I never call from the same phone twice, and never more than once a week unless the information is critical."

"How much have you told him?" Vincent asked, shaking his head to clear it of the shock of Eric's revelation. "And why the hell didn't you tell me sooner?"

"Would you have, in my place?" Eric countered calmly, though a part of him feared Vincent's reaction. He did not want to lose his lover, but he very much feared this could be the moment when he did. "I don't know the identity of Marcel's other spies, but I'm pretty sure I'm the highest placed one he has. I can't afford to jeopardize that. And until very recently, I wasn't sure telling you would be safe. I'm sorry if that hurts you—that certainly wasn't my intention—but winning this war is my first priority."

Heedless of the injuries Eric had suffered earlier that day, Vincent rolled the big man beneath him with a growl. "Fuck that," he muttered. "Fuck the war and the Milice and Serrier and everything else outside this bed. I'm your first priority and you're mine."

Eric felt like he should dispute that statement, but words had deserted him the moment Vincent's weight landed on top of him. When his lover ground down against him, coherent thought evaporated as well, leaving him capable only of groaning and surrendering to Vincent's claim.

Flush with power at Eric's submission, Vincent tore at his clothes, stripping away the layers of fabric that separated them until they lay skin to skin once more. Eric's hands flew over his body, urging Vincent on, adding to the heady sense of domination. Vincent had a feeling he would not experience that often so he cherished it now, reveling in the freedom to do to Eric as he pleased, for no other reason than because Eric was willing to let him.

The big body was hard beneath him, pushing up to meet every downward thrust of Vincent's hips as he ground their cocks together, bringing them both to aching hardness. "What other secrets are you keeping?" he demanded.

"None," Eric swore immediately, "or at least not intentionally. Ask. Ask anything you want and I'll give you a truthful answer."

"Not good enough," Vincent growled. "I want the whole truth, not just a partial one."

"Ask," Eric repeated, lying perfectly still beneath Vincent in a rare show of submission. He had just placed his very life in the other man's hands. He had to convince Vincent of his sincerity.

"How much of what you told Serrier was real?" Vincent asked harshly.

"All of it," Eric answered truthfully. "Danielle's death, my anger at Alain, even my frustration at the way it was handled. All of that was real, but I played it up, pretended it lasted far longer than it did. I always knew it was an accident on Alain's part, even in the depths of my grief. I blamed him, but once the worst of the grief had passed, I saw he was suffering as much as I was. Marcel convinced me to use my loss and anger as a reason to change sides, saying Serrier wouldn't buy anything less cataclysmic."

"So you've been passing information from the start?"

Eric nodded. "Just minor stuff at first. It was all I could find out, but Marcel's instructions were clear—do whatever it took to rise up through the ranks so I could get access to more critical information. So I did."

"Is that what this is?" Vincent asked, suddenly cold. "One more example of whatever it takes?"

"No!" Eric exclaimed, struggling now to get his hands free. "God, no! You're the one bright spot in this entire hellish two years." Finally breaking loose of Vincent's grip, Eric caught his lover's face between his palms. "If it hadn't been for your friendship, I'd have gone crazy within a matter of weeks, trying to figure out how to fit in while at the same time trying to deal with the leftover grief and everything else. This," he gestured helplessly between them, "whatever this is, wasn't planned. It just happened, and thank Merlin it did. I expected to die on this watch—I still expect it, honestly—because how could Serrier not find me out, and who would've cared when he did? And then you came along and gave me a reason to keep fighting, to stay alive in the hopes that there will be life after this war. Whatever emotions I've feigned in Serrier's service, our relationship is real."

Mollified somewhat, Vincent relaxed a little, his righteous indignation fading in the face of Eric's admissions. He wondered whether the other wizard had intended to reveal as much as he had, but Vincent was certainly glad to hear both that Eric's reactions to him were genuine and that his lover had finally come to the point of wanting and believing in a life together. "We'll survive," Vincent promised. "No matter who we have to call, we'll survive." He did not wait for Eric's reply, lowering his head to renew the kiss his questions had interrupted. Eric returned the embrace ardently, his head tilting, his lips parting for Vincent's tongue.

Vincent ravished his lover's mouth, wanting to wipe every thought from Eric's head that did not involve him and this bed. He resumed the seductive frottage, feeling their cocks swell between them again with their renewed desire. Soon, though, it was not enough for either of them. Eric mewled softly, a sound so at odds with his large stature and hypermasculine image that it brought a smile to Vincent's face. "What do you need, lover?" he teased softly.

"You," Eric replied simply. "In me, on me, around me, under me, I don't care. I just need you."

"You have me," Vincent promised.

Reparation in Blood   99

Chapter 15

ALAIN TOOK one step toward their target, the next to the last on the list from Raymond, and collapsed to his knees. He tried to rise, but his legs simply would not support him. Face twisting in desperation, he crawled another meter before his arms gave out as well. He lay face down in the mud, tears welling in his eyes with no choice left but to accept his inability to continue.

"You're exhausted," Thierry scolded for what felt like the hundredth time that day as he helped Alain rise to his knees. "You can't even lift your wand. How do you expect to fight the dark wizards, much less help Orlando?"

"I can't stop now, Thierry," Alain pleaded, his voice thin with fatigue. He knew his best friend was right, but admitting it meant admitting he had failed Orlando. Again. "There are only two more places left to search. I have to keep going."

"How?" the blond demanded. "You can't even stand, much less fight. Can you still cast a spell?"

Alain tried, but his magic did not respond to his call. The tears he had been fighting for days falling finally, he accepted defeat. "Take me home," he requested, his voice dull with despair. "Knock me out so I can sleep for a few hours. We'll keep searching after that."

"I have a better idea," Thierry said, a smile slowly dawning on his face. "Instead of going home, let's go to Notre-Dame. You'll recover faster there than anywhere else except maybe in Orlando's arms."

"Notre-Dame?" Alain repeated, confused. "Why?"

"That's right, you've been out of the loop for the past day," Thierry exclaimed with a shake of his head. "We made a bit of a discovery last night." He explained quickly as he helped Alain to stand. "The power in the church will restore you much quicker than just sleep alone. And you'll be safe there as well."

"If you say so," Alain replied skeptically. He trusted Thierry, though, so he let his friend cast the spell to take them to the parvis. Immediately, Thierry felt the welcoming call of the stones. "Do you feel it?" he asked Alain softly.

Alain shook his head, too weak to even stretch his senses. "It doesn't matter. I'm so tired, I could rest anywhere. Just take me inside and knock me out."

The lethargy in Alain's voice bothered Thierry more than anything else he had seen or heard since reuniting with his friend that morning at Eric's apartment. Helping the other wizard inside, he led Alain to one of the side chapels with a rug at the foot of the altar. "Lie down," he instructed. "You'll be safe here while you rest."

Alain collapsed onto the rough pile of the rug, eyes already closing as he fought sleep. "Come get me if anything changes," he requested. "I need to be there if… when we find Orlando."

"Sleep," Thierry ordered, not addressing Alain's comment. He understood his friend's need, but at the moment, it was truly a moot point. Desire aside, Alain simply had no more strength. A simple spell put him under, leaving Thierry to consider what to do next. After warding the chapel to make sure Alain would not be disturbed, he cast the displacement spell taking him back to Milice headquarters.

HE RACED through the streets behind the woman. Her face was not familiar, but he trusted her implicitly as she led him through underground passages and hidden tunnels, pausing periodically to chant a magical password under her breath, allowing them to cross pitfalls and traps unharmed on their way to Orlando. He would not have followed her alone like this for anyone else, but for Orlando, he would take any risk, any chance, if it would save his lover before he expired from hunger, exhaustion, or abuse.

He had long since lost track of where they were. Only the knowledge that he could use a displacement spell to escape if she played him false keeping him going. Left and right, up stairs and down, through twisting alleys and impossible mazes, he followed her, keeping her always in sight. Finally, they came out into open air, on the top of a hillside, looking down into a valley with a huge compound in the middle. "There," she told him softly. "That's where Serrier's holding him."

"So how do we get down there?" he asked.

"That's the hard part," she admitted. "I could bring you this far safely, but once we cross the wards, he'll know you're there. It'll be a question of who's faster—us getting to Orlando or him getting to us."

"I don't have a choice," Alain reminded her. "I can't leave Orlando there any longer. I can barely feel him now as it is."

The woman nodded. "Then let's go."

Alain braced himself for the displacement as she transported both of them to the edge of the compound. As she had at each of the previous wards, she began to chant softly until the spell unraveled to let them pass. This time, though, when he followed her through, alarms started going off.

"Hurry," she ordered, breaking into a run and leading him deeper into the warren of buildings.

Alain ran after her, hard on her heels. He drew his wand so he would be ready if it came to a fight, but she seemed to have a knack for avoiding the dark wizards. Finally, she led him into a sort of mechanics' garage, outfitted with various tools and gadgets. A closer look, however, revealed the sinister intention of the room. These were no ordinary tools, but rather instruments of torture. Instruments Alain was sure had been used on his lover. "Where is he?" he demanded.

The woman pointed to an odd, egg-shaped container on the other side of the room, the opaque white plastic concealing its contents. Alain's eyes widened as he looked at it, realizing Orlando would have to curl up in a fetal position to fit inside. Anger growing to cosmic proportions, Alain crossed the room, forcing open the screws that held the container's two sides shut. Inside, he could hear a whimper, a mixture of fear and pain, and it tore at his heart. "It's me, Orlando," he called as he freed the first screw and went to work on the second. "It's Alain."

The sounds of distress only increased, spurring him to increase his speed. His fingernails tore in his haste, but he did not even notice the pain. He had one thought only, now: getting to Orlando. The second screw came loose and he ripped the final one free, the casing falling away to reveal the bruised and battered form of his lover. Orlando's eyes were vacant as he shrank against the back wall of his prison. "Orlando," Alain cajoled. "It's me. Come on, let's get out of here."

Orlando shook his head violently. "You're another trick," he spat. "You'll hurt me just like all the others. Go away and let me die."

A sob catching in his throat, Alain reached inside, enfolding Orlando in a tender embrace. To his relief, the dark eyes slowly focused on him and a blood-covered hand lifted to his cheek. "Alain?" Orlando's voice trembled querulously.

"That's right, angel," Alain soothed. "I'm here. We're going to get you out of here now. I promise."

He turned back to his guide as the doors burst open and dark wizards came in from every direction. Common sense dictated that he get the hell out of there, but he could not take Orlando with him and he would not leave his lover alone. Keeping his body between Orlando and danger, he cast an Abbatoire at the nearest wizard. Before he could cast a second one, the woman had worked a displacement spell on him and Orlando, sending them to safety.

Relieved, he reached for his lover, tenderly embracing the battered form. Beneath the sweat and blood, he could still smell Orlando's sweet scent. Tenderly, he stroked the long locks, ignoring the matted blood. There would be time to clean up, time for Orlando to heal. Right now, Alain just needed to hold his vampire close. Orlando clung to him like a drowning man to a lifeline, the contact easing Alain's deep-seated fear that the torture he had endured would keep the vampire from being able to enjoy physical comfort again. Taking a deep breath, he tipped his lover's chin up, needing to kiss him before offering his neck for his lover to feed. He lowered his head, only to encounter empty air rather than the soft lips he loved. "Orlando!"

The sound of his voice roused Alain from his dream, a quiet sob escaping his lips as he realized where he was. He did not know why he was awake, because he could clearly remember Thierry's spell knocking him out. His dream must have been powerful enough, real enough for him to throw off that magic.

He wanted nothing more than to sink back into the dream, to find Orlando again and hold him, kiss him, feed him, even if only in his mind— but sleep proved elusive, the last image of Orlando slipping away from him too prominent for him to ignore. With sudden panic, he realized he could not feel Orlando's presence in the back of his mind the way he had been able to do any time he lowered his shields. Fighting down the bile rising in his throat, he tried to focus his senses, reminding himself he had drained his magical resources to nothing and that was surely why he could not feel Orlando's touch right away.

Unmindful of where he was, a long, keening wail escaped him as seconds passed with no trace of Orlando. Heart pounding, mind racing with worst-case scenarios, he fought the nausea that threatened to overwhelm him. Orlando could not be gone. It had not been four days yet. Sebastien had said Orlando could go four days without feeding, and while Serrier's magic could hurt Orlando, it should not have been able to destroy him. Surely if they had staked him out in the sun or set him on fire, he would have felt it, even if he could not have stopped it. Unless that was the source of his dream? He curled in on himself, delving deeper and deeper, tapping not only his own resources but the resources of the locus around him until he finally felt it again, a tiny flicker of contact that assured him of Orlando's continued existence.

Holding onto the little flame with all his strength, he tried to strengthen the bond, to reestablish the link that kept him sane. Slowly, far too slowly for his peace of mind, it came to life again, until he could feel Orlando without concentrating. Then searing pain sliced through him, stealing his breath and leaving him trembling.

It was different this time. That was the first thing he realized when he could get past the gasping, wrenching nausea that struck him along with Orlando's pain. He could not have said what was different about it or how he knew, but he knew it was, and that only added to the worry wracking him.

Thierry had said Notre-Dame was the site of a locus, and Alain could feel the power singing in the air now that he was less exhausted. He wondered if he could draw on it to strengthen his bond with Orlando, perhaps even to the point of sensing his location. He was down to only two places on the list Raymond gave him—though Serrier could have moved Orlando since yesterday, a tactic he had used in the past—but he wanted more certainty than that. He needed his lover at his side again. Now. Taking a deep breath, he focused on the energy in the air, channeling its power as he began to search.

STUMBLING TO his knees as his guards released him, Orlando stayed where he was until he heard the door to his cell close behind them. Once he was sure he was alone, he crawled forward to the cot, dropping onto its lumpy surface, trying to find a position that did not hurt. The torture had not been magical this time, but physical. His back stung viciously from the whip his torturer had used, bringing back vivid memories of his days at his maker's mercy. At least it had all been physical, not sexual this time. For Alain, he could hold on, endure the beatings and whatever else the dark wizard inflicted on his body, but he did not know if even the thought of his lover would carry him through another rape.

Finally getting as comfortable as he could with his back on fire and no way to heal it, he let himself drift into his memories, the days and nights at Alain's side over the past few weeks. He had never imagined he would find a lover, never let himself hope for one. He had his friendship with Jean and he had convinced himself that would be enough. Not until Alain had appeared on his horizon had he realized how much he was missing, how much more he could feel.

Eyes closing, he slid his hand over his chest, imagining it was Alain touching him, comforting him, healing him. He knew his lover's magic would not work on him, of course, but just the feel of Alain's fingers on his body would heal something far more important than the weals on his back. Over the time they had been lovers, Alain had started to heal his heart.

His fingers found his nipples, currently unscathed, although Orlando did not know how long that would last, and circled them gently. His maker had discovered early how sensitive they were and had frequently focused on them as part of his torture. He chose not to dwell on those memories, though, concentrating instead on remembering Alain's hands and mouth teasing them to hardness, lavishing loving tenderness on the aching buds.

Gentle, kind Alain who patiently held himself in check no matter the cost to himself so that Orlando could take tiny steps forward until he could trust again. Orlando bit back a sob at everything he had denied them in his fear. He could blame his inexperience with tenderness, but at the root of it all was his unwillingness to give control to anyone, even someone who would never abuse it.

It had taken being back again at the hands of a monster for him to realize the true extent of the difference. Faced with cruel insanity once again, he remembered its signals, the little mannerisms that gave away the dark wizard's intentions, much as they had given away Orlando's creator a hundred years ago. Mannerisms that were completely absent from Alain's demeanor. How he could have confused the two was beyond him now, though his fears had seemed perfectly reasonable at the time. He did not know how much longer he could survive, but if he did escape or if Alain rescued him, he would not make the same mistake again.

Letting his hand drift lower, he concentrated on eclipsing the pain his body still felt with happier memories, softer sensations. He imagined Alain's hands on him, stroking over his abdomen, down to his cock. Rarely had he let his lover touch him this way, but the memories of those few times warmed the vampire now. He focused on the love that had always imbued Alain's caresses, even before they had spoken the words. Their lives had been bound, it seemed, from the moment they met, the chemistry between them physical, emotional and magical. Nothing short of Alain's death could break those bonds, but Orlando wondered briefly if they could make their vows legal as well. Pushing that consideration aside until they were reunited, Orlando focused on what he was feeling, on projecting those feelings outward so that even if he never saw Alain again, his lover would know his final thoughts were of him.

Starved of gentleness after three days of magical and now physical abuse, Orlando's body roused quickly to the tender touch, incendiary memories sparking the vampire's blood and setting his loins on fire. He stroked more rapidly now, actively bringing himself physical pleasure to match his memories, needing that barrier between himself and the torture the dark wizards had inflicted.

A part of him warned against depleting what little strength he had left in self-pleasure, but Orlando needed this one link to sanity, to love, to a world outside of pain and isolation. If it meant his end came sooner, at least he would greet it with a smile on his face and the surety of having loved and been loved. He did not want to cause Alain the pain of his loss, but that seemed inevitable now. As much as Orlando tried to hold onto hope, he knew he would not last much longer, especially if he continued to lose blood. Perhaps he would simply pass out of existence as he climaxed. A smile ghosted across his lips at the thought. If he had to leave Alain, he could not think of a better way to do it.

His body twitched as it found release, but his back continued to ache, his lungs continued to work, and once it came down from its sexual high, his mind continued to function, his bond with Alain coming into sharper focus again. Clinging to that touch, he projected his emotions back toward his lover, hoping Alain would sense his thoughts.

The wave of strength and love that poured back left Orlando gasping. Pain, despair, fatigue faded in its wake. He reached behind himself, fingers seeking the marks left by the dark wizard's whip. They were still there, but closing, as if he had fed instead of masturbating. He felt stronger as well, to his surprise. He had no explanation for what he was feeling, but he knew undeniably that it was real.

"Thank you," he whispered to the empty room, hoping Alain would realize the contact had helped. Even if he did not, it only made Orlando love his wizard more.

Chapter 16

"CALL EVERYONE in," Serrier ordered, pacing the room like a caged lion. "Anyone who isn't here in an hour, cut them loose. I don't know how in the hell the Milice has figured out the location of our most secret bases. Payet didn't know about them. Monique didn't know about them, and I seriously doubt that bumbling boy knew about them. However Chavinier's doing it, though, he's getting too close for comfort. We're going to regroup somewhere they'll never think to look."

"Where?" Vincent asked, deliberately not meeting Eric's eyes as he considered what this news could do to their plans. They had not succeeded in reaching Chavinier after their frantic lovemaking, but Eric had assured him the old man would be back in his office in the evening. They had planned to call again, but now Vincent wondered if they would be able to get away.

"You'll find out when we get there," Serrier replied. "Until I know how Chavinier's doing it, I'm not telling anyone anything. And once we move, no one leaves until his attacks stop. I won't let everything I've worked for fall apart now!"

A restless murmur passed through the room, but no one voiced their concerns. "What about the vampire?" Simon asked.

"We'll take him with us. We can stake him out just as well where we're going as we can here," Serrier replied. "I don't want to leave him here for the Milice to find."

"They're far more likely to ease up on their pursuit if they get him back," Eric ventured, calculating the risk of speaking up.

"That would be admitting defeat!" Serrier roared. "I won't give Chavinier what he wants."

Another wave of murmurs circled the room, a little louder this time as hints of Serrier's madness began to show—but even the massed wizards did not dare to challenge him, none of them sure the others would back them up, or even simply let them fight.

"Let's go," Simon barked, breaking the tension in the room. "Contact everyone you can think of. You have an hour."

The crowd dispersed. Vincent met Eric's eyes over the heads of the departing wizards, but Eric shook his head slightly. Whatever happened next, it looked like they were on their own after all. They would simply have to stay alert and take advantage of any opportunities as they arose.

"GET SOME rest," Jean told Raymond. "Mireille said monsieur Lombard would be back tonight. I'm going to wait for him. If I learn anything, I'll come in immediately."

"You're just going to sit on his doorstep?" Raymond questioned.

"That's exactly what I'm going to do," Jean agreed. "We're out of options and out of time. Our only hope is whatever arcane knowledge resides in Lombard's head or in his library, and I don't want to wait any longer than absolutely necessary once he returns."

Raymond frowned, but he could hardly argue Jean's assertion that they were out of options. Alain's searches had turned up nothing, leaving him exhausted but no closer to finding Orlando. The hit-and-run attacks around the city had stopped, leaving an eerie calm and no hint as to Serrier's whereabouts. Sebastien had no new ideas, even with his more intimate knowledge of the bond Alain and Orlando shared. If they were going to rescue the captured vampire before his strength gave out or before Serrier got bored tormenting him, they needed a new plan. "Fine, but take this with you," Raymond urged, pulling his coat from its hook. "It's spelled to stay warm, no matter how cold it gets outside. I know you aren't as sensitive to temperature as I would be, but I don't want you to suffer any adverse effects from the exposure."

Jean smiled gratefully and pulled the coat on, immediately feeling its warmth like a tender embrace. "I'll come back as soon as I see if he knows anything," he repeated.

"Be careful," Raymond warned, buttoning the coat and then cradling Jean's cheeks between his hands. "I don't know what Serrier's up to, but I don't trust this lull. He went after the vampires once before. He could be after them again."

"I'm not looking for a fight," Jean assured him. "I just want to find Orlando."

Raymond snorted in disbelief. "Tell me another one. You might not be actively looking, but I know you want revenge, for Karine and for Orlando, so don't give me that line about staying out of a fight if one comes to you."

"I'll be safe, I promise," Jean vowed, touched by Raymond's concern. "Yes, I want revenge, but I've got a reason to survive this war—and that's even more important than vengeance."

Raymond smiled softly. "Good to know." He kissed Jean tenderly, barely a brushing of lips, but the vampire had other ideas, latching onto his lover's mouth and ravishing it thoroughly before finally pulling back.

"Get some rest. If this goes as I hope it will, you'll need it before the night's over."

Letting Jean walk out the door alone was one of the hardest things Raymond had ever done, but his lover was right that he needed to rest. The entire Milice was overextended, but he and Alain and Thierry had borne even more than their share of the work: Alain because of his desperation to find Orlando, Thierry because he would not let Alain fight alone, and Raymond because his experience with Serrier in the past gave him an insight the others did not have. If Jean was right and monsieur Lombard could help them find Orlando, they would need every edge they had to beard the lion in its den. Raymond did not want to be the one slowing them down. Sinking onto the couch, he stifled a smile, Jean's voice in his head scolding him to make it a real bed so he could sleep properly.

Out in the cold winter air, Jean felt the warmth of Raymond's coat— Raymond's magic—around him like a lover's embrace, protecting him as the wizard had promised from the cold and the wind. He pulled the collar up against the slight drizzle, wishing the coat had a hood. He would have to huddle in the entryway and hope the rain did not pick up any more, or coat or not, he would be soaked before long.

The trek to his mentor's house took longer than it should have, a strike on the subway snarling the bus routes and thoroughfares. Jean was tempted to get out and walk, knowing his preternatural speed would get him there faster than public transportation or the cab he'd hailed in hopes of avoiding the weather, but the sun was only just now setting. He did not want to draw attention to himself before full dark, on the off chance Serrier or one of his minions was watching.

Monsieur Lombard's house was still dark when he finally arrived there, but that was not terribly surprising. The old vampire still eschewed electricity, preferring the warm light of a fire or lamps to the cold artificiality of light bulbs. Night having fallen completely by the time he wended his way through the narrow streets of île St-Louis to his destination, he knocked hopefully on the door, but no one answered. Fortunately, the rain had eased up. The night was still cold and misty, but Raymond's coat was enough to protect him from that, making him glad once again that he had a wizard for a lover, partner, and friend.

He shook his head to think of it. They had come so far in such a short time. It gave him hope for the future, for the alliance and beyond. If two such disparate individuals, two such loners, as Raymond and himself could come together and forge a partnership that worked to the point of beginning to build a life together, surely others could do the same. With that expansion of understanding, tolerance would spread beyond the wizards to society as a whole. He was not naïve. He knew it would not happen overnight, but he was a patient man. Even if he had to wait the lifetime of a mortal man, he would survive to see the change.

Marcel had updated him earlier that night on the progress of the equal rights bill, saying it would go before Parlement within a day or two for the up or down vote he had asked for. The news had cheered him as much as anything could, given the rest of the current situation. Whatever else the alliance succeeded or failed in doing, he would have achieved his goal in securing legal equality for his kind. He knew getting the law passed was, in many ways, the first step rather than the last—but it was a huge step forward, one that would give vampires a leg to stand on as they demanded the respect their age and experience deserved. With wizards like Marcel and Raymond, Thierry, and hopefully Alain on their side, they would win those battles as well, in time. First, though, they had to defeat Serrier or all the rest would be in vain. If the dark wizard won, laws passed in Parlement would be worth less than the paper they were written on or the ink used to print them. Serrier's behavior had already proven he believed himself above the law, and the fact that the vampires—most of them, anyway—had actively sided with the Milice would make them a target of revenge if the dark wizards won the war. Jean did not see that happening anymore. It had been a very real concern when they formed the alliance, but the long-reaching effects of the partnership bonds had done far more to aid their efforts than simply putting more fighters on the streets. He had felt the power Raymond had summoned and channeled during the Piège-Pouvoir and again as he searched for Orlando. Serrier would have to be powerful indeed to stand against even one such pairing, much less the amassed might of the entire Milice.

If only they could find him.

"WHAT ARE we going to do?" Vincent hissed, pulling Eric into an empty hallway as soon as they were far enough away not to be overheard.

"I don't know," Eric muttered. "I can't get away to contact our friend and even if I could, I don't know where we're moving to give him that location."

"So we just go along?"

Eric shrugged helplessly. "Do you have a better idea? I don't dare push right now, not after earlier. He doesn't trust me at the moment, and if we're not careful, he'll stop trusting you by association."

"I don't give a flying fuck if he trusts me," Vincent spat. "I just want to grab the vampire and get the hell away from him."

Eric nodded, mind racing. "Try to be the one to move Orlando when the time comes. When Serrier gives the orders, cast your spell and go. Take him to Milice headquarters—you know where they are. You don't need me. The vampire will be enough to get you inside and protected. I'll join you when I can."

"No way in hell!" Vincent retorted, his voice sharp despite being low. "I'm not leaving you to face Serrier's wrath when he realizes he's lost his prize. You said it yourself—he already suspects you. If the vampire goes missing, he'll kill you even if you're still there."

"That's a risk I took when I agreed to do this," Eric replied, brushing off the concern.

"It's not a risk I agreed to," Vincent countered. "We do this together or not at all. I won't leave you behind to pay the price for my defection."

"It would be worth it to know you were safe," Eric said softly.

"I'd rather die with you at my side than live without you," Vincent protested. "We do this together or not at all."

"Not at all" was no longer an option in Eric's mind. His wards had detected Alain and Thierry's presence, mere moments after he had left. When he had returned to his apartment later, the vampire's ring was missing, solidifying his determination to reunite the two men he had unknowingly separated. He remembered all too clearly his grief at losing Danielle. He would not condemn Alain to that if he had any other choice. "Then I guess we'll have to do it together."

"We could go now," Vincent suggested. "Just grab him and disappear."

"We'd never get past the wards," Eric replied. "Can't you feel that Serrier has strengthened them? They'll still let people in, but until he's ready to leave, they won't let anyone out. Whatever he's planning, it's his last big gamble, the roll of the dice that will either win it all or lose the war entirely."

"Are you having second thoughts?" Vincent asked cautiously.

Eric snorted. "Not likely. If Serrier wins, Blanchet's torture would be the norm. I couldn't live with myself if I let that happen."

Vincent smiled. "Good. Let's go get the vampire. Maybe we'll be able to use your original suggestion—together—when Serrier drops the wards."

THE NIGHT grew colder as Jean waited, rising to pace now and then, only to return to his vigil on monsieur Lombard's stoop. His stomach churned painfully whenever he let himself dwell on the passage of time, his awareness of Sebastien's predicted deadline for Orlando's survival weighing heavily on his thoughts. If Serrier thought Orlando had reached the end of his usefulness, the dark wizard would surely seek to dispose of him. He would know by now that most things would not hurt him, so the dark wizard would surely turn to more tried and true methods of ending a vampire's existence. Sunlight and fire. Jean had revealed those methods by his own words, never thinking they would be turned against his best friend.

He hoped Orlando would be unconscious by then, if it came to that. Jean had seen vampires burned by the sun before. Not often, fortunately, but the memories were etched into him, the suffering they experienced if they were not immediately destroyed as their bodies turned to ash inch by painful inch. The thought of such torment being inflicted on Orlando tore at his soul. He had saved the young vampire from torture once, only to have him suffer it again—and this time, Jean was helpless to stop it.

"Jean?" Lombard's voice cut through the frigid air. "What are you doing here?"

Rising stiffly to his feet, Jean faced his mentor and predecessor. "I've come to throw myself on your mercy. Serrier's wizards kidnapped Orlando three days ago and we can't find him."

Chapter 17

ERIC AND Vincent arrived at Orlando's cell only to find Simon there ahead of them. "Get upstairs," he ordered. "Pascal will be ready to go soon and you don't want to get left behind. He's decided to displace everyone himself so he doesn't have to worry about anyone getting lost along the way."

Vincent had reached for his wand, obviously intending to take Simon out, but Eric shook his head. "Thanks for the warning," he said simply, tilting his head to indicate Vincent should come with him.

"We could have taken him," Vincent hissed when they were alone.

"Yes, we could have," Eric agreed, "but when we went upstairs with the vampire, Serrier would have demanded an explanation I'd rather not give, even if he didn't hear us fighting and come to investigate. It's only midnight. We've got a few hours until dawn. We'll figure it out once we get wherever we're going."

Vincent did not look convinced, but he let Eric lead him back to the large room where everyone had gathered for Serrier's latest round of insanity. A few moments later, Simon came in, the vampire slung over his shoulder, clearly immobilized by a spell.

As if that were the cue he had been waiting for, Serrier began casting spell after spell, the first sealing the doors leading into the room so no one else could enter or leave. A second spell started flames licking along the walls, spreading outward for the moment, though Eric knew eventually they would devour this room as well. The third spell bound the massed dark wizards as surely as the spell Simon had put on Orlando, making Eric's stomach roil nervously. Unable to reach for their wands, they would not be able to do anything to counter Serrier if he did something they did not like, nor to escape if he chose to leave them there at the mercy of the flames. Eric hoped the dark wizard was not so far gone that he would kill his followers that way, but honestly, he would not put anything past Serrier.

One final spell wrapped itself around everyone in the room, moving them on Serrier's command from the slowly crumbling building to their still-unknown destination. When the spells holding them eased finally, Eric looked around their new headquarters, trying to place it amid the myriad of bases Serrier had used over the two years he had been with the dark wizard.

He saw nothing that gave away their location, though, a fact that unnerved him slightly. It was much harder to cast a displacement spell from an unknown location. "Where are we?" he murmured to Vincent, hoping his lover would recognize the building since he had been with Serrier from the beginning.

"Just north of the Seine, near Beaubourg," Vincent replied just as softly. "It was one of our first bases, and one of the first abandoned."

Before he could say more, Serrier started shouting orders for strengthening the wards, for preparing for battle, and for the execution of the prisoner. "Lock him in a room somewhere until it starts to get light. We'll deal with him then. In the meantime, we have other things to do."

Vincent and Eric trailed behind Simon as he found a place to stash Orlando. There were too many people around for them to do anything at the moment but take note of the location, but at least they knew where to find the vampire when—if—the opportunity to rescue him arose.

Instead, so as not to arouse suspicion, they threw themselves into making the building as secure as possible against outside threats. If they knew exactly how the wards were cast, they would know exactly how to penetrate them when the time came to rescue Orlando. More than that, if they did not succeed in attempting the rescue, the wards would have to hold against whatever attack came once the Milice realized what had happened to their operative. And Eric had no doubt Serrier would make sure they realized. He was just crazy enough to provoke them that way.

"I THINK you'd better come inside," monsieur Lombard declared, brow furrowing at Jean's announcement. "And start at the beginning."

Nodding, Jean followed the elder vampire inside, waiting with thinly disguised impatience as monsieur Lombard removed his coat and scarf, hanging them with the precision of years on their hooks in the closet. He offered to take Jean's coat as well, but the chef de la Cour declined, not wanting to be parted from that link with his partner.

Leading Jean into the library, monsieur Lombard lit the fire in the grate, waiting until the wood caught before turning back to the other vampire. "Now, tell me what's going on."

"Three days ago, we got word of an attack targeting the Cour, centered around place Pigalle," Jean recounted. "We took measures to protect everyone we could, of course, and then we met Serrier's force in battle. We defeated them, but near the end of the fight, two of the dark wizards cast a spell on Orlando and disappeared with him. We've been searching for him ever since, to no avail."

"He hasn't been destroyed?" monsieur Lombard verified.

"No, thank God," Jean replied. "His Avoué can still sense his existence, but not his location. Serrier must have found a way to block the magical tracking devices the Milice uses, because that didn't work, nor did any of the wizards' searching spells. I've gone through every book in my library, and in my partner's, but we can't find anything else to help us. There has to be something, though. We can't just lose him!"

Monsieur Lombard regarded Jean for a long moment, his gaze fixed on the chef de la Cour's agonized visage, but his thoughts were in another time and another place, desperately seeking another kidnapped man.

Unsuccessfully.

Then, though, it had been the mortal taken and the vampire left to search in vain until the dark wizards who attacked Reims killed him as they retreated rather than leave him behind to be rescued. Eyes closing, monsieur Lombard fought back the memories of finding his Avoué's body, broken and lifeless, amid the ruins of the Alamanni camp, making their victory hollow and cutting short a relationship that should have lasted decades longer. Feeling his anger returning as if his loss had occurred only yesterday, he opened his eyes again. "Who wants to find the boy?" he asked. "You and his Avoué, or the Milice as a whole?"

"If we knew with certainty where to look, Chavinier would surely commit the Milice to the task," Jean assured him, "because where we find Orlando, we're sure to find a large number of Serrier's wizards and perhaps even Serrier himself."

"Not to mention the rogue," monsieur Lombard added.

"Not to mention him," Jean agreed. "He is *extorris* now so he will not last much longer regardless of Serrier's sanction. He killed a woman under my protection and as such has lost the indemnity of the Cour."

"That is Cour business," monsieur Lombard declared, "and you will handle it as such. Kidnapping the boy is personal. I refuse to see history repeat itself."

Jean nodded. "Living through torture once is more than anyone should have to endure. Suffering through it twice is unacceptable."

That was not the history monsieur Lombard had intended to refer to, but Jean had not even been made when he lost his Avoué so there was no reason for the other vampire to be aware of those circumstances. Nor did he feel like talking about them now. "We need the boy's Avoué and such wizards as Chavinier will send with us for his rescue."

"Then let's go to Milice headquarters," Jean said, surprised monsieur Lombard would volunteer to participate. "Marcel will be there and can gather a squadron, and he'll know where Alain is if he isn't there."

Retrieving his coat, monsieur Lombard gestured for Jean to precede him. "Lead the way."

ORLANDO PACED the length of the room where he had been confined after the jump from his previous prison. He did not know where they were now anymore than he had known before, only that he had exchanged one cell for another. The spell that had bound him during the displacement had incapacitated his body but not dulled his senses, leaving him able to hear everything Serrier said—so he knew what the dark wizard intended come dawn. He would fight, of course, but if they used a spell on him, he would be helpless against their foul intentions. He still held out a faint hope that Alain would find him or that Eric would find a way to rescue him, but that hope faded with each passing minute. Aware to the core of his being of the cycle of the sun, he knew exactly how long he had until its rays lightened the horizon again. And once that happened, his existence would be cut short and his bond with Alain destroyed forever.

The room he was in had clearly been some sort of office in the past, with papers scattered across an old desk. Orlando debated looking for a pen and writing a letter to Alain in the hopes Eric would be able to deliver it even if he could not save Orlando. When he sat to write it, though, he found he could not make his hand stop trembling long enough to put words on paper.

Abandoning that idea as fruitless, he imagined instead that Alain was there with him, but unable to change his fate. If he put his feelings into words, perhaps they would translate in some small way through the bond, helping Alain to understand that while he had not embraced his fate willingly, he had accepted it.

"Good-bye, my love," he whispered to the empty room, eyes closing so he could imagine Alain in front of him. "I'm sorry we didn't have longer together, but I don't regret the bond we formed. I don't regret having known you and loved you. You showed me what it meant to love, and for that, my soul will be eternally grateful.

"I know there are things we didn't say, that we didn't do, and I wish now that I hadn't held back so long, ruled by my fears. It doesn't do any good to tell you this now, with dawn just a few hours away, but those fears are all in the past. I want every touch you could give me, and everything I denied us. If only we had more time, I'd let you show me how good it feels to give yourself to a lover. I'd let us discover how powerful it would be to make love as I fed. I'd cover you with proof of my devotion, little love bites everywhere you wanted—"

His voice broke on a sob, throat closing tight with tears that could not come. He buried his head in his hands, trying to stay strong, to project his love, not his fear, through the bond, but it seemed he was not as sanguine about his fate as he wanted to be. "Hurry, Alain," he begged. "I don't want to face the sun without you at my side. I'm not ready to be separated from you. Oh, please, God, don't do this to me. Don't do this to him. He's already lost everyone once. Don't make him suffer that loss again."

The sound of the lock opening startled him to silence, his eyes growing wide as he waited for it to open. *Too soon!* his mind shouted. *It isn't dawn yet.*

Don't make me wait for first light outside. Just leave me here until you can take me outside and destroy me instantly. Dear God, I'm not ready!

ALAIN PACED the chapel in the nave of Notre-Dame, the odd mix of emotions from Orlando leaving him more than a little baffled. From intense pain to sexual euphoria to the depths of despair, his lover's emotions had fluctuated wildly, making Alain question what he was feeling. Had the link been corrupted somehow? Was that even possible?

He did not know, nor did he know who he could ask, for even Sebastien would not be able to tell him for sure. No living vampire had formed an Aveu de Sang with a wizard, and they had already seen far-reaching consequences from the simple involvement of wizard and vampire without the additional magic of the Aveu de Sang.

Alain hoped the pain was somehow skewed by their bond, but he feared that was in fact the most accurate of the sensations he felt from his lover. He had no explanation for the orgasm he imagined he felt, though the surge of love that accompanied it was unmistakable. He had tried to return the love, but he had no way of determining what Orlando could feel.

It was the despair that scared him most, though. Injuries that caused pain could be healed, but if Orlando gave up, if something had happened to make him believe he would not survive, Alain would lose him. He could heal many things, but not death. He had experienced a terror like nothing he had ever known when the bond had snapped for a moment, sure Serrier had finally found a way to destroy his lover. His howl had been loud enough to rattle the windows in the cathedral, the very air vibrating with the power of his grief as his magic coalesced around him in response to his wildly fluctuating emotions.

A few seconds later, though, the bond was back in place again, making Alain wonder what had happened. The despair had followed hard on the return of their bond, distracting him from one worry and filling him with another. He had felt a variety of emotions prior to that moment, but nothing like this wretched resignation. Whatever had happened, Orlando had stopped believing he would be rescued. That frightened him like nothing else. If his lover was convinced his destruction was imminent, Alain was out of time. "Where are you, Orlando?" he cried in frustration, the words trailing off into a pained shout as panic broke through the despair. And then nothing.

Frantically, Alain reached for the elemental magic, drawing it into him, stretching his senses wider and wider, the combined power breaking through ward after ward as he searched for his lover. He could feel himself growing thin as he spread his magic across the elements. Ignoring those warning bells, he drew deeper on his connection with the air, wind whipping around him in the usually still cathedral, then spiraling out across the city as he targeted the two places left on his list from Raymond. The wards crumbled beneath his determination, but he did not find Orlando. One building was empty, the other destroyed by flames, but neither bore any trace of his beloved.

"No!" he bellowed, the whirlwind of his grief and anger overturning statues and shattering windows. "You can't take him from me!"

"Alain!"

Thierry's voice, sharp with command, drew the other wizard's attention. "Don't do this. We know how to find him."

"WHAT DID you do to me?" Orlando accused as soon as he saw the wizard at the door. "Why can't I feel Alain anymore?"

"Shhh," Eric hushed. "We're getting you out of here, but I have no idea what kind of tracing spells Serrier might have put on you and we can't take the risk of alerting him. I used a simple *Vide* spell that doesn't let magic pass through. As soon as I lift it, any spells on you will go back into place."

"This isn't a spell," Orlando insisted, though he moved toward the door, more than ready to be free again. "It's far deeper than that."

"If it's magical, the *Vide* will still block it," Eric replied. "Come on. Vincent's guarding the hallway."

Orlando nodded and stepped into the corridor, hoping his days of confinement were truly behind him this time. "Where are we?"

"Near the Beaubourg," Eric said.

Orlando's mind raced as he considered where he could go this close to dawn where he would be safe. Alain's magic had long since worn off, leaving him as susceptible to sunlight as any other vampire. He could go west toward Jean's apartment and hope his friend was there. Or he could go to monsieur Lombard's house on île St-Louis. The old vampire was more likely to be home than the chef de la Cour, but less likely to answer his door in daylight, not having the protection of a partner.

"And where are you taking me?"

"Wherever you want to go," Eric replied, "as long as it's far from here and protected by the Milice."

His apartment was Orlando's first impulse, but he doubted Alain would be there, and even if he was, Orlando did not want to lead any pursuers to his home. Milice headquarters would be the safest place, though he had no idea how he would get the two wizards in through Marcel's wards.

"Hey!" a voice behind them shouted.

"Don't stop," Vincent muttered under his breath. "Keep going and don't look back. We'll join you if we can, but get out because Serrier will kill you if you don't."

"What is it, Blanchet?" Eric demanded impatiently, turning to face the sadistic wizard. "We're a little busy right now."

"I was supposed to get to take him outside," Claude whined.

"Yeah, well, plans have changed," Vincent snapped. "Abbattez!"

Eric's eyebrows shot up as the killing spell hit the wizard who had tortured so many innocent souls, but he said nothing as they turned to follow Orlando out of the building.

"One less pest to worry about," Vincent explained as they rounded the corner. The exterior door was open, giving them hope that Orlando had escaped, but a wizard blocked their path. They exchanged quick glances, raised their wands, and prepared to fight.

Chapter 18

"How?" Alain demanded, turning on Thierry. "We have to hurry. I can't feel him anymore."

"Give me your wrist, then," monsieur Lombard said, stepping forward, his presence brooking no resistance.

"But...." Alain hesitated, eyes flying to Jean and Sebastien standing next to this unknown vampire. "But what about the Aveu de Sang?"

"That's how we'll be able to find him," Jean assured him. "Monsieur Lombard won't feed. He just needs a taste so he can lead us to Orlando."

Terribly uncomfortable with this perceived infidelity, Alain pulled his sleeve back and offered his hand to monsieur Lombard. With great reverence, the vampire inclined his head, bringing sharp nails to the skin of Alain's wrist. He could sense the wizard's restlessness, the uncontrollable urge to be reunited with his lover, but monsieur Lombard would honor the wizard's vow not to let any vampire but his Avoue feed from him. Slicing the skin with his nails, he turned the wizard's wrist, coaxing a few drops of blood from it onto his palm. "Some things are sacred," he declared before licking the blood from his hand.

It took a moment, his eyes closing as he concentrated. Then he turned to the others. "Let's go."

Turning north as they left Notre-Dame, they raced through the streets, driven by their urgency and by the vampires' awareness of the upcoming dawn. Those who could had fed before they left Milice headquarters at Jean's insistence, but many who gathered had no partner. They insisted on coming, nonetheless, declaring they would fight until daylight drove them inside but that they would not allow anyone to hurt one of their own.

Jean had considered ordering them to stay behind, but he doubted they would have listened anyway. Had their positions been reversed, he would not have stayed behind either. He had been amazed at how quickly Marcel summoned the Milice once he heard monsieur Lombard's news. The two men had stared at each other for a long, fraught moment before organizing the wizards and vampires as if they had been working in concert for years.

Now, as they tore up rue d'Arcole and across the river, Marcel moving nearly as quickly as monsieur Lombard, Jean wondered if the old vampire had finally met his match. All around him, he could hear wizards casting spells to allow them to keep up with the vampires' speed. A quick glance revealed Raymond pacing him perfectly, stride for stride. It should have been impossible, but he had learned much about magic in the past month—enough to know that impossible was quite a relative term.

Free of the pont d'Arcole, they flowed north, a terrible, silent wave of wizards and vampires, all set on the same goals: saving Orlando, and punishing those who hurt him. Early morning traffic on the rue du Renard parted for them, drivers finding their cars suddenly on the sidewalks with no explanation for how or why. Horns honked wildly behind them, but they ignored the noise, moving relentlessly up the boulevard until they passed the Centre Georges Pompidou. Monsieur Lombard made a sharp right on rue Rambuteau, then an almost immediate left into the Cité Noël.

The narrow cul-de-sac only had a few buildings on it, and at the end, Alain saw the most wonderful sight he could possibly imagine. Orlando stumbled down the steps, falling to his knees as he reached street level. Racing ahead of the others with the last reserves of his strength, the wizard ran to his lover's side, scooping him into an ardent embrace, ignoring the shredded clothing, the blood on his face and arms, the oozing welts on his back. "You're alive."

Orlando smiled weakly, already feeling the effects of the growing daylight, though no rays had yet topped the surrounding buildings. "Eric... let me... go," he gasped, trying to keep his eyes open. His vision was graying, though, everything narrowing to the welcome sight of his lover's face. And then darkness descended completely.

The sun broke free of the horizon.

"Get him inside," Jean ordered. "It's been too long since he fed for him to be outside."

"Thierry!" Alain shouted. Immediately, his best friend was at his side. "Send us to Orlando's apartment."

Thierry shook his head. "Go back to Notre-Dame. Let the magic there help you both."

"Then send us there," Alain snapped, eyeing the ashy color of Orlando's skin worriedly. "He won't last much longer outside. And don't kill Eric. He helped Orlando escape. Capture him and we'll sort it out later."

Thierry nodded and cast the spell, Alain and Orlando disappearing immediately. "He isn't the only vampire who won't last much longer," Thierry warned Jean before turning to spread the word concerning Eric.

"Then let's get inside and deal with the rest of our business." The chef de la Cour's voice was cold as he spoke, the sight of his young friend so gravely injured enough to snap every bit of control he had. He would find the bastards who had hurt Orlando and they would face vampire justice.

"Général Chavinier," monsieur Lombard intoned, holding out his hand, "if you would do me the honor?"

Marcel smiled and extended his arm, palm up, for the elder statesman to feed. The old vampire did not linger, taking what he needed and then releasing the wizard's arm. The general's magic washed over him, strengthening him and ending the tingling sensation from the earliest rays of the sun. "Now, let us see justice done."

"And not before time," Marcel agreed, marshalling his forces and leading them toward the building Orlando had just exited.

The one wizard at the door fell to a spell from the inside just as the Milice reached the stoop. As they burst inside, Eric stepped in front of Vincent, eyes looking around frantically for someone he recognized. Catching sight of Marcel, he relaxed, taking a step forward, only to be caught in an implacable grip by the older man at Marcel's side. "Did you find Orlando?" Eric asked, not even trying to struggle. He did not want anyone to mistake his actions for an intention to harm anyone, especially Marcel.

"We found him," Marcel related. "He's safe with Alain now."

Eric breathed a sigh of relief. "Vincent helped me get him out. He's on our side."

"*Our* side?" David questioned, catching the choice of words. "Since when is it our side?"

"Since always," Marcel intervened. "Eric's been providing me information from the beginning." He turned to Vincent. "While I trust Eric's word, I'm afraid I'll have to put you both in protective custody until we can investigate more carefully."

Vincent nodded, his wand pointing carefully at the ground. "Do what you have to do."

Marcel cast a quick binding spell, then sent the two wizards back to a holding cell at Milice headquarters. They would be safe there until this battle was over. Stepping past the dead body of one of the dark wizards, Marcel gave orders for the squadron members to spread out and work their way through the building, capturing when possible or killing anyone they met. "This ends now," he added.

Making sure the unpaired vampires were among the first inside, Jean murmured, "*Extorris*," to every vampire who passed, reminding them that the rogue was his should they find him inside the building. Those who might have challenged the ostracism on Karine's behalf alone stayed silent now, having seen the way Orlando was abused. Even Luc Cabalet, the chef de la Cour d'Amiens, who had been summoned along with his partner accepted the pronouncement. If the rogue was indeed here, he had accepted Orlando's treatment by not opposing it, even if he had not engaged in it actively.

They swarmed through the building, securing room after room, Marcel and monsieur Lombard at the head of one group, Thierry and Sebastien leading a second, and Jean and Raymond with the third. Thierry had never encountered such fierce resistance from the dark wizards, whose usual mode of operations was to wreak havoc and then flee. "They know this is their last stand," he murmured to Sebastien as they stormed a small room where two wizards had holed up.

"And so they fight all the harder because of it," Sebastien agreed, executing an elegant roll to one side to allow a spell to sizzle harmlessly in the plaster behind him. "Do they truly fear capture that much that they would choose to die rather than surrender?"

"I think Serrier has them so convinced Marcel will torture them or worse, just as he would do for failure, that death is the safer option," Thierry explained before returning the volley of spells that came his direction. "This is ridiculous. We can't get in and they can't get out. We're going to be stuck here for hours at this rate."

"I can go in," Sebastien volunteered. "Their spells won't work on me."

"Their killing spells won't work," Thierry countered. "Other spells will, and they know that now."

"You'll just have to make sure they don't hit me then, won't you?" Sebastien challenged, muscles bunching in preparation for his assault.

"Merde!" Thierry cursed as Sebastien launched himself forward, tucking and rolling, using every bit of his preternaturally enhanced speed and flexibility to avoid the cascade of incantations. Thierry fired spells as quickly as he could, trying to neutralize anything the dark wizards might send at his partner. One slipped by his guard, hitting Sebastien in the chest. The dark-haired vampire stumbled to his knees but then got up again. Thierry's muttering grew dire as he threatened all manner of retribution against his brave lover. First, though, he had to deal with the dark wizards.

The pain in his chest shocked Sebastien momentarily, but he reminded himself it was just magic, not a real injury, and that ultimately it could do him no lasting damage. Pushing it aside, he continued his inexorable progress into the room, ducking behind a plush, high-backed chair to escape another barrage of spells from the dark wizards. Gauging the moment, he launched himself at the nearest wizard, tackling him to the floor and knocking his wand out of his hand. He could hear Thierry shouting for the other wizard to surrender. The dual shouts of "Abbattez!"

that followed stopped his breath until he heard Thierry's voice again, casting a binding spell on the wizard beneath him.

"You scared me!" he accused, rising to his feet.

"*I* scared *you?*" Thierry demanded, grabbing Sebastien's shoulders and shaking them roughly. "I'm not the one who dove headfirst into the middle of a spell battle with no protection!"

"I had all the protection I needed," Sebastien assured him, kissing his wizard lightly. "I knew you wouldn't let anything happen to me."

"But it did," Thierry insisted. "I saw that spell hit you."

"It either wasn't a very strong spell or it doesn't work as well on vampires as they thought," Sebastien replied, "because the pain's already fading."

"The wizard who cast it is dead," Thierry explained. "That sort of spell doesn't linger long if its caster dies. Others do, so be more careful next time."

Sebastien just smiled, letting Thierry interpret that as he chose. His wizard's scowl informed him that Thierry did not believe he intended to do anything differently should the situation arise again.

"Let's go. We've got the rest of this floor and then upstairs to secure," Thierry said after a moment. "We don't have time to stand around."

Sebastien grabbed Thierry's shoulders, kissing him once more, before letting him go to lead his patrol farther down the hall.

The deeper they got into the building, the more rooms they found empty. Those that did have people in them were full, as if the dark wizards hoped that by sticking together they could defeat their attackers.

"We're not going to be able to root them all out, Captain Dumont," one of Thierry's subordinates worried aloud when they found a room with thirty wizards inside. "They outnumber us."

Thierry considered various tactics, but in the end, none of them were worth the risk. "Seal the room," he ordered instead. "If they try to come out through the door, we can pick them off a few at a time. Otherwise, we'll deal with them later, after the rest of the building is secure."

David nodded and cast the spell, making it impossible for anyone inside to use a displacement spell to escape the four walls confining them. Only the door now offered any chance of escape.

Thierry left four wizards and two vampires on guard at the door to ensure sufficient numbers to keep anyone inside from escaping. Then he ordered the rest of the patrol to move on. Though he did not say it aloud, he hoped they would find Serrier as they searched. He wanted a piece of the dark wizard's hide, for all the lives lost, but especially for the anguish Alain had suffered these last few days. That did not seem to be in the cards for him, though. Despite finding groups of wizards all over the building, Serrier remained elusive. He just hoped the other patrols were having more luck. They had to take down Serrier or he would find a way to rebuild his forces and start the conflict up again.

He lost track of how many wizards they fought and captured, even more so of those they killed, as they finished securing their wing of the building. He would have preferred to take more of them alive, but he knew what justice looked like under Serrier's command and understood that many of them probably preferred death over torture. He didn't know why they didn't displace away from the fight, but he didn't have time to worry about that at the moment. That Marcel would never stand for such things must either have been beyond their comprehension or had simply not occurred to them, because they fought to the death unless one of the vampires managed to disarm them, leaving them vulnerable to a binding spell.

Thierry's respect for the vampires, paired and unpaired alike, grew exponentially as they continued to fight through the building. They threw themselves selflessly into battle with no concern for their own well-being, taking spells that would have felled a mortal and rising again to continue fighting, trusting the wizards to protect them to the best of their ability and to their undead nature to deal with the rest. That they captured any dark wizards at all was a tribute to the bravery of their allies, and Thierry intended to make sure the public knew it. He paid little attention to the political aspect of the Milice, but he knew Marcel's plans, and a little detail like this could do wonders for the vampires' reputation.

Sebastien's hand on his shoulder drew Thierry's attention back to his immediate surroundings. "There's another group up ahead," he warned. "They seem to be trying to make it to the exit."

"Why don't they just use a displacement spell?" Thierry wondered aloud. "If they're going to run rather than fight anyway, why not just disappear?"

"I don't know," Sebastien answered, "but they looked pretty desperate, like they'd used up most of their options and didn't like the ones they had left."

Thierry frowned. That did not bode well for any wizard trying to capture them. Nothing fought like a scared, cornered animal, but they had no choice. Marcel had been clear. *This ends now,* the general had said, and that meant securing everyone in the building as rapidly as possible so the insurrection would not continue.

"Can we get someone behind them?" he asked. "If we block their way out and they realize they're surrounded, maybe they'll surrender."

"I don't know if we can or not," Sebastien replied. "The halls in this place are crazy. I have absolutely no sense of orientation at this point. I can try to take a few people around if you want, but I think we risk more in getting separated than we do in going at them just on one front."

"Yeah, you're probably right," Thierry agreed after a moment. Glancing behind him to make sure everyone was ready, he shouted, "Milice! Throw down your wands and nobody will get hurt."

A predictable volley of spells met his words. His patrol hunkered down, letting the magic fly over their heads, waiting for the right moment to retaliate. "Binding spells first," Thierry ordered softly. "Let's try to take them alive. I have some questions for them."

His patrol nodded their understanding, bursting around the corner as one, binding spells flying from their wands. The vampires ran ahead, Sebastien in the lead, tackling and disarming as many wizards as they could.

When the dust settled a few minutes later, they had brought down the entire group, either physically or magically. Thierry frowned, though, to see some of his own patrol also down.

They were all still breathing, a positive sign, but it was obvious they would not be able to continue the fight. "Can you get everyone back to the infirmary, David?" he asked.

"I think so," David replied.

"You're signing your own death warrant if you do," one of the dark wizards sneered. "This place is warded so tightly you'll smash yourself to bits trying to leave magically."

That answered Thierry's earlier question, but it did not help him now—and his people definitely needed medical attention. "Putain," he cursed softly. "All right, Hugues, pick two vampires and you all get David, Stéphanie, and Jérôme out of here and back to base. Rejoin us if you can, but getting them treatment is more important. The rest of us will finish up here. Go back the way we came. The route should be secure."

"I'll go with you," Sebastien offered quickly, "and of course, Angélique will want to go with her partner." He did not want to leave Thierry, but the unpaired vampires would be susceptible to sunlight now, which meant only paired vampires would be able to help. "I'll be back before you know it," he promised Thierry who looked ready to protest. "Watch your back."

Thierry glowered, but he could not exactly order his partner to stay. "Hurry," he said simply, turning his attention back to dealing with the captured wizards. One of them needed medical treatment as well, but Thierry was not willing to risk his patrol by decreasing their numbers even more. The dark wizard would just have to wait until the building was secured and the wards brought down.

With the help of the rest of his patrol, they got the newly captured wizards into a room, sealing the door behind them so their prisoners would still be there when they got back. "There are two more rooms on this floor, then we move upstairs," Thierry told his patrol, stifling a groan. He could feel his magical reserves depleting with each spell he cast, and he doubted the others were in much better shape. They had to keep going, though. This was a chance they could not squander.

Chapter 19

LANDING AWKWARDLY in the narthex of Notre-Dame, just inside the main doors, Alain went to his knees rather than fumble his precious burden. Rising to his feet again, he rushed toward the chapel where he had rested earlier, Orlando's lax features and shallow breathing making him desperate for a place to set his lover so he could tend to him. Reaching the chapel, he laid Orlando gently on the carpet, pulling his sleeve back and tearing at the barely-scabbed wound where the old vampire had scratched him earlier to find Orlando.

Guilt wracked him as he watched the blood well sluggishly to the surface. He prayed he had not broken their bond by allowing another vampire to taste his blood, even if that had not involved an actual bite. He would have to explain it to Orlando when he awoke and hope his lover understood it was the only way. Even with Eric's assistance in helping Orlando escape, the sunlight would have destroyed him before he could reach safety since Eric had not followed him outside to transport him magically somewhere out of the sun's reach.

Finally getting the blood flowing enough for it to drip into Orlando's mouth, Alain turned his wrist over, pressing it to Orlando's slack lips. He massaged the skin on either side of the vampire's mouth, trying to get the blood to flow more quickly until Orlando had taken enough to wake and begin to feed on his own.

Seconds passed, then a minute, with no response from Orlando, no sucking on his wrist, no fangs elongating, no reflexive swallowing. Frowning, Alain dropped his other hand to the vampire's chest, searching for the familiar heartbeat, the reassuring rise and fall, but the body beneath his hands was completely motionless.

"No!" he howled, his voice echoing off the high arches. He pulled Orlando's body into his arms, cradling the beloved form against him, rocking back and forth on his heels as he sobbed with grief. After all they had gone through, after all they had risked, he had arrived seconds too late. Tears streamed down his face, wetting Orlando's slack cheeks, dampening his eyelashes with droplets the dark eyes could no longer produce, even before Alain failed him. "You can't do this to us," he raged. "You can't do this to me!" His shouts rent the relative silence of the cathedral and brought a passing priest running to his side.

"What's wrong?" the priest asked. "Do you need help?"

Alain's face fell as he continued to rock Orlando's unmoving form. "No," he said brokenly. "Just leave us alone."

"I can call the paramedics," the minister offered.

"It won't do any good," Alain replied. "He's a vampire. They can't help him. I could have, but I was too late."

The priest took an instinctive step back upon hearing the word vampire—the man on the carpet was obviously harmless now, regardless of how dangerous he might have been once upon a time, and the one holding him needed human comfort, something the priest could provide. "Then his soul is in God's hands now," he said softly, coming to kneel next to Alain. "We must pray for him to find peace."

"He always said he was damned," Alain sobbed, "but he was an angel for me, bringing light to my darkness." He raised tear-filled eyes to look at the priest. "Surely that will count for something, won't it? He was a good man. Being a vampire didn't change that. He fought for what he believed in. He never hurt anyone, even when he had a reason." His voice broke as he buried his face against Orlando's neck, the tears falling freely as he mourned his lover's passing.

"It all counts," the priest promised. "God sees all things, considers all things, and forgives all things. If he was the man you say he was, I'm sure he's already numbered among the heavenly host." It occurred to the man of the cloth that the two men before him were either brothers or lovers for the blond to be exhibiting such grief, and given the complete lack of resemblance, he rather thought it was the latter. Many of his colleagues would have something to say about that, but it was not the priest's place to judge. The mourning man was clearly devoted to the deceased one, and that was far more important than any question of gender as far as he was concerned. The blond had lost a loved one and needed the assurance that he was with God, a comfort the priest was more than willing to give. "What happened to him?"

"Serrier's bastard wizards tortured him until he was too weak to survive anymore," Alain spat, unmindful of his language in his grief. "I thought all he needed was to feed, but he won't swallow." His voice caught again as he faced Orlando's loss. "He can't be gone. He just can't be."

"He lives on in your heart and mind," the priest reminded him. "I know it's hard to hear that now, but his soul survives, and as long as you remember him and love him, he's a part of you. And when your time comes, you'll be reunited in God's grace."

Alain tried to take comfort in the words, but the thought of having to live out his life without Orlando at his side after only a few weeks of being together was too much to bear. "I have to go. I have to help end Serrier's butchery once and for all," he declared. He would fight the dark wizards for all he was worth, and if he was killed in the process, he would be reunited with Orlando that much more quickly. "Will... will you stay with him until someone comes for him?"

The priest frowned. "I'll stay with him until you come back, my son. You must come back and see to him properly. He deserves a better tribute than your death."

"I'm a wizard," Alain replied dully. "My place is with the Milice. He wouldn't want me to neglect my duty. I can just hear him telling me there's nothing I can do for him now, but I can keep Serrier and his minions from hurting anyone else. Will you stay with him?"

"If you insist on leaving him, then yes, I'll stay with him until someone returns, but I'm no wizard. I won't be able to protect him," the priest warned.

"The cathedral herself will protect him," Alain assured the other man. "The elemental magic is stronger here than anywhere else on the continent. The dark wizards can't get inside now that the locus knows about them."

The priest's eyebrows jumped in surprise, but he accepted the assertion without challenge. He had prayed since he was a child to be posted here, at Notre-Dame, feeling it somehow the strongest seat of faith despite the commercialism brought about by the huge influx of tourists each day. He had read and seen enough in his life to know that there were more things in heaven and earth than were dreamt of in the philosophy of his faith. That line of thought would have some vilifying him as they did any who questioned the Church, but his horizons were broader than that, his understanding deeper, and this assertion that Notre-Dame was a seat of inherent power seemed only fitting. "Then I will stay with him and pray for him while you do what you feel you must. But you must promise to come back for him yourself, for I will release him to no one else."

"And how would you stop another wizard or a vampire from taking him? You said yourself you would not be able to protect him," Alain challenged.

"And you said the cathedral would protect him," the priest replied. "It only knows you, so how would it know to let anyone else near him?"

"Any wizard could communicate with the elemental magic, could explain their intentions," Alain began.

The priest shook his head. "Do what you need to do, but *you* must come back for him."

Deciding that arguing would lead nowhere, Alain nodded. "It may be some time, though, if the battle goes ill."

"I have time," the priest promised. "Go now and come back safely."

Looking down at Orlando one last time, Alain gave in to the urge to kiss his lips, knowing it would be the last time. They were still soft, supple, as if Orlando were only sleeping, but no breath whispered between his lips, no animation, nothing but that deathly stillness. "I love you, mon ange," he whispered. "I'm sorry I was too late."

He waited, as if expecting the dark eyes to open, to meet his own tear-shimmered gaze, but they stayed closed, the dark lashes highlighting the livid circles beneath his eyes. Biting back another sob, Alain pushed to his feet, wand clenched in his hand as he returned to the place he had just left.

"Alain!"

Turning, the wizard saw Sebastien outside Serrier's base with David, Angélique, Mathieu, Jérôme and Stéphanie. "Where's Thierry?" he asked immediately.

"Inside, still fighting. I volunteered to help get the wounded back to Milice headquarters," Sebastien explained. "Where's Orlando?"

"Gone," Alain rasped. "We were too late. I tried to get him to feed, but he didn't swallow, didn't wake up."

"Where is he now?" Sebastien asked urgently.

"At Notre-Dame."

"Protected from the sun?"

Alain nodded.

"Then find Jean. There might be a way to help Orlando if any of his line are still in existence. You just have to make sure his body survives until the right blood can reanimate him," Sebastien explained. "I don't know Orlando's history, but Jean will. He keeps records on all the vampires in Paris. It's part of his position."

"Sebastien, we need to go," Angélique interrupted urgently, growing more concerned as David sagged against her.

"Find Jean," Sebastien repeated, turning back to the others. "Let's go."

Lt. Fouquet cast the spell and the small group disappeared, leaving Alain even more shell-shocked than when he had arrived. Hope warred with doubt in his heart. Sebastien seemed to think there was a way to help Orlando, but Alain was afraid to hope again. Losing his beloved once was hard enough. To hope again and have that dashed would destroy him entirely. He wavered between making sure Orlando was safe from any light and finding Jean as quickly as possible. Indecision tore at him, leaving him uncharacteristically immobile. He knew that Orlando's maker had been destroyed when Jean rescued the younger vampire from hell, but he knew few details of his lover's past. He wanted to believe there might be a way, but with Thurloe gone, it seemed a long shot indeed. A shout of pain drew his attention, and he pushed all thoughts aside except for the fight at hand.

Running inside, his eyes searched frantically for any sign to indicate which way Jean might have gone, but while he could see dark wizards down—dead or bound—everywhere he looked, nothing pointed him in one direction over another. He would simply have to quarter the building logically until something gave him a direction to go. Starting down the hall to his right, he passed room after room, the doors warded with Milice magic, but never with the same wizard's signature. While some of the wizards were part of

Thierry's usual patrol, others were not, obscuring the path Alain had hoped to follow. He was sure that if he could find Raymond's magic, he would find Jean at his partner's side. Raymond's signature was conspicuously absent, though.

Coming to the end of that corridor, he looked right and left, trying to decide which way to go. He could sense more of Thierry's magic to the right. He could join his best friend, fight as they had always said they would do, and find Jean when the smoke cleared, or he could go in the opposite direction where he sensed no Milice magic and hope he ran into friendly faces before he encountered more foes than he could deal with alone. Self-preservation won out, and he turned to the right, coming across a group of wizards and vampires standing guard outside a warded door. "What's going on?" he asked.

"There are too many dark wizards inside for us to storm the room," Lt. Raynaud de Lage replied. She did not mention his partner, but the vampire's conspicuous absence at Alain's side spoke volumes, and her heart ached for him, unable to imagine what it would feel like to lose Justin. "Captain Dumont ordered us to guard the door and pick them off if they came out. He said we could deal with them last if we had to."

"Were Raymond and Jean with you?" Alain inquired, seeing the logic in Thierry's decision. He ignored the flicker of sympathy that crossed her face, not wanting to deal with the emotions he had forced down. Trying to explain what he thought had happened, what Sebastien had suggested, would stir it all up again and leave him unable to function.

She shook her head. "No, they were leading a different group, with Marcel and the old vampire—I didn't catch his name—leading a third."

"Lombard," Justin interjected. "That was monsieur Lombard."

"I've got to find Jean," Alain said doggedly, already itching to continue. "Do you know which way they went?"

Catherine shook her head. "Sorry, Alain. We left first and I didn't see which way the other two patrols went."

Alain nodded. "I'll just keep looking then."

"Don't go off alone," Catherine admonished. "Find Thierry and get at least someone to go with you. There are dark wizards everywhere, and usually not alone."

Alain shook his head, still too afraid to believe Sebastien could be right—or that they could find someone in Orlando's line—to care about much of anything except finding Jean and doing his best to end Serrier's reign of terror once and for all. He would not take unnecessary chances, just in case Orlando could be saved—if Orlando did come back to him, he wanted to be alive and healthy to enjoy it—but even if time was irrelevant to Orlando, it weighed heavily on Alain, driving him to hurry as he continued down the hall, searching until he found Thierry and his patrol.

"Alain, what are you doing here?" Thierry exclaimed. "Where's Orlando?"

"At Notre-Dame," Alain said shortly. "I have to find Jean."

"He's in another part of the building, but I have no idea where now. What do you need him for?" Thierry asked, sensing Alain's distress. He had no idea what had driven his friend to return to the fray rather than staying by Orlando's side, but whatever it was, it could not be good. "Is Orlando all right?"

Alain shook his head. "I thought he was gone, but Sebastien said there might be a way to bring him back. I have to find Jean to know for sure."

Thierry glanced toward the last two doors in the hallway he was currently securing. He did not even debate his course of action. Orlando needed help. Alain loved Orlando. Therefore, Thierry would do whatever it took to make sure Orlando got the help he needed, and that meant finding Jean. Now. "Seal the rooms," he ordered his patrol. "We'll come back and deal with the occupants after we've found Jean."

Immediately, members of Thierry's patrol cast the spells, sealing the two rooms so no one could escape while they were elsewhere. "Let's go," Thierry directed, pointing Alain back in the direction they came. "Jean and Raymond took the west wing of the building, so we'll head back to the entrance and work our way through until we find them."

The hope in Alain's heart that he feared so desperately to acknowledge grew a little bit stronger. With Thierry at his side, the two of them working together, they simply could not fail. Now it remained to be seen if Jean could provide the answers they needed to save Orlando again.

Chapter 20

"WE WILL go down," Marcel declared as the three patrols split up. He had studied Serrier's ways long enough to know the man's habits, and in every building they had searched, they had always found a bolt hole, a safe room in the basement of the structure warded even more heavily than the rest of the building. Often, they could not even penetrate it, though Marcel thought they had finally mastered that knack in the past few months. If such a room existed here, Serrier would be in it.

And Marcel intended to be the one to face him. In the heat of battle, the vampires would not be able to feed to strengthen their partners, and that left Marcel the most powerful wizard in the Milice, meaning the one most likely to defeat the rebel leader. The war had dragged on too long as it was. It would end this morning.

The narrow steps and corridors leading to the basement forced the wizards and vampires to walk no more than two abreast, often even having to go single file. They worked their way down methodically, disabling every trap they found as they passed it. Marcel let his subordinates do the work, knowing he would need all his strength and cunning when the time came to fight Serrier.

They encountered surprisingly little human resistance, but a mental catalogue of the spells they had countered as they made their way deeper into the bowels of the building suggested it was because Serrier had every confidence his traps would keep the unwary far away. A less organized, less disciplined attack would have cost them greatly. Marcel thanked all the gods and goddesses that Raymond had willingly shared his knowledge of Serrier's more twisted spells so that they knew how to counter them now.

Even as careful as they were being, though, a shout of pain slowed their progress. Marcel turned back to see who was hurt, his gaze landing on Georges Pantin, the wizard prostrate on the floor in pain. "Marie, get him out of here," Marcel ordered immediately. "When you've cleared the wards, send him and his partner to the infirmary. Then get back here as quickly as you can."

"What hit him?" Marie asked, knowing the medics would want the most detailed information they could get so they could begin treating Georges as expeditiously as possible.

Marcel cast a quick diagnostic spell. "Internal bleeding," he muttered.

Behind them, Fabienne blanched, thinking of her own partner's injury. Mathieu had insisted she join the fight even though he had been unable to accompany her. "André, bite him now rather than waiting. It will help slow the spread of the dark magic, even if it doesn't undo all the damage. The medics are sure we'd have lost Mathieu if I hadn't done the same when he was hurt."

"Here?" André repeated, eyes widening. He had heard rumors of certain taboos loosening because of the alliance, but he had not imagined this possibility.

"You're a vampire," monsieur Lombard interrupted. "Your partner needs you. What are you waiting for?"

Marcel looked surprised at the old vampire's insistence since he had not been part of the alliance or of the resulting partnerships until a few hours ago, but that did not seem to matter now. However Lombard had come by his information, he carried sufficient clout to sway André. The vampire lowered his head to his partner's neck immediately, drawing blood and dark magic into his mouth.

"Can you carry him and feed at the same time?" Marie asked. "We can't cast a displacement spell inside Serrier's wards."

André glanced up at her, his lips still working on his partner's throat. Carefully, he juggled Georges in his arms until he could stand. Marie steadied him with a hand to his elbow, but André brushed it off, gesturing for her to lead the way out. Geneviève, Marie's partner, flanked him from the other side, not willing to let Marie out of her sight for even a short time.

Marcel watched them until they disappeared around the corner of the hallway. "Let's go," he ordered. "They'll catch back up with us if they can."

Rounding the next corner, they encountered a magical shield completely blocking their path. Caroline stepped forward to counter it, but the moment the ward felt her magic, it exploded. She raised her hands to cover her face, too late. Triggered, the trap sent shards of glass flying, cutting her hands, embedding in her face, her eyes. "Caroline!" Mireille screamed, catching her partner as she fell.

Marcel cursed under his breath. "Go!" he ordered. "Catch up with Marie. Tell her to stay outside so she can provide emergency transport for anyone we need to get back to base."

Nodding, Mireille scooped her partner into her arms, taking off at a run in the direction they had come.

Casting a protective shield of his own, Marcel ordered everyone else back as he began untangling the complex spell. He detected Serrier's handiwork in the cruel knots of magic, each one set to deploy another nasty attack. For a moment he wished Raymond were there with him so he could call on the other man's expertise, but he understood Jean's need to find the rogue, and he knew better than to separate partners at a time like this except under the most dire of circumstances. Closing his eyes in concentration, he let his magic wrap around the dark wizard's trap, feeling its knots and crannies, until he could find the point where it began. He began unraveling it slowly, letting his magical senses guide him rather than trusting to his vision, which could be fooled by clever illusions.

Behind him, the assembled wizards held their breath, waiting to see if Marcel's magic was strong enough, deft enough to deal with the trap. Layer by vicious layer, Marcel tore down the wall impeding their progress. A strangulation spell escaped his grasp, but his shield stopped it before it could hurt anyone, much to Marcel's relief. The near miss brought a frown to his face as he slowed his attempts even more, determined not to let anything else escape to hurt the wizards behind him.

Not entirely sure he wanted to bring himself to the attention of the oldest vampire he had ever heard of, much less met, Jude swallowed down his nerves a couple of times before approaching monsieur Lombard. "The general is your partner, right?" he asked hesitantly.

Monsieur Lombard nodded.

"If you feed from him now, while he's using his magic, you'll make him even stronger than he already is," Jude explained. "I don't know how long the effects last, but even if all it does is keep him from exhausting himself now, we'll all be safer for it."

Monsieur Lombard raised a questioning brow.

"He's telling the truth," Fabienne chimed in. "Like everything else, we don't know why it works—but it very clearly does."

Jude hid a scowl at the thought of all the benefits of his partnership denied to him because his partner could not admit she enjoyed their bouts of rough sex. Her blood told a different tale, reducing her to a hypocrite and a cocktease in his eyes. In this forum, he doubted those sentiments would be well received. It infuriated him that she would accept the restraining spell Chavinier had cast on them, accept being separated from him at a time when being together had strengthened every other partnership. Her acceptance of her assignment to Jean's patrol was one more betrayal, one more proof that she was good for nothing but fucking.

"Général?"

Holding his magic stable for a moment, Marcel turned to look at the vampire.

"I think I might be of some assistance," monsieur Lombard stated softly.

Nodding, Marcel tilted his head to one side, wanting to keep both hands free in case of another attack. He jumped slightly at the feeling of fangs sliding beneath his leathery skin, then gasped as the power of their partnership fell into place, glutting him with magic. The remaining layers of Serrier's spell appeared as child's play to him now, even the complexity of the ward no match for Marcel's newfound strength. The ensorcellment crumbled beneath his assault, leaving the way clear for them to continue.

Regretfully, monsieur Lombard raised his head. "Lead on, Général," he said with a sweep of his hand. "I'll be but a step behind you."

For the first time since the war began, Marcel felt completely confident of his ability to overcome Serrier. With his partner at his back, nothing could defeat them.

He took another two steps forward before he encountered another ward much like the one he had just dismantled. Beyond it, with his magic still augmented by his partner's feeding, he could sense the bolt hole they were seeking. He turned back to face the patrol.

"Serrier's safe room is just down the hall," he informed them, "but the confines are too narrow for us all to face him with any effectiveness. You'll all be at risk of spells going astray if you remain. Monsieur Lombard will stay with me, of course, and I'd like Magali and her partner to stay as well, in case we need backup, I want the rest of you to find Raymond or Thierry and add to their numbers. This has always been a fight between Serrier and me. I don't want anyone else caught in the crossfire."

"Of course we'll stay," Magali replied immediately.

"Don't just expect the rest of us to go, though," Charlotte protested. "What if you fall? Would you make Magali face him alone?"

"He won't fall," monsieur Lombard insisted. "You have no idea how powerful he is, how powerful he already was even before I bit him. And he's even stronger now."

"And if the rogue is there with Serrier, maybe even feeding from him to strengthen him as well?" Charlotte pressed.

"Do you really think he'd let any vampire close enough to him to actually bite him?" Magali scoffed.

"And even if he did," Luc added, "a vampire's power is a direct function of his age. No vampire could stand against monsieur Lombard for long, so I doubt Couthon would be as much help to Serrier as monsieur Lombard will be to the general."

"Serrier wouldn't share his safe spot with anyone else," Marcel assured the others. "Raymond and Thierry aren't nearly as likely to encounter lone wizards, and I don't want to lose anyone if we can help it. You've trusted me this far. Trust me just a little bit longer. I know my own strength, and I know what my partner has added to it."

Beneath his implacable stare, the others slowly scattered, making their way back up the stairs and into the upper floors in search of the other patrols. Charlotte was the last one to go, but eventually even she relented, leaving Marcel, Magali, Luc and monsieur Lombard facing the ward and the bolt hole. "If I might impose on you again?" Marcel asked his partner, gesturing Luc and Magali to move back around the corner so they would be safe from any backlash should he fail to contain part of the spell.

"Of course," monsieur Lombard replied, returning to his place directly behind Marcel, his fangs finding the marks they had left moments ago.

Everything else faded into the background as Marcel felt the ground swell of power within him. The very stones around him came to his aid as he strove against the second barrier, Serrier's magic slowly giving way beneath Marcel's unswerving assault.

He grimaced as each new layer revealed its vicious secrets, making Marcel glad he had sent everyone else away. Any one of the spells could have incapacitated his patrol in a heartbeat, and many of them were far worse than that. As his disgust grew, so did his determination to finish with Serrier once and for all.

Finally, this barrier crumbled as the first had, leaving only Serrier's safe room between them and victory. As soon as the second barrier fell, monsieur Lombard released Marcel's neck, taking a respectful step back. "What now?" he asked.

"Now we beard the lion in its den."

They had taken only one step forward when the first spell flew through the closed door at them. Marcel countered it with a wave of his hand. "You'll have to do better than that if you intend to take us down," he goaded.

"You think two old men are enough to defeat me?" Serrier jeered, though his voice seemed to come from everywhere and nowhere at once.

"No," Marcel replied. "I think one old man will be more than sufficient." He cast a spell of his own, the magic sparking harmlessly off Serrier's wards. The dark wizard laughed derisively again, but Marcel smiled. His spell had done exactly what he wanted it to do, revealing the texture of the protective wards. Gesturing for Lombard to step back for a moment, Marcel began a murmured chant, drawing layer after layer after layer of power into himself. With a flick of his wrist, he sent it out through the building itself, dissolving the walls of the room where Serrier had hidden, trusting to the stones to keep him safe.

"Abbatez!" Serrier shouted immediately, his panic causing his spell to go astray, striking the ceiling above Marcel's head. Small shards of plaster showered down, dusting Marcel's shoulders as white as his hair, but otherwise doing no harm.

"You'll have to aim better than that if you want to have any hope of defeating me," Marcel declared calmly, the power that still pulsed within him seeking an outlet. Without even voicing a spell, he let the pure magic flow out of him, seeking to bind Serrier for trial.

The dark wizard jumped aside at the last second, sensing the unusual flow of magic. "Now who needs better aim?" Serrier taunted, rolling to his feet.

Behind Marcel, monsieur Lombard frowned. He had tasted his partner's power and could not imagine Serrier standing against it for long, but strength aside, all it would take was one badly blocked spell and even Marcel could fall, particularly since Lombard could see the physical toll the fight was taking on the general. He might be far more spry than the average man his age, but he was not thirty any more, probably not even sixty anymore, and that was enough to goad Lombard into action. The first *Abbatoire* had missed, but that did not mean the next one would be so poorly aimed. Edging carefully to the side, he kept a close eye on Serrier, making sure the dark wizard's attention remained fixed on Marcel.

As he had expected, the dark wizard dismissed him as a threat, seeing only the apparent age of a body turned late in mortal life without giving any thought to the resilience or agility that all vampires possessed, regardless of their seeming physical age. Lombard's own long existence and experience only enhanced those traits, making him even more formidable. As the spells flashed back and forth across the room, he worked his way around behind the dark wizard. He could tell from the spells Marcel was casting that he wanted to take the dark wizard alive, but Lombard was too aware of time passing to let the battle continue indefinitely.

He remembered with disturbing clarity how the wizards had dismissed the vampires as unimportant the last time they had interfered in a mortal war. Then, Clovis had sent them into battle at the side of his soldiers, expending their existences as casually as he did the lives of his men. They had fought as hard as they could, against magic and against steel, but with only mortal men to protect them, they had not fared well. Clovis had eventually won the war, securing his place as the first king of France, but the scars of his victory had not soon faded from the memories of the vampires who had survived the confrontation. Lombard had suffered even more than most, for not only had he lost friends that day, he had lost his Avoué, a soldier who had a sufficiently discerning eye to see past Lombard's aged exterior to the vital, vibrant man who dwelled within. The years they had together had been far too short, would have been too short even without Auberon's premature death, but his execution by the Alamanni wizards had been enough to haunt Lombard for many, many years. The wizard fighting for their future now was not his Avoué, was barely even his partner, but Lombard refused to lose the chance to see where that connection might lead.

Waiting until he was sure Serrier's attention was fixated on Marcel, Lombard sprang forward with the trademark speed and agility of the vampires, hands closing around Serrier's wrist as he grappled with the wizard, hoping to disarm him. The wand fell quickly from the dark wizard's grasp, but the spells did not stop, directed this time at Lombard himself rather than at Marcel. The elder vampire felt the wash of dark magic, felt a ghost of the pain it should have engendered in him, but the combination of his inherent power and the magic flowing through him from Marcel were enough to neutralize Serrier's spell before it could do any harm.

Marcel's pulse pounded as he watched the two men locked in a struggle. Serrier's first spell seemed not to have had the desired result, but that was no guarantee others would not. "You can't defeat us both, Serrier. Surrender now while you still can."

"Va te faire foutre!" Serrier cursed. He spat another spell in Marcel's direction. This one connected, despite Marcel's counterspell, blood gushing from his nose and ears as the incantation damaged the capillaries there.

"You shouldn't have underestimated us," Lombard growled, seeing the rampant madness in the dark wizard's gaze. "You lost every chance of winning this war the moment the Milice solicited our aid."

"And what do you think you can do against my magic, old man?" Serrier sneered. "Vampires might have different weaknesses than mortals, but you have them all the same. Your sniveling little brat proved that to us before we destroyed him. All I have to do is get you outside and you're dead."

"I died a long time ago," Lombard contradicted, determined to keep Serrier talking and focused on him rather on Marcel, "and as long as we fight at the side of the Milice, we have nothing to fear even from daylight." As Lombard spoke, Magali jumped forward, clearly working a healing spell as Marcel's bleeding slowed and then stopped. "But I'm far more human, even now, than you will ever be."

Realization fought with madness, and a trace of pity flickered across Lombard's face as he understood that whatever demons had Serrier in their grasp, he would never be anything other than what he was. Hands moving almost too quickly for human sight, he caught Serrier's chin in one hand, the dark beard scraping his palm, and his neck in the other, twisting sharply and breaking his neck.

"I wanted to take him alive," Marcel protested, brushing aside Magali's smothering concern as the rebel leader's body slumped lifelessly in monsieur Lombard's grip. "We needed to put him on trial to show the world the war was over."

"You don't put a rabid dog on trial, Général. You put him down," Lombard disagreed.

Chapter 21

LOOKING AT the people ready to follow him and Jean, Raymond came to the uncomfortable conclusion that they would have to simply seal rooms as they passed and hope they did not encounter a large contingent of dark wizards. He and Adèle alone could only face so many at a time, even with all the unpaired vampires who had insisted on staying close to Jean. "We only fight if attacked," he told the patrol. "Our goal is the *extorris*. Adèle and I will seal doors behind us so anyone inside stays inside until we're ready to deal with them. Other than that, we're after the rogue."

"Is this a good idea?" Adèle asked Raymond softly.

Raymond shrugged. "It doesn't matter. You saw Orlando. Jean won't be able to deal with anything else until the rogue is in Cour custody."

"But just the two of us?"

Raymond's lips quirked. "It'll be a definite test of our abilities. I'm not worried about dark wizards, honestly, because they'll see our numbers, not that you and I are the only two wizards here. I'm more concerned about the traps Serrier has surely laid. Jean's not exactly thinking straight at the moment."

"Will he let us go first to deal with the traps?" Adèle asked.

"Probably not, since there are so many nonalliance vampires here, but he might agree to letting us flank him," Raymond replied.

"He won't do much good against the rogue if he gets caught in one of Serrier's traps," Adèle pointed out rationally.

"It's that whole saving face thing," Raymond explained. "He's the chef de la Cour so he shouldn't need anyone else's help."

"That's bullshit."

"That's what I told him," Raymond laughed. "He was less than impressed."

"Are you two done?" Jean asked caustically. "We've got a rogue to catch."

Raymond just grinned at his partner unrepentantly. "Don't run ahead," he ordered. "It won't do any of us any good if you set off Serrier's traps before Adèle and I can neutralize them. You can't fight the rogue if you're injured, and I won't be able to help you unless you'd like to feed in front of half the Cour."

Jean scowled but limited his speed to one the wizards could maintain, trusting Raymond to either secure the corridor as they passed or stop him if they needed more time.

Raymond blanched as he identified some of the spells affixed to the walls and doors. He wanted to take his time and counter each one, but he knew Jean would never brook that kind of delay, not after seeing the state Orlando was in when they found him. He settled instead for covering them with a protective layer of magic so that even if someone brushed against them accidentally, it would not set them off. Many of them were illusory, but not all, and it took very little logic to figure out the pattern. Struck by a spell that befuddled the senses, a wizard would be more likely to bump into another hex, then another until they finally hit one that would do them serious injury. That the majority of the patrol following him were vampires offered no consolation, because Raymond doubted their undead nature would offer them any protection from this battery of enchantments. He hated leaving the job half done this way—it went against his very nature—but he understood Jean's urgency and knew no other compromise would convince his partner to wait any longer.

Jean's anger grew as they wended their way through the building, chafing at the restrictions of having to wait for his partner and Adèle to secure each stretch of corridor before they entered. Images of Orlando collapsing at Alain's feet haunted him, fueling his desire for revenge. He wanted Edouard, but he would settle for finding Serrier instead, or even the bastard Blanchet whom Raymond had credited with most of the torture Karine had experienced prior to her death at the rogue's hands. He had grown sufficiently attuned to Raymond's magic to sense the amount of strength his partner was expending in the effort to move forward at this speed, but Jean's instincts had never been influenced by such practical matters. They drove him to find the *extorris,* and nothing else mattered.

Movement in the hallway ahead of him caught Jean's attention. "There," he hissed to Raymond. "Can you block the corridor so he can't get away?"

Raymond frowned. "I can try, but without knowing what kind of spells Serrier used on that hallway, I could set off a chain reaction to kill us all."

Jean scowled. "Then we need to move faster."

Raymond nodded. "Tell everyone not to touch the walls under any circumstances. If we only have to worry about the floors and any spells that block the way, we can move faster."

Jean gave the order, making clear the possible consequences of not following those orders. The vampires clumped closer together to decrease the likelihood that they would accidentally brush the walls and trigger a spell.

"If he's in that hallway, don't you think it's safe to move faster?" Adèle asked Raymond softly.

Raymond hesitated. "Probably," he admitted after a moment, "but if I'm wrong, if Serrier's given the rogue some way to avoid his spells, we could be walking into a trap."

"Traps be damned," Jean spat. "Keep up or catch up, but I'm going after him now." Before Raymond could try to stop him or ask Adèle to do the same, Jean had rounded the corridor where they had seen movement.

"Couthon!" Jean bellowed. "Give yourself up to the Cour or face the wrath of both the Cour and the Milice."

"Why should I?" a taunting voice replied, though Jean could not see its source. "What has the Cour or the Milice ever done for me? When Serrier wins this war—"

"Serrier will never win this war," Jean insisted, moving stealthily toward the sound of the voice. "He is outnumbered, outclassed, and outmaneuvered. And you are *extorris*." He lunged around the corner, expecting to find his target, but Edouard was nowhere to be seen.

"And you are the last, feeble remnant of a dying society," Edouard spat from farther down the hall.

The ridiculousness of that assertion surprised a laugh from Jean's throat. "Then explain why the Cour has followed me rather than turning to Serrier," he challenged, stalking toward where he had last heard the rogue's voice.

Behind Jean, Raymond warded the worst of the traps he passed, his need to be at Jean's side overriding his ingrained caution. Fortunately, Adèle seemed to understand without him having to say anything, trailing behind a little to deal with the spells he had bypassed.

"Jean, wait!" Raymond shouted as the chef de la Cour started to take a step forward into one of Serrier's more devious snares. Whether Jean did not hear him or whether his warning came too late, Raymond could not have said, but his partner triggered the spell, falling to the ground, hands covering his ears as he writhed beneath a deafening screaming that seemed to puncture his eardrums with each pulsing sound. He tried to scramble away, hoping to distance himself from the noise, but the magic had latched onto him, the sound coming from inside his head so that no amount of distance lessened it.

"Adèle!" Raymond screamed, running to Jean's side to hold him in place so he would not set off any more magical mines. "I need help!"

"What is it?" the wizard asked as she skidded around the corner.

"An *Assourdi*," Raymond replied, trying to get his wrist to Jean's mouth so his partner could feed. "He can't even hear me to understand that I want him to feed to undo the damage."

Adèle frowned. "Let me see if I can break the spell. At least with the noise gone, he might be alert enough to follow your gestures."

Raymond nodded his permission and Adèle cast the spell.

"Sniveling excuse for a leader," Edouard sneered, stepping out into view.

Without even looking up from his struggles with Jean, Raymond cast a binding spell, but the rogue sprang out of the way with that damnable speed and grace the vampires possessed. As much as he hated to admit it, Raymond was afraid Jean would have to be the one to deal with the rogue. Even double-teaming, he doubted he and Adèle were fast enough.

His attention returned to the vampire in his arms as his partner's writhing eased. Stroking Jean's forehead to get his attention and encourage him to open his eyes, Raymond waited until he was sure Jean was with them and then lifted his wrist to his partner's lips again.

Jean nodded and bit into the smooth skin, healing blood rushing into his mouth, easing the pain in his head and restoring his hearing. "What was that?" he asked when he released his lover's hand.

"An *Assourdi*," Raymond replied. "It deafens you, and if it isn't broken quickly it can cause enough brain damage to kill you. Well, maybe not you, but it could certainly kill a wizard caught by it for too long."

Jean shuddered at the memory of the searing pain in his ears and head. "I think, if nothing else, it would quickly drive many of us to seek the sunlight rather than suffer it for long."

"Can you go on?" Raymond asked solicitously. "We can send the others after the rogue and have them bring him back to you."

Jean shook his head. "No, I have to do this. I'm chef de la Cour and this is my responsibility." Carefully, monitoring his physical state with every small movement, he rose to his feet. "I think I'm all right, but maybe I'll stay a little closer to you this time."

Raymond grinned despite the tension of the situation. "That might be wise. He went that way. If I remember correctly, this leads to a rather large basement room. And if I further remember correctly, there's only one other entrance, which we can get to that way. If Adèle takes half the patrol and blocks him in from this side, we can go the other way and catch him between us."

Jean nodded and split the vampires into two groups, sending one with Adèle while the rest followed him and Raymond along a different path. As Raymond had predicted, the hallway led to a door that opened into a large, gymnasium-like room. Wand in hand, Raymond opened it carefully, coming face to face with the rogue.

"Don't move," he ordered, summoning his magic with the wave of a hand, but the rogue ignored him, springing away with the grace of a martial arts fighter and the speed of the undead.

"Let me by," Jean growled.

"Are you strong enough to take him?" Raymond queried, concern deepening his voice.

"I'll have to be," Jean replied. "Don't let him leave, but beyond that, don't interfere."

Watching Jean walk alone into the cavernous room ranked high on the list of hardest things Raymond had ever done. Only working up the courage to approach Marcel after he defected had been harder. His partner moved with the same deadly grace the other vampire had shown, but none of the theatrics. Raymond thought that made him even more menacing, the contained power beneath his stillness vividly evident to the wizard's eyes.

"There's no way out, *extorris*," Jean informed the rogue as he reached the center of the room. "Between the members of the Cour and the members of the Milice guarding the doors, you have no choice but to face me. You can either do so of your own will, or I can bring you to justice."

"I haven't broken any Cour laws," Edouard drawled. "Despite your vaunted ways, you haven't managed to force the Cour into making it illegal to drain our prey dry."

"That isn't why you're *extorris*," Jean replied. "I didn't like it when you were killing people off the streets, but I didn't come after you until you picked the wrong victim."

"And what victim would that be?" Edouard challenged.

"The one you left on the doorstep of Sang Froid," Jean retorted. "The one you led the dark wizards to. The one you raped and sodomized and tortured before you left her where you knew I'd find her because you knew her death would hurt me."

"I have no idea what you're talking about," Edouard bluffed.

"Liar!" Jean shouted, his composure breaking as he leapt at the rogue. Edouard dodged, but he had gotten lazy in his dealings with mortals and underestimated Jean's speed. Their bodies crashed together, Edouard using Jean's momentum to spin him around and throw him off.

"Prove it," Edouard retorted. "You can't prove any of it was me."

"A vampire betrayed Karine to the dark wizards," Jean spat, lunging again, hands and feet flying as he attacked in earnest now, the rogue's dismissive words enough to ignite his temper.

Edouard met him blow for blow, blocking every strike with an ease of years of practice, spinning and leaping with a preternatural grace that left Adèle and Raymond with wide eyes and gaping jaws.

"And a vampire killed her," Jean continued, his breath coming in harsh pants as he fought the weakness from the *Assourdi* as well as the vampire in front of him. "And even if you could convince me someone else did that, Serrier had a vampire in his custody and you did nothing to help. And that, *extorris*, is a crime you cannot deny."

"You make it sound as if I tortured him myself," Edouard sneered. "I didn't touch the sniveling whelp. He made his own bed quite well on his own, binding himself to a weak mortal so he couldn't feed to recover from Serrier's spells. Too bad he didn't think to tell Serrier that before he poured someone else's blood down the idiot's throat. Not that I'm complaining, of course. Since he didn't finish her off, I got that pleasure."

Jean's stomach churned at the thought of the pain Orlando must have endured, not just from the torture itself, but from having poison forced down his throat in the form of some poor woman's blood. "You have no idea the strength he draws from that bond," the chef de la Cour countered. "The strength even to face the dawn and survive, but you—you forfeited that chance when you chose to side with Serrier. This morning's sunrise was the last you will ever see."

He lunged again, managing to get a grip on Edouard's arm. The rogue fought him, using every trick he had learned in all his years of survival in an attempt to escape, but he had underestimated Jean's strength, the power that came from his age, his position, and most importantly, from his partnership. Within moments, Jean had subdued him, pinning Edouard's arms behind his back and beginning to march him toward the exit Raymond stood guarding.

"You can't do anything to me now," Edouard goaded. "You're as much a prisoner of the daylight as I am."

Jean just laughed, though the harsh sound conveyed no amusement at all. "Little do you know, *extorris*. This ends now."

"Jean, don't," Raymond said softly. "Don't lower yourself to his level."

"You saw Karine," Jean replied just as softly. "You saw what he did to her, and you saw Orlando this morning. He's committed crimes beyond the pale."

"I'm not saying you're wrong," Raymond insisted, "just that you don't help your cause doing it this way. You told me vampires had ways of dealing with these things, but you're not following them. The discrimination law hasn't passed yet. If you do this and word gets out, you've just proven the naysayers right by showing that you can't even respect your own laws."

"What says the Cour?" Jean called, turning to the vampires who had filed into the room after he subdued Edouard. "What fate does he deserve?"

"That isn't the way a *judicium* works," monsieur Lombard interrupted from the hallway. The throng of vampires parted to let him pass.

Jean's eyes dropped like a scolded child.

"Your dedication to your friend does you credit, but you gain nothing by bypassing our laws," the old vampire continued. "You have him in your custody and you have the means, thanks to your partner, to keep him in custody until such time as the Cour can be convoked formally and a true *judicium* can take place. The result will be the same, but the impact on your bid for equality will be far greater this way."

"You can put him in one of the holding cells at Milice headquarters," Marcel offered, reaching Lombard's side. "They're all interior rooms so you don't have to worry about daylight. And I can set the wheels in motion to give you a formal venue in which to hold the *judicium* to add to its validity in the eyes of the rest of the country."

"Do this in a way that gives dignity to your friend's death and legitimacy to your authority," Raymond requested softly.

Unable to stand against them all, Jean nodded slowly. "I will need someone to be *accusator* in my place since I cannot be both judge and complainant."

"Surely someone will volunteer," Marcel commented as the rest of the patrols arrived. "There is no shortage of vampires here."

Jean frowned, for while Marcel was certainly correct, the chef de la Cour was not willing to trust that role to just anyone. He wanted there to be no doubt as to the outcome of the trial.

"Will you let me stand in your stead?" Sebastien asked deferentially.

Jean stared hard at the other vampire, all of his mixed emotions about Sebastien swirling through him; but as Thierry joined his partner, Jean accepted that the chain of attachments—Sebastien to Thierry, Thierry to Alain, Alain to Orlando—would make Sebastien the vampire most vested in seeing justice done, bar Jean himself. "I can think of no one I would trust more," he declared firmly, offering his hand in a peace offering intended to lay the past to rest once and for all.

Sebastien smiled and took the outstretched hand.

Chapter 22

"JEAN!"

A commotion in the crowd drew the attention of those gathered around the captive rogue.

"Where's Jean? I've got to find Jean!"

"Alain? What are you doing here?" Jean asked when the blond wizard pushed his way through the crowd. He had expected it to be hours, if not days, before he saw Alain again. "Where's Orlando?"

"At…" Alain's voice broke.

"He went too long without feeding," Sebastien interrupted.

"I tried," Alain added, holding up his wrist, savaged by his nails as he had fought to draw enough blood to tempt Orlando, "but he never woke up, never swallowed. It just trickled out of his mouth. He wasn't breathing anymore. I tried, Jean."

"So you're the one whose trap the weak-willed fool fell into," Edouard sneered. "You've condemned him, you know, letting him be captured that way. If he'd been smart enough to resist you, he'd have been able to feed the last few days and he wouldn't be gone now."

Edouard reeled back under a blow from Sebastien that would have knocked him off his feet if the chef de la Cour had not been standing directly behind him. "Shut your filthy mouth," Sebastien growled. "You don't have the slightest idea what you're talking about."

"Make me," Edouard goaded.

Sebastien stepped forward, intending to silence the rogue physically, when three different silencing spells hit the vampire from three different directions. Raymond quirked an eyebrow. "That should keep him quiet for the time being."

"Was Sebastien right?" Alain asked, bringing the conversation back to the only subject he truly cared about at the moment. "Can you help Orlando?"

"I don't know," Jean admitted, mind racing for every scrap of information he had ever read about reanimating a vampire who had gone too long without feeding. If he or any of the vampires present had made Orlando, it would not have been a problem at all, but Orlando's maker was destroyed a hundred years ago. "Sebastien was right that there's a way to help him, but I don't know who made Orlando's maker, and without that, there's nothing I can do."

"What about the genealogies?" monsieur Lombard asked. "You have been keeping them up, haven't you?"

"Of course I have!" Jean protested. "But Orlando knew nothing of his maker's history besides his name and I didn't take the time to ask after I saw the shape Orlando was in. We dispensed justice and that was the end of it. Maybe one of the other British vampires would know. Many of them came here about the time Thurloe did because his behavior made life in England difficult for all of them."

"Whatever you decide needs to be done," Marcel interrupted, "you can't do it here. Serrier's dead and you have the rogue in custody, but there are still dark wizards around, some of them loose. We need to secure the building, deal with the prisoners, and update the president."

"Not all the vampires can leave," monsieur Lombard reminded the Milice general.

"There are enough wizards to transport them magically wherever we want them to go," Marcel assured him. "And plenty of places at Milice headquarters where they'll be safe until Jean's gotten all the information he needs and we can send them home."

"I have to get back to Orlando," Alain insisted, feeling like a caged lion.

"Bring him back to Milice headquarters as well," Jean suggested. "If the vampire we need isn't here in Paris, it may take some time to track him or her down. He'll be safer there, or maybe at home, than he will be in the open church."

"How long does he have?" Alain asked, worry clear in his face and voice.

"As long as his body is protected from sunlight, there is no time limit," Jean assured him.

"Go on," Thierry said, seeing the expression on Alain's face. "Go to him. I'll join you as soon as we get the rest of the vampires settled so I can help you take Orlando wherever you want to go."

Alain nodded and started to cast the displacement spell. "Not from in here," Thierry warned quickly. "You can't get through the wards."

Alain aborted the spell and ran for the door, the need to be with Orlando again growing irresistible.

"I guess we need to take Serrier's external ward down before we displace anyone from within the building," Raymond commented, sending a seeking spell into the walls. "Yes, it's set to keep people in or out, and once that's done, the dark wizards who aren't already contained will be able to leave, too. I can do it whenever you're ready, but I just want you aware of the cost when I do."

"Between the three patrols, we quartered the building fairly well," Marcel started, but Raymond shook his head.

"We didn't do anything but neutralize Serrier's traps enough to go after the rogue," he explained. "We didn't encounter any human resistance, but we didn't check rooms as we passed. They could all be full for all I know."

"Then we need to do that first," Marcel declared, his eyes expressing his apology to Jean. "We've worked too hard to let an untold number of dark wizards escape. Even with Serrier dead, we need to finish this right or the war could still drag out for weeks or months."

Jean bit back his protest. As long as Orlando was protected from the sun, his body could recover once they found the right vampire to offer his blood, and Alain knew not to let any sunlight near him. However urgent his need to help his friend, they really could afford to do this right. "Divide up," he instructed the other vampires. "Half with Marcel and monsieur Lombard, half with Thierry, Sebastien, Raymond and me. The faster we get the building secure, the faster we'll be able to help Orlando and all go home."

The vampires moved quickly to join one patrol or another. The entire army spread back out to finish the job they had started.

Across the city, Alain reappeared on the parvis of Notre-Dame, not entirely sure he could displace directly into the cathedral. Even if he could, he had too much respect for the sacredness of the location to appear that way. Wand still in hand, though loose in his grip and pointed at the ground, he went back inside, hurrying to the small side chapel where he had left Orlando. The priest still knelt there, just as he had promised, his hands resting on Orlando's head in benediction as he prayed for Alain's safety and swift return.

"Thank you, mon père," Alain said softly, kneeling next to the priest and pulling Orlando into his arms. "I will sit with him now."

The priest studied him with a critical gaze. "You seem calmer than when you left. Were you successful?"

"Serrier is dead, the rebellion ended, and the ones responsible for Orlando's torture are in custody," Alain replied. "All that remains is for the vampires to find a way to help Orlando."

"So he isn't dead?"

Alain chuckled softly, brushing Orlando's hair back from his face. "He's dead, and even if they can help him, he'll still be dead, but they think they can wake him up, restore him to his usual state before Serrier captured him."

"That's good news," the priest agreed. "Will you be all right alone with him now, if I return to my duties?"

"Yes, mon père, we'll be fine. My friend is coming for us soon, and we'll return your chapel to you."

The priest shrugged. "You are welcome here in God's house for as long as you need to stay. It's not for me to deny anyone the hospitality of this place, for protection, for succor, for repose, for solace." He rose to his feet. "God bless you both, my son."

Alain smiled down at Orlando's face as the priest's footsteps faded. "He already has," the wizard murmured, "the day you came into my life. Now we just have to keep you there."

He pressed a tender kiss to Orlando's forehead, wanting to kiss his lover's lips, however slack, but not wanting to profane holy ground. "You're going to be all right," he vowed. "Jean's going to find a vampire in your line and bring him or her to us—or we'll take you there—and we're going to get you the blood you need. And after that, we'll never be separated again. The war's over. Well, all but over. Jean captured the rogue vampire and Marcel killed Serrier. All that's left is to mop up, and then we can move forward, together. We have all our lives before us. We just have to decide what to do with them. What do you want to do? Is there somewhere you want to go? We can. Anywhere we want. Where do you want to go? Just name it and we'll go."

The silence that met his questions, while not unexpected, still tore at Alain's heart. The place in his mind where he had been able to sense Orlando was empty now, as cold and lifeless as the body in his arms. He clung with all the hope he had thought lost when Edwige and Henri died to Jean's promise to search for a vampire to help Orlando. He knew the chances were slim that Thurloe's maker could be identified, much less found, but the alternative—losing Orlando—was unthinkable. There had to be a way. He could not contemplate any other future.

He glanced up at the progress of the dancing reflections of the stained glass windows across the opposite wall of the cathedral, wondering what was taking Thierry so long. It should have been the work of only a few minutes to send the unpaired vampires back to Milice headquarters. As he waited, his mind churned up one scenario after another to explain his friend's continuing absence. They would have to undo Serrier's wards before they could displace the vampires, but Raymond was there. Such a spell should not have taken him more than five minutes. Alain had seen him take down far more complex spells unaided in less time than that. Was it some problem with the vampires themselves? Something keeping the displacement spell from working on them? Or had they encountered resistance after Alain left? Were they fighting again, besieged by some unsecured force of dark wizards?

Growing restless, he pushed to his feet, pacing the small chapel as he waited for Thierry's arrival, his concern growing with each passing minute until it transmuted to worry and then to panic. He had almost reached the point of leaving Orlando again and returning to Serrier's base when he caught sight of Thierry at the back of the church. He stepped out into the nave so the other wizard could find him without having to yell.

"What took so long?" he demanded when Thierry reached his side.

"We couldn't just drop the wards," Thierry explained. "We'd have undone all our hard work if we let everyone escape. We had to secure all the groups of prisoners and make sure we hadn't missed anyone before Raymond could undo the spell. But that's done now. Everyone is either back at Milice headquarters or on their way there but you and Orlando. So where are we going? To Milice headquarters or back to your apartment?"

Alain had spent some of his time while pacing contemplating that choice as well. While he wanted the privacy of their apartment so he could care for Orlando undisturbed after Jean found the vampire to help him, he would be better able to keep tabs on the progress of the search for said vampire if he was at Milice headquarters. He could always get Thierry or someone to send them back to their apartment after Orlando was awake again. "Milice headquarters, at least for now."

Thierry nodded and waited for Alain to lift Orlando into his arms. When he saw Alain was ready, he cast the spell and returned all three of them to the office he and Alain shared. "Put him on the couch," Thierry suggested. "He'll be comfortable and safe there with the volets closed until we can find a way to help him."

Carefully, Alain set Orlando on the couch, stretching his limbs out to the most comfortable position possible. If he ignored the blood staining his lover's clothes and the unnatural stillness of his body, he could almost believe Orlando was simply sleeping. He pushed away the thought that it was a sleep from which he might never wake.

"I don't want to leave him," Alain admitted. "Even knowing there's not a thing I can do until Jean finds out the identity of the vampire we need, I feel like I belong here."

"So stay," Thierry said. "I can go check in with Jean for you, let you know what kind of progress he's making. Or I can ask him to come here instead of meeting with the vampires in Raymond's office. That way you could hear exactly what he does."

"I don't want them all tramping in here, staring at Orlando," Alain decided after a moment. "If he needs me, you can call for me to come down there. Otherwise I'll just let you bring me news periodically."

"I'll go see what's going on, then," Thierry offered. "Do you want Sebastien to keep you company? Of us all, he has the best chance of understanding what you're feeling."

"Thanks," Alain replied. "If he's not busy."

Thierry smiled. "He won't be. Not if you need him."

He had no idea if Alain actually heard him, though, because his friend had drifted back to Orlando's side, hand tracing up and down the motionless limbs as if he could somehow revive the vampire through the devotion in his touch. Shaking his head, Thierry left them alone and went in search of his lover and then of Jean. He found Sebastien outside Raymond's office, obviously almost as anxious for news as Alain was. "Anything?" he asked.

Sebastien shook his head. "Not yet, but he's only talked to a couple of vampires, most of whom are honestly too young to know the information we need. Thurloe lived in the mid-seventeenth century. There aren't a lot of vampires extant from that time, at least not in Paris."

"So who is?" Thierry asked.

Sebastien shook his head. "Honestly, I don't know. I've been away from the Cour for too long. I'm afraid Jean's going to have to contact his equivalent in London and hope they have records from that time, despite the disruption Thurloe caused which led to a fairly sizeable mass migration about a hundred years ago."

"Who can I at least go looking for to help Jean?" Thierry asked. "Jude, and who else? Unless Jean's talked to Jude already."

"No, Jude hasn't been through yet," Sebastien replied, "and what am I supposed to be doing while you're hunting up vampires to talk to Jean?"

"Keeping Alain sane," Thierry replied seriously. "He's in my office with Orlando, and he's holding it together for the moment, but I keep expecting him to lose it any second now. He wasn't even like this after Henri was killed, and I thought then that he couldn't grieve any harder without going mad."

Sebastien smiled sadly. "I never had children, so I can't imagine what it would be like to have one die, much less killed, but I know what Alain will suffer if we can't help Orlando. I'll go sit with him. I'm pretty sure Jude is older than Thurloe would have been. If he doesn't know the answer, he might have an idea who would."

Thierry nodded. "I'll see if I can find him."

"Your best bet will be just outside whatever room Adèle is in. He can't be in there with her, but he can't seem to resist the lure of her presence either."

"That is so fucked up," Thierry said with a shake of his head.

"That's Jude for you," Sebastien agreed, kissing Thierry quickly. "I'm going to sit with Alain. Bring news when you have some."

Thierry watched Sebastien go and then went in search of Jude. He found him a few minutes later, as Sebastien had predicted, hovering just outside the periphery of the Ordre de restriction. "You need to come talk to Jean," he said firmly.

"Why?" Jude demanded. "Thanks to him, I can't even feed from my partner in private anymore. I don't want anything else to do with him."

"That wasn't a suggestion," Thierry countered, grabbing Jude's arm. "You have a better chance of being able to help Orlando than anyone else."

"And why would I want to do that?" Jude snarled. "He's a child without enough sense to stay out of a situation where he couldn't get to his Avoué."

"Because if you don't," Thierry growled, "I'll change the Ordre de restriction so that you can't get to her at all. The war is all but over. We wouldn't miss you at this point. And I'd be willing to bet that if Jean finds out you refused to help, he'll put you on trial the same way he's planning on doing with the rogue who helped Serrier. He made it very clear that not helping was the same as actively hurting in his mind."

"You wouldn't!" Jude protested.

"Are you sure enough of that to test me?" Thierry challenged.

"Arsehole," Jude spat, but he followed Thierry back toward Raymond's office nonetheless.

"You called?" he mocked when he walked in to see Jean sitting with his partner at the desk in the crowded broom closet that passed for Raymond's office. Another day, he would have been amused at the incongruency of the chef de la Cour holding court in such mean surroundings.

"Sebastien suggested he was from the right time to know something useful," Thierry explained with a shrug. "I thought I'd get him here so you could question him."

"So what exactly am I supposed to know that can save your precious Orlando?" Jude drawled.

"The identity of his maker's maker," Jean explained.

"And his maker was?"

Jean glared at the insolent vampire. "Thurloe. He was Cromwell's spymaster."

Jude quirked an eyebrow. "Now there's a name I never thought to hear again."

"You knew him?" Jean asked, leaning forward with excitement.

"I had the unfortunate honor. He's the only vampire I ever regretted making."

Chapter 23

"WHY DIDN'T you say something sooner?" Jean shouted. "You knew we were searching for a vampire in Orlando's line!"

"I dropped Thurloe as soon as I realized what he was," Jude defended himself. "I didn't keep track of all the bastards he spawned. He turned them like it was nothing. Most of them didn't survive. For that matter, many completely unrelated vampires didn't survive because of his cruelty. Victoria ordered a purge of vampires on British soil because of him, and those who could not leave fast enough were captured and executed. I assumed all of his get had disappeared with him."

"He wasn't destroyed in England," Jean corrected. "He immigrated to France and hid here for another thirty years, probably, before I found out about Orlando and put a stop to Thurloe for good."

Jude shrugged. "I wasn't in Paris yet. I stayed in Rouen until after World War I. So where is the poor boy? I'm assuming you have him stashed somewhere safe."

Thierry clenched his fists to keep himself from punching Jude in his insolent mouth.

"Shut the fuck up, Jude," Jean growled. "You're not impressing anyone with your insults."

"Oh, but it's so much fun watching you all splutter and fume," Jude crowed. "Do you think you can stand it, Jean, being beholden to me for your friend's recovered well-being?"

"Watch it, Jude," Jean warned. "Refusing aid to a vampire in need would see you called before the Cour as well. With emotions as high as they are because of the *extorris*, I doubt you would fare very well."

"So you would threaten me into submission?" Jude challenged. "You risk much, chef de la Cour."

"It's a risk I choose to take. So what is your decision, Leighton? Will you help him or will you face the Cour?"

"I'll help," Jude relented, "but I want the Ordre de restriction lifted."

"That isn't something I can grant," Jean reminded him. "I'm no wizard."

"Maybe not, but your partner is. The boy's Avoué is. Get it revoked. The war's over. Morale doesn't matter anymore."

"The war's hardly over," Thierry scoffed. "We'll be hunting down the remnants of Serrier's forces for months."

"You don't need me for that."

"If we don't need you, then you don't need Adèle," Thierry countered. "And if you don't need her, then the Ordre de restriction is irrelevant. It doesn't keep you from feeding from someone else, only from abusing her."

"Abusing?" Jude snorted. "She loved every minute of it."

"That isn't the story she told."

"Lying bitch."

"This is ridiculous," Jean interrupted. "Help Orlando. I'll talk to Marcel and Adèle and see if they agree, but I won't let you hold Orlando's future hostage. If you help him, I'll do what I can as a way to say thank you, but I make no guarantees, and you'll help him first. Otherwise consider yourself convoked to the *judicium*."

"If you don't follow through, I'll see you ousted," Jude warned. "Where is he?"

"In my office," Thierry replied. "Alain and Sebastien are with him."

Jude rolled his eyes. "Well, let's go. It wouldn't do to keep him waiting."

They marched through the corridors to Alain's and Thierry's office, Thierry insisting on knocking before going inside. "You're bringing hope and help, but Alain's holding vigil. It's only polite to warn him before we go in."

"The boy's not fucking royalty," Jude snarled. "He's just a puerile, lovesick fool who bound himself to a wizard too weak to protect him."

That was more than Thierry could stand. He spun on his heel, reaching for Jude's lapels, his magic sparking around him in his fury, but Jean beat him to it, slamming Jude hard against the wall.

"One more word," Jean hissed. "One more word and I'll withdraw the protection of the Cour. You'll be on your own, whatever comes. Out of the alliance, out of the city."

"Do that, and your friend will lie there in limbo for eternity. I'm the oldest of my line."

"I can shut him up," Thierry offered, wand pointed at Jude's face. "It wouldn't hurt him. It would just stop his babble."

"We needn't tell Marcel I used a *Forçage* to ensure his cooperation," Raymond added. "Just say the word."

"Jude?" Jean inquired.

"Fuck you," Jude spat, pushing open the door. "Well, where is he?" he demanded to the room in general.

Alain scowled at seeing who had invaded his sanctuary, but since Jean, Raymond, and Thierry were with him, Alain imagined Jude must be the one who could help Orlando. "On the couch."

"You can stay," Jude said to Alain. "He might need you when he wakes up. The rest of you wait outside. I don't need an audience."

"And how do we know you'll keep your promise?" Thierry challenged.

"The boy will wake up. And then we'll see if the chef de la Cour is as good as his word."

Fed up with Jude's constant slurs, Raymond quietly cast a *Forçage*, the spell setting Jude's limbs twitching as it drove him to his knees. "That's where I'll keep you if you don't shut your mouth and help Orlando," he warned Jude. "I'm sure Adèle could think of all kinds of things to do to you while you're kneeling at her feet." Tightening the spell for a moment, he forced Jude's forehead to the floor in a mockery of a kowtow. Releasing the spell, he ignored Jude's sputtering. "Let's leave him to do his job."

When the other four had left, Jude crossed to where Orlando lay supine on the couch. "Are you sure you want me to do this?" he asked in mock concern.

"Of course!" Alain exclaimed. "I moved heaven and earth to get him back."

"Ah, but you're assuming you'll get him back," Jude warned. "I'm making him anew. He may not retain any of his memories. The Aveu de Sang may be completely broken. He may not be the Orlando he was before. Can you live with that? Are you willing to risk him not knowing you? Not loving you anymore?"

"Sebastien said it was just a question of waking him up," Alain insisted.

Jude shrugged. "He might be right. But what if he isn't?"

"At least he'll be awake," Alain said, a tinge of desperation coloring his voice. "I won his trust and his love once. I can do it again if I have to."

Jude smiled. "If you say so."

"What do you know?" Alain demanded. "Why are you trying to make me change my mind?"

"I'm not." Jude came to Alain's side, laying a consoling hand on his shoulder. "I just want you to be prepared for any eventuality. You're so sure it will work and I truly hope it does," he lied, "but I'd feel like I was doing you a disservice if I didn't warn you of what could go wrong."

Alain hesitated. Jean had not mentioned any risk. He had spoken of waking Orlando up like it was a sure thing, as long as they could find the right vampire. Jude would not be here, clearly at Jean's behest, if he were not the right vampire. Which meant either Jean had simplified the situation or Jude was playing him. He had no doubt Jude would stoop to that level, but he could also believe that Jean would gloss over the situation in his attempt to save Orlando, to save a vampire. Alain's gaze drifted to Orlando on the couch. His dark angel. Orlando had restored his broken heart, brought back his faith in the future, given him back his dreams of life after the war. He had a way to restore Orlando's existence. Even if it meant losing his lover, he could not simply leave the vampire this way.

"Do it."

"As you wish," Jude shrugged, having enjoyed his subtle revenge, the only one he could ever be allowed for Alain's part in his disgrace. Stepping to Orlando's side, he lifted his wrist to his mouth, his fangs tearing open the skin. When blood began to flow, he put it to Orlando's mouth, letting it drip into the brunet's throat.

After a moment, Orlando's hands moved suddenly, grabbing the source of renewed strength and holding it tightly to his lips. Jude pulled away roughly. "It's not my blood you need, boy. It's mortal blood." He turned to Alain and gestured him forward. "Hope the Aveu de Sang is still in place, or he will drain you dry without compunction." With that, he turned on his heel and left.

Alain fell to his knees at Orlando's side, head tilting back in offering. Blindly, voraciously, Orlando lunged at him, his fangs driving deep into Alain's neck as he rolled the wizard beneath him, sucking and sucking and sucking down the life-giving elixir.

The mindlessness of Orlando's actions frightened Alain. Orlando had never been this careless, this rough with him. Was Jude right? Had restoring Orlando fundamentally changed him? Concentrating on his love for the man above him, he lay back and let Orlando feed unhindered. If the Aveu de Sang held, Orlando could not hurt him and Alain's love would soothe him. If it did not, Alain would die in the arms of the man he loved instead.

Orlando clung to the body beneath him like a drowning man, the fierce hunger of his remaking burning within him as he feasted on the hot blood. As the beast within him calmed, appeased by satiation, feelings began to filter through Orlando's mind. Physical sensations first—the burning in his back, the aches in his joints from limbs stretched too far, the heat of the body beneath him, the tenderness of the fingers stroking his hair—then emotional ones—the love and desire he tasted in the man's blood, the slowly fading fear and desperation. His mind sifted lethargically through the haze that veiled his memories, until one name came clear. "Alain."

Tears sprang to Alain's eyes at the sound of his name in the beloved voice. His arms tightened. "You remember."

Slowly, Orlando nodded. "I remember you." His hand moved reverently to the brand on Alain's neck. "You love me."

"I do," Alain swore. "I always will."

More memories surfaced, a hodgepodge of recent and distant, of people and places long gone and of Alain. "You saved me."

Alain shook his head. "I couldn't. I searched and searched, but I couldn't find you. Monsieur Lombard had to do that."

Orlando silenced the flow of words with a kiss. "You saved me. Eric set me free because of you. You saved me."

Alain started to protest again, knowing he would have to explain about the marks on his wrist, but it could wait. For now, he would be satisfied with holding Orlando, with kissing him.

"I'm still hungry," Orlando said apologetically.

"Take all you need," Alain offered, his head dropping back again, gasping as Orlando's fangs connected with his stubbled skin. Passion rose hot and swift in his veins. He fought it for a moment before giving that effort up as futile. From the first bite in the Père Lachaise cemetery, he had never been able to resist the seductive lure of Orlando's fangs. He laughed with the pure joy of having Orlando in his arms again, the future spread out before them in all its glory. Orlando remembered him, loved him, wanted him still. Closing his eyes, he let his desire grow until it exploded in his head, his heart, his lungs, spinning out of him in creamy fluid, in joyous groans, in the gentle stirring of the air around them in the otherwise still room. "I love you," he chanted softly.

The litany of words, the rich promise in Alain's tone, the depth of passion in his blood drove the fog from Orlando's memories until every moment was as clear in his head and heart as if it had just happened. Feeling his hunger momentarily sated, he lifted his head again, staring down into the royal blue eyes.

"The last thing I remember is telling you Eric had saved me," Orlando said. "I have no idea how much time has passed or what has happened since then."

"Serrier is dead, the rogue is in custody, and the war is essentially over," Alain recounted. "That was—" he glanced at the clock on the wall "—eight hours ago."

"So I awake to a brand new world," Orlando mused.

Alain nodded. "One we can shape as we please."

"How did you find me? Or was it just luck?"

Alain flinched away. "No, monsieur Lombard knew of a way. I'm sorry, but there wasn't any other choice."

The sudden absence of warmth in Alain's voice concerned Orlando. "Why are you sorry?"

"He said the only way to find you was through my blood. I… I let him taste it so he could lead us to you. I'm sorry."

Orlando's possessive instincts howled in protest at the thought of any other vampire touching his Avoué. "Where did he bite you?"

"He didn't," Alain replied swiftly. "He cut my skin and let some of the blood fall onto his palm. I didn't want to let him do even that, but I could feel you getting weaker and the pain you were in kept increasing. Time was passing and Sebastien said you only had hours left. I didn't know what else to do," Alain explained desperately, panic welling as he faced the possibility of regaining Orlando only to lose him by breaking the promises of their Aveu de

Sang. The vampire could not feed elsewhere, but he could withdraw his trust, his love, and that would be nearly as fatal a blow as losing him to death.

Taking a deep breath, Orlando forced aside his instinctive reaction and considered the situation as rationally as he could. Monsieur Lombard, as the oldest of the vampires and a former chef de la Cour, would not have approached his Avoué unless there was no other way. Orlando had felt Alain searching, had felt the growing desperation as avenue after avenue failed. If they said this was the only way, then he would live with that infidelity. "You did what you had to do."

"I didn't want to break my promise," Alain swore. "I refused at first, because how could I give him what belongs only to you? But it was that or let you go, and I couldn't do that. I couldn't lose you."

Orlando understood that. The knowledge that Alain was mortal never completely left him. He would make any sacrifice and break any taboo to delay the moment of separation a little longer. That was a worry for another day, though. "If monsieur Lombard said it was the only way, then it was the only way," he said firmly.

A sudden pounding at the door drew their attention.

"That will be Jean," Alain predicted. "He's been nearly as worried as I was."

"I've fed enough for now," Orlando decided. "Let's reassure him. Then I want to go home, take a bath, and sleep in our bed."

"I can't think of anything I'd like more," Alain agreed vehemently.

Orlando grinned impishly. "Not even making love with my fangs deep in your neck?"

Alain's eyes flashed dark and his body hardened at the mere thought. "What are we waiting for?"

"Come in," Orlando called, pushing to a sitting position and drawing Alain up to sit next to him. The door flew open, Jean pushing in ahead of the others in his eagerness to see Orlando restored. "Are you all right?"

"Not yet," Orlando replied honestly. "It will take more than one feeding to heal all the damage Serrier did with his magic and his whips, but I will be. The damage is only physical. Enough time and enough of Alain's blood will set that right."

Jean studied Orlando's face, seeing the lines of pain and exhaustion around his lips and eyes, but the umber gaze was clearer than Jean could ever remember it being. Whatever Serrier had done, he had not succeeded in breaking Orlando. Everything else could be fixed in time. "Good. I'd hug you, but frankly, you stink."

"That didn't stop Alain," Orlando teased lightly.

Jean rolled his eyes. "Go home. Take a shower and rest. I don't want to see you before sundown tomorrow. You'll have to appear at the *judicium* for the *extorris*, when we decide when to hold it, but beyond that, you're off duty until you're well."

"What about Alain?"

"Marcel relieved him of duty for as long as you need him," Thierry answered. "Now that Serrier's dead, the fighting should taper off and eventually cease altogether. We can spare him for the time it takes you to heal."

"How's everyone else doing?" Alain asked, concern for his friends surfacing again now that his concern for Orlando was mostly eased. "Mathieu and David and—"

"Go home, Alain," Thierry interrupted. "I promise to come by tomorrow and answer all your questions, but despite the hours you spent at Notre-Dame last night, you're almost as exhausted as Orlando is. There's nothing that can't wait until tomorrow."

"I'm not in any shape to be seen in public," Orlando said, looking down at his torn and bloody clothes. "Can you send us home?" he asked Thierry. "I promise to make sure he rests."

"Remember my advice," Sebastien added before Thierry could cast the spell. "Now more than ever."

Orlando smiled, his eyes flashing as reached for Alain's hand. "I will. Just as soon as Thierry gets us home."

Deciding that was invitation enough, Thierry cast the spell.

"What advice?" Jean asked curiously, the change in Orlando's demeanor marked enough for him to wonder what had passed between the two vampires.

"To feed from his Avoué every time they make love."

Chapter 24

"I THINK I'm finally getting the hang of this," Orlando joked as he and Alain reappeared in their bedroom. "I didn't even stumble this time."

Alain smiled at the comment, but his mind was still on their conversation with Sebastien. "What advice was Sebastien talking about?"

"I'll tell you," Orlando promised, "but I need a bath first. Jean wasn't kidding when he said I stink." He glanced at Alain from beneath his lashes. "Want to join me?"

Alain's smile widened. He was not completely sure he wanted to see what had been done to Orlando, but he refused to hide from it. Having his pain acknowledged would help Orlando heal and perhaps keep Alain from making the same kinds of mistakes he had made before, not knowing what would bring back bad memories. "Absolutely," he murmured, kissing Orlando lightly.

The vampire led the way into the bedroom and from there to the bathroom. Closing the door behind them, he turned the water on hot and hard, letting it begin to fill the tub. Although his body had begun to heal, the hot water would certainly sting the closing wounds. He needed to soak, though, to hold Alain in his arms and let all the misery of the last four days disappear.

Swiftly, Alain stripped, clothes falling haphazardly to the floor. His eyes never left Orlando, keeping track of how stiffly his lover moved. When Orlando straightened, the wizard stepped forward to embrace the vampire from behind. Orlando tensed for a moment, but before Alain could draw back, he turned his head and kissed the blond. "I doubt even magic can clean these," Orlando said, picking at his tattered clothes.

Alain helped immediately, their hands brushing as they undid the buttons and pulled the garment off. Alain muffled a cry of despair as he saw the bloody mass of crisscrossed welts on Orlando's back. "I'll kill him," he growled.

"Eric and his friend already did," Orlando replied soothingly. "They'll heal. After a few feedings, they'll be nothing but scars and in a few weeks, they'll be gone entirely. Trust me. I know."

Alain knew that was the truth, although it made him furious to think of his lover suffering like this.

"Alain," Orlando cajoled, hands cupping his lover's cheeks and forcing their eyes to meet. "Yes, I hurt, but this is nothing compared to what Thurloe did to me. I'll heal and this will just be a bad memory."

Alain hoped Orlando was right, that the emotional scars would fade into memory as well as the physical ones. "I love you," he said helplessly, not knowing what else to say.

Orlando smiled. "I know you do. It kept me sane while Serrier had me. Nothing he said, nothing he did, could break that bond, and as long as I could sense you, I knew we'd be all right. Come on. The bath's calling me." He dropped his jeans to the floor as well, stepping into the tub and hissing as the hot water hit his bruised and abraded skin.

"Are you sure this is a good idea?" Alain asked, climbing into the tub behind Orlando. His jaw clenched at the sight of the welts continuing down over Orlando's ass and upper thighs.

"Very sure," the vampire replied. "I'm not very steady on my feet yet. I want to just lie in your arms and soak until the blood and grime float away."

"Maybe you'll let me wash some of it away for you?" Alain offered hesitantly, not sure how far Orlando's time with Serrier had set them back in terms of intimacy.

"Just be gentle," Orlando replied, handing Alain the washcloth. "Some of the cuts haven't closed yet."

Alain soaped the cloth thoroughly, urging Orlando to lean back in his arms. When his lover lay relaxed against him, Alain started running his hands over the smooth skin of Orlando's chest, frowning at the eddies of black and rust that swirled away from the vampire's skin, dirt and blood giving up their hold beneath Alain's tender ablutions. "Feels good," Orlando murmured. "Last night, when I thought I wouldn't see beyond sunrise, I lay on the cot in my cell and touched myself, imagining it was you. As good as it felt, nothing compares to your hands on me."

"I felt that," Alain replied, rinsing the cloth and starting over, trying not to flinch at every new injury he discovered. "I thought I was dreaming, because how could you possibly be feeling pleasure after so much pain?"

"I wish I'd tried it sooner," Orlando confided. "The pain lessened when I did, as if that connection fought the dark magic and strengthened me. Not as much as if I'd fed, but far more than just resting."

"You can feed as much as you need," Alain promised, "but if pleasure helps you heal as well, then we'll have to make you feel nothing but that from now on." Tentatively, he brushed his fingers, free of the cloth, over Orlando's nipples. They peaked beneath his touch, a gasp escaping the vampire's throat as his cock surged in the water.

"Do much of that and we won't finish my bath," Orlando warned.

"We can always take another one."

Orlando chuckled. "Get my back clean while I do my legs. The rest can wait until later."

Nodding, Alain washed Orlando's back as quickly as he dared, face tightening at the livid marks on his lover's flesh, two of them splitting open beneath the rag and oozing fresh blood into the water. He would have to swallow his pride and thank Eric for killing the beast who had done this.

Orlando scrubbed roughly at his feet and legs, the skin dirty but relatively unscathed by his ordeal. He ran a soapy hand over his cock and balls. He needed to feed again, but feeding would not be enough after the fear of the past few days. He needed Alain open and writhing beneath him, their bodies as joined as their hearts, reaffirming the strength of their bond, their love, and he refused to allow any remnant of Serrier's filth to touch what they shared. Pushing to his feet he turned to face Alain, already half-aroused at the thought of what the night would bring. "I need you again."

Alain rose immediately, water glistening on his skin as he stepped out of the tub and reached for a towel. "Don't," Orlando stopped him, joining him on the mat. "Let me."

Alain lifted an eyebrow in surprise but waited to see what Orlando intended. He did not expect the hot swipe of his lover's tongue across his shoulder, licking away the drops of water on his chest. Nor did he expect the quick nip of Orlando's fangs, barely even piercing skin as they passed, leaving Alain suddenly hard and aching with desire. Sebastien's words and Orlando's grinning reply came back to him again. "What did Sebastien tell you to do?" he asked hoarsely.

Orlando did not reply, sinking to his knees at Alain's feet and biting deeply just above the wizard's hipbone as his fingers curled around the hardening shaft. He had tasted desire in Alain's blood before, had even tasted his lover's climax on more than one occasion, but it had never been like this, never been a part of their lovemaking. Alain's blood was as rich, as flavorful as it had always been, with the added awareness that he would not have to pull back this time. He could leave his fangs where they were or bite Alain in any of a dozen other places, tasting, devouring, until they both climaxed from the sensation. He tasted the sudden awareness of that fact in Alain's blood, a bolt of pure desire so strong it nearly brought Orlando undone right there. He resisted, though, wanting everything he had denied them until now. His fangs sustaining their passionate lure, Orlando gathered the fluid already leaking from the tip of Alain's cock, coating his fingers well enough that he could begin preparing his lover to receive him again. He fully intended to take this to bed, to stretch Alain out on the smooth sheets and shower him in love bites, but that was for later. For now, he wanted to feel Alain come apart beneath his hands and his fangs as he had before the ill-fated battle at place Pigalle.

Alain gasped as Orlando bit him again, the contact obviously about his pleasure as much as if not more than about Orlando's hunger. He shivered with delight at the realization, groping blindly behind him for the sink, sure he would need its support. Before the night was over, he would truly know what it meant to be loved by a vampire. Already, his head spun with sensation, Orlando's hand on his cock, his fingers probing Alain's entrance, but most especially, Orlando's fangs driving deep into his belly, marking him not just as his Avoué but as his lover. As many times as they had done this, as many times as they had whispered heartfelt declarations, Alain had never felt this cherished.

"Orlando," he husked, his lover's name the only thought he could form as love and lust swamped him.

Orlando did not reply, only intensifying all his caresses, determined to taste and feel Alain's climax, the first of many that night if he had his way. He knew how close he had come to never waking. If Jude had not cooperated.... That did not bear thinking about. He and Alain were reunited now. Nothing else mattered except proving that in the most primal of ways.

Finding his lover's prostate, he massaged it deliberately, wanting to bring Alain undone beneath his hands. He did not even flinch when the wizard's hands tangled in his hair, tugging gently. Releasing his fangs' grip on his lover's flesh, he looked up into lust-crazed eyes, his own eyes asking the question. Alain shifted beneath his grip, bumping his cock against Orlando's lips in a silent plea.

"My fangs," Orlando warned. "I don't want to hurt you."

"You won't," Alain replied with complete confidence. "Please. I need...." He dared not put into words what he truly needed—Orlando beneath him, writhing on Alain's cock—but they had done this before, his cock in Orlando's mouth. He trusted Orlando not to bite him, but he suspected that even if his lover did score him, he would not protest the reminder of his love's supernatural nature.

Reminding himself that Sebastien said he could not hurt his Avoué even if he tried, Orlando parted his lips around the slick head, tongue probing the leaking slit as he tried to draw up his fangs. He did not expect to succeed, given how hungry he was for blood, but the sharp incisors retracted obediently, leaving Orlando free to suck as deeply and energetically as he desired. Working his fingers deeper into Alain's passage, he timed his swipes over Alain's prostate with the pulls of his mouth on his lover's erection.

"Orlando!"

The cry was plea, praise and portent all in one, giving Orlando only enough time to take a deep breath before Alain's cock disgorged into his waiting throat. He kept licking and sucking until the wizard's twitching stilled, his body entirely supported by Orlando's hand on his hip and the sink behind him.

"Ready for bed?" Orlando purred when he finally released his lover's cock. "I'm still hungry."

Alain nodded dazedly, his body buzzing in satiation. Orlando's voice, though, betrayed his continuing need. "I'm yours," he promised. "Take what you need."

Orlando smiled, rising slowly to his feet, though he could already feel the difference that just the little bit of blood and lovemaking had already made. It seemed Sebastien was right. He knew the effect of feeding on his injuries, at least the physical ones, and he had discovered the effect of sexual pleasure, but the synergy of combining them had strengthened him far more than he could have predicted. The claim that it would take him weeks to recover completely suddenly seemed ridiculously pessimistic. "I will," he agreed, "as long as I can give you what you need at the same time."

"All I need is you, safe in my arms," Alain swore, pulling Orlando into a tight embrace, forgetting about the wounds marring the vampire's back. Orlando did not pull away, though. He needed the contact as much as Alain did. Not letting any space appear between them, he waltzed them toward the bed, lowering Alain tenderly down onto it. Immediately, the wizard's legs parted to make space for Orlando, his head tipping back to offer his neck.

Orlando licked the already healing wounds on Alain's neck, but he did not bite again immediately. Now that he had released his fears, he began to see the body beneath his as a blank canvas on which to paint the picture of his devotion. Ultimately, he would feed from the pulsing vein as he slid home into his Avoué, but first he would feast his senses on the rest of the delights laid out for his delectation.

Pushing up on his elbows, he slithered up Alain's body, rubbing skin against skin at every point possible, wanting his wizard as needy as he was before he joined their bodies again. His lips sought Alain's blindly, skating across the stubble of several days—proof of how single-mindedly Alain had searched for him—until he found his target, kissing his lover passionately, desperately. Alain's lips parted for him, inviting him inside, a temptation Orlando had no hope or intention of resisting. He lingered, though, savoring each touch, each caress as if it were the first. If he had learned nothing else from his captivity, he had been reminded of how fleeting life could be, even for a vampire, and he intended to cherish every moment he and Alain were given. As their lips met, clung, then parted only to meet again, the world fell away until nothing existed beyond the meeting of hearts, minds, and souls made real in the meeting of their mouths. They drew breath from each other, completely lost in the communion of their lives, the tender indignities of teeth clashing, noses bumping, unnoticed as the kiss continued unabated.

Finally, though, more powerful needs made themselves known. Panting, Orlando drew back, smiling at the resurgent erection he felt against his stomach. He dropped another quick kiss on Alain's lips before rocking back on his knees to stare down at his lover's body, considering where to lavish his attention first. As if reading his mind, Alain bent one knee, opening himself more fully to Orlando's gaze, Orlando's touch, Orlando's bite.

Hunger suddenly riding him hard, Orlando reached swiftly for the lube, coating his fingers as he bent his head to the inside of Alain's thigh. His fangs penetrated the hard muscle at the same time as his fingers sought the tight sheath, beginning to stretch it in earnest now. Their earlier play notwithstanding, he knew he would have little or no control when he finally got inside Alain again and he would not risk hurting his Avoué.

Alain cried out in delight as he felt Orlando's fangs sheath themselves in his flesh again, the pinch as nothing compared to the glorious knowledge that Orlando had set aside his fears. He almost wished it were summer so he could go out wearing just shorts, to let everyone would see how thoroughly his vampire had claimed him.

Orlando could taste Alain's rising desire in the delicious blood that filled his mouth as he fed, each brush of his fingers across his lover's prostate echoed by a jolt of passion. Silently, Orlando berated himself for denying them both this pleasure before, but he pushed those feelings aside, focusing on Alain's gratification, on this moment when they truly became one.

With increased awareness of Alain's pleasure, Orlando set out to drive his lover so high he would never come down, finding the touch, the rhythm that best pleased the wizard without ever letting him reach the pinnacle of rapture that would delay their joining. Sebastien had told him once that he would find making love to his Avoué almost as addictive as feeding from him. Orlando suspected they were, in fact, one and the same. Certainly, the nourishment he was receiving was necessary to his body, but the connection had become necessary to his soul. He could only imagine what it would feel like in a few minutes when they added another layer to that connection.

Alain writhed on the bed, caught between Orlando's fingers and his fangs, inundated with pleasure, so hard it hurt in the best possible way. Orlando had fulfilled all of Alain's desires, stated and unstated, in this moment. All that was missing was his vampire's pleasure. "Please," Alain gasped. "Make love to me."

"I thought that's what I was doing," Orlando teased as he released his bite on Alain's leg, licking the wound lightly to stop the bleeding.

"I want you in me," Alain specified, reaching for Orlando to draw him up so their lips could meet. "Your cock deep in my ass and your fangs deep in my neck."

Control shattered by the inflammatory words, Orlando acceded immediately. His cock slipped into the slick sheath as if made to fit there, his fangs finding the brand that marked his first claim without conscious thought, completing the circle of their lives and love. Alain convulsed almost immediately, the dual sensation too much for his overtaxed synapses to process.

"Again," Orlando insisted, releasing Alain's neck momentarily. "Come for me again."

Alain would have said that was impossible, but then Orlando's fangs returned to his neck, Orlando's cock moved in his passage, and his body responded, clenching again as Orlando drove him higher and higher. He sobbed aloud with the force of their merging, fingers tangling in Orlando's hair as he tried to keep from grabbing his vampire's shoulders, knowing how badly they were torn up.

Orlando wanted to draw out their lovemaking, to make their reunion last for hours, but his body had suffered too much abuse in the past days to allow for that kind of control. Feeling Alain contract around him again, he gave in to his own need, thrusting hard and fast until he climaxed deep inside his lover's body. His fangs tore the skin of Alain's neck slightly, eliciting a hiss from the wizard.

Orlando pulled back, starting to apologize, until he caught sight of the look of utter bliss on Alain's face. He would not diminish that pleasure by apologizing for anything that caused it. Instead, he lowered his head again, lapping tenderly at the torn flesh until the bleeding stopped and the wound began to close.

"I never dreamed," Alain said slowly, his eyes opening to look down at his lover's dark head.

Orlando looked up, meeting Alain's gaze. "Neither did I. I didn't hurt you, did I?"

Alain shook his head. "I've never felt so thoroughly ravished as I do right now. What about you? Are you all right?"

"I'm feeling better all the time," Orlando promised, and it was true, he realized as he rolled to the side. Craning his neck, he peered over his shoulder, trying to see the wounds on his back. When he could not see to his satisfaction, he turned the other way, presenting his back to Alain. "They don't hurt as much. Do they look better?"

Alain's eyes widened as he stared at the expanse of skin. Where before the whip marks had been barely scabbed, some of them even bleeding a little, now all of them were closed and several of them were merely raised marks. "It looks like days have gone by. How is that possible?"

"You love me," Orlando replied simply. "You gave me your blood, your magic, and your heart. I think anything is possible for us."

Alain smiled, the expression overtaken by a yawn as the adrenaline-enhanced strength of the past four days deserted him, the lack of sleep catching up with him and leaving him heavy lidded and yawning.

"Sleep," Orlando said immediately. "I'll still be here in the morning."

"Don't make me wait that long," Alain requested through another yawn. "I'll need you again long before that."

Orlando grinned and kissed Alain softly. "Sleep," he repeated. "I'll guard your dreams."

Chapter 25

"I SHOULD check on the wounded," Thierry said when Alain and Orlando were gone. "I had several from my patrol, and I'm sure there were others as well. With Alain off duty and Marcel at l'Élysée, I'm the ranking officer on duty."

"I'll come with you," Sebastien offered immediately, not wanting to let Thierry out of his sight. He imagined that feeling would fade eventually, when the danger had well and truly passed, but for now, the thought of Thierry being farther than arm's reach set every instinct he possessed to screaming.

"I should check to see if any vampires are injured as well," Jean decided. Now that Orlando was awake and safe in Alain's arms and the *extorris* was confined awaiting trial, all Jean's other responsibilities came back to him. He glanced over at Raymond. "If you aren't too tired?"

"I'll be fine for a few more hours," Raymond assured his lover, though he could feel fatigue pulling at his limbs.

"Hopefully it won't take hours," Jean replied quickly, wanting Raymond in his bed, even if only to sleep.

"It shouldn't," Thierry agreed, leading the way toward the infirmary. "Unless someone is far more injured than I realized. But even then, there's little we could do that the medics won't have already done. It's more about morale than about anything medical."

"It might be worth making sure the medics know about the benefits of having vampires feed from their injured partners," Raymond mused as they neared the sick ward. "Even if all it does is ease the pain the wizards are feeling, that can make a huge difference in the patient's mindset."

"As long as there isn't already blood loss involved," Thierry agreed. "Otherwise the risk might outweigh the gain."

"As often as most of the vampires have fed from their partners in the past few days, I wonder if there isn't something in the bond that protects you," Jean mused aloud. "Not to the point of an Aveu de Sang, but I know I shouldn't have been able to feed from Raymond the way I've done—yet he doesn't seem to be suffering for it."

"Yet another of those questions for which we have no answers," Thierry said with a shake of his head. "We probably won't have to worry about it, though, since the number of battles should decrease steadily as we hunt down and take out Serrier's remaining forces. We'll have to interrogate the captured wizards to see what kind of numbers we're talking about, but with Serrier dead and given the number we took down today, I just don't see it being anything more than mopping up at this point."

"The end of the war gives us flexibility in exploring the implications of our partnerships," Sebastien agreed, "but I don't see very many vampires walking away from their partners simply because the war's over. For all that it's only been a little over a month, the effects of the alliance are going to be more far-reaching than this brief time would suggest."

"Could you really walk away?" Raymond asked Thierry seriously. "Could you just say 'thanks, it's been fun' and let Sebastien walk out of your life for good?"

"Could you walk away from Jean?" Thierry countered.

Raymond shook his head. "It hurts just to think about it."

"Could you?" Sebastien asked, suddenly nervous at his partner's lack of answer.

"No," Thierry admitted. "Not unless something changed drastically now that our partnerships aren't magically necessary."

"What's to say they aren't?" Raymond inquired. "We already know they contribute to the magical equilibrium. They strengthen the wizards involved. They give the vampires an otherwise unknown freedom. What's to say those things aren't as magically necessary as winning the war? Yes, we could go back to the old way of doing things, performing a Rite d'équilibrage each time we sensed an imbalance. Or we can go forward with the partnerships, explore them to their fullest potential, and see what kind of new world we can create. It isn't Serrier's revolution, but it may well be ours."

"I never knew you were such an idealist."

"I'm not," Raymond defended himself. "I'm a historian. But that gives me a broader perspective on events sometimes. We're at a crossroads. Serrier's vision of a new regime was flawed to the core, but that doesn't mean we live in a perfect world now either. Public opinion will swing hard in our favor with the cessation of hostilities, and we can use that to shape a different future than simply more of the same. Marcel's already started it with the equality legislation that will surely go to vote in a matter of days, if not hours, now that the vampires have proven themselves such capable allies. The question now is what else we need to change, how else we need to transform society so that we can guarantee a better future for all of us."

Looking away from Thierry for a moment, Raymond was arrested by the hungry look on Jean's face. "Sorry," he said, squirming a little. "I tend to get carried away."

Jean did not even look at Thierry and Sebastien, just excused himself and Raymond, pulling his partner down the hall and into an empty room.

Sebastien chuckled. "It always amuses me to see what turns other people on."

"And what turns you on?" Thierry asked, only half joking.

"Watching you on duty," Sebastien answered immediately. "Let's check on the wounded and then I have plans for you."

Thierry swallowed roughly, suddenly hard at the thought of what Sebastien had in store for him. If Sebastien had not specified wanting to watch him on duty, Thierry would have said to hell with the injured and dragged his vampire back to the office where they could lock the door and have some privacy—but his own sense of duty and Sebastien's statement of interest kept him from giving in to that desire. If nothing else, he could enjoy Sebastien's company later with a clear conscience and could go straight to Alain's and Orlando's apartment the next day with news, rather than having to return to Milice headquarters first.

Schooling his face to hide his desire, Thierry pushed open the door to the infirmary and led Sebastien inside. Far too many beds had occupants for the wizard's peace of mind, but most of those he could see were conscious, many of them even sitting up, particularly those with a vampire by their side.

"Captain Dumont," the head medic said with a nod of his head. "You don't look hurt."

"I'm not," Thierry assured him. "I just wanted to see how everyone was doing."

"We've been busy," Dr. Périssé replied honestly, "but I think everyone's stable at least. The vampires have been of great assistance, both in taking care of their own partners and in lending a helping hand wherever one was needed."

"Jean will be glad to hear that," Sebastien said. "I know he was planning on coming by at some point as well, but he had another matter to handle first."

Thierry suppressed a snicker at Sebastien's choice of words, quite sure he knew just how Jean was handling Raymond. "I take it from your comment that someone let you know about the effect of a vampire feeding from his or her partner?" he asked, preferring not to dwell on Jean's and Raymond's sex lives.

Dr. Périssé nodded. "I would have lost at least a few wizards if it hadn't been for that," he admitted freely. "It seems the alliance has tapped into magic far stronger than anything available to most magical practitioners. Now if only every injured wizard had a partner.... Fortunately, those who aren't partnered have injuries I can heal in time. It won't be fast, and in a few cases, it won't be pretty, but I think everyone will recover eventually."

"Can I see David?" Thierry asked. "He was hurt the worst from my patrol."

"Of course," the medic replied. "He's in the back with his partner. The last bed on the left."

Thierry and Sebastien walked down the aisle to the curtained area the doctor had indicated. "Knock, knock," Thierry said, rustling the curtain but not drawing it back. He had no idea what kind of détente David and his partner had come to, and he certainly did not want to walk in on anything personal, even if Angélique was simply feeding.

"Come in," the vampire called.

Thierry pushed the curtain aside and gestured for Sebastien to precede him. "How's David?" he asked when the curtain fell shut behind them.

"Sleeping, finally," Angélique replied softly. "The doctor said that's what's best for him now."

"Did he say what kind of spell David took?" Thierry asked. "I didn't see in the chaos."

"He was bleeding into his abdomen," she explained. "The doctor was afraid he wouldn't make it, but he seems to have pulled through."

"You fed, right?" Sebastien asked.

Angélique nodded. "Dr. Périssé said it would help him heal faster."

"As strange as it sounds, it seems to be true, at least when it's a magical injury," Thierry agreed. "How long do they want him to stay?"

"If he continues to heal as fast as he is now, they said he could go home with supervision in a day or two."

"With supervision sounds ominous," Sebastien said.

Angélique shook her head. "I'll just take him to Sang Froid and not let him out of my sight," she replied. "I can give him whatever nonmagical care he needs. If he needs something I can't provide, I'll either call for the medics to come to him, or I'll bring him back in."

"With you taking good care of him, he'll be fine in no time, I'm sure," Thierry commented with a grin. "We should check on everyone else, but if you need anything, just let the medics know. If they can't get it for you, they'll let me know and I'll arrange it."

"I'll have to talk to my manager at some point," Angélique replied. "He needs to know what's going on, but I doubt he knows where Milice headquarters are, and even if he does, he wouldn't be able to get inside."

"When is he at Sang Froid? We can get him an escort," Thierry offered.

"He usually works daylight hours because he deals with the business side, the paperwork and such, not with the customers usually," Angélique replied. "His name is François Roche."

Thierry nodded. "I'll send someone over as soon as we're done here. Is there anything you need him to bring? A change of clothes? Anything else?"

"A change of clothes would be nice," Angélique replied, looking down at her battle-torn outfit. "I seem to be somewhat the worse for wear at the moment."

Thierry glanced down at his own dirty attire. "You're hardly the only one. I haven't seen anyone looking their best since we got back. Even those of us who could use magic to repair our appearances are too tired to bother, I guess."

"It's not particularly important," Angélique agreed. "At some point I'd like a shower—but it can wait until later, when I know David won't wake up and miss me."

"I'm sure one of the orderlies would wait with him while you went to clean up," Thierry offered. "Things seem to have settled down here at the moment."

Angélique smiled. "I'll ask one of them later, after I've talked to François and David wakes up at least once. I don't want the first person he sees to be anyone but me."

"You've settled your differences then?" Thierry asked. Jude's demand to have the Ordre de restriction lifted was a reminder that not all the partnerships had jelled as well as his and Sebastien's.

"We're making progress," Angélique replied after a moment's consideration. "Far more than I imagined possible a few weeks ago."

Thierry smiled. "Good. I'm glad to hear it. We need to check on everyone else, but we'll send someone for your manager. In the meantime, let someone know if there's anything else you need while you're keeping vigil."

"I will. How is Orlando?" Angélique asked quickly, realizing Thierry was about to leave. "Have they had any luck?"

Thierry's smile was radiant. "I sent them home just before we came to the infirmary," he assured Angélique. "He was awake, talking, even teasing. I imagine he has a long road ahead of him just like everyone else who suffered from Serrier's spells, but it looks like he'll be fine."

"Oh, that's wonderful news!" Angélique exclaimed. "Tell him I asked about him next time you see him, since you'll certainly see him before I do. Unless Alain brings him in here."

"All he needs is Alain's blood," Sebastien chuckled. "I don't see either of them going anywhere except bed until Orlando has to appear at the *judicium*."

"Jean caught the *extorris* then," Angélique observed with a nod. "Good. We'll all rest easier knowing he's off the streets."

"They haven't decided when to have it yet," Sebastien replied, "but I don't see it being anything more than a formality with Orlando hurt as badly as he was."

Angélique nodded, more than a little pleased to have the individual guilty of the torture that had been inflicted on the woman left on her doorstep facing justice. David stirred on the bed, drawing her attention.

Seeing the direction of Angélique's gaze, Thierry said good-bye as he and Sebastien left her alone with her partner. As they started back toward the front of the infirmary, they noticed Mireille sitting outside a cubicle, her head in her hands.

"Mireille?" Sebastien asked. "What's wrong?"

"It's Caroline," the vampire replied. "She got hit with a spell. They managed to remove the glass from her eyes and stop the hemorrhaging, but they're not sure they can undo the damage. She may never see again."

"Did you feed from her?" Sebastien asked immediately.

"Not yet," Mireille replied. "They said it could help her, but there was so much blood. I was afraid to take anymore. She insists I'm fretting over nothing, that her eyes will be fine in a matter of days, but the doctor didn't seem at all optimistic to me."

"Definitely feed from her as soon as she wakes up next time," Thierry counseled. "For whatever reason, it seems to help aid in healing."

Mireille frowned. "That's what the medic said, but I didn't believe him. I mean, what about Laurent? Blair fed from him almost immediately after he was hit and it didn't help him. He still died."

Thierry shrugged helplessly. "I don't know what made the difference. I doubt anyone does, honestly. We're floundering around in the dark where the partnerships are concerned. Maybe the bond was too new. Maybe the damage was too great. Maybe it was because Blair was actually trying to turn him. I just don't know, but Caroline's not in danger of dying, is she?" Mireille shook her head.

"Then what have you got to lose by trying?" Sebastien continued. "You have to feed one way or another and I don't imagine you want to start hunting again when you know Caroline would be perfectly happy for you to take what you need. If it helps her, all the better, but even if it doesn't, you haven't lost anything. You've still strengthened your bond, still taken care of her and of yourself. And she may be right about her eyes."

Mireille sighed. "I don't want to say anything that might discourage her. I know how important it is for her to keep her spirits up, but it feels to me like she's grasping at straws rather than dealing with the reality of her injury, and I'm afraid what it will do to her when she realizes the doctors were right instead of her."

"First of all, you don't know that the doctors are right," Thierry reminded her. "Even if the medics here can't do anything for her because the injury is physical, not magical, there are specialists of every kind in the city who might be able to help her. And even if they are right, that doesn't mean she can't lead a rich, fulfilling life. She'll have to relearn how to use some of her senses, but she's a wizard. She's not without resources. L'ANS has all kinds of retraining programs for wizards who have to change fields due to disability. And with the war ending, we'll be able to devote time and resources to those civilian concerns again."

Mireille took a deep breath, visibly fortifying herself. "I know all of that. It's just a shock. I have to be strong for her because I don't want her to lose her positive attitude, even if she's wrong about her eyes, but I needed a few minutes to deal with it myself."

"You aren't in this alone," Thierry promised. "Don't be afraid to ask for help. For either of you."

"I've already thought about seeing if she would come live with me at monsieur Lombard's house," Mireille admitted. "It would mean another pair of eyes watching her as she learns how to function without her vision and someone else for her to talk to while she recovers."

"That sounds like a good idea," Sebastien agreed, having gained even more respect for the old vampire in the last day. "Although she may prefer to be in her own place for awhile, just for the familiarity."

"You don't have to decide right away," Thierry added. "Whatever you decide, you can always count on our help."

"Merci," Mireille said, summoning a smile.

"Don't give up hope," Sebastien admonished again. "Orlando was gone. Inanimate from hunger. But we managed to restore him. Caroline isn't nearly as bad off as that."

A rustle inside the curtain drew Mireille's attention. "I think she's waking up. I'll let her know you came by. And tell Orlando I'm glad he's safe when you see him." Without waiting for their reaction, she disappeared into the cubicle and they could hear her voice greeting Caroline cheerfully.

Sebastien took Thierry's hand and drew him toward the exit. When they were out in the hallway, he squeezed Thierry's hand before releasing it. "They'll be all right. Mireille's stronger than she looks."

Thierry nodded. "So's Caroline. We'll just have to make sure they get the help they need, especially if Caroline is blind permanently." He leaned against the wall, heaving a sigh.

"Have you fulfilled your duty?" Sebastien asked seriously. "You look almost as bad as some of the patients in there. You need to rest." As much as he had joked about being turned on by Thierry doing his duty, the wizard was clearly beat, and that took precedence over Sebastien's desire. They had their entire lives ahead of them. They could wait until morning to make love.

"I need to eat," Thierry said. "I'm not sure when I last ate, to tell the truth. My stomach thinks I've forgotten what food is."

"Do you want to get something here or go home and find dinner there?" Sebastien asked.

"Let's go home," Thierry said. "I think there's stuff in the fridge that isn't too old, but even if there isn't, I can't go out dressed like this. I'll have to clean up."

"We'll order a pizza," Sebastien decided. "That way you don't have to go back out. You can rest and I'll wake you when it gets there."

"Once I fall asleep, I'm not likely to wake up for a good twelve hours," Thierry warned. Sebastien did not reply, but he suspected that was a low estimate.

"Let's go. Either way, we're wasting time standing here."

Thierry pushed away from the wall and started toward the main entrance. He was eager to be home, to be clean and fed, and to finally get some untroubled sleep.

Chapter 26

"JEAN!" RAYMOND protested laughingly as the vampire pushed him into an empty room. "I thought you wanted to check on the injured."

"I did," Jean purred, nuzzling Raymond's neck enticingly, "until you got all earnest on me. Then I got other ideas."

"Like what?" Raymond teased, relaxing beneath his partner's caress. He knew, of course—or at least he was pretty sure he did—but he wanted to hear Jean say it.

"Like molesting you," Jean drawled, his hands moving freely, swiftly, over Raymond's body, cupping his buttocks, cradling his cock. "You don't mind, do you?"

"Mind?" Raymond repeated dumbly, his body arching into the demanding touches. "I don't mind anything you do to me. You should know that by now."

Jean grinned, leaning in for a kiss. "It never hurts to hear you say it." He did not give Raymond the chance to reply, taking his lover's mouth with tender forcefulness.

Raymond returned the kiss eagerly, the fear and danger of the past twenty-four hours heightening his need. They were safe now. Serrier was dead. The *extorris* was taken. For the first time in two years, Raymond could sleep easy, knowing the price on his head had been lifted with the dark wizard's demise. Fingers tangling in Jean's dark hair, he molded their lips together, clinging to his lover as if that contact could ensure his continued existence. After only a moment, Jean's hands mimicked his, the same desperation claiming him.

"We need to go home," Raymond rasped, lifting his head slightly. "I need more than just another quick tumble in my office."

"It's an awfully long subway ride," Jean delayed, hands moving in ways intended to steal Raymond's concentration.

He underestimated his partner.

"There's still a wizard on duty in the Salle des Cartes," Raymond replied single-mindedly. "We can be home in a matter of minutes."

Giving up with a laugh, Jean released his hold on Raymond, settling for taking his partner's hand instead. "Fine, but you get to explain to the duty officer what the rush is."

"I'm too exhausted to take the long way home, but I don't want you on the subway alone, so would he please send you to where I'm going," Raymond said as if it were the most logical explanation in the world.

"If I hadn't tasted the passion beneath the surface, I might even buy that," Jean laughed as they walked toward the Salle des Cartes. "The question is whether the wizard on duty will."

Raymond shrugged. "Does it matter if he believes me? I don't care what he thinks as long as he sends you to me. It's not as if I really have to worry about my authority at this point. Thierry would argue, but the war's basically over."

Jean had to admit Raymond had a point. "What about my authority?" he asked, speeding up as he pulled Raymond along behind him.

"I doubt there are any vampires hanging out in the Salle des Cartes, now that Orlando's safe and the Milice is regrouping and deciding what to do next," Raymond reminded him as they entered the spacious room. Raymond was right. The only other occupant was the wizard on duty, who came wearily to his feet at the sight of the two men.

"Can you send my partner home after me if I keep my repère?" Raymond asked simply, not providing any explanation.

"Of course," the wizard replied. Raymond glanced at Jean, who nodded, then cast the displacement spell to send himself to his vampire's apartment. Moments later, Jean appeared at his side.

Raymond took a step forward, intending to continue the embrace they had begun at Milice headquarters, but the effort of that last spell had stolen what little energy he still retained after the battle. He stumbled, grateful Jean's reflexes were fast enough to keep him from falling.

"What happened?" Jean asked immediately, scooping Raymond into his arms and carrying him into the bedroom. "You were fine at headquarters."

"I've used more than my quota of magic in the past day," Raymond explained, charmed by Jean's actions. His mind told him he should be uncomfortable with the display, but he ignored the little voice, tired enough and relieved enough at the outcome of the night to let down the walls he usually kept high around his heart. "I'll be fine after some sleep."

Lust still driving him after listening to Raymond's earnest oration, Jean looked down at the man in his arms. He suspected Raymond would fight to stay awake if he pressed his desires, but he could see the exhaustion in his partner's face. Dark circles ringed the hazel eyes; the usually imperceptible lines around Raymond's mouth were etched deeply. Jean had been selfish more than once in his life, but he could not bring himself to be that way tonight. "Can you stay awake long enough for me to clean you up a little?" he asked considerately.

"I can try," Raymond said as Jean set him on his feet again, peeling away layers of dirty, sweaty clothes.

When he was down to just his underwear, Jean pulled back the covers on the bed and urged him to sit. "Let me wash you up a bit. You'll sleep better."

Raymond chuckled as Jean hurried into the bathroom. As if there were any doubt how he would sleep tonight! He did not protest, though. The warm cloth felt good against his skin, lifting away the grit of the day and the feeling of filth Raymond always had after coming in contact with Serrier's magic. "Thank you," he said softly after a few moments. "Some days, I don't think I'll ever be rid of his evil."

"He's dead," Jean declared, setting aside the washcloth and cradling Raymond's face in his hands. "He can't touch you ever again. Even more than that, you rid yourself of him when you switched sides. You don't need me or anyone else for that."

Raymond smiled. "But I do need you. Maybe not to win free of Serrier's influence, but they all still doubted me, except for Marcel, until you vouched for me. You've rehabilitated my image completely since the alliance began, and I have no doubt that will continue as we move forward. People won't see the wizard who fell for Serrier's propaganda. They'll see the partner of the chef de la Cour. And that is a very different thing indeed."

Jean hated the thought of Raymond being judged that way, but he also knew it was human nature. "You are far more than just my partner," he insisted, "and you can be sure I'll tell that to anyone who'll listen."

"Jean," Raymond said softly, stopping what was clearly gearing up to be a rant. "It's all right. I'm perfectly content to be an unknown history professor with an important lover. I don't care that the public will care more about the scar on my back than about the record of what I truly did in the war. You know the truth. Marcel knows the truth. I'm generally accepted within the Milice now, which means I'll have that support when the war is over and I try to go back to my job. I don't need the press or public opinion to turn in my favor. It doesn't matter."

Deciding nothing would be gained by debating it tonight, Jean let the subject drop, easing Raymond back onto the bed instead. "Let me get cleaned up quickly and then we'll rest," he promised, starting back toward the bathroom. "I'll be right back."

Raymond watched with drooping eyes as Jean disappeared for a moment, the sound of running water enough to lull the wizard almost to sleep while also letting him keep track of his partner's progress. When he heard the taps turn off, he forced his eyes back open so he could watch Jean come out of the bathroom. A black silk robe hid his body from Raymond's view, bringing a slight frown to the wizard's face.

"What are you thinking?" Jean asked.

"You're wearing clothes," Raymond muttered petulantly.

The tone was so at odds with Jean's image of his partner that he smiled. "You're too tired for me to do anything but snuggle up next to you and sleep anyway. You can take it off me in the morning."

"Wanna feel your skin," the wizard said, the words almost entirely muffled by a huge yawn.

"Go to sleep," Jean chided, slipping the robe from his shoulders and climbing into bed behind Raymond. He pulled his lover close, spooning up against him firmly, and kept vigil as his wizard slept.

SEVERAL TIMES as they rode the train back out to Versailles, Sebastien wondered why Thierry had not asked someone to send him—or them—home, particularly seeing how the wizard closed his eyes and leaned against the window of the train. Eventually, Sebastien reached for the blond, urging the wizard to lean on his shoulder so his head would not keep bouncing against the glass. Thierry sighed and shifted into Sebastien's embrace, leaving the vampire even more confused. He had listened to his partner insist to everyone they met that the war was not really over, yet Thierry seemed completely unconcerned by that prospect. Not because he was sleeping now—he had been on high alert for four days and had not slept in over twenty-four hours—but because he had let his guard down so completely as to take the train. Deciding to play it safe, Sebastien let his eyes scan the car constantly, on guard against any threat.

When they reached their stop, Thierry roused somewhat, enough to walk off the train and down the street toward his house, but Sebastien suspected he acted on instinct, familiarity rather than conscious thought guiding his feet to the gate. His fingers fumbled with the keys until Sebastien finally took them gently and opened the portal, letting them inside. As soon as the gate shut behind them, protecting them from curious eyes, Sebastien bent and lifted Thierry into his arms. His lover mumbled a protest, but Sebastien ignored it. Thierry could berate him later, when he could keep his eyes open and form a coherent sentence. For now, he needed to sleep.

Carefully, not wanting to jostle Thierry awake, Sebastien set his lover on the bed, pulling off his shoes, opening his shirt collar as far as it would go, and sliding off his jeans. Hopefully, that would allow Thierry to sleep comfortably enough. Pressing a tender kiss to his wizard's forehead, he went into the bathroom to take a shower.

The hot water felt good on his cool skin. The weather had turned sharply colder over the course of the day, as if Serrier's defeat had set everything back in balance and the seasons were rushing to catch up with where they should have been already. Closing his eyes as the water ran down his face, Sebastien pondered the whirlwind of change that had struck his life in the past month. He had known even before the alliance formed that the war was going on, but it had seemed irrelevant to him, a fight between two factions of wizards, neither of which cared about the other magical races.

Marcel and the alliance had proven him spectacularly wrong, for which he would always be grateful.

He had lived his life in the shadows, not simply because of his innate sensitivity to light, but also because of his somewhat shaky status in the Cour because of his history with Jean. The alliance had changed all that, bringing him fully into the Cour again as well as giving him the unexpected immunity to sunlight. It had brought him far more than that, though, a fact witnessed by his presence in this house and his welcome in the bed and arms of the wizard who slept in the next room. He had not been looking for a new lover, a new love, but fate had seen fit to find one for him anyway. He smiled as he reached for the shampoo—Thierry's shampoo—and began to wash his hair.

He had not clicked with anyone the way he did with Thierry since Thibaut. The thought still caused his heart to clench, but now as much in anticipation of the future as in pain at the memories. Thierry was still young, though not as young as Thibaut had been, but he was a wizard and would live far longer than Thibaut had…. They would have many, many years together before age or infirmity forced Sebastien to look elsewhere for sustenance. He shuddered. He had gone through this once when Thibaut died. The thought of loving and losing again tore at him, but it was either that or let Thierry go now, and every fiber of his being protested that choice. He had survived losing Thibaut. He would find a way to survive losing Thierry when that time came. And in the meantime, he would cherish every moment, storing up memories against his eventual return to the shadows.

Pushing aside such morbid thoughts when he should be celebrating their victory, he finished his shower and dried off quickly, slipping back into the bedroom on silent feet so as not to disturb his partner. He slid into bed behind Thierry, spooning against the wizard's warmth and settling to rest, only to have his lover turn in his arms and press a sleepy kiss to his lips.

"You need to rest," Sebastien evaded.

Thierry mumbled a reply the vampire could not quite make out, but his hands moved deliberately over Sebastien's bare skin, igniting his passion. "Thierry," he said discouragingly.

Thierry shook his head, eyes opening. Making sure Sebastien was watching, he thumbed the vampire's nipples, rubbing at them until they stiffened. "Make love to me."

Sebastien gasped at the unexpected sensations, then again as one of Thierry's hands wrapped around his erection, stroking him firmly. It only took a moment before the vampire was fully hard. Thierry rolled to his other side again, pressing his buttocks against the hard shaft. "Make love to me," he repeated, his voice, though sleepy, brooking no disagreement.

Turning away only long enough to find the lube, Sebastien shifted a little so he could slip his hand between them in search of Thierry's opening. He slid his other hand beneath his lover's body, wrapping it around his torso and caressing wherever he could reach: chest, belly, swelling cock.

Lazily, Thierry undulated between Sebastien's hands, forward into the channel made by his clenched fist, then backward onto the fingers stretching him tenderly. His eyes closed again, doubling the darkness and wrapping him in a cocoon of desire. After a few moments, Sebastien's cock replaced his fingers. "Bite me," he pleaded, missing the feeling of Sebastien's fangs as they made love.

"It's too dangerous," Sebastien protested. "I've taken too much in the past few days and you're already exhausted."

"Bite me," Thierry repeated.

Marshalling his control, Sebastien lowered his head to Thierry's shoulder, letting his fangs penetrate, giving his lover the sensation he desired without drawing any blood into his mouth. The temptation to suck was strong, but he forced himself to resist, not wanting to weaken Thierry. His hips rocked languidly against Thierry's backside, ratcheting the tension between them slowly. Thierry writhed against him enticingly, but Sebastien kept the pace deliberately slow and sultry. There would be other chances for fast and hard. Tonight he wanted the tenderness of this warm, sleepy coupling.

The mood seemed to work for Thierry as well, because within minutes he climaxed over Sebastien's hand, his clenching passage triggering the vampire's orgasm as well. Withdrawing his fangs and licking at the wounds to heal them, Sebastien kissed the nape of Thierry's neck, just behind his ear. "Sleep now," he urged, his slowly softening cock still buried in his lover's body.

Thierry nodded, the connection between their bodies relaxing him enough that he could finally let his guard down and truly rest.

VINCENT PACED the confines of the holding cell in the depths of Milice headquarters, the incessant crossing and recrossing of his arms betraying his nerves even more than his inability to sit still. "Surely the battle's over by now," he said finally, turning to face Eric, the only other occupant of the cell. "Why haven't they come for us?"

"Because even if the battle is over, we're hardly top on their priority list," Eric replied calmly. "They have to see to the injured on both sides, deal with the other wizards they captured—the ones who are going to actual jails as opposed to here, where Marcel can deal with us on his own. But first he has to report to the president and probably to Parlement about the battle and whatever transpired there. I don't think Serrier would let them take him alive, but either way, his fate has to be reported. They haven't forgotten about us, I promise."

"Easy for you to say," Vincent said uneasily. "You were working for them all along. When they get around to dealing with us, you'll be released. But what about me?"

Eric rose and went to Vincent's side. "Marcel's a fair man," he began, his arm going around Vincent's shoulder and drawing him toward the cot where he had been sitting. "He'll listen to what you did and take it into consideration. And I'll vouch for you, something I won't be doing for anyone else."

"They'll want to separate us," Vincent predicted.

"They might," Eric agreed, "but it will only be temporary if they do. I don't know what influence I'll have, but I'll use every bit of it to make sure you get out as quickly as possible. We can work out some kind of bond agreement, maybe, especially if I agree to be responsible for you."

"You think I'll have to stand trial."

Eric shrugged. "I don't know, but I think it's likely. Not because Marcel will want to see you punished, but because he can use you—and Monique for that matter—as a way to finish discrediting Serrier entirely. If even his supporters were deserting him, then he was truly a madman, not someone working for true change."

Vincent nodded slowly. "That makes sense. I'd be willing to testify against him if that would help."

"It might," Eric agreed. "All we can do is talk to Marcel when he gets here and throw ourselves on his mercy."

"You don't need his mercy," Vincent reminded his lover. "You were on their side all along."

Eric shrugged. "I might not need mercy, but I do need their forgiveness. Maybe not Marcel's, but Thierry's and Alain's. I hurt them. By changing sides, by fighting against them, by taking Alain's lover from him."

"You didn't know," Vincent reminded the other wizard.

"It doesn't make it hurt less," Eric said softly. "Alain didn't know what he'd done when he killed Danielle and the children, but it didn't make the loss less real. His fear wouldn't have been any less when Orlando was missing just because I didn't know who I captured."

"You saved him in the end," Vincent reminded him. "You just have to make sure Magnier knows that."

"We saved him," Eric amended. "I might have been able to get him out by myself, but I wouldn't have made it out without you. If Blanchet hadn't gotten me, the wizard at the door certainly would have."

Vincent smiled and kissed Eric softly. "We make a good team. Now we just have to make sure the Milice realizes it."

"We will," Eric promised, returning the kiss. "I won't let them separate us for long."

Chapter 27

THE SOUND of the cell door opening woke Eric from where he dozed against Vincent's shoulder. Even backlit, he immediately recognized Marcel's slender, erect carriage. Nudging Vincent gently awake, he rose to his feet, waiting to see what the general would say.

"Serrier's dead," Marcel began unceremoniously. "Thank you, son. We couldn't have done it without you."

Eric shrugged, as uncomfortable as he always was when Marcel highlighted his role in the war. "I couldn't have done it without Vincent," he said immediately

"So you said yesterday," Marcel affirmed. "Would you care to be a little more specific?"

"It was Vincent's idea to rescue Orlando, hoping that it would be a measure of good faith so you'd take us in like you did Raymond and Monique. He didn't know, obviously, that I was working for you at that point," Eric explained. "I'd have tried to do it anyway when Serrier decided to stake him outside, but I don't know if I would've succeeded. Given how it went down, I would've died trying to do it alone."

"I can guess why you'd want to rescue Orlando, Eric," Marcel said with a smile, "but why would you care, Mr. Jonnet?"

Vincent cringed slightly. "Please, call me Vincent, Général. As for why I wanted to rescue Orlando, it was a couple of things. I felt responsible, in a way, since I'd helped bring him in. And I grew to admire him when he didn't give in to Serrier's experiments. His body reacted, but he didn't. I'd been dissatisfied with the way Serrier handled prisoners anyway—Eric can tell you. I'd made several comments about Blanchet and his torture. And then Monique got out. And given the way the Milice reacted, I was sure she'd brought information about Orlando. I wanted out—I wanted us to get out. Serrier was getting crazier with each passing day and I wasn't willing to go down with his ship. And Orlando seemed like our ticket out. That sounds mercenary, and maybe it is, but it was the chance I'd been looking for. A way to get out and not be hunted down like a dog, either by Serrier or by the Milice."

"There's nothing wrong with self-preservation," Marcel assured the bald man, "particularly when your self-preservation also saved one of our valued operatives."

"So what happens now?" Eric asked, broaching the subject that they were all avoiding.

"You're free to go," Marcel replied immediately. "Everything you did was done in the service of the Milice in order to give us an advantage in the war. You may be asked to testify at the trials of the wizards we captured, but other than that, your life's your own again."

Eric shook his head immediately, reaching for his lover's hand. "I'm not leaving without Vincent."

Marcel sighed. "So that's where things stand," he murmured, juggling plans in his head once again. "As noble as that sounds, it won't help Vincent," he told Eric. "Regardless of your actual relationship, when it comes to a trial—and yes, both he and Monique will have to stand trial—he needs you to appear unbiased so you can talk about how he came to you with a plan to save Orlando and switch sides, preferably taking out as many of Serrier's rebels as possible in the process. If you stay here with him, you'll lose all credibility as a witness, and I don't know when Orlando will be well enough to testify on Vincent's behalf. I'll push for a plea bargain and a reduced sentence, but it will come down to your testimony. You can't appear biased."

Eric started to shake his head, but Vincent interrupted. "He's right, Eric. I don't like it, but he *is* right. It won't be forever. I'll be fine. Nobody's going to mess with me in prison."

Marcel suspected Vincent's statement was correct, but he could do this much at least. "That isn't even a worry," he promised. "I've already spoken to the Ministre de Justice because of Monique, and I feel it well within my authority to apply everything related to her to you as well. If you agree, you'll stay here as a guest of the Milice until your trial takes place. Monique's has already been scheduled to begin in about two weeks. I should be able to get yours on the docket almost as quickly. I would suggest you limit your contact, but I don't see why Eric can't come visit a friend occasionally."

Eric took a deep breath. "You know this isn't just about friendship."

Marcel smiled. "I'm not blind, boy. But I also know what we'll be up against in getting Vincent a lightened sentence or even a pardon, and proclaiming your true relationship isn't going to help that. It's only for a few weeks. Surely you can behave yourselves for that long. Now, I haven't slept in too many hours to count, so I'm going to set the ward on this door to let you leave when you're ready, Eric. I doubt anyone will come looking for either of you for several hours at least, since everyone else is even more exhausted than I am, but don't linger too long. Remember what I said about appearances."

With a flick of his wrist, Marcel adjusted the ward and was gone, leaving the two wizards alone again.

"Do you think he's right?" Vincent asked. "I mean, that it can be that simple?"

Eric shook his head, not to discourage, but to express his surprise. "Marcel's always right. That doesn't mean it'll be simple, but I think it'll come right in the end. Will you be all right here if I leave, like Marcel says?"

"I'm a big boy," Vincent replied with a laugh. "I'll be fine here, and he said you could come visit, although that might look like we're trying to get our stories straight for trial. Maybe it would be better if you didn't."

"I guess it'll depend on how people within the Milice feel about us," Eric said slowly. "Since you're here, it's not like the public or whomever would know I'm visiting. As long as the Milice wizards follow Marcel's lead, we can do whatever we want here without it being a problem. If you were in a public prison, that would be a different matter."

"Are you worried about how they'll react?" Vincent asked bluntly.

"Not most of them," Eric replied honestly. "Most of them will accept Marcel's word and move on. I'm worried about Thierry and Alain. I said some terrible things to them, in my grief and then as I started my charade. They have every right to hate me, even more for my part in taking Orlando. God, if I'd known, I wouldn't have picked him."

Vincent hugged Eric tightly as his voice broke. "We didn't have any choice," he reminded his lover. "He was the only vampire who moved away from a wizard long enough for us to pick him off."

"We could've waited for someone else," Eric suggested feebly.

Vincent shook his head. "The battle was already turning in their favor. I understand why you feel the way you do, but you know we couldn't have done anything differently at that point without either giving ourselves away or disobeying orders."

"Maybe we should have."

"Eric, stop!" Vincent ordered. "You heard the general. Orlando will recover. He and Alain are reunited. If we'd disobeyed orders, we'd both be dead and another vampire—maybe even Orlando—would've been taken anyway."

Eric knew it was the truth, but he knew what it felt like to lose the people he loved, and he hated himself for having caused Alain that grief, however temporarily.

"Talk to them," Vincent urged. "Don't let this stretch out between you."

AWARENESS RETURNED slowly for Raymond, the exhaustion of the previous days eased by—he glanced at the clock—twelve hours of sleep. Jean was warm beside him, bringing a smile to Raymond's lips. He had no idea how he had gotten so lucky, a sentiment that amused him given his initial reaction to the alliance in general and his partner in particular. Turning his head, he brushed a kiss across Jean's forehead, smiling when the dark eyes opened.

"Good morning," Raymond said, his voice scratchy from sleep.

"Good morning yourself," Jean replied. "How are you feeling?"

"Better," Raymond said. "Less tired. I could probably sleep for another twelve hours if I didn't know Marcel will need us today, but I've slept enough to face the day. How about you?"

"I don't feel exhaustion the way mortals do," Jean reminded him. "As long as I've fed, I can keep going pretty much indefinitely. And I've fed far more in the past few days than I usually would, so I'm fine."

"Good," Raymond declared, rolling so he lay facing Jean. "That means you feel well enough to finish what we started last night."

"And what would that be?" Jean asked, voice dripping with amusement.

"Fucking me silly."

Lust hit Jean hard at Raymond's words, but he shook his head. "That wasn't my intention at all last night. Now if you'd said making love to you until you screamed, I'd be glad to oblige."

Enchanted, Raymond tilted his head, meeting Jean's lips in a tender kiss. "I certainly won't say no either way," he murmured against his lover's mouth.

"We've had too many hard, fast fucks, driven by fear or instinct or magic," the vampire replied. "Monsieur Lombard told you what happens when vampires fixate on someone, but you haven't really felt that yet. It's past time you did."

Raymond shivered at the husky promise in his lover's words. The times they had come together already had been mind-blowing. To think Jean had something even more powerful in store for him was enough to have Raymond throbbing before they had even gotten started. "I'm not sure it can get any better."

Jean chuckled, the sound rubbing along Raymond's spine like warm velvet. "Trust me," he drawled. "Let me show you what it's like to truly have a vampire as a lover."

Raymond nodded, rolling to his back and baring his neck, but Jean shook his head. "Not today. You're worn down as it is and I fed yesterday. I don't need my fangs to worship you."

Surprised, Raymond pushed up on one elbow. "But I thought—"

"That I couldn't make love to you without biting you?" Jean interrupted. "Certainly I often combine the two pleasures, but just as I can feed without sex, I can make love to you without feeding."

"Then why, the first time…?"

"Because I didn't know you as a lover," Jean explained, "didn't know for sure that you really wanted me. Your blood gave me that reassurance. And then later, it just seemed to happen because we both wanted it to. But that doesn't mean I can't control myself if necessary."

"I'm feeling better," Raymond protested. "I'm sure you could—"

"No," Jean said firmly. "Not before tonight. There's no reason to take that risk." He ran his hand down Raymond's smooth chest. "Surely I can make you feel good without it."

"I just don't want you to feel like something's missing," Raymond explained.

Jean chuckled. "It seems to me you're the one feeling that way, not me."

Raymond flushed. "Well, every time we've had sex, you've bitten me."

And that told Jean all he needed to know. "Ah, but this time we aren't just having sex. We're making love."

"So does that mean I have to settle for 'just sex' if I want you to bite me?" Raymond joked, uncomfortable with the suddenly serious turn the conversation had taken.

"Raymond," Jean chided seriously. "I'm not going to bite you this morning whether we make love, have sex, or fuck like rabbits. I'd rather not make myself sick either, if it's all the same to you, and as often as I've bitten you over the past week, I'm completely gorged. Now, are you going to let me make love to you or are you going to keep arguing with me?"

Raymond's smile spread slowly across his face. "Maybe I want to make love to you instead."

Jean's eyes flashed as he pounced, pinning Raymond's wrists to the bed in an implacable grip and using the weight of his body to ensure the rest of his lover stayed in place. "You are *the most* infuriating man," he growled, body reacting to Raymond's nearness. "You're not getting your way this time."

Raymond chuckled and undulated slowly beneath Jean, deliberately rubbing their erections against one another. "I don't think I'll be complaining about the results," he assured his lover. "Not if it involves the two of us naked in bed." He paused as his hands slid down Jean's back to squeeze the tight muscles of his buttocks. "Or on the couch. Or up against a wall. Or anywhere else, as long as we're together."

"I didn't know you were such an exhibitionist," Jean teased, beginning to grind down against Raymond. His lips coasted over his lover's features, tracing every line, every chiseled plane, until he found Raymond's mouth. He could tell from Raymond's reactions, even without tasting his blood, that his partner would not complain if he simply slipped between the widespread thighs and took the wizard now. They would no doubt both enjoy it, but he had made a promise to himself to take his time with Raymond, to cherish his partner the way he had not done with Karine, so that Raymond would never doubt his place in Jean's life, never doubt the devotion he would show every day but never speak of. It was not his way, particularly, nor did he think Raymond would want to hear it. Feel it, yes, but his lover was not comfortable with expressed emotions.

Jean was right, Raymond thought dimly, as he sank deeper and deeper into their kiss. He really had no idea what it meant to be the center of a vampire's attention. Until now. His lover stoked the passion between them with consummate skill, tender caresses interspersed with the occasional harder squeeze, gentle kisses alternating with little nips—just enough to keep him constantly off-kilter, not knowing what would come next.

His head spun from the multitude of assaults on his senses. Jean seemed to have sprouted an extra set of hands and probably lips as well, for surely one man could not touch him in so many places at once. Raymond wanted to reciprocate—but every time he tried, the vampire caught his hands again, pressing them back against the mattress with that low growl that made Raymond shiver in delight. Finally, he accepted that Jean was determined to make this about him. Deciding to enjoy it now and return the favor later, the wizard relaxed onto the bed, moving at Jean's direction as his lover worked him over from head to toe.

Eyes closing, Raymond let himself float, every touch taking him higher, every kiss reaffirming his place at the center of Jean's life, just as monsieur Lombard had foretold. Before long, he found himself begging, pleading for more of Jean's touch, for more of his kisses, for more of *him*. He expected the vampire to give him that infuriating, inviting grin and refuse, but apparently the devotion monsieur Lombard had spoken of went beyond the surface, leading the vampire to indulge his lover's every whim. The moment Raymond's entreaties began, Jean slid up over the larger body of the wizard beneath him, soothing him, reassuring him. Taking him with such tenderness that Raymond was left gasping with it. Never before had a lover lingered over him this way. Never before had a lover put his pleasure at the forefront of their intercourse with no thought for anything else. Never before had a lover made him the center of the universe.

And Raymond understood why monsieur Lombard could assure him with such confidence that Alain would never question whether he had made the right decision in accepting Orlando as his Avoué.

Heart pounding in his chest, he bit back the plea that sprang unbidden to his lips as his release caught him unaware. Panting through his climax, his always-busy mind analyzed this new, sudden desire to be Jean's treasured one and stifled it as suddenly as it had arisen. He could not saddle the chef de la Cour with a dark-horse wizard whose loyalty would probably always be in question. History might eventually decide in his favor, but that would do Jean no good now. Even with a wizard's longer-than-usual lifespan, he did not expect to see his own rehabilitation. Having the Cour know about him would be bad enough, but with all the new responsibilities that would come with the equal rights legislation and the integration of the vampires into wider society, the last thing Jean needed was the millstone of Raymond's disgrace around his neck. He would be content to live in the vampire's shadow, supporting him quietly, easing what burdens he could and doing his best to avoid any problems arising from his past.

Stroking Jean's hair as the vampire climaxed inside him, Raymond brushed his lips across his lover's, waiting for the dark eyes to open. "Whatever the future brings," he said softly, "I want you to know now that I'll always support your position as chef de la Cour. In le Jeu des Cours, in Parlement, within l'ANS or in the media."

It was not a declaration of love, but it was a declaration of devotion, far more than Jean had ever expected from his reserved partner. He returned the kiss tenderly. "And the chef de la Cour will always support you," he replied.

Raymond started to shake his head, but Jean overrode his protests. "Think of it as just another way you're protecting my position. After all, if someone says something about you, that reflects on me."

Raymond frowned, wondering if perhaps he should cut the ties between them for Jean's sake, but even as the thought crossed his mind, he knew he would never be able to walk away like that. For good or for ill, he was bound to Jean in ways that went far deeper than either of them would probably ever understand.

"Soit."

Chapter 28

THIERRY TOSSED restlessly on the bed, images of the day before and of other battles haunting his sleep. Time after time he found himself facing Eric, drawing his wand, casting the spell that would end the other wizard's life, only to hear Orlando's shout a moment later that Eric had saved him.

A hand on his shoulder roused him finally. "Thierry, what's wrong?"

Thierry blinked a couple of times, bringing the vampire's concerned face into focus. "I need to find out what happened to Eric," he said slowly. "I know Marcel sent him back to Milice headquarters, but in all the rush yesterday, I didn't check to see what Marcel decided to do about him."

"The spy?" Sebastien verified.

Thierry nodded. "I owe him an apology, if nothing else," he admitted. "I believed he'd switched sides. Of everyone in the Milice, I should have known he'd never do such a thing, even in his grief, without there being another reason. I shouldn't have doubted him."

"You had an awful lot of evidence to prove his change of loyalty," Sebastien pointed out, instinctively defending his partner even against himself. "I don't think anyone will blame you for believing what he and Marcel wanted you to believe."

"I still owe him an apology," Thierry insisted mulishly. "And I'm not going to be able to relax until I've made it."

"Well then," Sebastien said with an indulgent shake of his head, "let's get up and go to Milice headquarters so you can. I had other plans for the morning besides politics, but I can wait."

"What plans?" Thierry asked as he pushed out of bed, noticing the stickiness between his legs for the first time. Memories of their late-night sleepy lovemaking rushed back, his cock twitching at the thought.

Sebastien grinned as he watched Thierry's body react. Grabbing his lover in a strong grip, he tumbled the wizard to the bed, stroking the swelling erection firmly. "Getting better acquainted with this."

"How much better acquainted can you get?" Thierry gasped.

Sebastien's grin widened. "I still don't know what it would feel like inside me."

"Putain," Thierry groaned. Images of flipping Sebastien beneath him, of Sebastien above him riding him, flickered through his mind, eroding his need to see Eric. "Don't say things like that to me when my mind is supposed to be on duty."

"It's up to you," Sebastien said, and it was. He understood and respected Thierry's need to settle things with his former friend, to see if anything could be salvaged of that relationship or if the intervening years had changed them beyond recognition. He knew as well that he would have far more of Thierry's attention if they waited until Thierry was no longer distracted. Given how long it had been since Sebastien had let anyone top him, an attentive, focused lover would not be a bad thing at all.

Forcing himself to sit up, to ignore the temptation of Sebastien's offer, Thierry scrubbed at his face with his hands. "I need to go see Eric," he repeated, as much to convince himself as to convince Sebastien, "but I can't go like this."

Sebastien smiled. "There are other ways of taking care of your problem, in case you've forgotten. Come on, join me in the shower and I'll help you take the edge off while we're getting ready. Then later, when you aren't distracted anymore, we can see about making love properly."

Thierry let Sebastien lead him into the bathroom and the small cubicle that only fit both of them if they stood very, very close together. Thierry was not complaining. Sebastien turned the water on hot and hard, washing away the remnants of the previous night's loving and the day's exertions. He squirted some soap into his hand, rubbing it over Thierry's chest, then down to circle the wizard's cock. With a groan, Thierry leaned back against him, trusting Sebastien to support his weight.

Shifting so he could lean against the wall while Thierry leaned against him, Sebastien rubbed provocatively against his lover's buttocks as he stroked the growing length of the wizard's erection. Before long, Thierry was moaning and pushing back against him hard, making Sebastien wish they had time for more than a quick hand job in the shower. While it would be easy enough to push Thierry against the other wall and drive deep into his welcoming heat, his lover had not agreed to that—and Sebastien did not want to push, knowing how important it was to Thierry that he make amends with his friend. Increasing the strength of his grip and the speed of his movements, he worked Thierry's cock until it disgorged its load.

Thierry collapsed against the vampire in repletion, his breath harsh as he panted through his climax. "I swear, I come harder every time you touch me," he murmured when he could speak again. He turned slowly in Sebastien's arms, bringing their lips together in a tender kiss. "Now, lover, what can I do for you?"

Sebastien shook his head. "I'll be fine until we get home. I'd rather wait to come until you're inside me." He squirted more soap into his hand, offering the bottle to Thierry. "Now get cleaned up. Your friend is waiting."

Thierry had no idea how Sebastien found the patience to wait, but then, the span of his existence had surely taught him many things. "As soon as we get home," Thierry promised, finishing his shower and going to get dressed.

He figured the promise of Sebastien's ass would be enough to keep him moving through the day's ups and downs. He was sure there would be many.

Sebastien followed more slowly, willing his erection to subside. The promise in Thierry's voice was distracting, and Sebastien wondered if he had made a mistake in deciding to wait. He did not really want to meet this Eric for the first time with a tent pole in his pants. Whatever came of the meeting, that was not the impression he wanted to give. It was too late now, though. Sebastien recognized the determined set of Thierry's shoulders. There would be no luring him back to bed until after he had satisfied his sense of duty. Shrugging into his clothes, Sebastien resigned himself to ogling his lover and fantasizing about things to come until they could be alone again.

As Thierry finished getting ready, he mulled the upcoming meeting over in his mind. He had so many things to say to Eric, so many things he needed to hear from his former friend. He hoped they would be able to put the last two years aside and pick up the threads of their friendship. Glancing back over his shoulder to where Sebastien dressed in silence, Thierry contemplated his partner. His lover. He had no idea how he was going to explain the vampire to Eric. Not that he expected Eric to disapprove. It was just… complicated. He sighed. "You don't have to go with me," he offered after a moment. "There's no reason for you to ride all the way in to Milice headquarters, only to sit around twiddling your thumbs until I'm done meeting with Eric. You could just stay here and relax."

Sebastien raised an eyebrow slowly. He had expected many things of this meeting, but not to be excluded entirely. "I don't mind riding in with you," he replied simply. "Besides, it'll let me check on Orlando and the rest of the vampires. And I'd like to meet your friend."

Thierry shrugged. "I'm not sure we're friends anymore," he admitted softly.

"All the more reason for me to meet him," Sebastien growled, the thought of anyone hurting his lover enough to make him bristle. "You shouldn't see him alone if you aren't sure how he'll react."

Thierry doubted Eric would hurt him. That would hardly help his contention that he had supported the Milice all along. It was more a question of whether they still had anything to say to each other. It annoyed him to no end, though, that Sebastien still seemed to doubt—after everything they had been through together—that he could take care of himself. "If you're determined to go with me, let's go then," he said tersely. "It'll take us at least thirty minutes at this time of day to get into town, maybe more."

The ride into Milice headquarters passed in tense silence, neither man wanting to start an argument in public nor to back down from his position. When they arrived at the base, Thierry went immediately to the holding cells to find out where Eric was.

"The general released him during the night," the wizard on duty informed Thierry apologetically. "The other one he was with is still here, but Simonet left early this morning. I don't know where he went."

"I guess the conversation will have to wait for another day," Sebastien commented as they walked back toward Thierry and Alain's office.

Thierry shook his head. "He won't have gone far. Under the circumstances, it's hardly safe for him to just wander around. Why don't you go check on the vampires in the infirmary while I see if I can find him? That way, once I'm done, we can leave right away. I have a promise to keep," he added, waggling his eyebrows in a bid to lighten the mood between them.

Sebastien's scowl suggested the levity was not appreciated. Giving up with a shrug, Thierry marched out, heading toward the Salle des Cartes without looking to see if Sebastien followed him.

The wizard on duty there was more helpful. "Yes, he came through here before he left. Général Chavinier sent word that he could leave but to make sure he had a repère in case we needed to find him. He's...." the wizard looked at the board. "It looks like he's just down the street."

Thierry thanked the woman and left, ignoring the little voice that insisted he should at least let Sebastien know where he was going. His own repère would show on the map if his partner was that determined to find him.

He found Eric in a little café three blocks down, cigarette forgotten between his fingers as he stared out into space. "That stuff'll kill you. Not even magic can cure cancer," he said as he took a seat at the next table.

Eric snorted, snuffing out the cigarette but not meeting Thierry's eyes. "It's the first one I've had in months. The first time in months I've felt like I could sit down and have one."

"I know the feeling," Thierry agreed, searching for a way to continue the banter or to broach the subject that hovered between them with all the subtlety of a bull in a china shop. Nothing came to mind, so he let the silence stretch.

A waiter came by to take Thierry's order, breaking the tension for a moment as Thierry ordered an espresso.

"I guess you want an explanation," Eric began after the waiter left.

"If you have one to give me," Thierry replied.

Eric sighed, knowing that as hard as this was, it would be the easier of the two conversations he would have to have before he could leave the last two years behind him. "You remember what it was like when the war first broke out. The immediate reaction was that it would be over in a matter of weeks. And then it suddenly got worse and it looked like we might lose before we ever started. Raymond hadn't defected yet and we didn't know that he would. Serrier had some really powerful, resourceful people on his side and we couldn't seem to stop the chaos from spreading."

"I remember." And he did. After the initial widespread incredulity that Serrier would try such a stunt, the government had scrambled to pull together a cohesive reaction to what was then a much better organized force. They had ordered the formation of the Milice and asked Marcel to head it. He had agreed, but it had taken time. Time Serrier took advantage of to gain an upper hand.

"And then Danielle and the kids died."

Thierry flinched. "You know—"

"It was an accident," Eric interrupted. "I know. I've always known, but I was grieving. Marcel came to me, pointed out that my grief—and the ability to blame it on Alain—would allow me unquestioned entry into Serrier's ranks. Even as just a foot soldier, I'd have access to some information, and anything would be better than what we knew then. I saw the opportunity to avenge their deaths, but I balked anyway because I would have to blame Alain for what I did. Marcel and I went round and round, but in the end he convinced me it was the only way Serrier would believe me."

"You could've told us," Thierry insisted.

"I wanted to," Eric replied, "but Marcel was adamant. No one could know, because if you knew, you might react differently if you met me in battle. That would have jeopardized my position in Serrier's army. It was as much for my protection as for the information I'd be able to get."

"We could've killed you!" Thierry protested. "We would have if we'd met you in battle."

"It was a chance I took. I didn't expect to survive, to be honest. I just wanted my death to mean something," Eric admitted. "I never expected to see the end of the war. I probably wouldn't have if it hadn't been for Vincent. I might have gotten the drop on Blanchet when I was trying to save Orlando, but I couldn't have taken out the wizard guarding the door on my own."

"Orlando told us you helped him escape. Did you…?" Thierry trailed off, not sure how to put the question into words.

"Aguiraud and Serrier experimented on him, and Blanchet tortured him," Eric said, anticipating the question. "I witnessed more of it than I would've liked, but I didn't participate other than to carry him back and forth to his cell when Serrier had him bound. He's quite a man. Is Alain happy with him?"

"As happy as I've ever known him," Thierry replied immediately. "How did you know?"

"Orlando told me. Not at first, of course, but once he realized who I was, he was determined to convince me to change sides. He even spouted that code we developed."

Thierry chuckled. "That sounds like Orlando. So I guess he convinced you."

Eric shrugged noncommittally. "He had help. Vincent was already trying to convince me. Not that I needed any convincing on the inside, though I couldn't have done it until it was a question of Orlando's life or death, but I couldn't let Serrier stake him out. Did he get his ring back?"

"Alain has it," Thierry answered. "I don't know if he's thought to give it back to Orlando yet or not. You took a huge risk bringing it to your apartment. It showed up on the locator map immediately. Alain would've killed you if you'd been there when we arrived."

"I figured it was a repère when he parted with it so easily," Eric agreed. "It was a calculated risk on my part. I hoped you'd find the wards unchanged and guess that I hadn't really changed sides."

"If we'd been capable of thinking clearly at that point, maybe we would have, but Alain only knew one thing while Serrier had Orlando, and that was that his lover was missing. And hurting."

Eric frowned, clearly confused.

"The bond between them lets them sense each other," Thierry explained, leaving it at that. "He felt every spell, every blow, as if he were the one suffering."

Eric blanched. "I didn't know. God, Thierry, I swear I didn't know."

"I'm not the one you need to apologize to."

Eric nodded. "I'll tell them myself, the first chance I get. I don't imagine Alain will ever really forgive me, but I'll tell them anyway."

"Two months ago, he probably wouldn't have," Thierry agreed, "but finding Orlando changed a lot of things. Give it time. You might be surprised how persuasive Orlando can be. He was the first of us to truly buy into the alliance, and I don't know that we'd have made it without him insisting we all stop circling around each other and work together. And he's already inclined to like you, since you helped him escape."

"I missed you," Eric said, so softly Thierry had to strain to hear him. "Everything else got easier in time, but not that."

"Imbécile," Thierry said fondly, pulling Eric into a tight hug. "We missed you too."

The sudden roar of anger startled the two men apart and drew the attention of every patron in the café as the dark blur of a figure stormed through the door. Eric reached automatically for his absent wand, but Thierry shook his head, recognizing his lover. "Sebastien, stop," he ordered sharply, not wanting a scene in front of Eric.

Temper snapping visibly in his eyes, Sebastien settled for glaring at the dark-haired man who had dared to touch *his* wizard. "Why? Tell me why I shouldn't tear him limb from limb," he demanded.

"Eric, will you excuse us for a minute? I need to speak with Sebastien in private."

Eric nodded mutely as Thierry rose from the table and propelled a fuming Sebastien toward the restroom at the back of the café. Pushing his lover into the small room ahead of him, Thierry shut the door and glared at the vampire. "What the hell was that? You know Eric and I are just friends. If that, at the moment."

"He put his hands on you," Sebastien snapped.

Thierry rolled his eyes. "Are you jealous?"

"No," Sebastien replied defensively.

Thierry snorted. "Sounds like it to me. You were my first male lover. You know that. You are my only lover. Eric isn't any threat to you. He wouldn't have been even if he hadn't been spying for the Milice. He's the little brother I never had. And that's all."

"That's not what it looked like to me," Sebastien muttered.

Thierry sighed. "I'm going to go finish my coffee and my conversation with my *friend*. If my *lover* would like to come join us, I'd be glad to introduce you. Otherwise, go back to Milice headquarters and I'll meet you there when I'm finished."

Turning, he walked back out of the restroom, leaving Sebastien feeling like an immature idiot. Taking a deep breath, the vampire took a moment to calm his raging emotions and went back into the café to meet his wizard's "little brother."

Chapter 29

"WHO WAS that?" Eric asked Thierry when the blond returned to the table.

Thierry sighed and shook his head. "That was Sebastien Noyer," he said as if that introduction were self-explanatory.

Eric arched an eyebrow, waiting for the rest of the explanation.

"My partner in the alliance," Thierry continued.

Eric waited in silence, knowing there had to be more for the other man to have reacted the way he did.

"My lover."

Eric's eyes widened and he blinked a couple of times in surprise. "Your...?"

"Yes, his lover," Sebastien interrupted, his hand settling possessively on Thierry's shoulder as he rejoined the other two men. "Get used to it."

"Sebastien," Thierry scolded. "Enough. Sit down and act like a civilized man or go home."

Sebastien subsided, taking the seat next to Thierry, his hand remaining visible on the wizard's arm.

Eric glanced back and forth between the two men, trying to make sense of the signals and words and reconcile them with everything he thought he knew about Thierry.

"There's more to the alliance than just the vampires fighting beside the wizards," Thierry began, not sure exactly how to explain the partnerships to someone completely outside the alliance. "We discovered—"

Next to him Sebastien snorted.

"Fine," Thierry amended, "we *stumbled upon* a magical resonance between wizards and vampires. The right combination creates a partnership, a bond between the two that protects the vampire from sunlight, helps restore the magical equilibrium, increases the wizard's power, and who knows what else. Every time we think we have it down, some other aspect pops up to surprise us."

"That explains the alliance and the oddities Serrier noticed after the vampires started fighting with the Milice, but it doesn't explain the bit about you being lovers," Eric replied, mind racing as he reconciled this revelation with everything he had seen but not understood in the last month of the war. "Last time we talked, you were straight and madly in love with your wife."

"She left me," Thierry revealed, his voice tight. Sebastien's grip on his arm tightened supportively and his glare returned, directed firmly at Eric for bringing up such painful memories. "She said she wouldn't take second place in my life to anything, even to the war. She died in an attack at Versailles in the middle of October."

"I'm sorry," Eric said automatically, still not sure how Aleth's departure and death had led to Thierry's current situation, but the vampire's intimidating stare suggested he should just accept reality rather than trying to get to the bottom of it. Maybe he could ask one of the other wizards later.

Thierry shrugged. "What's done is done. The important thing is that we've discovered this incredibly powerful bond that can exist between wizards and vampires. Sebastien is my partner now, just as Orlando is Alain's. You may even find a partner of your own now that you're back with us."

Eric frowned, thinking of Vincent still confined in a holding cell in Milice headquarters. "I already have a partner," he said discouragingly. "I'm not interested in finding another one."

"I can't imagine it being a necessity anymore," Sebastien commented. "Not that there won't still be advantages, obviously, but if a vampire or a wizard doesn't want a partner, I see no reason why they would have to have one. It *is* a more involved commitment than we originally imagined."

Thierry had to agree with that, though he did not regret making it. "That will be a decision for Marcel and Jean to make," he declared after a moment. At his side, he could feel Sebastien's tension increasing as they talked. Rising to his feet again, he offered Eric his hand. "It's good to have you back."

Eric shook Thierry's hand warmly. "It's good to be back. I've spent the past two years feeling dirty. It's nice not to feel that way anymore."

Sebastien nodded curtly at the dark-haired wizard as he and Thierry left the café. The moment they were out of Eric's line of sight, he spun Thierry against the wall, kissing him frantically. Thierry shivered beneath the onslaught, letting Sebastien work out his tension. When the vampire finally lifted his head, Thierry stroked his face tenderly.

"You left without telling me," Sebastien accused.

"I needed to talk to him alone," Thierry repeated. "I needed to explain about the alliance, the partnerships, even if I didn't get that far before you arrived. I needed to hear his explanation for the last two years. He wouldn't have talked to me as openly as he did if you'd been there the whole time, and I needed to know."

"You hugged him," Sebastien pointed out petulantly.

Thierry rolled his eyes. "You've seen me hug Alain before, and that never bothered you."

"Alain has a brand on his neck," Sebastien replied as if that explained everything. "He doesn't have eyes for anyone but Orlando."

Thierry shook his head at the idiocy of that statement. "As if I have eyes for anyone but you," he scoffed. "You've been feeding from me for a month, sharing my bed for the past two weeks. Have you really not figured out that I love you?"

The shell-shocked expression on Sebastien's face suggested he had not.

"I think we need to go home," Thierry declared. "I obviously haven't been doing something right."

"I did offer to let you top," Sebastien replied hoarsely, his anger and jealousy fading completely in the face of Thierry's unexpected declaration. His head spun and his heart pounded fiercely in his chest. Thierry loved him.

Thierry grinned. "Whatever it takes to convince you I want to be with you. Not Eric, not anyone else. Just you."

"This is one hell of a place to say such a thing," Sebastien groaned, vividly aware of the cars whizzing by behind him on the busy street, the pedestrians who glanced at them before turning their heads and hurrying on their way.

"Milice headquarters are two blocks that way," Thierry gestured, not making any real move to pull away. "I have an empty office. With a lock on the door."

"Lube?" Sebastien asked hopefully.

Thierry lost it, laughing so hard he had to hold his sides. The ridiculousness of the situation was just too much for him. Sebastien looked less than amused, though, so he straightened a little, poking his lover in the side. "Lighten up," he instructed.

Sebastien caught the wandering finger, lifting it to his lips and nipping at it, his fangs barely grazing the surface. "Careful," he warned, only half-teasing. "You're just asking for a spanking."

That just made Thierry laugh harder. He finally pushed away from the wall and grabbed Sebastien's hand. "Come on, lover. We're making a spectacle of ourselves."

Sebastien moved enough for Thierry to start walking, landing a light slap on his retreating backside. Not enough to hurt. Just enough to prove he was only partially teasing.

The blow startled Thierry and brought more laughter to his lips, the relief of Serrier's death, Orlando's rescue, even his own declaration to Sebastien bringing a lightness of heart and mind which he had not known since the war began. Grabbing Sebastien's other hand as well, he walked backward down the street, drawing his lover with him toward Milice headquarters, the look on his face a mixture of levity and desire.

Consciously letting go of his anger and jealousy, of the need to mark Thierry as his own so that Eric and anyone else who looked would keep their hands to themselves, Sebastien let Thierry lead him down the street. By the time they reached Milice headquarters, the only desire that remained was the need to feel Thierry moving beneath him, confirming the words he had said so lightly outside the café.

Once they were inside and in Thierry's office, Sebastien latched onto his lover, hands digging into the muscles of Thierry's ass as he held his wizard tightly against him, humping the thigh that pressed between his legs. "We need something we can use as lube," he ground out. "I can't take you dry."

"I really ought to start carrying some in my pocket," Thierry joked, rubbing lasciviously against Sebastien. "Let me check Alain's desk. Maybe he has some, or at least something we can use. As often as we've caught him and Orlando in here, I'd bet there's something."

Sebastien chuckled, releasing his grip on Thierry long enough for the blond wizard to search Alain's desk. After a moment, Thierry pulled out a tube, grinning as he tossed it to Sebastien.

"It's expired," Sebastien said after a moment.

"How expired?" Thierry asked, already imagining the conversation he could have with Alain.

"A couple of months."

Thierry snorted. "That's nothing. I'm sure it's fine. Although I intend to talk to Alain about keeping expired products around."

Sebastien rolled his eyes at his lover's mirth, but the good mood was catching, lightening the jealous tension the vampire had still felt moments earlier. "We should warn him of the consequences of harming a vampire."

"Somehow I think Orlando might object if we did that," Thierry retorted, coming around the desk and returning to Sebastien's side. "Now, I think you said something about me topping this time?"

Sebastien grinned and backed toward the couch, the tube clutched in his hand as he did. When his knees hit the edge of the couch, he dropped the lube on it and started pulling off his clothes, tossing them any which way in his eagerness to get rid of them. Thierry followed suit immediately until they both stood nude, the wizard still waiting for the vampire to take the lead.

Lying back, Sebastien handed the tube to Thierry, stroking his cock with one hand while the other reached lower to play with his sac and lower still as he waited for his lover to decide what to do with the gel. Thierry stared, mesmerized, for a moment before squirting enough of the clear lotion onto his hand to coat it completely.

"Half that would be enough," Sebastien teased lightly as Thierry knelt on the couch between his legs.

"I'm not taking any chances," Thierry husked, the mood turning suddenly serious as he considered what he was about to do.

Sebastien smiled, catching Thierry's hand with his and guiding it between his legs. "I'm so hard with just the thought of it that I won't need much foreplay. Take your time stretching me and I'll be ready to go."

Thierry groaned. "Don't say things like that to me if you expect me to retain any sort of control," he warned.

Sebastien was tempted to continue teasing until he pushed Thierry past his limits, but that would be better saved for another time, when it had not been four hundred years since he last bottomed for a lover.

Remembering how Sebastien had prepared him, Thierry worked a single digit into the furled ring, gasping in surprise at how tightly it squeezed him. "Putain, Sebastien, how long's it been?" he asked as he watched his lover consciously relax beneath his touch. Even then, the pressure on his finger was surprising.

"A while," Sebastien replied, not wanting to summon Thibaut's ghost now when he was celebrating a new love.

"Four hundred years?" Thierry ventured, marveling again at the depth of emotion that bound a vampire and his Avoué. He had seen it with Alain and Orlando, but Sebastien's devotion had driven home to Thierry the amazing power of that bond. He could barely comprehend the power of the bond that already bound him to Sebastien. The thought of something even more powerful simply boggled his mind.

"Give or take," Sebastien agreed, pushing his hips up so Thierry's finger slid deeper into him. He did not want to talk about Thibaut, especially not now.

Thierry let the matter slide, his attention drawn by Sebastien's wantonness. Focusing again, he worked his finger in as far as it would go, crooking it as he searched for his lover's prostate. A long low moan told him when he was successful, bringing a smile to his face and making him feel like the world's best lover.

Wanting to care for Sebastien as well as his lover had cared for him, Thierry slid his finger back and forth across the little bump, working it relentlessly until Sebastien started thrashing beneath him. "Enough," the vampire groaned. "Add another finger."

Rubbing his fingers together to make sure they were still slick enough, Thierry withdrew and then pushed back inside with two digits, crossing them to better work his way into the tight passage. Sebastien writhed on the couch, hips pushing up against Thierry's hand. Lowering his head, the wizard caught the leaking tip of his lover's cock in his mouth, sucking on it lightly as Sebastien had done for him so many times. The slightly salty flavor surprised him, but he forged ahead, scissoring his fingers to loosen the tight entrance as he drew more of the thick shaft into his mouth. He could not swallow Sebastien down the way the vampire could him, but he did his best, hoping to provide as much pleasure as Sebastien had always bestowed.

If the vampire's reaction was any indication, he was succeeding.

Sebastien's cock seeped bitter fluid, coating Thierry's tongue, distracting him enough that he forgot to keep shunting his fingers inside his lover's body. Sebastien could not decide whether Thierry was an astute enough lover to realize what he was doing to the vampire by leaving his fingers there, buried deep but unmoving, or if the wizard was simply so lost in his first blow job that he had completely lost track of his surroundings. Either way, the effect was devastatingly arousing, leaving Sebastien trembling between the dual caress. He tried to lie still rather than thrusting into Thierry's mouth, but eventually he could no longer resist the need to move, his hips lifting into the sucking mouth, his movement jostling the fingers inside him.

Thierry choked slightly and had to pull back as Sebastien's thrust drove his cock deeper into Thierry's throat. He knew it was possible to take the entire length, but he was clearly not going to manage tonight, so he pulled back instead, licking at the weeping slit, then moving down the long shaft to the heavy sac beneath. To his delight, Sebastien's thrashing increased. "Feel good?" he husked.

"Too good," Sebastien groaned. "I'm going to come too soon if you keep that up."

"Why too soon?" Thierry teased. "Why not come twice? You manage to do that to me most nights."

"Because I don't want to wait that long to feel you inside me," Sebastien replied honestly, reaching for Thierry's shoulders and drawing his lover up over him. He ran an appreciative hand down the length of Thierry's erection. "I want you to fill me up and give me a long, hard ride. And at the end of it, I want us to come together."

Thierry gasped at the hot hand surrounding his shaft. He fumbled for the lube, knowing he needed to coat himself before he tried to fit inside his lover's body, but Sebastien's attentions made anything except climaxing on the spot difficult.

Sebastien spread his legs and slid a little farther down on the couch. "Come on, lover," he urged. "Inside me now."

Running a shaky hand over his shaft, Thierry positioned the tip of his cock at the tight iris.

"Push the head in," Sebastien instructed hoarsely, feeling the welcome pressure. "Go on. You won't hurt me."

Thierry was not so sure about that, but he did as Sebastien directed, rocking against the furled portal until it opened to him, letting him into the tight inferno. "Putain," he groaned. "You feel so good."

Sebastien panted through the initial burn, reveling in the sensation of being stretched, being filled again after so long. "Slowly," he rasped. "Just rock slowly until you're all the way in."

Thierry nodded, his hips beginning to pulse in a repetitive rhythm. "Tell me if I hurt you."

Sebastien smiled even as he gasped again, the thicker shaft stretching him now. "You won't. Just keep doing what you're doing."

Thierry was not sure how long that would be possible, the heat and pressure of Sebastien's body enough to have him trembling with need already, and they had barely started. He gritted his teeth and swore to himself he would make Sebastien come before he did, whatever it took.

For his part, the joy of being filled again after so long had Sebastien already teetering on the edge of release. He had preferred giving himself this way to Thibaut, letting his Avoué take with his body while Sebastien took with his fangs, but it was a gift he had not given since.

Until now.

Now, his heart once more engaged, he could relish ceding control as he had only done with his Avoué since he was turned. Urging Thierry to lower his head, he captured his lover's lips, his tongue plundering Thierry's mouth with the same rhythm that the wizard's cock plundered his body. His hands flew over Thierry's back and buttocks, urging him on now that the initial burn of penetration had passed.

Thierry threw his head back as he fought for control, his hips pistoning faster as he strove to drive Sebastien over the edge. The motion offered his neck perfectly, a temptation Sebastien could not refuse. His fangs drove deep. The hot wash of blood rushed through his body and heart as he read, now with perfect clarity, the emotion he had previously been afraid to identify for fear he had misunderstood. Now, in the aftermath of the war and all that had occurred in the last twenty-four hours, the love Thierry had so casually professed washed over Sebastien with a clarity he had never tasted before, as if the ups and downs of the past day had erased all the fears, doubts, hesitations—everything except a devotion to rival anything Sebastien had ever tasted in Thibaut's blood.

Sucking harder, he let his climax take him, the emotion he shared now with Thierry enough to take him over the edge. It only took the first squeeze of his passage around the wizard's cock before Thierry joined him in release.

Licking gently at the wounds his fangs left behind, Sebastien cradled Thierry against him, ignoring the way the leather stuck to his sweat-damp skin. When Thierry finally lifted his head again, Sebastien cradled his lover's face in his hands. "I didn't say it earlier, but I should have," he said slowly. "I love you too."

Thierry smiled. "I hoped since you didn't go running for the hills that you felt the same way."

Sebastien chuckled and stroked Thierry's hair. "I do. I've only felt like this one other time in all of my years."

Thierry nodded slowly, fingers searching for Sebastien's. "I made myself a promise after Aleth was killed that I would do whatever it took to win the war, even if it meant a mark like Alain's. At the time, I saw it as a sacrifice." He took a deep breath. "I don't see it that way anymore."

Sebastien's eyes closed with regret. "I can't mark you that way. I'm sorry."

"Why not?" Thierry asked, trying to keep his head and not let the jealousy that wanted to explode within him come out.

"Because the magic of the Aveu de Sang only works once," Sebastien explained. "You'd feel all the pain of the brand without either of us gaining any benefit from it. I didn't think it mattered after Thibaut died because I couldn't possibly feel about anyone the way I felt about him, but I was wrong. If I could, if I were free to bind myself that way again, I wouldn't think twice about it, but all I can do is make a verbal promise to stay with you for as long as you want me."

"I want you," Thierry swore. Disappointment tore at him, but he reasoned that most couples never had the assurance of the kind of magical bond the Aveu de Sang represented. At least he knew Sebastien was capable of that kind of commitment. If he said he would stay, Thierry would be satisfied with that. "I'll always want you."

Chapter 30

"WE SHOULD go see Marcel," Raymond said eventually. He was reluctant to leave the comfortable warmth inside the heavy curtains that enclosed Jean's bed, where they had dozed after making love.

"We should," Jean agreed, making no move to rise, "but he was as exhausted as you were. It can wait a little longer."

"I just feel like we need to—"

Jean stopped the words by the simple expedient of kissing his wizard until Raymond subsided against the dark sheets. Jean rolled onto his elbow so that he hovered over his lover, claiming his mouth with a feral intensity that surprised them both. Panting harshly, he lifted his head.

"Where did that come from?" Raymond asked. "Not that I'm complaining. I just want to know how to get that response again."

"You were talking about leaving."

"Not leaving you," Raymond pointed out. "Just going back to duty. With you."

Jean shrugged and rubbed the back of his neck sheepishly. "That doesn't seem to matter where you're concerned. My instincts are screaming at me to keep you here. Permanently."

Raymond smiled. "That might make it a little difficult to run the Cour."

"You'll have to do better than that if you want me to let you go," the vampire declared, rolling Raymond onto his stomach and running tender hands down the strong back, lingering over the jagged scar. He bent his head and ran his tongue along its length, anointing it as if he could heal it as he healed his bite marks. Beneath him, Raymond shivered delightfully, reigniting the desire that simmered just below the surface of Jean's controlled façade.

"I didn't say that," Raymond said immediately, relaxing into the caress, spreading his legs slightly when he felt Jean's hips settle against his backside, slotting the vampire's cock into Raymond's crease. "Just that we'll have to move eventually."

Jean hummed in his throat. "Later. After I show you how grateful I am to have you at my side, acting as my voice of reason when I need it."

Raymond started to demur, to point out that it had taken monsieur Lombard's intervention to dissuade Jean from his destructive impulse to kill Edouard on the spot, but his lover's mouth distracted him, moving down his spine to the swell of his buttocks. The tips of Jean's fangs grazed his skin, not enough to even leave marks, but definitely enough to send another shiver of desire along Raymond's nerves. He wanted to beg Jean to bite him—there, anywhere—but his lover had been adamant that morning about not feeding before nightfall, and that was still some hours away. Instead he pushed back against the vampire's lips, wanting, needing more contact.

Jean might have smiled at Raymond's eagerness had he been able to concentrate on anything other than the musky smell of his lover's desire. As it was, he had only one focus: wringing more of the delightful squirming and delectable sounds from his wizard. Parting the muscular cheeks with his thumbs, he nuzzled between them, pulse pounding as his actions garnered another wanton groan from Raymond's lips. Turning his attention to the tight pucker he had so thoroughly plundered only a few hours earlier, he swiped his tongue across the sensitive skin, wishing he could truly taste its full flavor. He settled for burying his tongue deeper, sucking eagerly at the crinkled skin as Raymond writhed on the bed beneath him.

Raymond whimpered. As much as he would never admit to it later, there was no other word to describe the sound that escaped his lips when he felt Jean's mouth on him. He was no blushing virgin, but neither did he have a string of notches on his bedpost. His devotion to his research had driven away the few lovers in his past before they could begin to get creative in their lovemaking, and so this was a new pleasure to him. With someone else, he imagined he would feel intensely the vulnerability of his position, but that feeling did not even register now. This was Jean above and behind him, his affable, determined, masterful vampire who had proven already that he would never hurt Raymond and who, when Raymond let him have his way, could absolutely blow his mind. Fear no longer entered the equation between them, and so Raymond could simply experience the indescribable pleasure his lover bestowed upon him with none of the nervousness he might have otherwise felt. "M-more," he stuttered, trying to get his knees under him so he could press back against Jean's mouth.

Strong hands moved to Raymond's hips. Jean helped him adjust his position until his knees were directly beneath his chest, his arms braced on the bed as he rocked back and forth, trying to get Jean's tongue deeper inside him. Wordless cries fell constantly from his lips now, all coherency stolen by the emotions assailing him, as Jean began to actively fuck him with his agile tongue. In and out, in and out, until Raymond could do nothing but hang his head between his elbows, panting and begging and moaning. He could not even have said what he needed. He just knew he needed something.

The sudden cessation of sensation made him cry out in protest, but before the sound had even resonated through the room, Jean's cock replaced his tongue, driving deeper than it ever did before. It plunged all the way inside, burning Raymond from the inside out, leaving him feeling hollowed out, burned up and built anew, claimed from the tips of his toes to the top of his head, until he existed for only one purpose: to love the man behind him with every fiber of his being.

Then Jean's fangs pierced his skin at the top of the terrible scar that traveled the length of his back, and Raymond cried out deliriously, his entire body clenching. Jean's movements never faltered, driving the wizard higher and higher until he sobbed his release a second time. His body said he was done, but the magical connection between them had snapped into place—pushing his mind further and further until his senses were glutted with lust and love and magic and need, and it all exploded out of him in a rush, stealing his consciousness.

Jean felt Raymond go limp beneath him as he climaxed, Jean's body shaking with the power of his release combined with the flavor of Raymond's orgasms in his blood. Only when Raymond did not stir beneath him did Jean realize it was more than simple satiation keeping his lover still. Withdrawing carefully, he licked the wounds on Raymond's back to seal them, then rolled his lover to his side. The wizard's features were slack, his breathing still harsh but slowing. Jean nuzzled Raymond's neck, waiting for the hazel eyes to open. Finally, slowly, they did, the emotion stealing Jean's breath.

Words hovered on his lips, but they had already said all he dared to say earlier, so he settled for kissing his lover tenderly, letting that contact speak what he could not.

"We need to go see Marcel," Raymond said after a moment, uncomfortably aware of how low his usual shields were, how close to the surface his emotions were.

Jean shook his head. "We need to sleep some more. We can go see Marcel in a few more hours."

Raymond wanted to protest, to bring up duty, but the bed was warm and safe and Jean was pressed up against him, holding him like he never intended to let the wizard go. Insisting was just too much work. With a soft sigh, he let his eyes close again, forced his mind to settle, and drifted back off into sleep.

"YOU LOOK better than the last time I saw you," Marcel commented when Raymond and Jean entered his office some hours later.

"So do you," Raymond replied. "It's amazing what twelve hours of sleep will do for you."

Marcel glanced at the clock. "Just twelve hours?" he teased lightly, enjoying the flush that rose to Raymond's cheeks and the smug smile on Jean's face. That was one of his boys taken care of. Now he had only to settle the other three, although if he read the situation with Eric and Vincent correctly, that had taken care of itself already.

Raymond considered several different possible replies to Marcel's teasing—but every one of them could have been turned into more fodder, so he simply turned to Jean and waited for the vampire to bring up the reason for their visit.

Taking pity on Raymond's unease, Jean addressed Marcel, drawing the general's attention. "Have you had a chance to look into a venue for the *judicium*?" he asked. "I know you've been busy, but if we hold the rogue for long, we'll have to find a way for him to feed, and I don't know that we want to open that can of worms."

"We can use one of the courtrooms at the Palais de Justice tomorrow night," Marcel replied. "Tell me about the *judicium.*"

"It's a trial, just like any other," Jean explained, "but instead of a jury, the Cour assembles and makes its decision based on information presented by the *accusator.* As chef de la Cour, I will preside and enforce the decision of the Cour."

"And what kinds of decisions does the Cour usually render?" Marcel inquired.

"There are only three penalties: banishment, incarceration, or extinction."

"Incarceration?" Marcel questioned. "What about feeding?"

"No feeding," Jean said coldly. "If that's the sentence, he'd go into hibernation, like Orlando did. When the sentence is up, he'd be reanimated— if someone is still around who can. I only know of one case where the malefactor was actually reanimated."

"You don't find that harsh?" Marcel inquired.

"If they ran afoul of the Cour, that's their fault, not mine," Jean insisted. "Every vampire knows the penalties for violating vampire law."

"It gives some validity to the concerns for integrating vampires into our legal system, though," Marcel mused. "We don't have the death penalty— and I don't see the legal system accepting your version of incarceration, either."

"All the more reason to have the *judicium* as quickly as possible then," Jean declared. "The *extorris* will face vampire law and the consequences of his actions. Any sentence a French court would impose would be a drop in the bucket compared to the length of a vampire's existence, and I will not have him on the streets to threaten us again."

"That will work now, before the equal rights legislation goes for a vote," Raymond agreed, not completely comfortable with this vindictive facet of his lover's personality, "but what about after? These are issues we're going to have to address, and the Conseil des Ministres is going to look to you and Marcel for the answers."

Jean snorted, meeting the general's eyes in amusement as they remembered their last conversation about that illustrious group of politicians. "This isn't an everyday problem," he insisted. "In the four hundred years I've been chef de la Cour, this is only the second time I've had to convoke a *judicium.*"

"But what about all the little infractions that might land someone in our courts but wouldn't trigger a *judicium*?" Raymond asked. "We talked about the limits of vampire law when the rogue started his killing spree."

Jean shrugged. "I don't have all the answers," he admitted, "but at the moment, I'm primarily concerned with this infraction. Once we've dealt with the *extorris* I'll think about the rest." Seeing the concern on Raymond's face, he added, "We will deal with it. We'll hammer out all the details logically and coherently so that if the issue ever arises, the Cour and the rest of society will both be well served by the process, but I don't intend for the *extorris* to be a test case. He's not representative in any way of vampire society and I won't have him held up as an example. We'll deal with him inside the Cour as we always have."

"What do you need from us in order for the *judicium* to go forward?" Marcel asked, heading off the incipient argument. Raymond was right, but Marcel had dealt with stubborn men in the past and forcing the issue now would not help the vampires, the Milice, or any of them in the room at the moment.

"Sebastien will need to talk to Orlando," Jean said. "As *accusator*, he'll be the one responsible for presenting the situation to the Cour. Honestly, all Orlando has to say is that he saw Edouard at any time while he was in Serrier's hands. Not rendering aid to a vampire in need is comparable to hurting another vampire in the eyes of our law."

"He could argue that he didn't realize what they were doing to Orlando," Raymond warned, "or that he believed it was in Orlando's best interest to change sides."

Jean snorted. "Not after what he said openly when we captured him. He made his opinion of Orlando and the situation quite clear."

"Sebastien just has to bring that up," Raymond maintained.

"This is the Cour, not a jury with no experience in le Jeu des Cours. They'll see through his lies," Jean insisted. "Enough of them were there when we captured him to make sure the others know what he said, what his attitude was."

A knock on the door interrupted them.

"Come in," Marcel called.

To everyone's surprise, Alain and Orlando came in, both of them still looking more than a little wan, but the smiles on their faces and their intertwined fingers telling Jean everything he needed to know.

"You said to come in tonight for the *judicium*," Orlando reminded Jean when he saw the question in his friend's eyes.

"We postponed it until tomorrow," Marcel apologized. "We just finished talking about it, but with everyone exhausted, we were afraid Sebastien wouldn't have time to prepare."

"Sebastien will be your *accusator* this time," Jean explained, remembering the last time he had convoked a *judicium.* "You'll need to talk to him so he can present the case tomorrow night."

"What will happen to the rogue?" Alain asked, anger still very close to the surface despite nearly twenty-four hours spent sleeping, making love, and feeding his vampire. Orlando was safe now, but Alain wanted the ones who hurt him to suffer the tortures of the damned. Blanchet was out of his reach now, but he would make sure the rogue paid the ultimate price as well.

"That will be up to the Cour," Jean replied, "but their options are banishment, incarceration, and extinction."

"That's too good for him," Alain spat. "He should suffer the way Orlando suffered."

Orlando laid a soothing hand on Alain's arm. "It's over, Alain," he said softly. "They can't hurt me anymore, and torturing Edouard won't make me get better any faster."

"It might make me feel better," Alain grumbled, thinking about the days of panic and grief as he suffered alongside Orlando through the strength of their bond. Jean sent him a sympathetic smile.

"He'll be executed," Jean assured the blond wizard. "Most of the Cour heard the filth he was spewing yesterday, but even those who didn't will take one look at Orlando, hear that the *extorris* did nothing to stop it, and will make their decision. This is as cut and dried as the last time we called the court into session, when we dealt with Thurloe and his crimes. There is only one punishment for that kind of abuse."

"He never actually touched me," Orlando warned Jean, "not like my bastard maker."

"Did he see you?" Jean countered. "Did he know they were hurting you?"

"He laughed in my face when they tried to make me drink someone else's blood and realized I had an Avoué," Orlando remembered.

Alain's and Jean's faces tightened.

"That alone will see him destroyed," Jean promised.

"I wish I believed that would make me feel better," Alain admitted. "I don't like feeling this vindictive—but I look at Orlando and I remember how he suffered, and I want to tear the rogue limb from limb myself."

"It's hard to believe in the rule of law when the victim is someone you love," Marcel agreed, "but that's why we have laws. So that calmer heads rule our angry hearts."

"I spent the last two years fighting for the rule of law," Alain said, "but I'm glad the vampires will deal with this, not the French court. I want to see the bastard burn."

"He will," Jean promised. "As Orlando's Avoué, you might even be allowed to help us see to it."

Orlando looked at Alain sadly, understanding the anger all too well, but knowing as well how that emotion could eat him from the inside out. He shook his head. "I don't want any part of it this time," he informed Jean. "It didn't help when I watched Thurloe turn to ash. It only made me angrier that his destruction didn't heal all my wounds. Knowing the *extorris* is gone will be enough for me this time. I don't want the anger. I have too many other things to focus on."

Alain was torn. He wanted to watch the rogue burn, to see with his own eyes that the threat was ended. But he did not want to disappoint Orlando, and he sensed his lover wanted to move on rather than lingering over the past. He would have to see what the following night brought.

Chapter 31

AS THEY left Marcel's office, Orlando slipped his hand into Alain's. "You know I'll be fine, Alain," he said softly. "You can let it go now."

"I just hate that they hurt you in the first place," Alain protested.

Orlando smiled, squeezing Alain's hand gently. "It's not an experience I'm eager to repeat either, but I'd far rather devote my time and energy to loving you than to hating them."

"I want to do the same," Alain admitted. "I know revenge is empty. Killing the wizard who killed Edwige and Henri didn't make me feel better. I just feel so helpless. I almost lost you and it took a turncoat to save you."

"Are you sure?" Orlando asked. "Not that he saved me, because he certainly helped me escape, but that he really is a turncoat?"

"What else could he be?" Alain demanded.

"Marcel's spy."

The new voice entering their conversation startled both men. Alain's expression tightened as he turned to face the voice that had once been as familiar as Thierry's, which he had not heard in two years. "What are you doing running around loose?"

"Alain," Orlando scolded. "Eric saved me. At least give him a chance to explain."

"Explain what? How he kidnapped you and set you up to be tortured for four days?"

"It wasn't like that," Eric protested. "I didn't know who he was or anything about the partnerships. I was given an order to capture a vampire. I had to follow those orders or I'd have been tortured, maybe even killed myself, and I was under orders from Marcel not to let that happen. If I'd known who he was, I wouldn't have taken him. I never meant to hurt you."

"That isn't what you said before you defected," Alain reminded him angrily.

"After Danielle and the kids died, I went a little crazy," Eric defended himself, "and when I started to calm down, Marcel approached me, suggesting I use that grief, that craziness as a way to get Serrier to accept that I'd change sides. Everything I've done since then has been so I could stay far enough in his good graces to feed Marcel information."

"Orlando could have been destroyed because you wanted to stay in Serrier's good graces," Alain spat.

"And Eric got me out before that happened," Orlando interrupted. "Why don't we find somewhere for you to talk that isn't the middle of a hallway where anyone could walk by? And while we're doing that, you can both calm down and stop being defensive."

Neither wizard had an answer to that, but Alain started walking toward his office, taking Orlando's suggestion. He did not really want to fight with Eric. However much it galled, he owed the other wizard his gratitude for helping Orlando at the end, even if he was also responsible for Orlando's capture in the first place. He paused outside his office, the rather distinctive sounds inside stilling his hand as he reached for the knob.

"Maybe we should find somewhere else to talk," Orlando suggested, a droll smile on his face. "I doubt Thierry and Sebastien would appreciate our interruption at the moment."

Eric's eyes widened. "I don't have any desire to disturb them," he said quickly. "One run-in with that vampire is enough for today!"

Orlando laughed. "We vampires do tend to be a rather possessive bunch when it comes to those we care about," he agreed. "Is there another room we could use, Alain?"

"There's a conference room down the hall."

Gesturing for Alain to lead the way, Orlando deliberately kept himself between the two wizards. When they reached the room, he walked inside but stayed on the threshold. "Now," he said sternly. "I'm going to step outside and you two are going to clear the air between you. I'll come back in ten minutes and I expect you to be done acting like sulky boys."

Both wizards stared at him in shock, but he simply stepped back into the hall, leaving them alone. Neither of them spoke for a long minute, followed by another. Finally, Eric broke the silence, spreading his arms. "I'll give you one free shot. You deserve that much after everything I put you through."

Alain glared for a moment, thinking of all he had suffered in knowing that his actions had ended the lives of three innocents and driven his good friend to change sides, of the anguish he had felt while Orlando was missing. His hand closed around the wand in his pocket, fingers clenching reflexively as he imagined all the ways he could take revenge, but magic seemed somehow impersonal in the face of an incredibly personal pain. Releasing his wand, he took a step closer, his fist lifting to strike a blow that would knock the bigger man backward even if it did not send him to the floor.

He started to swing, all the anger, frustration, pain, grief welling up inside him again, searching for an outlet. He could tell Eric saw the blow coming, but he did not flinch, did not try to avoid it, and that was enough to stay Alain's hand.

Collapsing into a chair, a deep scowl on his face, he glared at his former friend. "Just tell me the truth, for God's sake. What really happened?"

Taking the seat next to Alain's but keeping a respectable distance, Eric scrubbed at his face with the palms of his hands. "I'm not sure where to start," he admitted, raising apologetic eyes to meet Alain's gaze. "I mean, I already told you the gist of it. Marcel heard the stupid things I said in my grief and approached me with the idea of using that to insinuate myself with Serrier."

"But why didn't you tell us?" Alain demanded. "It's killed me the past two years believing I'd not only done the unthinkable but had also driven you to Serrier's evil because of it. You could have told us."

Eric shook his head. "I wanted to. I told Marcel I'd do it on one condition—that he let me tell you and Thierry. He refused. He said I couldn't afford for anyone to know because you might do something, or not do something, that would give me away if you knew. If I was going to take the risk, I wanted to last as long as I could. If Serrier found out, not only would he kill me, depriving Marcel of that source of information, but he'd also be that much more suspicious of any new spy."

"You walked in there alone. You're either incredibly brave or incredibly stupid."

Eric shrugged. "I went fully expecting to die, despite Marcel's orders to stay alive. I just hoped I could take a few of them down with me and help Marcel in the process."

"And yet here you are," Alain said. "What happened?"

Eric shook his head. "Vincent happened. I would never have expected it and I didn't go looking for it, but I found someone to watch my back. Without his help, I know I wouldn't have survived and I'm not sure Orlando would have. I'd have tried to get him to safety, but time was running out. Serrier had already decided to execute him at dawn, and then there was the sudden change in locations. When we finally reached his cell and got him loose, Blanchet found us. If I'd been alone, he might well have finished me off before Orlando could escape. Even if he hadn't, the wizard guarding the door would have if I'd been alone. I owe Vincent my life, and we probably both owe him Orlando's, because that's how Orlando escaped."

His anger slowly dissipating, Alain chuckled a little, glancing toward the door. "I know all about not expecting it. It doesn't seem to matter, though. When it happens, it happens. Tell me about Vincent. I didn't really know him before the war started."

Eric quirked an eyebrow. "I don't really know how to explain it. We've known each other from the moment I joined Serrier's side. He was assigned to keep an eye on me, although that's not what he called it. We became friends, even partners in the war effort, leading attacks together, that sort of thing, but that was it. And then about a month ago, I guess, maybe not even that, something changed. It was right after the attack on Sainte-Chapelle. It felt like I was seeing him for the first time. We ended up together that night and everything changed. He started opening up, talking about switching sides. And then Serrier ordered us to get a vampire. We did, but that was the final straw. It was just a question of finding the right moment so we could get him out and escape ourselves."

Alain's mind raced as he compared Eric's descriptions to his own experiences. "Samhain," he said softly. "When the Rite d'équilibrage went wrong and wild magic escaped. We knew it wreaked havoc within the alliance. I guess it makes sense that it would strike in Serrier's camp as well."

"What do you mean?" Eric asked, tensing slightly.

"The elemental magic latched onto Thierry," Alain explained. "Raymond and I managed to get him free, but we were so worried about him that we didn't end the Rite correctly. A huge vortex of wild magic spun completely out of control and it latched onto several of the partners in the alliance that we know of. Between partners, it manifested as sex magic, rough sex in at least a few of the cases. It sounds like it hit you and Vincent as well."

The thought that what he felt for Vincent might somehow be a side effect of some magical vortex and not his own emotions struck Eric in the gut. He shook his head in automatic denial. "No, it's not like that. It's not some freak magical thing. He risked his life to help me get Orlando out, to help us get out."

"Calm down," Alain said soothingly, the rawness of Eric's response more convincing of sincerity than any reasoned explanation. "The magic might have been the catalyst, but it can't sway your emotions. You know that. It's the same with the partnerships. The blood magic creates a resonance that's incredibly powerful, but whatever the catalyst, the reactions of the people involved are still their own. Adèle hates her partner, despite the partnership bond."

"Thierry mentioned a magical resonance between vampires and wizards," Eric said slowly, still trying to assimilate everything Alain had told him, "but he didn't really explain it."

Alain smiled ruefully. "I don't think any of us can explain it, not really. It started with Orlando and me, I guess. We discovered that my blood would let Orlando walk in the sunlight and not get burned. But it's so much more than that. We made promises to each other that enhance the effects between us, but even with other pairs, we've seen additional effects. I swear I've learned more about magic since the alliance formed than I did in all the time I spent learning about it as a child. And there's still so much we don't know."

"So tell me what you do know," Eric requested. "If it's somehow spun outward to affect Vincent and me as well, I'd like to know what we're talking about."

"I don't think it has," Alain insisted, the need to reassure Eric overriding the last of his acrimony. "What you felt was just the wild magic getting loose, and it's been contained again. The partnership bonds are something entirely different. The resonance between partners can increase a wizard's strength exponentially, but we have no idea what the limits of it are.

We know it keeps a wizard's magic from working on his or her own vampire. But there could be so much we still don't know. It boggles the mind. And I know that it brought me new love and new hope when I'd given up on ever having either again."

"It doesn't bother you to have that much magic mixed up with your emotions?" Eric asked, remembering how he had given up hope after Danielle died only to find it again in Vincent. "Thierry mentioned that you could sense what Orlando was feeling when Serrier had him," he added remorsefully.

Alain shook his head. "Maybe the partnership bond sped up my realization and acceptance of what I feel for Orlando, but you know magic can't force your feelings. There's no such thing as a love potion. If you feel something for Vincent, no matter how it started, it's real. As for sensing his emotions, at least I knew he hadn't been destroyed."

Eric was surprised at how much Alain chose to downplay what he must surely have suffered while Orlando was being tortured, but since it appeared Alain was disposed to forgiveness, Eric would not dwell on it anymore. He had other things to worry about. He knew Alain's comment about his feelings for Vincent was true, but away from the dark desperation of the last weeks of Serrier's rebellion, he also felt himself questioning the ability to finally let go when he had never expected to want to move on. "I expected to die as a spy in Serrier's ranks," he murmured. "And now that I suddenly have my life in front of me again, it doesn't look anything like the one I left behind."

"It's a new world," Alain agreed. "All you have to decide is what you're going to make of it."

"I think that'll depend on what kind of deal Marcel can work out for Vincent," Eric admitted. "I can't envision a future without him."

Alain smiled. "I know the feeling. Trust Marcel. He's a wily old fox. He'll find a way to make everything come right."

"We did some pretty horrible things," Eric reminded Alain. "And Vincent didn't have the assurance that he was doing it as a means of helping the Milice. I could at least attempt to justify my actions as a means to an end."

"And that will make the difference when you go before the court," Alain replied with complete confidence. "Serrier and his followers believed the means truly did justify the ends. The fact that you never quite succeeded in believing it is what separates you from the rest of them. Raymond switched sides for the same reason, and we couldn't have won the war without his assistance and insight. Don't count your contribution—or Vincent's—short. I wouldn't have survived losing Orlando, if that's any consolation to you."

"Ten minutes are up," Orlando interrupted, opening the door and coming back inside. He took a moment to examine both men carefully. "Well, there isn't any blood, so I guess that's a good sign."

"I didn't even swing at him," Alain informed Orlando self-righteously. "Besides, I don't want anyone near my blood but you."

Orlando did not even try to resist the desire to kiss his lover. He bent over completely uncaring of their audience as he captured Alain's mouth with his own, nipping gently at the bottom lip until he could taste just a hint of copper.

"He didn't even shout at me," Eric added when the two men separated. He would never have believed anyone who told him that both Thierry and Alain would find new loves, much less with vampires, but he could hardly deny the proof before his eyes.

"I'm in trouble now, aren't I?" Orlando asked. "With you and Thierry and Eric all ganging up on me?"

"Sebastien won't let Thierry gang up on you," Alain said with utmost confidence.

Eric snorted. "Does he really have that much influence on our hothead?"

Orlando laughed. "I think they're pretty much both hotheads, but Alain's probably right. Sebastien won't want to share Thierry's attention with anyone for a while."

"And you're comfortable sharing Alain's?" Eric asked, not sure where the difference lay.

"He knows he'll never have to share my attention for long," Alain explained, tipping his head to draw Eric's attention to the brand on his neck. "The ties that bind us go far deeper than any legal contract or any spoken vow. He can't feed from anyone but me."

"And what do you get out of it?" Eric inquired.

Alain's smile lit the room. "Orlando."

Chapter 32

"ARE YOU ready to go?" Angélique asked David as he sat on the edge of the hospital bed, dressed again, but still looking wan. The medics had assured them both, however, that he was out of danger and could heal as well at home as in the ward.

"Are you sure I won't be an imposition?" David asked for the tenth time at least.

For the tenth time at least, Angélique replied, "Of course I'm sure. François set everything up for you so all you have to do is rest and recover until you're well again. It's been some time since I last needed to cook, but I haven't forgotten how. And if you don't like what I make, we'll have something delivered."

"Are you—?"

"David," Angélique interrupted, her voice heavy with warning. She sat down next to him and kissed him, cradling his face between her hands. "You took care of me when I needed it, after the *extorris* killed Jean's friend. Let me take care of you now."

David had no chance to reply before the medic came in with last minute instructions and an offer to transport them to their destination. Angélique accepted before David could protest and gave the address of Sang Froid. After reminding them to call if David experienced any new symptoms or reversal of his progress, the medic drew his wand and cast the displacement spell to send them home.

As soon as they arrived at Sang Froid, Angélique insisted on helping David undress and tucking him into her bed. When he was settled, she bustled around the room, checking to make sure everything was organized the way she wanted it. She smiled softly to see some of David's clothes in her drawers next to her own garments. Even knowing it would only be temporary, it gave her a small thrill to have him with her for the time being.

"How are you feeling?" she asked, perching on the edge of the bed, level with his waist. Now that they were alone, she allowed herself the luxury of touching him—something she had limited while they were in the infirmary, not sure how David would react if others came in and saw them. As she waited for his answer, she trailed her fingers up his bare arm, lingering at the crease of his elbow.

"Fine right now," David replied, voice breaking a little as Angélique worked her wiles on him. He recognized the intent behind her actions, though he was not sure she did, but her past had lost its power to haunt him when he had watched her fighting to save his life.

"Good," she purred, her fingers walking slowly up his arm to his bare shoulder, tracing along the edge of the duvet covering his chest. "I have a treat for you, if you're interested."

David's body was certainly interested, his cock hardening and his nipples peaking beneath the heavy comforter. "What treat?" he asked hoarsely.

"The last time I decorated myself with henna, I did it for me. Tonight, I want to do it for you."

David bit back a groan at the seductive image. "You don't have to do that," he insisted.

Angélique smiled. "I know, but I want to. And then tonight we'll sleep side by side, and in the morning you can explore all you want. Just lie back and watch, knowing that no one will see these tattoos but you."

David's eyes darkened, pupils dilating with lust as he rolled to his side so he could see her better. She left the room for a minute, coming back with everything she needed to prepare the henna. When the paste was ready, she pulled the cheval mirror from its place near the wall, repositioning it so she could look into it to check her strokes while still giving David a clear view.

The duvet slipped from his shoulders as she made her preparations. Coming back to his side, she pulled it up so he would not catch a chill, but he caught her hand before she could pull away, lifting it to his lips and tracing the henna marks permanently imprinted on her skin with his tongue. Her eyes closed in anticipation of feeling that same exploration on other parts of her body tomorrow morning.

When David finally released her fingers, Angélique's stomach was churning with desire. She took a few steps back, just enough to be out of his reach, and began slowly divesting herself, scarf and blouse first before removing her skirt, shoes, and stockings. When she stood before him in nothing more than a lacy bra and panties, she walked back to the bed and kissed him once more. "When I was in the harem, I didn't have any choice in whom they painted me for, but tonight I do. Tonight I'm painting myself for you."

David was tempted to say to hell with the tattoos and simply pull her into bed and ravish her now, but after all the tension between them because of the unassuming marks, he hoped this would finally lay all the negative associations to rest. He settled for trailing his fingers along the edge of her bra strap where skin and fabric met, his thumb brushing lightly over one cloth-covered nipple. "I can't wait."

Angélique backed away with a smile on her face, stopping when she stood in front of the mirror again. Unfastening her bra and dropping it to the floor, she reached for the brush and dipped it in the henna, tracing over the fading tattoos with careful strokes. She could feel his eyes on her, devouring her bare skin covered with the thin greenish-brown lines. As she redid each decoration, she could feel her skin heating, glancing at him periodically to make sure he was watching, understanding the tacit admission in her recreation of the existing marks. These adornments were—had always been—for him.

David's eyes stayed fixed on every seductive move of the vampire's hand, his gaze a caress as he imagined following each stroke with his fingers, his lips, his tongue. His temperature went up with each dip of the brush into the thick paste, with each pass of the bristles across her pale skin. "You're beautiful," he whispered. "Absolutely perfect."

Angélique's expression softened as she looked up from her work. "Not yet," she replied, "but with your help, I will be soon."

David's face conveyed his confusion, but Angélique just shook her head as she worked her way lower, across her stomach to the top of her panties. Satisfied with the decoration to the front half of her body, she found a clip from her dresser and swept her hair up onto the top of her head. "Now it's your turn," she explained, coming to the bed with the henna kit in hand. She handed him the brush and turned her back to him, the long expanse of skin on offer. "Paint me as you wish."

"I've never done this before," David protested.

Angélique shrugged. "You'd never been bitten by a vampire before the alliance started, either. There isn't any trick to it, I promise. Just paint the henna on in whatever design is pleasing to you. It doesn't have to be a traditional pattern, or even a pattern at all. When you're painting a lover, it's the experience itself that matters."

"Is that what we are?" David asked, hand shaking slightly as he dipped the brush and began to work, painting a long, thin stroke down the center of her back, over every vertebra, until he reached the edge of her underwear. Feeling daring, he edged them down so he could continue the line to the top of the crease between her buttocks. Her head turned, drawing his attention as he froze, afraid he had trespassed, but she simply held his gaze as she shimmied slightly, working the silky swath down and off.

"I hope we will be," she answered honestly, completely unselfconscious in her nudity. For the moment, her body was the canvas of a joint work of art.

David was once again tempted to say to hell with the henna, with waiting, and simply pull her in bed with him. But he was still weak from his injury, and there was something unspeakably erotic about being the one to decorate her, knowing it was for his own pleasure. He wished he had the artistic talent to do justice to her beauty, but he would settle for worshiping her to the best of his ability. Dipping the brush again, he returned to her shoulder, beginning at the outer edge and working down over her shoulder blade, across her ribs, the dip of her waist, the flare of her hip, and down across the swell of her buttock. She bent forward just a little so he could continue down the back of her thigh if he wanted, but the picture she presented was too much for his control. Reaching for her, he pulled her back toward him until he could run his lips over the other, still unmarked cheek.

"Not tonight," Angélique scolded softly, stepping back out of the reach of his mouth. "Tonight you paint. Tomorrow you can touch all you want."

David nodded around the lump of desire in his throat, determined to use the paintbrush to touch her in all the ways she would not allow his fingers to do tonight. And then tomorrow, he would follow every line, explore every nook and cranny, and become her lover in truth. To that end, he returned to his pleasant task, mimicking the line he had just drawn on the other side of her body, urging her to part her legs slightly so he could follow the crease of her buttock between her thighs. She gasped when his knuckles brushed her folds, but he did not linger, so she did not repeat her injunction. The touch disappeared with the brush, returning to her shoulder again as he drew wavy lines across her back, connecting the lines he had already made.

Angélique closed her eyes, nerves humming in anticipation of where the next touch would fall. She forced herself to stillness so she would not ruin his design by jumping, but her skin tingled each time the brush made contact, sensitizing her flesh until even the most benign patches became erogenous zones. She lost track of time as she stood there, resisting the urge to pleasure herself or to turn around, straddle him, and ride them both to completion.

Finally, he set the brush aside. "What now?" he asked, voice tight with desire.

"Now we seal it and wrap it until morning," Angélique replied, handing David a bottle of spray gel. She turned to face him again, gesturing for him to start with her torso and work his way lower.

Gulping slightly at the tempting sight of her full breasts, David did as she directed, coating her chest and stomach with the sealant. When he was done, she rotated again so he could spray her back. When that was done, she gave him a roll of thin gauze to cover the henna.

He wrapped her body slowly, the delicate patterns disappearing beneath the protective covering. When he was done, he stared at her with a mixture of lust and longing that nearly broke her resolve. "Lie back and let me take care of you," she prompted when he did not move.

David scooted over in the bed so she would have space next to him as she lifted the covers and slid beneath, pressing the full length of her body to his so that the gauze rubbed against his bare chest and his cloth-covered erection rubbed against her bare folds. A soft moan escaped his lips as her hands coasted over his chest. "Relax," she urged, bending her head and kissing his collarbone. "Let me take care of you."

David let her move him as she wanted, his body putty in her hands. He might have protested when she rolled him away from her, but then her body pressed along his back and her lips found the curve of his shoulder again, sharp fangs piercing hard muscle. His back arched at the slight pain, but it subsided as her delicate hands smoothed over his chest, kneading at his nipples before moving lower to slip beneath the waistband of his one remaining garment. Then she slid that down as well, leaving him completely bare to her touch. His hips bucked forward instinctively into the channel created by her slender fingers, each suck and pull of her lips causing his cock to twitch again as if some invisible string connected them. He knew the medics had advised her to feed from him regularly to speed his healing, but this exchange did not feel at all clinical. No, whatever the side benefits, this was entirely about them, about the desire between them that nothing had been able to extinguish, not even their miscommunications and prejudices.

Angélique's hands moved with practiced precision as they layered sensation after sensation on David's body, but rather than being bothered by it, the wizard was finally able to relax and enjoy the benefits of her background. Her past was a part of her, but he had come to understand that it did not rule her. Gasping, he ground back against her, wanting to make her feel as good as he felt—but when he reached for her, she caught his hand, bringing it back to the sheets and holding it there for a moment, making it clear what she wanted without ever releasing his shoulder to speak.

Within moments, the accumulated stress and desire had built to uncontrollable levels and he climaxed in her arms, her fingers continuing to stroke as he came down from the orgasmic high. When even the aftershocks had faded, she finally withdrew her fangs, licking at the wounds to speed their healing. "Feeling a little more relaxed?" she breathed against his neck.

"Yes," he replied, turning in her embrace again. "Now, what can I do for you?"

"Nothing at all," she answered, guiding his hand to her wet folds. "Tasting what I did to you took care of me."

"But—" David protested.

"But nothing," Angélique interrupted. "You nearly died just thirty-six hours ago. Yes, I know, magical cures work faster than regular cures, but you aren't fully recovered yet. Sleep tonight, and tomorrow we'll see how you feel."

David wanted to protest again, but he recognized the tone of her voice. He could argue all he wanted. She would not budge. Deciding not to push, he let his eyes drift shut, his mind filled with images of what the morning would bring. He could easily envision peeling back the strips of gauze and washing away the henna paste to reveal the tattoos beneath. Angélique would be warm from the bath, her hair curling in wisps around her face, cheeks flushed with a combination of the steam and desire as he explored every inch of colored flesh, both the ones she had painted and the ones he had. They would end up back in bed so they could finish what they had started. Except that he already knew it would not be the end. He would not be able to make love to her in the morning and then let her go. He had no idea where they would go from here. With the war over, he feared what the future would bring. The alliance would no longer bind them together, and he worried that the concern Angélique felt at the moment would fade when his injuries healed. Would she still want him when political necessity did not dictate their partnership? He did not know the answer, but he desperately wanted it to be yes.

Next to him, Angélique shared his worries. She had no doubt what the morning would bring. She welcomed it so that she would finally know what it felt like to make love with the man who had haunted her fantasies since the alliance formed, but she had no idea what came next. David had scorned her from the moment they met—for her past, for her tattoos, for her choice of livelihood. He seemed to have set that aside in the past few days, but she did not know how much of that was political expediency and how much of it was real. She could taste more acceptance in his blood than before, and certainly his desire for her increased each time she fed, but that was not enough to guarantee them a future together. She needed more than simple desire to let a man into her life again on a more permanent basis. She wanted David there, but only if he could return her feelings fully. She suppressed a sigh as she snuggled against him more closely, resenting the gauze that kept her from feeling his skin against hers, even though she knew the payoff would more than make up for the momentary absence. She could be patient a few hours longer. Her years in the harem had taught her that.

Chapter 33

SUNRISE DISTURBED Angélique's rest, the instinctive need to hide bringing her to wakefulness even though David's blood and the closed shutters each provided plenty of protection. Rolling to her back, shivering at the loss of David's warmth, she peeled back one little strip of gauze to check the henna. It looked set, unmarred by her movement during the night. Glancing at the man still sleeping next to her, she slipped quietly from between the sheets. While he looked better than he had the day before, his face was still drawn from pain, even in sleep. She would shower while he slept and wake him when she was done, presenting him with the finished result of their combined work the night before.

Over the course of her long existence, Angélique had prepared for many seductions, some eagerly, others with much trepidation, but never had she experienced such mixed feelings as she did now, standing in her bathroom, peeling away the gauze David had wrapped around her body the night before. David already had a place in her life that no man had ever occupied, for even when she had taken lovers in the past, she had never limited her feeding to just one person—yet since the alliance began, she had only fed from one other person besides David, and then only once. To add the further gift of her body would bind the ties between them even more tightly, a step she both dreaded and desired. The night before, everything had seemed clear, her path forward obvious. Now in the cold light of day, removed from David's presence, she doubted the wisdom of what she had undertaken.

Annoyed at herself for her indecision, Angélique tore away the rest of the gauze and stepped into the shower, turning the water up as hot as it would go. She grabbed a bathing brush and scrubbed at the sealant keeping the henna in place on her skin, letting the vehemence release some of her frustration.

Gentle hands pulled the brush away from her reddening flesh. "You don't have to hurt yourself to get it off," David scolded lightly, stepping into the enclosure with her. "Soap and water will do fine." He picked up a washcloth, squirted some soap on it, and proceeded to demonstrate, running the cloth tenderly over her body, washing away the gel and the henna, leaving only the stains on her skin as a reminder of their presence. The last time David had bathed Angélique, he had kept his touch as clinical as possible, not wanting to take advantage of her while she was upset. This time, however, he had no such qualms, his hands lingering on her breasts as he washed away the henna, eventually letting the cloth drop from his hands so that his palms caressed her directly. She leaned back against him, her arms lifting over her head, opening her body completely to him. He imagined she knew exactly how that posture put her body on display, but that thought had lost its power to upset him. She was displaying herself for him. Nothing else mattered.

He took advantage of it, pressing along the length of her back as his hands explored every inch of her breasts and belly, all the way down to the triangle of curls at the apex of her legs. He was tempted to slip his fingers between them and return the favor she had bestowed on him the night before, but he wanted to finish revealing the tattoos, the ones he had painted. Turning her in his arms so he could reach her back, he could not stop his smile as she rubbed provocatively against him. "We'll get there," he promised. "I won't be able to simply hold you this time, but first I want to see our creation."

Angélique nodded breathlessly as his hands went to work on her back. She had felt him painting the designs the night before, but she had yet to actually see them, and the thought of his marks decorating her body made her stomach jump with delighted anticipation. She left her mark on him every time she fed. Now he had marked her in return. The feeling of his hands cradling her buttocks as he washed away the henna he had put there the night before sent lusty shivers through her, anticipation growing with each pass of his palms, each squeeze of his fingers. "In my harem, a girl's back had to be as elaborately, or even more elaborately, decorated than her front," she told him breathlessly, "because she always greeted the sultan or his guests on her knees with her forehead to the floor, and so his first sight of her was of her back and buttocks, displayed for his pleasure. If he liked what he saw, he would choose her for the night, thus raising her status in the harem. If he did not like what he saw, he would pass over her and pick someone else." She pulled out of his embrace and turned so he could see her back. She had sworn when she left the harem never to kneel to any man again, but that did not stop her from making the offer on her feet. "Do you like what you see?"

"Yes," David replied hoarsely, reaching for her, but she shook her head, turning off the taps and pulling away.

"Not here," she said as she stepped out of the shower. "We'll be more comfortable in bed."

She handed him a towel, intending to get another one for herself, but he pulled her back against him again, wrapping the thick material around her and rubbing her skin through it to catch all the droplets of water. "You'll spoil me," she warned teasingly. "I'll start expecting this kind of treatment all the time."

David smiled. "Maybe you should."

Angélique's eyes widened and she turned to look at him questioningly.

"Are you suggesting…?" she trailed off, not wanting to put words in his mouth.

"I don't know what tomorrow will bring, much less next month or next year," David said, "but I do know there's nowhere I'd rather be than here where I am. I'm willing to see where this takes us if you are."

"I'll still own Sang Froid, and with the war over, I need to give it my full attention again," she warned.

David nodded. "I have to hope my old job is still available and if not, I have to find a new one, so it's not like I'll be in your pocket all day every day. You and Jean have pounded it into my head that there's nothing questionable about the services you offer. You won't hear me complain about it again."

It all seemed almost too good to be true, but Angélique decided to push aside her doubts and trust in the strength of the partnership bond. It was more guarantee than she had ever had with previous lovers. "Then take me to bed and spoil me some more."

David chuckled and dropped the towel to the floor. He slid his hands into her hair, dislodging the clip that still held her long tresses off her shoulders and back. They tumbled down to curl wildly around her, dancing across her collarbones and the tops of her breasts. David lowered his head and kissed her, waltzing her back toward the bedroom without ever parting their lips.

He pushed aside the covers already mussed from sleep and lowered her onto the bed. Instead of following her down, though, he simply stood and stared at her for a long moment, taking in every voluptuous curve and hollow on her body, from the tips of her toes, up long, slender thighs, over her smooth belly and narrow waist to her full breasts, and then on to her elegant features. When he met her eyes finally, she was smiling, clearly both amused and aroused by his perusal. "Is everything to your satisfaction?" she teased.

"I don't know," he replied hoarsely. "I've only seen one side."

Laughing, Angélique rolled to her stomach, craning her neck to look down her back at those tattoos. She did not get much chance to examine them, though, before David had leaned over her, his tongue finding the first of the marks on the lower curve of her buttocks and tracing them up her back until he could reach her lips, kissing her eagerly, his tongue delving deep to claim her mouth.

She let him.

When they finally broke apart, the need to breathe and the awkward position enough to end their kiss, they were both panting heavily. David tried to roll her over, but Angélique shook her head, pushing up onto her hands and knees. "This way," she directed, "so you can see what you did to me."

David groaned deep in his chest, his eager cock sliding between her cheeks and down toward her entrance as she moved. Until she spoke, he would have said he wanted a long, drawn-out round of lovemaking to cement the bond between them permanently, but he could not resist slipping deeper into her wet folds when she pressed back against him, taking him in all the way to the root. Steadying her hips with one hand, he reached beneath her with the other to knead at her breasts, trying to take her as high as the wet heat of her body had taken him.

Much to his delight, she reared back, straddling his thighs so she could thrust down as he thrust up into her. "Look," she murmured, pointing to the mirror on her dresser. "Watch how perfect we look together."

They were quite the contrast, he had to admit, his eyes fixed on the sight of the two of them in the mirror across the room. His pale skin stood out vividly against her slightly darker flesh, the henna tattoos only adding to the contrast. In their new position, both of his hands were free to wander, and they did—over her breasts, across her stomach, and into the nest of curls, finding the hidden nubbin and rubbing at it until she cried out. With her lips parted, her fangs glistened in the lamp light that pushed back the shadows in the room, making him wish they were facing each other so she could bite him. But that could wait. Instead, he lowered his head and bit lightly at her shoulder, wringing another cry from her as his lips and fingers worked in concert to send her soaring.

In only moments, she was writhing and begging.

"Let me feel you come apart around me," he whispered, nipping at her earlobe as he spoke.

It was the encouragement and permission she needed, her release bubbling up inside her and spreading out, her contractions enough to trigger his climax as well. She shivered with delight as she felt his cock spurt inside her, the fluid hot and thick, marking her from the inside out. She sagged back into his embrace, letting him support her weight as she came down from her orgasmic high.

Passion sated, David felt the lingering weakness from his injury return to the fore. Choosing to lie down rather than fall down, he tipped them to the side, the movement separating their bodies. Angélique snuggled against him immediately, though, turning in his arms so her head rested on his shoulder. "I'll have to check with Jean and see when the *judicium* is, but other than that, we have nothing to do but rest and recover. Sleep now. I'll be here when you wake up."

"HOW ARE you feeling, Orlando?" Sebastien asked when his fellow vampire joined him in the office Alain and Thierry shared.

"Better," Orlando replied, summoning a smile. He understood why this interview was necessary, but being separated from his Avoué even long enough to tell Sebastien what he would need to know for the *judicium* tonight frayed his nerves nearly to the breaking point. The case was not as clear-cut this time as when he had last been the material witness for a vampire trial, and he knew Sebastien's presentation of the case would be critical. He just wished Alain could be with him. "A lot better than I expected to be feeling, honestly. I don't know how much of it is the partnership and how much is the Aveu de Sang, but I didn't recover nearly as quickly when I finally escaped my maker."

"The torture didn't last as long this time either," Sebastien reminded him.

"No," Orlando agreed, "but my creator never let me get as close to starving as I did this time. Either way, I'm feeling well enough to attend tonight. I didn't see Serrier fall, which is all the more reason why I need to know the vampire won't hurt anyone else."

"He won't," Sebastien replied with utmost confidence. "He's made too many enemies within the Cour. Not coming to your defense is the final straw. Now, can you tell me anything he said or did to suggest he knew what was happening to you?"

Orlando related the confrontation with Edouard when Serrier tried to force him to feed, including the other vampire's disdain for the Aveu de Sang, which had kept him sane even while it had made his captivity much more dangerous.

"So he knew you'd been separated from your Avoué," Sebastien verified.

Orlando nodded. "He was the one who told them that I obviously had an Avoué and what that meant, at least in terms of feeding and my eventual usefulness to them without Alain. He was very scornful."

"He would be," Sebastien agreed. "He clearly has no respect for any of our institutions or traditions. Which would be fine if he didn't go around hurting people. Anything else?"

Orlando shook his head. "I didn't see him again after that, but Serrier referred to him as his pet vampire. A couple of different times, he made comments about asking the rogue about something related to how I reacted or didn't react to his spells and later to Blanchet's physical torture. He might not have witnessed what they were doing, but he knew about it."

"And when he says he couldn't get to you to help you?" Sebastien inquired.

"I wasn't guarded when I was in the room where they held me prisoner," Orlando replied. "Eric and his friend managed to rescue me when they put their minds to it. The *extorris* could have done the same if he'd wanted to. He chose not to."

"And that will be the last mistake he ever makes," Sebastien declared coldly. "Go find Alain. I can only imagine it's killing you to be away from him. Jean's going to try to make an exception to the vampires-only rule tonight so he and Marcel can attend. As your Avoué, Alain shouldn't pose a problem. We'll see how the Cour reacts to including Marcel."

Orlando nodded. "Thank you for doing this. I probably could go without Alain, at this point, but I don't want to. I just want it behind me so Alain and I can go on with our future."

"Just a few more hours and it'll be over," Sebastien promised. "In the meantime, remember you aren't facing this alone. I don't know what kind of support you had the last time you did this, but this time you have the entire Milice, most of the Cour. Even more than that, you have Alain. With him at your side, there's nothing you can't face."

"I know that," Orlando replied. "It's the only thing that kept me sane this last week. He's waiting for me. I'll see you tonight."

Sebastien nodded and watched Orlando go. He could not help but admire the other vampire's collected demeanor. Sebastien doubted very many other vampires could have endured what Orlando had undergone with the same dignity.

Outside the office, Orlando walked into Alain's waiting arms. "Sebastien said Jean thinks you'll be able to attend tonight," he said without preamble. "I know it'll be hard hearing everything again, but if they'll let you, will you come with me?"

"Of course," Alain replied immediately. "There's nowhere I'd rather be than at your side, even in the midst of a vampire trial."

"I need to feed before it starts," Orlando said softly. "I don't think I can face it without that boost."

Alain suspected he would need the reassurance as much as Orlando did, given what he was likely to hear over the course of the night, but he did not voice that sentiment. His sole goal now was to help Orlando through the next few hours. Once the *judicium* was over and the sentence carried out, he could fall apart. For now, though, he had to be strong for Orlando. "Sebastien's using our office, but we could probably find an empty room. Marcel's running on a skeleton staff at the moment to give everyone a chance to recover from the final battle. We'll find an office of someone who's on sick leave."

"They won't mind?"

"We'll pick someone who will understand," Alain promised, mentally running through the list of wounded he had gotten from Thierry earlier in the day. "I'm pretty sure Caroline will still be out of commission. She won't mind if we use her office. We can go by the infirmary to check if you want. Thierry didn't expect her to be released for at least another three or four days."

"No, it's all right," Orlando said, not wanting any delays. "If you don't think she'll mind, then that's fine with me."

Alain led Orlando to Caroline's office, taking absent note of the feminine touches like the potted plants on the windowsill, but his real focus was his partner. Orlando seemed of the same mind, reaching for Alain as soon as the door closed behind them. Alain managed the presence of mind to turn the lock before everything but Orlando faded to nothingness.

His lover's lips and tongue prepared the skin on his neck. "They'll see this tonight," he warned Alain. "This one won't have time to heal."

"I don't care," Alain reminded him. "I've never cared."

"It doesn't matter one way or another most of the time, but tonight I want them to see it," Orlando admitted. "I want them reminded that the rogue didn't just threaten me, he threatened the most sacred bond a vampire can make."

"Then mark me well so they can't help but notice," Alain offered, drawing Orlando to the couch against one wall. He tipped his head back as he sat, giving Orlando complete access to his neck, indeed to his entire body if the vampire wanted. He would never deny his lover anything.

Orlando had never felt such a strong need to mark someone as he did with Alain at that moment. The brand on his lover's neck was just a start. He wanted to leave the expanse of flesh so covered with bites that anyone looking would have no doubt of Alain's place in his life. A month ago he would have fought that impulse with every fiber of his being, but Alain had given permission. Even more than that, Alain had never shied from his bite, never seen it as a mark of shame. Lowering his head, he bit deep, hot blood welling up immediately and rushing into his mouth, coating his palate with the rich bouquet of flavors that was uniquely his sustainer's. He hated the lingering fear and anger he could still taste, but only time would ease those emotions in Alain's heart. Love and desire flooded his senses, though, wiping away the other sapors. Licking the marks to close them, he moved his mouth down a couple of inches and bit down again, adding a second set of incisions.

The moment Alain felt the second bite, he knew what Orlando intended. He wondered idly how many bites would fit on his neck. He suspected he would find out. Each pinch of fangs added another layer of sensation to the ones already assailing him. Now that Orlando had finally abandoned his prohibition on combining feeding and sex, Alain found it hard to hold back. He wanted to pull away the clothes that separated them so he could reach bare skin, to make Orlando feel as good as he felt right now. He had no idea how long they had until they needed to leave for the Palais de Justice, though, and he did not want them to be late. He would have to settle for feeding now and making love later, once they knew the rogue vampire would never threaten anyone again.

Orlando's fangs in his neck had their predictable effect, causing Alain's cock to swell in his pants. He tried to ignore it, but Orlando tasted his welling desire. Shifting slightly, the vampire slid his hand down the front of Alain's shirt to his waistband, finding the zipper and undoing it so he could get a hand inside. Alain cried out when he felt the beloved hand close around his erection, drawing it out through the open placket into the cool air of the room. Soon, the strokes on his cock matched the pull on his neck, and Alain knew he would not last much longer. "Please," he begged, unable to put his desires more clearly into words.

Orlando did not need words to understand. He released Alain's neck, his body having taken its fill of blood, and lowered his head to his lover's shaft, sucking it deep instead so that Alain's release went down his throat as he came with a sharp cry.

"Less mess that way," Orlando teased, lifting his head and carefully tucking Alain back into his pants. "The sun is setting. The Cour will begin gathering. We should go."

"What about you?" Alain asked, his head spinning with amazement at the change in Orlando. His hand went to his neck, feeling the multitude of bite marks, proudly proclaiming their bond for all to see. His claim on Orlando was less visible, but he knew it was just as real.

"I can wait until tonight," Orlando assured him. "I'd rather wait until I'm inside you than settle for a quick climax now. Come on, lover. The Cour awaits."

Chapter 34

THE LIGHTS inside the Palais de Justice gave the illusion of daylight, but the denizens of the Cour de cassation were creatures of the night. Alain knew many of them from the alliance and recognized still more from the battle near the Beaubourg, but he saw at least as many whom he did not know, making him realize how much he still had to learn about the Cour and vampire culture.

As far as he could tell, he was the only nonvampire in the room. Marcel and Jean had discussed the possible advantages of having select news media there to cover the *judicium*, but in the end, they decided against it. Vampires were as protective of their rituals as wizards were.

He could feel the vampires watching him, some discreetly, some openly. He simply stayed at Orlando's side, letting proximity fill in the blanks for those vampires who did not know him or realize that Orlando had formed an Aveu de Sang. As minutes passed waiting for Jean to arrive and begin the trial, Alain noticed respect on more and more faces as word of what Orlando had suffered and survived flew around the room. Next to him, Orlando seemed oblivious to it all, standing serenely in his place as the tension in the room mounted.

A side door opened. André Perrot and Blair Nichols came in, the *extorris* held tightly between them, propelled forward by their grips on his arms rather than by his own impetus. Alain wondered if the vampire was still under the binding spells they had put on him when they captured him. It would serve the bastard right, he thought vindictively. The two guards stood the *extorris* in the defendant's box and then joined the rest of the crowd, the sour looks on their faces enough to make it clear who had their sympathies.

A moment later, another door opened and Sebastien came inside, nodding to Orlando and Alain as he moved to the prosecutor's table. Seeing the vampire without Thierry seemed odd, making Alain realize again just how completely the alliance had infiltrated their lives. He wondered how much of that would continue once the war was over. Obviously, his bond with Orlando would survive, and he suspected Thierry and Sebastien, and Raymond and Jean, would continue forward together as well—but despite all they had learned about the workings of the partnership bonds, he still did not know how much of that pull would lessen now that the magical necessity had eased. Some of the relationships had deepened to the point that the thaumaturgic bonds no longer mattered, but Alain could not say how many had not.

All noise and movement stopped when the door behind the judge's bench opened and Jean entered. He was dressed far more formally than Alain had ever seen him, though not in traditional judge's robes. The symbols of his rank hung around his neck, but even without them he radiated such power, such authority, that no one would have doubted his right to sit in that chair had he been in rags.

The Cour rose to their feet at his entrance, giving him all the respect due his position and the seriousness of their current endeavor. Jean nodded at Sebastien and Orlando, glared at Edouard, and started to gesture for the other vampires to sit when the main doors in the back of the courtroom opened. Every vampire turned, ready to do battle with whoever dared disturb them. Their eyes dropped quickly, though, every head in the room bowing, when they realized who stood on the threshold.

Monsieur Lombard strode in, flanked by Marcel on one side and Raymond on the other. "I trust you won't mind my guests joining us," he said, addressing Jean, though he already knew the opinion of the chef de la Cour.

"Not at all," Jean replied magnanimously, relieved beyond words to have this fight taken out of his hands. "Welcome, Général Chavinier, monsieur Payet. And of course, welcome to you as well, monsieur Lombard."

"I wouldn't dream of missing this *judicium*," monsieur Lombard intoned gravely. "It is the responsibility of every member of our Cour, even the retired ones, to see justice done."

And that, Alain thought, *was the rogue's death knell, whether he knew it or not.*

"Indeed," Jean agreed, "so let us begin. Monsieur Noyer, as *accusator* for the Cour, will you please lay out the charges against the *extorris*?"

Sebastien rose and moved to the center of the courtroom so everyone could see and hear him.

"The *extorris*, Edouard Couthon, is accused of conspiring with enemies of the Cour, specifically Pascal Serrier, to capture the former companion of the chef de la Cour. He is further accused of raping and murdering her. Additionally, he is accused of conspiring with Serrier to capture a vampire and of not rendering aid to Orlando St. Clair once said vampire was captured and tortured. Finally, he is accused of attempting to poison monsieur St. Clair with the blood of a mortal other than his Avoué."

The murmur that had started through the crowd when Sebastien mentioned conspiring with Serrier exploded into angry imprecations when the *accusator* stated the last of his charges, driving home to Alain once again how truly sacred the Aveu de Sang was to the vampire community.

Jean let the surge of noise die down in its own time. When it had receded again, he addressed Sebastien once more. "You have proof of these crimes?"

"I do, monsieur le chef," Sebastien replied, turning back to address the Cour again. "The body of Karine Gaudier, former companion of the chef de la Cour, was found on the doorstep of Sang Froid, clearly tortured, raped, and finally killed by a vampire."

"It could have been any vampire," Couthon interrupted, speaking for the first time. "How do you know it was me?"

"You're the only vampire in the city known to have killed anyone in recent memory," Sebastien answered coolly. "A fact you admitted within the hearing of everyone who participated in the battle we fought two days ago, where you were captured."

"I didn't admit to killing his whore."

Again the murmurs rose up in the crowd.

"Keep a civil tongue in your head," Jean instructed, face tightening. "You have the right to defend yourself, but not to insult the Cour with your vulgarities."

"I didn't admit to killing his *companion*," Edouard repeated.

"No, but you admitted to killing the woman used to poison monsieur St. Clair," Sebastien retorted. "You said, and I quote, 'Since he didn't finish her off, I got that pleasure.' Don't bother denying that. Too many of us heard you."

"I didn't know he had an Avoué until I saw his reaction to the woman's blood," the rogue sneered. "I was trying to provide what little assistance I could to a fellow vampire."

"Furthermore," Sebastien continued, ignoring the interruption from the rogue and from several vampires in the Cour who made their disbelief volubly known, "monsieur St. Clair will testify to the fact that you knew he was being held and tortured by Serrier and you did nothing to help him."

"Sniveling whelp," Edouard muttered.

Monsieur Lombard rose from his seat, towering over the vampires around him. He glanced at Jean for permission as he stalked forward to grab Couthon by his collar, hauling the slighter vampire off his feet so they were face to face. "You listen to me, boy. You think because you've killed, it makes you a man. Think again. The deaths you caused are just more proof that you aren't man enough to have the power of life and death over the people you feed from. You see our self-control as weak, but you're wrong. It takes far more power, far more maturity, to contain our instincts than to give in to them. And it takes even more courage to enter an Aveu de Sang. If there's a sniveling whelp in the room, it's you. Orlando has more than earned the title of man."

Edouard opened his mouth to respond, but before he could, monsieur Lombard turned back to his two companions. "Would one of you shut him up? I'm tired of listening to his whining."

"I will," Alain interrupted, rising to his feet. "I'm the one he's insulting when he insults Orlando."

Monsieur Lombard inclined his head deeply in Alain's direction. "My apologies. I didn't see you sitting with your Avoué."

Alain glanced in Jean's direction, quite sure they had disrupted the usual order of the *judicium*, but the chef de la Cour watched impassively, no sign of irritation on his face. Taking that for permission, Alain cast the spell, silencing Edouard again.

"Monsieur St. Clair," Sebastien said when monsieur Lombard had regained his seat, "would you please tell the Cour about your experience in Serrier's hands, particularly as it relates to the *extorris*?"

Squeezing Alain's hand for support, Orlando rose and walked to the witness box. The hitch in his stride was still noticeable enough to speak to the horrors his body had undergone during the four days he was held prisoner. "I didn't see him at first," Orlando began. "I knew he must have been there, because we had news of a vampire working with Serrier's forces. Serrier kept me locked in a cell, so it wasn't like I could go looking for him, but he had to have known I was there almost from the first. Serrier made too big of a deal about my capture."

"Did you ever see him?" Sebastien asked.

Orlando nodded, swallowing hard as bile rose in his throat at the memory. "It was probably two days into my ordeal, although I don't really know for sure. I never saw a window, and with the protection of my Avoué's blood, I don't notice the sunrise the way I used to. Serrier had been at me pretty hard, trying spell after spell on me to see what worked and what didn't, and I was exhausted, hurting, and hungry. Serrier came in with a woman and made her offer her arm, saying he knew I'd need to eat because he wasn't done with me. I refused, obviously, but he forced the matter, cutting her wrist and using a spell on me so I couldn't escape the blood she poured down my throat. When I started retching, Serrier called for the *extorris* to come explain why I was sick. He specifically said that he'd gotten the information that I would need blood from the accused."

Alain shuddered, remembering all too well the sudden pain, the different kind of pain he had felt from Orlando. The thought of his lover drinking anyone's blood, however forced, brought all his rage back to the surface, directed squarely at the vampire across the room from him. If he could have done so without outraging the entire Cour, he would have summoned fire and burnt the bastard to a crisp, but he consoled himself with the knowledge that the rogue would endure that fate as soon as the sun rose.

"Did you see him again after that?" Sebastien prompted.

"No," Orlando replied. "He made a few snide comments about the fact that I had an Avoué and then he left. Two wizards, defectors from Serrier's ranks, rescued me just before dawn on the day Serrier had decided would be my last. I didn't see the *extorris* again until today."

"Did you see anything to suggest he was in any way a prisoner of Serrier just as you were?"

Orlando shook his head. "He gave every indication of being on Serrier's side when I saw him. No signs of duress at all."

"Thank you," Sebastien said, gesturing for Orlando to step down.

The vampire walked gratefully back to Alain's side, sinking into his seat and reaching again for his lover's hand. Alain wanted to call a halt, to take Orlando home, tuck him into bed, and make love to him while he fed, but they had to see this through.

"Do you have other evidence to present?" Jean asked Sebastien, who nodded.

"A number of vampires were present when the *extorris* was captured. They agree unanimously that the *extorris* was not in any way restrained in Serrier's base and that he fought his capture violently, making very clear through his words that he was in league with the dark wizard, who deliberately targeted vampires in his attack on place Pigalle. Further, if the word of a mortal will hold any weight with the Cour, one of the Milice's spies in Serrier's ranks corroborates all the above evidence," Sebastien finished, "including that Serrier targeted the companion of the chef de la Cour on the advice of the accused and that the accused was responsible for her death, although not for the entirety of her torture."

"And the others who tortured her? And Orlando?" a vampire in the crowd demanded.

"Dead," Marcel assured them from his seat. "Monsieur Lombard rid the world of Serrier. My agent ended the life of the worst torturer while helping Orlando escape. The only one still requiring justice sits before the Cour now."

"Thank you, Général," Sebastien said, inclining his head. "The Milice assistance in this matter has greatly facilitated the process."

"Does anyone else have anything to add?" Jean asked, addressing the rest of the Cour. "Questions, evidence, or arguments?"

A smatter of shouts in support of Sebastien's statements as to what the other vampires had witnessed as well as derisive insults thrown in Edouard's direction rang out, but no one had anything concrete to add.

Jean turned to Alain. "If you'll release the silencing spell, he has the right to defend himself—but I'm warning you now, *extorris*. If you abuse the court again, you will not get a third chance."

Edouard glared as Alain released the spell. "You've already condemned me," he accused Jean, turning to face the Cour. "You've all condemned me already. I could speak for days and you wouldn't hear a word I said, so why should I waste my time and energy defending myself? You think you're making progress, but all you're doing is condemning yourself to a mockery of what we were intended to be. We're vampires, not some tame pet to follow around on a wizard's leash." Every vampire involved with the Milice shouted in protest. Jean waited for the protests to die down.

"What says the *accusator*?" he asked when silence settled over the room again.

"Guilty," Sebastien intoned solemnly.

"What says the injured?"

"Guilty," Orlando repeated firmly.

"What says his Avoué?"

Alain's eyes shot up in surprise. He had not expected to have a say in the matter, not being a vampire, but he did not hesitate. "Guilty."

"Monsieur Lombard?"

"Guilty."

"What says the Cour?"

"Guilty." The roar of voices was deafening.

"Is there anyone who would speak in defense of the *extorris*?" Jean inquired. "Anyone who would request clemency?"

The silence was nearly as deafening as the shouts had been.

"Edouard Couthon, the Cour de Paris has found you guilty of violating vampire law. You will be sentenced and the sentence will be carried out immediately. What sentence would the *accusator* propose for the crimes?"

"Extinction," Sebastien answered firmly. "Banishment would leave him free to transgress again, against another Cour, and incarceration is not harsh enough considering the deaths he caused."

Jean skipped the formality of asking each member of the Cour this time, knowing how hard it had been for Orlando to demand Thurloe's extinction the last time the Cour had sat in a *judicium* when the case was far graver than this one. Nor was he sure Orlando needed to hear Alain make the request. Instead, he simply asked, "What says the Cour?"

"Extinction," they agreed with one voice.

"Would any request a lighter sentence?" Jean had to ask, though he hoped an argument would not ensue. No one spoke.

"Edouard Couthon, you have been sentenced to be executed at sunrise," Jean declared. "Your victim will decide the means."

Orlando flinched. Even knowing the words were coming, he flinched. The last time he had pronounced sentence, he had survived a hundred years of cruel torture inflicted by the vampire he was condemning, and he had relished choosing as cruel a method of execution as he could come up with. He was a different man now. "Make it as quick as possible," he said simply, rising from his chair as bile rose in his throat. "I want no more suffering."

Jean nodded and gestured for Alain to take Orlando out. More than a little alarmed at how pale Orlando had suddenly gone, Alain took his lover's hand and led him out into the hallway. "Are you all right?"

Orlando shuddered. "I never want to go through that again. Once was too much. Twice is unthinkable. Take me home. Please."

Back inside the courtroom, Jean rose. "The sentence has been pronounced. The *extorris* will be executed at dawn, as swiftly as we can manage. Any who wish to stay as witness may do so. The rest of you are free to go with my thanks and my sincere wish that it will be many, many years before we next have to gather in such a manner. Although, if Général Chavinier has his way, we may no longer need our own courts. He asked me to end this *judicium* with the welcome announcement that our labors have paid off. The equal rights legislation goes before Parlement tomorrow morning for an up or down vote as per l'alinéa 49-3. We will know by the following morning at the latest if our bid is successful."

"It will be successful," Marcel chimed in. "The contributions of the Cour to the war effort are irrefutable, a fact I have made and will continue to make clear to the esteemed members of Parlement as well as to the Conseil des Ministres. The Premier Ministre, monsieur Pequignot, has said he will attend the debate himself to lend his weight to our cause. We have a press conference scheduled for first thing in the morning, before the actual debate, but we felt we should tell you ourselves since you were already gathered."

A cheer went up when Marcel was done speaking. The vampires began milling about, André and Blair returning Couthon to his holding cell as others began discussing the trial, the execution, the legislation. Marcel nodded to his partner and the two older men withdrew, leaving the Cour to their discussions. Raymond shook his head when they waited for him. He needed to be with Jean. He doubted anyone else could notice it, but Raymond could see the toll the *judicium* had taken on his lover. They had talked about the likelihood of this outcome and what that would mean for Jean. As chef de la Cour he could have delegated the responsibility for the actual execution, but he refused to make someone else do what he would not do himself. He wished he could do this for his partner, but the Cour would never accept a wizard dispensing justice, even Cour-declared justice. He would simply have to stay at Jean's side, the silent support he had sworn to be.

Chapter 35

"*YOU HAVE committed the one unforgivable offense among our kind. You are condemned to dissolution.*" *Jean's voice was firm but cold. He had gathered the Cour within hours of finding Orlando, summoning them to Thurloe's house to pass judgment on the spymaster. He would have preferred it otherwise, would have preferred not to have to pronounce such a judgment on any vampire, but this one law was inviolate, and it was Jean's responsibility to enforce it. "Your victim will decide the means."*

Shock crossed Orlando's features first, followed by anger and then glee. The shock and the anger Jean could understand. The glee troubled him, but he said nothing. This was Orlando's right and he would not interfere. Later, perhaps, if the youngling would trust any of their kind, he would try to influence the lad to more... positive... ways.

Thurloe, though, had no such qualms. He flew at Orlando, intending to push past the younger, weaker vampire and disappear into the night. Accustomed as he was to controlling Orlando physically, he did not consider Jean in his flight. The elder vampire moved to intercept the criminal and the two powerful beings clashed violently, Thurloe's fear adding strength to his struggles. The other vampires convoked to the judicium watched passively, knowing better than to intervene unless Jean needed the assistance.

Eventually, though, Jean prevailed, forcing the condemned to his knees. "What is your decision?" he asked Orlando.

"I want him to suffer," Orlando replied, "the way he made me suffer. I want the end of his life to be as painful, as miserable, as he has made mine. Expose him slowly to sunlight, so that he dies little by little, burned by its rays."

Jean flinched, but nodded his agreement. "As you say, so it shall be done."

Thurloe's struggles increased, but Jean subdued him, pinning his arms at his side. "Find something to bind him," he told Orlando.

That was easy. Orlando knew, much to his dismay, what every drawer and cabinet contained. He removed a pair of silver restraints from one of the drawers and brought them to Jean. "Bind him," Jean directed.

Thurloe hissed threateningly, but Orlando refused to cower before him ever again. He fastened the chains around his maker and waited.

"Is there a window anywhere in the house?" Jean asked.

Orlando shook his head. "I don't know. I know only this room and my prison. Surely, though, there is one somewhere."

Jean nodded. "We will find one, or we will hold him until he can be taken somewhere else to be executed."

A quick search of the premises revealed a lone, east-facing window in one of the upper rooms. Despite Thurloe's howls of protest, Jean staked him to the floor, feet toward the wall so that they would be burned first as the sun edged its way along its path. None of the other vampires had stayed to watch the execution, trusting Jean to see to it as chef de la Cour.

The first rays of dawn light sent a shudder of fear and loathing through all three vampires, but Jean and Orlando stepped back to avoid the danger. Thurloe had no such choice. As the minutes passed and the deadly light grew closer, his protests turned to pleas, but the ears that heard them were as deaf to them as he had ever been to those of his victims.

When the pleas turned to screams of pain, Jean almost looked away. If he had been there alone, he would have, but Orlando's eyes never wavered and Jean could not do less.

The part of Orlando's heart that retained some inkling of compassion cried out in protest at the slow, tortuous death, but he reminded himself repeatedly that the writhing creature on the floor had brought this on himself. Never, in all the years Orlando had been with him, had Thurloe shown one ounce of kindness, of decency, of compassion. He deserved to die, and Orlando could feel the weight of his slavery falling away as his master slowly disintegrated into ash.

When the screams finally stopped, Jean turned to Orlando. "We must stay here until the sun sets, then you are free to go where you will. Do you have any idea what you will do now?"

Orlando considered the question. "None at all," he replied. "I know no one here, and nothing of the city in which I find myself. I have no skill other than soldiering, but I cannot fight now that I am a vampire. I... Perhaps I would be better off if I simply ended it now."

"Do not say that," Jean scolded. "There are always options, a way forward. Come home with me, if you like, for a few days, until you learn your way around."

"I will not exchange one master for another," Orlando hissed.

"Nor would I have you do so," Jean assured him. "You owe me nothing more than a simple merci. After that, you are free. I only offer my assistance. The choice is yours."

Orlando paused. Would it be so terrible to accept help? Would it be so awful to let this vampire guide him into his new world? Already, Jean had given him more choices than Thurloe ever had. He could accept Jean's help for a time, until he got on his feet, though he would never again allow anyone to dictate to him. He, and he alone, would control his life from now on. "Merci," he said. "I will accept your generous offer."

The first order of business, as far as Jean was concerned, was the injuries that dotted the vampire's body. Even if they had not already emptied Thurloe's dungeon, he would find no help there. None in the cachots would willingly offer their blood to a vampire after what Thurloe had done to them—Jean could hardly blame them—and he would not have Orlando start his new existence with the taste of fear in his mouth.

He doubted Orlando had the skill to seek his own prey either, having been at Thurloe's mercy since his making. He would have to learn, but that could wait. He needed blood to heal, and that meant a visit to Angélique and Sang Froid. The harem girl turned entrepreneur would have what they needed.

The hours passed slowly, neither vampire comfortable in Thurloe's lair, though for very different reasons. While waiting for the Cour to assemble, Jean had explored enough to find a set of clothes that would pass muster for Orlando. They were not of the highest fashion nor was the fit exact, but it had let the young vampire face the Cour with some dignity and would allow them to move through the city unnoticed until Jean could find more fitting garb for his new protégé. Finally, the sun set. "Come, my new friend," Jean said with a low bow. "Come discover the delights of your home."

Orlando paused on the threshold of his prison. He had been imprisoned for so long that he found himself out of his depth now that he once again had choices. "I don't even know where to begin," he admitted softly.

Jean smiled sadly. A vampire of any experience would never have made such an admission, knowing he would lose ground in le jeu des Cours. That this one, a century old already, had no such qualms said as much to the chef de la Cour about the privations Orlando had endured as the marks on his body. He would make sure the lad got the sustenance he needed to heal and then do his best to provide him the experience he needed to rise from the bottom of the heap. "Let's begin at the beginning," he suggested, leading Orlando away from the site of his nightmare and toward Montmartre where the vampires congregated. "You need to feed so you can heal. Since I don't imagine you feel up to hunting, we'll visit madame Bouaddi who specializes in finding willing donors for vampires who don't feel like seeking one themselves."

"I don't have—" Orlando began.

"You have everything that belonged to Thurloe," Jean corrected. "He created you. You are his heir."

"I don't want anything of his," the young vampire spat.

"So sell it and use the profits to buy new things." Jean shrugged. "It will be more than enough to provide for your needs. The house alone is worth a small fortune. In the meantime, tonight will be my treat, a gift to welcome you to Paris and to my Cour."

Orlando frowned at the unfamiliar term, but he already felt his lack of experience too clearly to ask for clarification. Jean summoned a carriage as if doing so were perfectly normal, as if cab drivers picked up vampires every night. "They see two young bucks out for a night on the town," Jean murmured as the hackney drove off toward the newly opened Moulin Rouge. "And given our destination, they imagine we are seeking the pleasures of the flesh. They are not entirely wrong."

Orlando shuddered. "I will not... I cannot...."

"Angélique is very particular," Jean confided. "She employs no one against their will. I imagine you know well the taste of fear, if what I saw in Thurloe's cachots was any indication. You will never taste that from her employees. She cares for and about them." The carriage rolled to a stop. "Come, I will introduce you."

"Jean," Orlando hesitated, "I'm not sure this is a good idea. I don't know how to do this."

"You have to feed in order to heal," Jean insisted, alighting from the carriage. "If you want, I'll stay with you, though perhaps you would rather be alone for such an intimate sharing."

Orlando snorted, following Jean to the ground. "Do you imagine Thurloe ever gave me any privacy?"

"Let's go inside and talk to Angélique," Jean suggested. "Between us, we'll find someone who appeals to you."

Privately, Orlando doubted anyone would ever appeal to him again. Thurloe had scarred him so deeply he had no interest in even looking for such a relationship. He needed blood to survive, though, so he would learn what he could from Jean, sell Thurloe's property, and become a regular patron of Sang Froid.

Inside, Jean conferred with Angélique, discussing who would be best to help Orlando. They had decided on a girl about the age the vampire would have been at his turning, but Orlando rejected the idea immediately. He had known little enough about girls before he was turned, and his experiences under Thurloe's yoke had only added to his unease.

"A youth, then," Angélique suggested.

"No," Jean intuited, watching Orlando's downcast face. "A man, someone with the experience and sensitivity to guide an innocent. Raoul, I think."

Angélique smiled. "I think you're right. Take Orlando upstairs. I'll find Raoul and join you."

Orlando let Jean lead him to a boudoir on the second story of the building. Inside were a couch, a chaise longue, and a bed. Immediately, Orlando began to shake his head.

"You don't have to touch him except to feed from him," Jean assured the skittish vampire. "You don't have to let him touch you at all if you don't want. Nothing will happen here that isn't consensual." A tap at the door interrupted them. "That will be Raoul and Angélique."

The proprietress came in, followed by a handsome man with shoulder-length dark hair swept elegantly back from his face. Orlando averted his eyes from the broad expanse of chest revealed by the open neck of the man's shirt. "This is Orlando," Angélique introduced. "Orlando, meet Raoul. We'll leave you alone."

Panic showed clearly on Orlando's face as the two elder vampires withdrew. "Relax," Raoul urged, sitting on the couch. "Angélique told me a little. I won't touch you. Just come sit next to me."

Slowly, Orlando did as the man suggested. Raoul turned so he leaned against the high arm of the couch and stretched his arm out to the vampire. "If it would make you more comfortable, you can feed from my wrist."

Orlando stared at the outstretched limb like it was a snake come to bite him. Raoul waited patiently until finally the vampire reached for his hand. "See the veins there, just at the base of my palm? Bite me there. You'll get the most blood and I'll get the most pleasure."

"Pleasure?" Orlando squeaked. "It won't hurt you?"

"Not at all," Raoul assured him. "Taste and see."

"I...," Orlando hesitated.

"Relax," the man urged again. "Lick my skin. Let your saliva prepare my wrist."

Orlando looked at the man doubtfully, but he did as his companion suggested, licking the patch of skin the man had indicated before biting hesitantly.

"Let your fangs go deeper," Raoul instructed. "You're not hurting me, and you'll get more blood that way."

Orlando closed his eyes and let his fangs sink all the way to the root. Blood like he had never tasted before rushed into his mouth. It took him but a moment to identify the difference. Raoul felt no pain, no fear, and its absence sweetened the man's blood. He swallowed and began to suck, letting mouthful after mouthful flow into his body. As he drank, a new flavor imbued the blood. Surprised, Orlando looked up to see the man's face slack with pleasure.

"You should stop now," he said finally. "If you need more, you must take it from someone else."

"I'm sorry," Orlando apologized, pulling back immediately. *"I didn't mean to trespass."*

"You didn't," Raoul promised, *"but you are not the first vampire to visit me tonight, and I know my own limits."* He held out his wrist again. *"Close the wounds with your tongue, and then I will take you back to madame Bouaddi."*

"Thank you," Orlando said fervently when he had done what he could to heal the marks he had left on Raoul's wrist. *"I didn't know."*

The man leaned forward, intending to kiss the vampire, but Orlando's hand on his chest stopped him. *"Don't,"* he pleaded, sensing what the man hoped for in the taste that lingered on his tongue. *"I can't— what you want—I can't give you. Not now."* Perhaps not ever, he thought, but he would not ruin the first night he had ever fed without fear by voicing that aloud. Not when he knew he would be returning the next time he needed to feed.

Raoul nodded sadly but stood. *"You're welcome here any time."*

A silent nod was Orlando's only reply.

It took Orlando a moment when he awoke to place his surroundings, to identify the warmth in bed next to him. When he finally did, he sighed in relief. He should have known the *judicium* would bring back memories of Thurloe's trial and execution, but he had not expected them to be so vivid or to include his first night as a free vampire. He smiled softly as he remembered Raoul. He had visited the man regularly for some years after that night, until Raoul was ready to retire. By that time, Orlando had learned to hunt and stopped using Angélique's services.

He had fond memories of Raoul. The man had helped Orlando see that he could feed without injuring, without causing fear, without killing. He had first tasted desire in the man's blood and for that, for the ability to recognize it in Alain's blood when he met his wizard, he would always be grateful to Raoul.

The emotions the long-ago friend evoked, though, were nothing like what Orlando felt for the man currently sharing his bed. He stroked Alain's blond hair gently, not wanting to wake him after the tension of the previous night. His lover had been his rock through the trial, but he was still clearly exhausted from four days of barely sleeping. The Aveu de Sang protected his body from the demands of Orlando's feeding, but nothing but time and rest could help with the other demands. Orlando hoped with the *judicium* over and the equal rights legislation about to be decided, Alain would finally have the opportunity to rest, not just for a few hours here and there, but for the days he needed to fully rebuild his strength.

"Why are you awake?" Alain mumbled, tilting his head into Orlando's caressing hand.

"A dream woke me up," Orlando replied honestly.

"Thurloe?" Alain asked.

"Yes," Orlando admitted, "and the first human friend I ever had as a vampire. I met him the night after the... Thurloe's execution." It cost him to use his maker's name after so many years of refusing to utter it, but he found it liberating at the same time, as if he had finally cast off the last chain his maker had impressed upon him. By refusing to say his name, he had continued to give Thurloe an importance he did not deserve. The time had come to put his demons to rest once and for all. He rolled to his back and pulled Alain on top of him, kissing his lover gently. "Make love to me?"

Chapter 36

"ANY TIME you want," Alain replied immediately, his hands sliding into Orlando's hair as he tipped his head back.

"Any way I want?" Orlando pressed.

"Of course," Alain assured him. "Just tell me how you want me."

Orlando shook his head. "Not this time. This time I want *you* to tell *me* how you want me."

"I don't want to make you uncomfortable," Alain hesitated.

"Putain, Alain. Are you going to make me spell it out for you?" Orlando said with a laugh. "I want to know what it feels like to have you inside me this time."

Alain's mouth moved, but no words came out as he tried to assimilate the request. He had hoped, certainly, that this day would come, but he had come to accept that it might never happen. To have it offered now, so unexpectedly, left him trembling with desire. "Are you sure?"

Orlando's smile was beatific. "Yes. Make love to me. I want to know what it feels like."

Alain's hand trembled as he stroked Orlando's smooth cheek, mind racing as he considered how best to respond to Orlando's invitation.

"It's not that hard a request, is it?" Orlando teased.

Alain flushed. "I want it to be perfect. After everything you've gone through, I'm afraid—"

"Don't be," Orlando interrupted. "You've never hurt me and you won't start now, but more than that, I'm perfectly capable of telling you if you do something I don't like. Trust me to do that and I'll trust you to show me what I've been missing."

Alain nodded and lowered his head, kissing Orlando tenderly, their tongues twining together sinuously as the kiss deepened and Alain's hands began to move. His body was already hungry for his lover, but he pushed that need aside. His primary concern had to be Orlando's pleasure. This could be his one and only chance to convince Orlando that his trust was well placed, and he did not intend to squander it.

Rolling to the side so Orlando would not feel confined by his weight, Alain ran his hands down Orlando's torso, suppressing a flinch each time his fingers encountered a healing mark. Orlando seemed not to notice, though, thoroughly lost in the kiss to the exclusion of all else. Keeping his touch light, Alain focused on the kiss, on exploring every nook and cranny of the hot cavern. Lips, teeth, palate, tongue. The inside of Orlando's cheek where he found a small scab, another injury to add to Serrier's tally. He forced himself not to dwell on the vision of Orlando biting the inside of his cheek to keep from crying out as he was tortured. They had enough ghosts in their bed already. They did not need one more. Instead, he drew back a little, nipping at Orlando's lower lip until the vampire's eyes opened. Alain felt himself drowning in the soft, dreamy look on his lover's face. He had put that expression in Orlando's eyes. No one else. That thought gave him the courage to intensify his other caresses, his fingers finding Orlando's nipples, tweaking one side, then the other, back and forth until Orlando was writhing against him.

Orlando had expected to feel nervous, the remembered pain of Thurloe's rapes a strong deterrent against letting anyone touch him that way again, but this was Alain in his bed. His lover. His love. His Avoué. Alain would not hurt him intentionally—and if he happened to do so accidentally, a single word would stop him. That assurance was strong enough to override everything else and to let him place himself completely in Alain's clearly competent hands. The welts on his body, nearly healed after his extensive feedings, no longer hurt when his wizard's hands moved over them, the marks on his skin meaningless when compared to the depth of his emotions, of his desire. Alain's hands found every sensitive spot, having learned them slowly in the time they had been lovers, exploiting them relentlessly until Orlando was a mass of tingling nerves and seething need.

Then the wizard started in with his mouth. Orlando shivered in delight as Alain's lips moved down the long column of his neck to skate across his collarbone, relearning every line of bone and muscle, sensitizing every inch of flesh. A low moan escaped his lips, causing Alain to pause and look up at him. Orlando smiled as best he could, his hands stroking Alain's hair in encouragement. Reassured, Alain returned to his explorations, his mouth closing over one peaked nipple, sucking gently. Orlando thrashed on the bed, trying to pull Alain closer, to meld their bodies into one new creation, one flesh as their hearts and minds were one.

He could feel Alain now, in the back of his mind, in a way he had not been able to before, as if their trial by fire had forged the bond so strongly that he was aware of it even when they were together. He could feel Alain's lingering worry along with his rising passion. Orlando focused as much as he was able with Alain's mouth doing wicked things to his chest and sent a wave of love and trust back in his Avoué's direction. Beneath his hands, he felt Alain relax marginally as he accepted the truth of Orlando's desire.

"Bite me," Orlando murmured. "Not hard, but let me feel your teeth."

"Are you sure?" Alain asked, surprised. That had been one of the earliest and most rigid taboos.

"I'm sure," Orlando said. "I refuse to let him stop me from experiencing something ever again. I almost lost my chance. I'm not losing another one."

Orlando was afraid Alain would still refuse, but the wizard simply nodded, returning to his current obsession, lips and tongue worrying one nipple until it tightened into a sharp point. Orlando was about to ask again, thinking Alain was ignoring his request, when the edges of Alain's teeth grazed his flesh, not hard enough to hurt, but definitely hard enough to send sparks zinging out from the point of contact. Silently, Orlando cursed the missed opportunities, the times he had denied Alain something out of fear.

To Alain's surprise, he realized he could feel Orlando's reaction to his bite in his mind as well as in Orlando's body. Experimentally, he bit again, concentrating to see if the effect reproduced itself. When it did, he let the awareness guide his actions, helping him know where to linger and where not to bother. The line of Orlando's ribs, though by no means unpleasant, created no particular spark. The hollow beneath Orlando's navel, however, resulted in such a jolt through their connection that Alain lingered for long minutes, licking, sucking, nipping until he had raised a dark bruise to the surface. It would fade in a few hours, but for that short time, Orlando was marked as well as Alain was.

"You can darken it again whenever you want," Orlando offered, sensing Alain's satisfaction at seeing the passion mark on his skin. "I won't complain about any marks you leave on my body."

"It's not like anyone will see it but us," Alain pointed out sensibly.

"So mark me somewhere people will see."

If he had been standing, Alain would have fallen, his knees giving out completely at the thought of leaving marks on Orlando to match the ones that so often decorated his neck. Bestowing one last nip on Orlando's belly, he scooted up the bed so he could reach his lover's neck. "Tell me if you want me to stop."

"I will," Orlando promised as Alain's lips found his skin again. The last time Alain had bitten his neck, Orlando had reacted badly, the memories stirred by the bite enough to send him running. Not this morning, he swore to himself. And never again. He would never run from Alain again, never again let memories keep him from judging an experience based on how it felt now rather than on how it had felt in the past. The wizard started by merely sucking on the tender flesh, his lips drawing heat to the surface. Eventually, though, he nipped slightly, hesitating in order to gauge Orlando's reaction.

"It feels good," the vampire assured his lover. "You can bite harder."

Alain applied a little more pressure, sending a shiver down Orlando's spine as Alain's teeth worked his skin. He could feel a bruise forming and reveled in the thought of everyone seeing it and knowing he had been well-loved. "Again," he said. "I want everyone to see it and know how much I love you."

Alain's teeth worried the spot over and over until Orlando gasped and shivered. "What does it look like?" he asked.

"Like a bite mark," Alain said with a soft laugh.

"Get the mirror," Orlando said. "I want to see it."

Alain rose from the bed, heedless of his nudity, and crossed to the dresser where Orlando kept an old-fashioned hand mirror. Bringing it back to the bed, he offered it to his lover, trying to hold back his amusement at Orlando's preening as he turned his head this way and that to check how well he could see the bruise from different angles.

Setting the mirror aside, Orlando sent Alain a radiant smile. "It may not be as permanent a mark as the one I left on you, but it means as much to me. I'm yours as fully as the Aveu de Sang makes you mine. Or I will be by the time we're done this morning."

"You don't have to do this," Alain insisted. "I don't want you to do this because you think I want you to."

Orlando covered Alain's lips with his fingers, stilling his words. "Close your eyes and concentrate. You know what I'm feeling. I want this because I don't want to hold back anymore. I want to know what it feels like. I want you to know what it feels like. Even if it's just once, even if we decide to go back to the way things were before, I want to make a rational decision, not one based on fear and conditioning. You aren't Thurloe and I'm not the man I was then."

The truth of Orlando's words resonated through the bond between them. Such surety, such confidence filled his mind that Alain stopped questioning and accepted that this was what Orlando wanted. Turning to the night stand, he found the lube and set it on the bed next to him for later. The sight of it changed nothing in Orlando's expression or in the emotions Alain could feel. With a sigh of relief and an eager smile, he reached for Orlando again, bearing him back onto the bed to kiss him hungrily. Orlando responded as wildly as Alain could have wished.

Hands moving freely now that all his doubts were laid to rest, Alain caressed Orlando's side, his back, over the curve of his buttocks and down the backs of his thighs, pulling one of his lover's legs over his hips. Immediately, Orlando lifted up into him, the offering so blatant, so bold, that Alain nearly forgot what a huge step Orlando was taking. Reminding himself to take his time and stay in control, Alain reached for the lube with trembling hands. He had to prepare Orlando properly, and he did not know how much longer he would be able to wait.

He propped himself on one elbow so he could look down at Orlando. "Look at me," he requested softly. "I want to see your eyes so I know I'm not hurting you or rushing you."

Orlando's eyes opened, luminous with love and desire, stealing the breath from Alain's chest. Slowly, reverently, he slid trembling fingers toward their destination, burrowing between the smooth cheeks in search of the tightly furled portal he had never thought to have the right to touch. Orlando pulled one leg up toward his chest, opening himself to make Alain's task easier and to remind his lover that he truly did want this.

For all of two seconds, Alain considered suggesting Orlando turn over so he could prepare the vampire more easily, but he abandoned that thought almost as soon as it formed. He needed to see his lover's face, needed the intimacy of looking into the deep brown eyes and knowing that his touch brought pleasure to the man who shared his life. Slick fingers found the puckered opening, massaging the skin around it firmly. Orlando's eyelids fluttered momentarily, but otherwise, his expression did not change; his body did not tense in fear or rejection. Moved beyond words at the implicit trust, Alain pressed one finger against the rosette, waiting for the muscle to give in to his silent request.

Orlando had expected to have to fight his instinctive reactions to these new, more intimate touches, given how hard it had been for him to adjust to having a lover in the first place, but apparently his love for Alain was so powerful that his body did not even equate these loving touches with Thurloe's vicious abuse. He felt no instinctive need to retreat, to protect himself, only an ever-increasing desire to have Alain continue, to feel his lover's fingers and then his cock inside him, claiming him. Nothing else mattered. Not now. Not ever. "Give me another," he requested huskily.

Alain complied immediately, working a second finger inside the tight passage alongside the first. Orlando squirmed, but a quick glance at his face assured Alain that his lover was not trying to get away, just to get more comfortable on the bed. Running his fingers along the walls of the channel he was plundering, Alain sought the bundle of nerves that, he hoped, would provide as much pleasure for his lover as they did for him. When he found them, Orlando cried out sharply, fingers digging hard into Alain's biceps. "Oh, merde, do that again!" the vampire pleaded.

Alain grinned and settled in to play, his fingers massaging Orlando's prostate mercilessly, driving his lover higher and higher until the vampire was trembling, pleading, begging. Not relenting at all in his manipulation of the little node, Alain lowered his head and captured the leaking tip of Orlando's cock in his mouth, sucking on it lightly as his lover thrashed beneath him.

Orlando thought he had found heaven. Alain's fingers were tormenting him with pleasure he had not dreamed possible. And when he felt the wet heat of his lover's mouth on his aching cock, he lost all semblance of control, his body seizing in release, every muscle taut as he spasmed long and hard down Alain's throat.

When Orlando's cock finally stopped twitching, Alain lifted his head and smiled up at his lover, waiting for the dark eyes to open again. As soon as they did, he crooked his fingers once more, renewing his attentions to Orlando's pleasure center. "We're not done yet," he purred, withdrawing his fingers enough to add more lube and a third finger on his way back in, stretching the now-relaxed guardian ring even more.

"Definitely not," Orlando agreed, voice breaking on a gasp as Alain's fingers teased him again. "You haven't made love to me yet."

"I haven't been inside you yet," Alain corrected. "I've made love to you every time we've touched since the first day I spent in this bed."

"Then come inside me and complete what's been building between us since that first night in Père Lachaise," Orlando offered, tugging on Alain's hips to urge him between the vampire's widespread thighs. "Make us one in every way."

Alain stared down at the vision beneath him in the bed, marveling at the amazing reality of this lover, this love, this moment. Then Orlando's hand closed around his cock, guiding the tip to the portal his fingers continued to stretch automatically. "Come inside me," the vampire repeated.

Alain withdrew his fingers carefully and rocked against the clenching hole. It relaxed for him again, letting him in, enveloping him in tight, slick heat. Alain bit his lip, trying not to thrust with all his might into the snug sheath. He could not hold himself completely still, though, the temptation of Orlando's glorious body too much for him to resist entirely. The hand that had guided his cock moved to his hips, setting the pace, giving Alain an indication of how best to make love to his vampire.

He undulated his hips slowly, forging deeper with each movement until finally he was fully seated inside his lover's body. His lover's virgin ass. He knew Orlando would argue that, given Thurloe's predilections, but this was the first time Orlando had given himself willingly. As far as Alain was concerned, that made him as untouched, as innocent, as any boy with his first lover. Reverently, he lowered his head, joining their lips, pouring all his love into their kiss.

Orlando returned it, but eventually, he wanted more. He nudged Alain's jaw until his wizard raised his chin, revealing the line of his neck, covered in healing bites. He licked across the brand that would never fade, relishing the shiver of delight that ran down Alain's back and caused his cock to twitch deep inside Orlando's passage. Carefully placing his fangs just where he wanted them, he bit down hard, piercing the brand with his teeth. Blood rushed into his mouth as Alain lost all semblance of control, his body bucking wildly as he drove repeatedly into Orlando.

The combination of the suddenly feral pounding and the soaring rapture in Alain's blood sent Orlando back to full boil, his body clamoring for a second release. Alain seemed determined to give it to him, his cock hitting Orlando's prostate with every pass, prodding it relentlessly. One hand encircled Orlando's resurgent erection, stroking in time with the energetic thrusts. The other hand grabbed roughly at Orlando's ass, his knuckles white from the force of his grip. Orlando did not protest the additional layer of sensation, not when he could taste how out of control Alain was. Never before had his lover been this unrestrained, this wild with his passion. Knowing he had inspired it gave Orlando an extra thrill, enough to shatter his control and wring a second orgasm out of him. His passage contracted, milking Alain's release from him as well, the hot flood a welcome reminder to Orlando of how much everything had changed. How much Alain had changed everything.

Lovingly licking the new bite marks, Orlando carefully withdrew his fangs. When he felt Alain start to pull back as well, he wrapped his ankles around his lover's hips, stopping him. "Stay right here," he requested. "I want to feel you, your weight, a little while longer."

"We'll stick together," Alain warned, but his body belied his apparent reluctance, relaxing immediately against Orlando's.

Orlando shrugged. "And this would be different from usual how?"

Alain just laughed. "Fine. Have it your way."

Orlando kissed the laughing mouth. "I will."

Chapter 37

"WAKE UP, Alain," Orlando said, shaking his lover softly. "It's getting ready to start."

Alain blinked a couple of times before sitting up. He was as sticky as he had predicted they would be, but he found he did not mind. "What?" he asked, his brain still muddled from sleep.

"The television coverage on the debate in the Assemblée," Orlando reminded him. "It's about to start."

"Have you seen Thierry yet? Or any of the others from his patrol?" Alain inquired. "Did they convince the gendarmerie to let them supplement the defenses just in case?"

"I don't know," Orlando replied. "I haven't seen anyone I recognize, but that doesn't mean they won't let them in. The news media is hardly interested in a few random spectators, and you know that's all they'll see."

"That's all Thierry will let them see," Alain agreed. After he and Eric had cleared the air between them, they had found Thierry and the three of them had spent hours comparing the list of captured and killed dark wizards with Eric's memory of wizards who had fought for Serrier over the time Eric had been spying for Marcel. There were surprisingly few combatants unaccounted for, but one was more than a little worrisome. Somehow, despite Eric's insistence that Aguiraud had been at the base right before the final battle, he had not been captured and his body had not been found. They had debated back and forth about whether the dark wizard could pull together the resources from Serrier's decimated ranks to dare an attack to stop the equal rights vote. While they could not agree on that, they did agree that he had the ingenuity for it, and that was enough for Thierry to insist on a full complement of wizards and vampires to defend the députés if an attack materialized.

"You realize you're probably worrying for nothing," Orlando said as they settled in to watch the news coverage. "It's only been three days. Aguiraud can't have recouped that fast."

"We can't assume that," Alain insisted. "He was the only wizard besides Serrier that I would have worried about facing in battle. I wouldn't have wanted to fight Eric, but if it had happened, I wouldn't have worried about being able to win. Aguiraud is a lot like Raymond, only without his decency. Even if it's purely a symbolic gesture, if the vote happens without any interference from the remnants of Serrier's forces, they've admitted defeat. And I don't see Aguiraud letting that happen if he's still alive."

"Could they have missed a body?" Orlando asked.

"Maybe," Alain replied, "and if he was wounded and escaped, he could well have died from his injuries. If I remember correctly, he wasn't much of a healer. There really isn't a way to know as long as he stays hidden."

"Then we'll hope the possibility of hitting the Assemblée, the head of the Milice and the chef de la Cour with one blow is sufficient to draw him out," Orlando said. "That is the point of having everyone there, isn't it?"

"Yeah," Alain agreed, sitting on the couch and pulling Orlando into his arms as they waited for the debate to begin.

Precisely on schedule, the Président de l'Assemblée called the session to order, laying the proposed law out before the gathered députés and reminding them of the procedure for today's vote. They would have a short time for debate followed by an up or down vote, with a rejection by the Assemblée leading to the dissolution of the current government. A murmur ran through the crowd as they considered the import of both the legislation and their vote.

"Here goes nothing," Alain said softly as he waited for Marcel to give his speech.

As expected, Marcel rose and took the podium, waiting for the murmurs to fade before he spoke. "I know there are skeptics in the room today who are wondering why this legislation is so important that it comes to you to vote on in this manner. Still others of you are probably wondering why I have anything to do with an issue that does not directly impact wizards."

Alain and Orlando both snorted their disbelief at that comment. Their lives could not be any more intertwined. Anything that affected the vampires directly impacted every wizard with a partner.

"The answer to both those concerns is simple. Without the vampires' assistance, we would still be fighting the war against the rebel wizards. Instead, thanks to the vampires, Serrier is dead and the rebellion is ended. We are not so naïve as to think there will not be aftershocks, the remnants of Serrier's forces trying to regroup, but we took out all but about fifty known combatants in a decisive battle three days ago that ended with Serrier's death at the hands of a vampire and with the capture of the rogue vampire who has since been tried and sentenced. After two years of combat, the alliance ended the war in six weeks—thanks to the power of the partnerships that formed between wizards and vampires."

Another murmur, louder this time, ran through the assembled legislators. In Orlando's living room, Orlando shuddered as he thought about the trial and its aftermath. "It's over," Alain soothed immediately, his arm tightening around Orlando's shoulders. "He's gone. We can put it behind us and move on."

On screen, Marcel gestured for someone to join him. The cameras panned to the side in time to catch Jean rising to his feet. The chef de la Cour took his place at Marcel's side. None of the weariness from the night before showed on his face, but Orlando hoped his friend had found at least a few moments alone with his partner between the execution at dawn and the beginning of the debate.

"I'm sure you all recognize monsieur Bellaiche," Marcel said by way of introduction, "but for those of you who don't know him, he is the chef de la Cour parisienne, the leader of the vampires here in the capital. He felt it appropriate to be here today since your decision affects him and his people most of all."

"How is he here?" one of the députés called out. "It's daylight."

"It's magic, you see," Jean drawled in reply, eliciting a chuckle from the Milice operatives in the room and from some of the sympathetic legislators. Orlando and Alain laughed as well, Orlando turning his head to kiss Alain lightly before giving his attention back to the TV screen. "One side benefit to the vampires involved in the Milice is protection from sunlight," he added. "We, the general and I as well as all the wizards and vampires in the Milice, have great hopes that our military collaboration is nearing its end, but the alliance has brought many things to light concerning the possible relationships between vampires and wizards. The partnerships, the friendships we have formed since the alliance began will not disappear simply because the rebellion has been put down. We stand on the brink of great discoveries with magical implications that reach far beyond the individuals involved. The efforts of this body will recognize that reality and allow us to move forward as equal partners in this endeavor."

A smattering of applause met Jean's speech.

"They don't get it, do they?" Orlando asked Alain as Jean returned to his seat. He was relieved to catch a glimpse of Raymond in the seat next to Jean's. At least the wizard was there to support his partner.

"Marcel will do his best, but even if the legislation fails, the wizards won't. L'ANS will keep working on the vampires' behalf until it passes," Alain promised. "Marcel won't let this drop."

Orlando smiled, squeezing Alain's hand. "I know. And even if it never passes, things won't be the same as they were because the partnerships won't let them be."

"No, things won't ever go back to the way they were," Alain agreed. To prove his point, he leaned over and kissed Orlando enthusiastically, his hand wandering into his lover's long hair and then down his back.

The Président de l'Assemblée had just risen to open debate to the rest of the députés when the sounds of shouting broke the relative quiet of the hall. The commentators' alarmed shouts startled Orlando and Alain out of their kiss.

"What's going on?" Orlando asked.

Alain frowned. "Aguiraud. I'd bet on it."

"Are they going to be all right?"

"Thierry's there with a patrol, ready for just such an event," Alain reminded him, "and Marcel and Raymond aren't exactly helpless. Look. They're already setting up a protective net."

Orlando concentrated on the screen, but he could not see whatever it was that reassured Alain. "How can you tell?"

"I can hear the spell they're casting," Alain explained. "They'll enclose the members of the Assemblée so that they're protected if anyone gets past Thierry and the others."

Justin appeared suddenly next to the commentator, urging him to move deeper into the hall. "There's a patrol outside, but the farther from the door you are, the safer you'll be," he insisted calmly.

"So the attack was expected?" the commentator pressed.

"The Milice's job is to be ready, vampires and wizards alike, whatever the threat," Justin replied simply. "We take our responsibilities seriously."

Orlando could not stop the chuckle that escaped at Justin's acerbic comment. "He isn't going to let anyone forget us, is he?"

"None of us are," Alain replied, but his eyes never left the screen as he searched for signs of the progress of the battle. With the media confined like the députés, they only saw and heard speculation and worried shouts.

"What's taking so long?" Orlando asked after a short time. "Shouldn't we have heard something by now?"

Alain shrugged. "It depends on how many of them there are and what their plan was," he replied, his mind racing as he went mentally through the preparations they had made, imagining where each wizard and vampire was posted, how they could react to the different threats. He hoped the gendarmes stayed out of it. They would have no defense against a magical attack.

Finally, after several endless minutes, the cameras focused back on Marcel, Raymond and Jean, Thierry and Sebastien joining them. They were too far away for their conversation to be picked up by the microphones, but just the sight of his friends still standing reassured Alain. Thierry's body language was calm so Alain assumed the threat was contained. They simply had to wait and see how many of the remaining dark wizards were captured or killed and more importantly, whether they'd captured Aguiraud.

After conferring for a few moments, Thierry and Sebastien left again, presumably to resume their patrol outside while Marcel, Raymond and Jean returned to their places.

"Is everything in order, Général?" the Président de l'Assemblée asked when they returned inside.

"It is," Marcel reported firmly. "We suspected Simon Aguiraud might try to disrupt the vote, a final gasp before the rebellion dies for good. The ringleaders are now all captured or killed. All that remains is to make a few arrests based on the intelligence we've gathered during the interrogations and then the rebellion will truly be over."

"Then we can continue with our debate undisturbed?"

"You may, monsieur le Président," Marcel replied with great dignity.

"Thank God," Alain sighed. "I hope we didn't suffer any casualties, but we'll have to wait until we check in at headquarters to find that out."

"Thierry didn't seem upset," Orlando reminded him. "If we'd lost anyone or had any serious injuries, he wouldn't have been so calm."

Alain was not so sure, but he let Orlando's words soothe him for now.

The Président opened the floor for debate. The député from Marseille, part of the Front National delegation, rose first. Alain rolled his eyes. "How xenophobic do you suppose he can get?" he asked rhetorically. Orlando did not reply. He did not need to. They both knew the answer. The man had the right to speak, though, however much his conservative opinions grated.

"Monsieur le Président," the député began with a respectful inclination of his head, "Général Chavinier, monsieur Bellaiche, honored colleagues, I'm sure the Premier Ministre has proposed the current legislation with the best intentions, but I fear it would be irresponsible on our part to pass it without considering all the issues it raises. We are not an institution created to rubber stamp the agenda of any organization, even our own government. We have only Général Chavinier's word on the contribution of the vampires in the war effort—"

"Bullshit!" Alain exploded. Orlando caught his waist before he could rise to his feet, as if shouting at the screen would change the other man's attitudes.

"—but even if he has told us the unadorned truth, we must consider the impact of this law on our society," the député continued. "Vampires do not function the way the rest of us do. They skulk in the shadows—" Jean's cough interrupted him. "Very well, they used to skulk in the shadows, unable to function in any respectable sense, not contributing to society in any way, and feeding off those around them. To give that kind of behavior legitimacy…. We simply cannot in good faith do that to our citizens."

A few of the other legislators applauded, but most sat in stony silence. Visibly incensed, Raymond rose to his feet. "May I address the député's concerns?" he asked.

"Oh, they're in for it now," Alain murmured. He had heard Raymond speak before the war began and knew the passion the other wizard could bring to anything he believed in strongly. The Assemblée was about to get an earful.

"This is highly unusual," the Président de l'Assemblée hesitated.

"So is the situation," Raymond reminded them.

The Président nodded his permission.

"You need not take the général's word for anything," Raymond said, turning to the other members of the Assemblée. "You all sat here just now, protected from the attack by a mixed patrol. Look up in the balconies. Every one of them is guarded by a vampire, and you will notice that no one penetrated any of them. As for the way vampires function, I can assure you from personal experience that they contribute to society on a regular basis. They own and run businesses, some of which cater primarily to vampires, but many of them have human clients as well. I have been in clubs, traditional cafés, internet cafés, and more. True, the proprietors themselves can only come out after dark, but many business owners employ nonvampire managers to run the day-to-day aspects of the business. Regardless of when they are there, their businesses pay taxes, pay rent, pay their employees, purchase supplies from other businesses, and make all the other contributions to the economy that any business does. With very few exceptions—in centuries, mesdames et messieurs, not at any one time, but in *centuries*—vampires only feed from willing partners, and that exchange of blood does not do any harm to the donor of the blood. If it did, I wouldn't be here talking to you now. Furthermore, in partnering with wizards as they have done, vampires have given us a new, more effective way of addressing magical disequilibrium. Unless you plan to drive them out completely, *our citizens* are already used to their behavior and benefit from it, even if they don't realize it."

Raymond's speech drew applause from the vampires in the balconies and from many of the legislators. "Damn, he's good," Alain observed admiringly. "He's wasted as a historian and researcher."

Raymond started to sit down, but the Président stopped him. "What's this about the magical disequilibrium, monsieur Payet? If it's not classified information."

Raymond glanced at Marcel, who nodded his permission. "The alliance wasn't simply a matter of vampires fighting with us. We formed partnerships, a vampire and a wizard working together, and those partnerships have a variety of impacts. One of them is that the exchange of blood between partners protects the vampire from sunlight. That exchange also helps restore and maintain the balance of elemental magic. By virtue of as simple an act as feeding from the right person, the vampires can contribute to the safety of the entire world."

"Thank you, monsieur Payet," the Président said before acknowledging another député who wanted to speak. Alain breathed a sigh of relief when he recognized one of the Parisian députés from the Parti Socialiste who had been among Marcel's staunchest supporters since the war began.

"The situation seems simple to me," the woman began. "We have a group of people who have materially contributed to the war effort, who are already part of the fabric of our society, and who have now been shown to contribute to a far greater effort as well. The legislation before us today does nothing more or less than recognize their right to exist and to do the things they are already doing. To deny that is to pretend they somehow do not exist. I'm sure some of you would probably prefer they didn't, but we aren't here to legislate them out of existence. I've heard some of my colleagues hint that the vampires are ungovernable, but just last night they governed themselves quite well, bringing to justice one of their own who had broken their laws. So I have a question for the chef de la Cour who joins us today. Monsieur Bellaiche, if this legislation passes, will vampires abide by French law?"

"We already do, madame," Jean replied with great dignity, "because if we don't, we're persecuted for it. The only difference this legislation will make in that respect is that we'll be protected from such persecution if we haven't broken any laws."

"Then I don't see what the problem is," she continued, turning back to the rest of the legislators. "The only thing the vampires gain is protection, and we gain their assistance in all the ways we've listed. To deny them that protection is as fundamentally wrong as denying protection to someone because of the color of their skin or their religious beliefs or their gender or because they immigrated from another country. We don't allow discrimination for any of those reasons. Why should we allow discrimination in any form?"

"Mesdames et messieurs," the Président de l'Assemblée declared when she had finished, "we've heard from both sides, from those affected by the proposed law and from those who helped propose it. While we could debate for days, perhaps even more, the Premier Ministre has set us a deadline by invoking Article 49, alinéa 3 of the Constitution. The time has come to vote."

One by one, the board lit up indicating the votes as they were cast. The first several votes came in against the bill. "They can't be serious," Alain muttered as the "no" votes mounted up.

"Look at whose votes they are," Orlando said soothingly. "Give the others time. It won't stay that way."

Then the tide started turning, more and more députés voting "yes" until finally they had reached the number for a majority. As the Président de l'Assemblée declared the bill passed into law, Alain turned to Orlando, hugging him tight. "We did it!"

Orlando smiled and kissed Alain deeply. When they broke apart, his face was radiant. "I knew we would. From the moment you told me Marcel would help, I knew it would work out."

Chapter 38

"IT HAS been four days, chef de la Cour," Jude snapped when Jean, Raymond, and Marcel returned to Milice headquarters. "Four days since I've seen my partner. Four days since I've had the protection of her blood."

"There have been a few things going on in those few days," Jean replied coldly.

"There have," Jude agreed, "but the *judicium* is over and the equal rights legislation has passed. I believe you have a bargain to keep."

"Marcel, if I could have a few more minutes of your time?" Jean said with a put-upon sigh. "Leighton has some concerns."

"Of course," Marcel replied, leading the others into his office. "What's going on?"

"Leighton was the vampire who reanimated Orlando," Jean explained, "and he seems to believe that merits having the Ordre de restriction lifted."

"We certainly appreciate what you did," Marcel agreed, "but that doesn't excuse your earlier behavior."

"The alliance is ending. You said it yourself this morning at the Assemblée. And with no alliance, the military issues you cited in placing the Ordre de restriction on us no longer apply," Jude countered.

"That is perhaps true," Marcel replied, "but civil law is even less forgiving than the Milice of the kind of behavior you exhibited toward Adèle. I can release the Ordre de restriction, but if you continue to act as you did, you could well find yourself in a French court facing serious charges. And, while I can release the Ordre de restriction on you easily enough, I can only release the one on Adèle with her permission. Do you expect she'll give it?"

"It doesn't matter if she does or not," Jude insisted. "I want it removed from me."

"As you wish." Marcel cast the counter spell without any further discussion. "You will find, however, that the spell still on Adèle will keep you apart as effectively as if you were both still bound," he warned. "You won't have any more luck approaching her unsupervised now than you did before."

"I'm not the only one who could end up in court over this," Jude threatened. "I believe I could make a case against you for keeping me illegally from my partner."

Marcel chuckled. "I'll talk to Adèle, but that's the best I can do for you. If you want the Ordre de restriction lifted, reconsider your own attitude first."

"We're not in the sixteenth century anymore," Jean reminded the other vampire. "If you have any hope of any kind of partnership with Adèle, you're going to have to adjust your attitude. With the alliance ending, the military necessity of the partnerships will fade—and if she chooses not to continue to see you, that's her choice."

"She'll continue it," Jude declared with utmost confidence. "She's as invested in this as I am."

Jean was skeptical, but he let it go. Jude would discover the truth eventually. And if Jude really was right, he and Adèle would have to work things out between themselves.

"Don't underestimate her," Marcel counseled as Jude made to leave. "She's more than just a Milice wizard. She's part of the gendarmerie in the Morvan on loan to the Milice. She knows how to defend herself, and she knows what protections she has under the law."

"And you might consider that French law will be far more restrictive on you than vampire law," Raymond mentioned slyly. "A number of years in prison, even for a vampire, would not be a pleasant experience. Particularly since you wouldn't have any access to your partner while you were confined."

"Yes, but she wouldn't have access to me either," Jude retorted.

"And yet you're the one here demanding the Ordre de restriction be lifted, not her," Jean reminded him. "You got what you wanted. Now get out."

When the door closed behind Jude, Jean shook his head. "His arrogance never fails to astound me. You'd think after all this time I'd at least remember to expect it, but it's the triumph of hope over reason, I guess. I keep hoping he'll learn."

"Maybe Adèle will be the one to teach him," Raymond suggested. "The partnerships have wrought changes in others. Look at Orlando. Look at us."

Jean chuckled and reached for Raymond's hand, pretending not to see Marcel's indulgent look. "Self-interest might be enough to motivate him to temper his behavior even if he doesn't truly change his attitude," he mused aloud. "Jude is most definitely self-interested."

"He's also correct that I don't really have the right to leave the Ordre de restriction in place beyond the end of their involvement with the Milice," Marcel observed. "That gives Adèle some time to decide what she wants to do, but the Milice was never intended to be a permanent institution. With the war essentially over, it won't be long before the Milice will be decommissioned. And when that happens, I'll lose all legal grounds for maintaining the spell."

"Unless she files a formal complaint between now and then," Raymond agreed. "The question is, will she?"

Jean shook his head. "The question is whether she really wants to," he disagreed. "However inappropriate their interactions seem to the rest of us, she's as attracted to him as he is to her. She may hate him, but he gets her off. They just have to find a balance that gives them what they both want."

"Ask for something difficult, why don't you?" Raymond quipped.

"Honestly, it's no longer even our concern," Marcel admitted. "I just worry about her."

"She's a grown woman. Tell her what's going on and then let her make her own decision," Raymond advised. "There's nothing else you can do."

"I know," Marcel sighed, "but that's a bitter pill for me to swallow. It always has been."

And that, Raymond thought, *was what made Marcel such a pivotal leader of l'ANS and what made him successful in the war against Serrier. He never accepted not being able to help.*

"If you'll excuse us, Marcel, it's been a long night and longer morning," Jean said. "I could use some rest."

"If you're going home, let me send you so you don't have to deal with the subway after all the publicity we got this morning," Marcel offered.

"Merci," Jean replied gratefully. "Home would be wonderful."

"I'll meet you there in a minute," Raymond said, gesturing for Marcel to cast the spell.

The older wizard sent Jean home, clearly curious why Raymond had lingered. "What can I do for you, my boy?" he asked when they were alone.

"Am I naïve to think I can make a life with the chef de la Cour?" Raymond asked after a moment.

"That's an interesting question," Marcel commented. "Why didn't you ask me if you could make a life with Jean?"

"Because I know I can make a life with Jean," Raymond replied with utmost confidence. "It's the public side of things that worries me."

"Then I'm about to make things even more complicated for you," Marcel apologized. "Or perhaps it will make things easier. Who knows?"

"What are you talking about?"

"I'm an old man, Raymond. I'm ready to retire and live out my golden years in peace," Marcel explained.

"You've more than earned it," Raymond replied automatically, "but what does that have to do with me?"

"The Milice will cease to exist soon, but l'ANS will require a new head. I want it to be you."

"Me?" Raymond exclaimed. "Marcel, I couldn't!"

"Why not?" Marcel asked calmly. "You've proved yourself a capable speaker today, although I didn't need today's speech to prove your abilities to me."

"What about the fact that I sided with Serrier at the beginning of the war?" Raymond reminded Marcel.

"What about the fact that without your knowledge of Serrier's hideouts and spells, we never would have defeated him?" Marcel countered.

"What about the fact that my partner is the chef de la Cour of Paris? I'm not exactly unbiased."

"None of us from the Milice would be unbiased," Marcel reminded him. "At this point, even I'm not unbiased given that I discovered my partner in monsieur Lombard. That doesn't mean you're unfit to lead. On the contrary, it makes you a better leader of an organization whose purview is about to expand considerably. Instead of simply representing wizards from now on, the mission of l'ANS must expand to represent the entire magical community, and the partner of the chef de la Cour is the perfect person to represent that new mandate."

"You wouldn't do that to me," Raymond pleaded.

"Who else is there?" Marcel asked. "Thierry and Alain are wonderful captains, but neither of them have the subtlety for public office. They'll support you and I'll be around to guide you at first, although I suspect Jean will be a more than capable guide as well, given the complexity of vampire society. Trust yourself, Raymond. The rest of us do."

Raymond coughed to cover the sudden rise of emotion that left him unable to speak. Marcel simply waited him out. "Go home to Jean," the general directed. "Talk to him. Love him. And let me know what you decide. I can't force this on you, but I do hope you'll think about it seriously."

"I'll think about it," Raymond agreed, "but taking this on… it doesn't affect just me now."

"I know," Marcel replied, "and that is a truly wonderful thing. Go home. I'll see you tomorrow."

Raymond cast his own displacement spell, leaving Marcel alone in his office. With a sigh, the general picked up his phone and called Adèle, asking her to come in as soon as possible.

Moments later, she appeared in his office. "Congratulations," she said as soon as she walked in the door. "I saw the news about the legislation."

"It is good news," Marcel agreed. "Have you recovered from the last battle?"

"I'm feeling well rested," Adèle replied. "Have *you* gotten any rest?"

"A little," Marcel assured her. "And now that the legislation has passed, I should have a little more time before the big trials start." He gestured for her to sit. "We need to talk. Your partner left a few moments ago. He's demanded that I remove the Ordre de restriction. I can delay, but with the war winding down, I won't be able to refuse outright for long. I've already removed it from him."

Adèle nodded, trying to digest the information. "You did what was best for the alliance, for the Milice, and I appreciate it. I'll just have to watch my own back from now on."

"You don't have to put up with him, Adèle," Marcel reminded her. "The legislation passed. He's bound by the same laws as the rest of us now. If you say no and he doesn't listen, that's rape."

And therein lay the problem, Adèle knew, because saying no to Jude was nearly impossible. She could fight him, insult him, prick his temper and drive him wild, but she had very rarely managed to utter the word no. "I know," she said simply. "I can take care of myself. I've been doing it for a long, long time."

"Don't go slinking back to Château-Chinon thinking you're alone now," Marcel admonished. "First of all, the Milice hasn't been disbanded yet, so you're still one of my soldiers until that happens. And even after you go home, Paris is still only a quick spell away. Don't banish yourself to the countryside just to avoid him."

"I wouldn't...," Adèle began, only to realize that she probably would have had Marcel not called her on it. "I don't want to create problems for l'ANS, or for Jean and the Cour. It's just better for me to go quietly home and let Jude forget about me."

Forgetting about him would be far more difficult.

Marcel frowned. "I can't order you to do anything once the Milice disbands, but I hate the idea of you feeling like you can't even come visit without being under siege."

Adèle smiled softly. "Undo the spell, Marcel. I'll handle whatever happens from here on out."

"Are you sure?"

She was not sure at all, but she pasted on her most confident smile. "Of course. He's just a vampire with the maturity of your average five-year-old. I handled worse than him every day on the force."

"Very well." Marcel cast the counter spell against his better judgment, but he did not know what else he could do when Adèle had asked him to remove it.

"Thank you, Marcel. For everything," Adèle said softly, rising to her feet and hugging the old wizard. "It'll be all right. You'll see."

Leaving his office, Adèle walked slowly through the halls of the Milice headquarters, stomach jumping as she half expected to hear the familiar drawled *"Hello, pussy"* from one of the empty conference rooms or offices, but she made it to her office without encountering her partner.

She could not decide whether to be disappointed or relieved that she had escaped his notice this time. She was sure he was somewhere in the bowels of headquarters, unless one of the other wizards had taken pity on him and sent him home. She could not check, though, without revealing an interest she was not ready to own up to. She despised his attitude, but she could not deny, to herself at least, that he made her react like no one else. One touch and her body went up in flames. One bite and she wanted more and more and more until the wanting devoured her and she gave in, however reluctantly, in order to get more of the sensations only he could provide. It hardly seemed to matter that she hated him. It did not even seem to matter that she hated herself when it was over. The moment he touched her, her body was his.

The simplest thing to do would be to retire to the country and forget about him. Except she had a feeling that there would be nothing simple about it. The past four days had passed in a mixture of relief in knowing he could not get close to her without her being aware of it and frustration at the absence of the frisson of nerves from always wondering when he would find her next. Nothing in her staid existence in Château-Chinon would come even close to replacing that little bit of excitement. Before she came to Paris, before she knew the twisted thrill of vying with him, she had been satisfied with her situation. She had earned the respect of her peers, even the relatively conservative older men. She had a house she loved and a job she enjoyed.

Then she met Jude.

She determinedly pushed him from her mind. He would stay in Paris when she returned home, and that would be that. Now if only she believed it.

She picked idly at the sleeve of her sweater, the form-fitting shape hidden beneath her coat. He would have something to say about that as well if he were here, insisting that she chose it because she was a slut determined to catch men's eyes. No, it was definitely better that she leave. Nothing about her would ever please him, not in any real way. Better to simply disappear than to live with this eternal fight. The sound of footsteps caught her attention. She glanced toward the door. It swung open, an all too familiar shadow appearing on the wall even before she could see who was there.

She knew it was cowardly, but she could not face him. Not now, not like this, when she was already discombobulated. Whispering quickly, she cast the displacement spell as he stepped inside.

"Adèle."

She was not there to reply.

Chapter 39

"IT'S TIME to go home. You can't stay here any longer," Mireille told Caroline. "You don't need more medical treatment."

"I can hardly go home like this," Caroline protested bitterly. "I can't even get myself dressed, much less do anything else. How am I supposed to go home by myself?"

"Who said anything about going anywhere by yourself?" Mireille asked. "You're coming home with me. I talked to monsieur Lombard about it and he agreed. Between the two of us, we can help you get used to taking care of yourself again."

Caroline frowned, hating the thought of being a burden on anyone, much less on Mireille and her employer. "You shouldn't have to babysit an invalid," she groused.

"You aren't an invalid," Mireille insisted, handing Caroline her shirt. The blonde pulled it over her head automatically. "You lost your eyesight, not your ability to live your life, and the medics said even that could come back in time, at least somewhat. And see, you just put your shirt on fine without my help."

"Only after you gave it to me," Caroline reminded the vampire. "If you weren't here, I'd still be sitting here in nothing but my underwear."

"Stop feeling sorry for yourself and put your pants on," Mireille ordered, throwing them in Caroline's face. "One of the medics is waiting to send us home so he can clean this room."

Caroline fumbled a little with getting the right foot in the correct pants leg, but Mireille refused to help her, standing with arms crossed in front of her partner while Caroline struggled with the recalcitrant garment. Eventually she figured it out, though, and stood up triumphantly.

"I told you you could do it," Mireille said when Caroline was done. "And it will get easier every time."

"I'm still going to have to relearn everything," Caroline complained.

Mireille shrugged. "So you relearn it. That doesn't mean you won't be able to function normally. You just have to give yourself time."

"I'm not a very good patient," Caroline warned, slipping on the shoes Mireille gave her. "I'll probably drive you crazy." Hand out in front of her, she took a step forward. Mireille caught Caroline's hand and tucked it in the crook of her own arm, guiding her partner out of the room and down the hall to the entrance of the infirmary.

"You're ready to go," the medic declared, casting the displacement spell for them.

When they reappeared in the foyer to monsieur Lombard's house, Caroline had tears in her eyes. "What's wrong?" Mireille asked immediately.

"Am I not even allowed to do magic anymore?" Caroline asked brokenly. "I know I can't see, but surely I could have cast my own displacement spell. I don't need to see to know where I'm going."

"Your eyes have nothing to do with it," Mireille scolded gently, pulling Caroline into a tender embrace. "He said you shouldn't do magic for another week because you're still weak from the blood you lost. Once you've recovered physically, you should be able to do magic like you always did. You just have to let your body heal."

Caroline let herself be held. She had tried so hard to keep her spirits up after waking up with bandages over her eyes, but that attempt was doomed to failure. No one had a truly positive prognosis for her, and that left her angry, bitter, and not a little bit depressed. Mireille had been the one bright spot in her life since then, refusing to let her wallow in self-pity, but Caroline wondered how long that would last before Mireille grew tired of babysitting her.

The door chime interrupted them. Mireille thought about ignoring it, but monsieur Lombard could not answer it himself and it might be important. "What are you doing here, Général?" she asked when she opened the door to see Marcel standing on the stoop.

"I'm following the doctor's orders," Caroline said bitterly before Marcel could reply. "I won't do any magic for another week. You didn't have to come check on me."

Marcel and Mireille exchanged sympathetic looks. "I didn't even know you were here," he answered truthfully. "As much as you might think otherwise, the world doesn't revolve around you. *My* partner lives here too, and I have yet to find the opportunity to speak with him about what that might mean. However, since I'm here, I'll mention that I just got the number of a good occupational therapist, one who specializes in working with wizards to use their magic to cope with their disabilities." He pressed a piece of paper into her hand. "I suggest you contact him immediately so you can start getting back on your feet. You'll have a certain amount of time off for disability, but the CNAF can't hold your job indefinitely. They have too high a caseload to do that."

"I didn't know you were a social worker," Mireille said admiringly. "All the more reason to get you back on your feet as quickly as possible."

Caroline nodded, not sure she wanted to start hoping again, only to chance having those hopes dashed. "I worked with the family allocations, trying to help people get the assistance they need."

"No, you *work* for them, unless you turned in your resignation without telling me," Marcel insisted. "Call the occupational therapist. You'll be back at work in no time. And now, Mireille, if you wouldn't mind letting monsieur Lombard know I'm here, I'd like a few minutes to talk with my partner."

"Of course," Mireille replied, a flush rising to her cheeks as she realized they were still standing in the foyer. She helped Caroline to a seat against the wall and went to find monsieur Lombard.

Returning a few moments later, she escorted Marcel into the library where her employer waited. After making sure neither of them wanted anything, she went back to the foyer to collect Caroline. "Come upstairs," she urged, putting Caroline's hand on her elbow again. "We'll get you settled."

Caroline let Mireille guide her up the front stairs to the attic. In her mind, she pictured the rooms she had seen once before, counting how many steps made up the staircase, how many to go down the hallway. "How many doors are there?" she asked suddenly.

"Five," Mireille replied. "The first four still are used for storage. The last one is mine. The workmen filled in the others when they made my quarters so there's only one door in."

Caroline committed that information to memory. If nothing else, a hand on the wall could guide her if she could make it back to this level of the house. They did not stop in the living room this time, Mireille leading Caroline straight through to the bedroom. She started to protest, though, when Mireille popped open the button on her slacks. "I've spent the past week in bed," Caroline groaned. "The last thing I want is to go back to bed again."

Mireille laughed, a low sultry sound that rubbed along Caroline's nerves like warm velvet. "But you've spent the past week in bed alone," she reminded the wizard. "You won't be alone this time."

"But—"

"But nothing," Mireille interrupted. "You don't need your vision for us to make love. Or do you mean to tell me you've never let a lover blindfold you? Never made love in the dark with only the sense of touch to guide your hands?"

"Yes, but—"

"No buts," Mireille insisted. "My bed is right behind you. I want to climb in it with you and not come up for hours. I want to remind you that we're both here, safe, and that whatever tomorrow brings, we'll face it together. I want to make you feel so good that you forget about your eyes, about the Milice, about everything but me. Now, are you going to cooperate?"

Head spinning with surprise and desire, Caroline nodded mutely. Mireille's hands were firm as they guided her back two more steps and helped her stretch out across the bed. Caroline felt the mattress dip as the redhead climbed onto the bed next to her. Her body tensed as she tried to anticipate where Mireille would touch her first.

She had been so afraid that her blindness would spell the end of her relationship with her partner. She feared Mireille would humor her in order to continue feeding but that the rest of their interactions would suffer. The assiduity with which Mireille kissed her—the first touch she had been anticipating—proved how baseless that fear was. The other woman could not possibly kiss her that way unless she truly meant it.

Caroline reached instinctively for Mireille's shoulders, finding cloth still covering her lover's skin. Not parting their lips, Caroline worked her hands between them, intent on finding the fastenings on Mireille's shirt so she could get it off. Not locating any, she slid her hands lower until she found the hem of the offending garment, working it up and off. Their lips met again, drawn together like magnets as Caroline's hands moved down Mireille's back to the clasp of her bra.

"You don't seem to have any trouble undressing me," Mireille teased as Caroline peeled the satin away from her breasts. She lowered her torso onto her partner's, rubbing the tender mounds together. "It's just a question of motivation."

"With you as my reward, I could probably figure out just about anything," Caroline admitted.

"Ah, but I *am* your reward," Mireille reminded her. "You aren't facing your recovery alone. I'll be here every step of the way, and you'll get your reward for every step."

"And what step am I being rewarded for tonight?"

"Tonight, you're being rewarded for being you," Mireille replied. "Or did you think I wouldn't want to make love with you anymore?"

"I didn't know," Caroline admitted, tipping her head up to seek Mireille's lips again. She found the smooth column of her neck instead.

"Silly girl," Mireille scolded, fingers tracing over Caroline's features tenderly. "Of course I still want you. Let me show you how much."

Caroline might have resented the appellation from anyone else, but Mireille was a vampire. Even if she was a relatively young one, she was still far older than Caroline herself. Then Mireille's fingers trailed along the underside of Caroline's breast and she forgot about everything except how good her lover could make her feel.

Mireille made love to her so thoroughly, so convincingly that Caroline forgot about her blindness, about the war, about everything except trying to make Mireille feel just as good. The vampire's fangs pierced Caroline's neck, pinning her in place as her hands drove the wizard to completion and beyond. When they finally lay curled together, sated and smiling, Caroline pressed a tender kiss to Mireille's shoulder. "Maybe I can do this after all."

Mireille laughed. "I know you can."

"I'm sorry I was so negative," Caroline apologized sleepily.

"We all have bad days," Mireille said. "I'll pick you up when you're down and you'll do the same for me. Let yourself rest now. We'll worry about tomorrow when it comes."

Caroline nodded and yawned again, her eyes drifting shut, the unfamiliar darkness of her blinded eyes giving way to the familiar darkness of preparing to sleep. More than once, she had felt her way around her apartment at night by touch alone rather than turning on the lights. She would just have to learn how to do that in the rest of her life as well. Then sleep overtook her, stilling all her thoughts and worries for the time being.

"YOUR VISIT is rather presumptuous, is it not?" monsieur Lombard said from the relative darkness of the library. "I don't remember inviting you to my home."

"You didn't have to see me," Marcel replied equably. "But we haven't had a chance to talk privately and I thought perhaps we should."

"I chose several hundred years ago to live in retirement. I have no desire to change that decision now," Christophe informed Marcel. "Certainly not to be the partner of Général Chavinier and the president of l'ANS."

"I appreciate that sentiment fully," Marcel assured the vampire. "I have no desire to be either of those things anymore. The Milice is already in the process of being disbanded, and I've chosen a successor for my position with l'ANS. In a matter of weeks, I'll be a private citizen again, nothing more."

"That doesn't tell me why you're here," Christophe insisted. "With Serrier defeated, there's no longer a reason for me to feed from you. I've lived so long as a vampire that I've truly lost the desire to see daylight again. The glimpse the other day only confirmed that."

"Perhaps I simply seek interesting company," Marcel suggested. "It's not often one has the chance to talk with a vampire of your age."

"I'm not an oddity to be studied at whim," Christophe growled, drawing himself to his full height.

"Nor am I a scientist to study you," Marcel retorted. "I've been in public life too long. Everyone wants something of me. I hoped perhaps in you I might find someone who would simply accept me as myself without thinking of what political agenda I can help you advance or what favor I can do for you. Retired as you are, all you could possibly want from me is my blood."

"And yet that, too, would be an ulterior motive," Christophe pointed out.

"But an honest one," Marcel explained. "One that would not require me to do or be anything special. Or do you think I have some kind of ulterior motive in seeking you out?"

"It would not be the first time," Christophe admitted.

"Then find out for sure," Marcel challenged, holding out his wrist.

Christophe raised an elegant eyebrow. "Why should I find out that way when it's so much more interesting to get to know a person the traditional way?" He glanced at the clock. "It will be dark in two hours. If what you truly want is a friend—nothing more, nothing less—meet me at Le Saulnier half an hour after dark. We'll see what happens from there."

Marcel nodded. He was more than a little surprised that Lombard could turn away from the partnership bond so easily. Having seen the near compulsion between the paired wizards and vampires, even Adèle and Jude who hated each other, he had come expecting the same influence to work on them. Certainly the explosion of power between them when the elder vampire fed during the battle with Serrier had led Marcel to believe the rest of the partnership bond would prove true for them as well. It seemed, though, that with great age and power came the ability to resist. Or perhaps the end of the war and the current equilibrium in the elemental magic had lessened the compulsion to create new bonds. It made him wonder if Adèle and Jude, or even some of the others who had not deepened their relationships as far as Raymond and Jean, would feel a lessening of the need now that the urgency of the situation had passed. He had no answers for those questions. Only time would reveal them. "I'll see you in a few hours, then. I'll show myself out. I don't want to disturb Mireille and Caroline."

"I'm sure they'll appreciate that," Christophe said drolly as the door shut behind Marcel. He could admit to himself that he had enjoyed the rather barbed exchange. So rarely did anyone dare speak back to him in any way. He found Marcel's lack of fawning admiration refreshing. He had no interest in most of the benefits the partnerships had brought to the other vampires and wizards involved in the alliance. He had reached a plane of existence where even sensual pleasures had lost most of their appeal—and while Marcel's blood had been incredibly rich, Christophe had known enough loss in his existence not to open himself up to more. He thought it might be nice, though, to have a friend again, for however long it lasted.

Chapter 40

"THANK YOU for agreeing to meet with us, monsieur le directeur-général," Marcel said, offering his hand to the head of the Gendarmerie Nationale. "With the Milice de Sorcellerie scheduled to be disbanded in a matter of weeks, I wanted to make sure the transfer of authority went smoothly."

"Definitely," Guy Sarraute agreed. "There's been, as you predicted, an almost complete cessation of active hostilities since Serrier's death."

"And we don't expect that to change," Adèle inserted. "Working with one of our covert agents and several other dark wizards who were willing to exchange information for lighter sentences, we've compiled a list of known operatives in Serrier's forces. Cross-referencing that list with the list of casualties and prisoners awaiting trial, we're down to about twenty-five wizards still at large."

"Do you have any leads on their location?" Sarraute inquired.

"We know they aren't in Paris anymore," Marcel replied. "I preferred not to send my people farther afield than that so as not to infringe on anyone else's jurisdiction. We have the list of fugitives as well as their known origins and associates. I believe you and your agency would be the best ones to handle the arrests from here on out."

"We appreciate your confidence, Général," Sarraute said.

"Perhaps you might accept Lieutenant Rougier's assistance," Marcel added. "She's been on loan to us from the Gendarmerie. While I know she's greatly missed in the Morvan, I believe her experience in the Milice would make her an excellent candidate for spearheading this investigation."

Adèle started to shake her head, to deny any desire to remain in Paris, but she bit back the protest. She was a wizard. She could work in Paris during the day and return home to Château-Chinon at night, thus avoiding contact with her erstwhile partner as surely as if she worked in the country. She had not seen him in the week since Marcel had released the Ordre de restriction, but she did not know how much longer that would last. The urge to go looking for him caught her at odd times. So far, she had managed to resist.

"Are you interested in a promotion, Lieutenant?" Sarraute asked. Adèle felt his eyes skim over her, but he seemed far more interested in her curriculum vitae than in her body, a refreshing attitude after dealing with her bastard of a partner for the past six weeks. It assured her as little else could have done that this would be one post she could accept with equanimity.

"Not a permanent one," Adèle demurred, "but I'd be honored to serve during this investigation. Eventually, though, I'd like to return home."

"Very good. When can you release her to me, Général?"

"Immediately, if you're ready to start," Marcel replied. "She has all the intelligence we have at the moment, and we'll communicate any new information to her as it becomes available."

"Bien," Sarraute declared. "Lieutenant, take today to get your affairs in order here at the Milice. We'll expect you at headquarters, rue St Didier, tomorrow morning."

"Thank you, sir," Adèle said. "I look forward to working with you."

"I'll have someone show you out, monsieur Sarraute," Marcel said, escorting the gendarme to the door. He called to a passing wizard to show the man back to his car. Going inside, he smiled at Adèle. "Well, my dear, that's settled. Are you pleased?"

"I think so," Adèle replied honestly. "It will be quite the different challenge than my sleepy village, but maybe that's what I need for a little longer. I can commute from home to start that transition back to my old life."

"Just don't be a stranger," Marcel insisted. "We want to see you occasionally."

"I promise," Adèle said, coming to give Marcel a hug. She had no idea what would happen, how things would resolve in the end between Jude and herself, but she would not let that uncertainty cost her the friends she had made during her stay in Paris.

ERIC SAT nervously in the back of the courtroom, waiting for Vincent's trial to begin. Marcel had been as good as his word over the past two weeks, letting Eric visit Vincent as often as he wanted. That had not reassured either of them, though, when the verdict came back on Monique's trial. Instead of time served and parole as the defense had requested as part of her plea bargain, she had received a year in prison. It was not that much, in the grand scheme of things, but it was enough to make Eric nervous. Vincent had been higher placed in Serrier's organization, making the list of crimes against him longer and more serious than the ones Monique had been accused of. The tender scene at the end of her trial—much of it held at night so that Antonio, Monique's partner, could attend—had torn at his heart. They had embraced, wizard and vampire, Antonio promising fervently to wait for her release, a year being nothing in a vampire's existence. Eric would easily make the same promise to Vincent, but watching them had driven home the very real risk of separation.

The bailiff brought Vincent in, giving Eric the first glimpse of his lover in two days. He was dressed conservatively, but nothing could disguise the breadth of his shoulders or the strength of his body. Eric wanted to go to him, to hug and kiss him, to assure himself that his lover was well. He restrained the impulse, not wanting to tip the scales against them by giving the impression of bias in his testimony. Vincent's fate rested on the jury being willing to accept Eric's account of Vincent's defection.

A moment later, the prosecutor entered followed by the judge. Everyone rose, ready for the trial to begin.

The prosecutor spoke first, outlining the list of crimes against Vincent. Eric flinched as he listened to the catalogue of charges. Illegal use of magic. Kidnapping. Torture. Murder. Treason. He had no idea how they would manage to make all of that go away to just time served and parole, but Marcel seemed confident that they could.

"How does the defendant plead?" the judge asked.

"The defendant has entered a plea bargain," the defense attorney explained. "In addition to working with one of the covert agents of the Milice, he helped a captured agent escape and has since then provided information leading to the arrest of a number of other dark wizards. In light of his contributions to Serrier's final defeat, we have asked for the treason, murder, and torture charges to be dropped."

"Does the prosecution accept the plea?" the judge asked.

"We do," the prosecutor replied. "The defendant's information has been vital in the cases we're building."

"That leaves illegal use of magic and kidnapping," the judge declared.

Eric flinched when he considered who they had kidnapped. He could see Alain and Orlando toward the front of the courtroom. He and Alain had made their peace, but he doubted that acceptance would ever extend to Vincent. He knew the defense attorney intended to have Orlando testify in Vincent's favor, speaking of the fact that Vincent had helped him escape, but Eric feared Vincent's role in Orlando's initial disappearance would weigh heavily against him. That they were just following orders hardly mattered against everything Orlando had suffered.

The first day of the trial involved the opening arguments and several long-winded speeches by both sides about their views on the value of Vincent having changed sides at the end. Eric did his best not to roll his eyes in frustration. Vincent had only waited until the end to change sides so he could make sure to save Orlando in the process. Unfortunately, that would be considered hearsay since Eric was the only witness. He did not care. He fully intended to make the jury aware that rescuing Orlando as a way to escape Serrier's control was Vincent's idea, just as soon as he was called to the stand.

It took three days of listening to witnesses describe all the terrible things Vincent had reputedly done before Eric was finally called to the stand. He stated his name for the record and waited for the interrogation to begin.

"How long have you known the defendant?" the prosecutor asked.

"Two years."

"In what context did you meet him?"

"I met him soon after I went undercover for the Milice," Eric replied. "I befriended him hoping to work my way up in Serrier's ranks so I would be able to provide more information to Général Chavinier."

"So he was a member of Serrier's rebels."

"A fact he hasn't bothered to deny," Eric pointed out. "The salient point is that he switched sides. And not just at the final battle. For several weeks prior to that, he tried to persuade me to switch sides. Obviously I resisted because I had a mission to complete, but that doesn't negate his intentions."

"Then why wait until the last minute?" the prosecutor challenged.

"It was becoming increasingly obvious that Serrier was going insane," Eric explained. "He'd captured a Milice operative, a vampire, and was torturing him for the pleasure of it by that point. Serrier intended to execute the vampire at dawn the morning that ended up being the day of his demise, but we didn't know that. We just knew we had to save Orlando—the vampire. We'd seen too much death to stand idly by and not do anything to stop another one."

"Why did you choose this operative to save and not any of the others?" the prosecutor asked.

"I already told you," Eric said. "Serrier was clearly losing it and we were afraid if we didn't get out—Orlando as well as us—that we wouldn't get another chance. Général Chavinier sent me to spy, but he didn't send me to die, even though I knew that was a risk. Serrier had started suspecting everyone, so I wasn't going to be able to do much more good for the Milice anyway. Vincent wanted out. Orlando was dying. It seemed the perfect opportunity. Neither Orlando nor I would have survived without Vincent's assistance. I realize my life might not matter much, but the Milice invested serious resources in finding and saving Orlando so his life obviously means something."

"No further questions, Your Honor."

Eric breathed a sigh of relief as the defense attorney rose to pose his own questions. "You mentioned that saving monsieur St. Clair was the defendant's idea. At what point did he first mention that to you?"

"Less than a day after Orlando's kidnapping," Eric replied, careful not to remind the jury unduly of his and Vincent's involvement in that unfortunate event. "Another of Serrier's agents switched sides, and it was obvious she was under Milice protection. And from subsequent Milice actions, it was obvious to us that the Milice was actively searching for Orlando. But while it wouldn't have been possible to think of saving Orlando before that, it wasn't the first time Vincent had mentioned wishing for other options. You have to understand that Serrier didn't brook any kind of opposition, and he had no qualms about torturing people who disobeyed him. It wasn't enough to simply want out. Leaving meant going to jail—or being killed if Serrier found him first—unless Vincent could find a way to convince the Milice to offer their protection. He didn't know that I could have left at any time. He was trying to find a way to get us both out safely. Orlando's situation provided the means, but not the desire."

"So you're saying that the defendant was disillusioned with Serrier's message and methods some time before he actually defected?" the defense attorney asked.

"Objection. Leading the witness."

"I was merely paraphrasing the witness's statements."

"Sustained."

The defense attorney glared at his opponent before turning back to Eric. "When did you first suspect that the defendant was becoming disillusioned with Serrier's message and methods?"

"It wasn't something we talked about, but even before the alliance with the vampires was formed, I noticed Vincent had stopped volunteering for assignments. He still followed orders when they were given, but he didn't seek them out anymore. And more than once, he counseled against Serrier's wilder plans. The first time he actually said something to me was a day or two after Samhain, but it only confirmed what I already suspected about his feelings on the matter."

Eric did his best not to let his emotions show on his face as he thought of everything else that had changed since that night. The night they became lovers. Suddenly, instead of facing a bleak future with no hope, no life, he had the possibility of a real partner in life again, someone to love and support as he was loved and supported. They just had to get through this trial and whatever sentence the court assigned.

"And what did he say to you on that occasion?"

"He asked me if I ever thought about getting out," Eric replied. "I told him that I didn't see any way out without Serrier hunting us down, but that if I knew we would be safe, I'd consider it. Things hadn't gotten as bad yet as they did before the end. I thought I could still do some good as a spy, so I didn't reveal my hidden loyalty at the time. Vincent, though, took my answer as an invitation to find a way out. And he did."

"You also mentioned that neither you nor the other Milice operative would have survived without his assistance. Could you explain that statement, please?"

Eric nodded, remembering the fraught night and morning leading up to Orlando's rescue. "The Milice was closing in on Serrier's remaining hideouts. Serrier called everyone in and transported us all to the location of the final battle, including Orlando. Vincent and I took advantage of the confusion upon our arrival to release Orlando from his cell, but Blanchet, one of the other dark wizards, stumbled upon us. Vincent kept him from killing me and stopping Orlando from escaping. We fought our way out together. I might have taken out Blanchet, but I couldn't have gotten Orlando and myself out alive without assistance."

"Merci, monsieur Simonet," the defense attorney said.

Eric returned to his seat, hoping he had not done too much damage to Vincent's cause with his testimony. His stomach churned nervously as the lawyers called Orlando to the stand.

"Monsieur St. Clair," the prosecutor began, "when did you first see the defendant?"

Orlando frowned, but he had sworn to the truth. "He was one of two wizards who kidnapped me from place Pigalle during a battle aimed at vampires."

"So he took you to Serrier?" the prosecutor pressed.

"Yes," Orlando admitted. Eric's stomach fell at the words.

"And did you see him again once he had brought you to Serrier's base?" the prosecutor pressed.

"A few times," Orlando replied. "He was occasionally sent to bring me to or from the room where Serrier interrogated me."

"So he used magic on you?"

"Only binding spells," Orlando answered quickly. "He never participated in any of Serrier's interrogation sessions or in Blanchet's later torture sessions. And then I saw him again when he helped me escape, the morning Serrier had intended to stake me out in the sun. The partnership bonds protected me for a period of time, but my partner's magic had long since worn off. I wouldn't have survived that. I'm only here to testify today because he and Eric set me free."

"And yet he was the reason you were in Serrier's hands to begin with," the prosecutor reminded him.

"He was following orders," Orlando insisted, "and I saw what Serrier did to people who crossed him. I hadn't been there ten minutes when he executed another wizard who admitted to spying for Marcel. And at the same time, he tortured another wizard who was, at that point, still loyal to him simply because he suspected she might also be a spy."

"So you're saying you don't blame him for what happened to you?" the man asked incredulously.

"That's exactly what I'm saying," Orlando replied firmly.

"No further questions, Your Honor."

"Of everyone who has testified against the defendant," the defense attorney said, rising to his feet, "you would seem to have the most reason to want to see him punished, yet you appear to hold him blameless."

"I'm a vampire," Orlando said as if that explained everything. "I tend to take a longer view of things. The fact of the matter is, I wouldn't have had a future at all if Vincent hadn't chosen to switch sides when he did."

"And in your eyes, that mitigates what he did?"

"Yes."

"No further questions."

Eric watched with quiet jealousy as Orlando returned to Alain's side, their fingers lacing together in silent communion. Eric wanted to be able to join Vincent and offer his own silent support, but they had to wait until Vincent was released, whenever that was, before he could let anyone else see the truth of their relationship.

Another day passed in closing arguments before the jury retired to deliberate Vincent's fate. Eric tried to get in to see his lover that night, to promise him that no matter what happened, Eric would be there waiting when Vincent got out, but not even Marcel could arrange a visit at that point.

Finally, the jury returned. Eric sat in the front this time, within reach of Vincent so he could hopefully get one last touch in should the verdict go against them. The guilty plea had already been entered, so the only deliberation the jury had to decide was what Vincent's sentence would be.

"Has the jury reached a verdict?" the judge asked.

"We have, Your Honor," the head juror replied.

"And what have you decided?"

"Time served and five years parole," the juror declared.

Eric slumped forward in relief, eyes going to his lover, drinking in the welcome sight. There would still be paperwork to process, but Vincent was coming home.

Chapter 41

ORLANDO LOOKED over at Alain, shaking his head as his lover stood in his office door, staring at the space as if it would somehow magically disappear or transform.

"Just because it's our last official shift doesn't mean we can't come back for the stuff that's here," Orlando reminded him. "Your desk will still be here later. I promise. Come on. You're tired and we both need a shower."

That brought a smile to Alain's face. "Frankly, we stink?" he asked with a tease in his voice.

"Exactly," Orlando replied. "Do you suppose someone's still on duty to send us home?"

"I doubt it," Alain replied, "but we can check. If not, it's not that far to the apartment by Métro."

Orlando could hardly argue with that, even if he was eager to be home more quickly than even the efficient Paris subway system could arrange. Alain was right. The Salle des Cartes was empty when they checked, the locator map dark. Orlando did not know when the next patrol would come on duty or even if another patrol would come on duty, but he did not want to stand around waiting. "The Métro it is," he declared.

Hand in hand, they walked through the silent corridors until they reached the exit. After glancing back inside once more, Alain let Orlando lead him through the streets to the subway stop, the reverse of the first time they had come to Milice headquarters together. How far they had come since then!

"Can you believe it's all over?" Orlando asked as they descended into the tunnels again to wait for the train that would whisk them to their destination.

Alain shook his head. "It's not over. It's just beginning."

"The war, I meant," Orlando elaborated.

"No, I can't quite believe it," Alain admitted. "It's been more than two years. I haven't had time for anything else. It will be odd, not being on patrol all the time."

"So what will you do?" Orlando wanted to know.

Alain shrugged. "I still have a job with l'ANS. I guess I'll go back to work for Marcel, just in a different capacity than over the last two years. What about you? Now that you have the freedom to move in daylight again, your options are pretty much limitless."

"I haven't even thought beyond the end of the war," Orlando admitted ruefully. "Until a few weeks ago, there weren't all that many options for me anyway. I don't need a job. Thurloe's estate passed to me when he was destroyed, so as long as I'm relatively frugal I don't need a larger income than what I earn off the interest from his investments. The apartment is long since paid off so that hasn't been an issue."

"I wasn't thinking about that as much as I was about how you'd fill the hours while I was at work," Alain explained. "I don't like the thought of you home alone with nothing to do while I'm away. Unless you want to come to work for l'ANS too."

"I'm sure I can find something to keep myself busy," Orlando teased. "All the places I've never been able to visit except at night. All the art I've never been able to see except in books. All the stores that have always been closed to me. But I like the idea of working for the greater good."

"I think I've created a monster," Alain quipped affectionately. Orlando laughed, as Alain had intended, amusement lighting up his face with an inner joy so radiant, so inviting that Alain could not stop himself from leaning forward and kissing his lover. He ignored the other commuters, letting their conversations eddy around him unnoticed. His only focus was the vampire currently returning his kiss with seductive ardor. "Can't this train go any faster?" he muttered, breaking the kiss breathlessly.

"Just a few more minutes," Orlando assured Alain as the subway neared the Père Lachaise stop. To ease the tension between them, he took Alain's hand, stroking the knuckles lightly, and changed the subject. "What did you do with your free time before, when you had it?"

"I tended to work around the house," Alain said. "Little repairs, that kind of thing. Henri and I used to talk about buying an old house in the country and fixing it up ourselves on the weekends. It was a child's dream, really. One we never got to fulfill."

"It wouldn't be with Henri, but there's no reason we couldn't do it now," Orlando said softly. "A big old house with a huge yard. We could work on it a little at a time. I know you say our apartment is fine, and it has been so far, but I think it would eventually start feeling crowded with us both living there. A house would give us more space, let us have friends come visit now that I actually have people to invite."

The train rolled to a halt at their stop. They exited the subway automatically, barely paying any attention to their surroundings as they discussed their future.

"I don't know," Alain hesitated. "I'm not sure I could do it now, without Henri. It was always our dream."

"I understand," Orlando replied immediately. "We don't have to rush into anything. Just think about it, that's all. If at some point you decide it's something you want again, know I'm interested."

Alain nodded, not sure how these suddenly revived dreams fit into his slowly healing psyche. Having Eric back in the fold helped with some of the sense of loss, but nothing could replace his son. Perhaps if he had fallen in love with a different woman after Edwige died, he would have felt differently, but Orlando, a male and a vampire, could certainly not give him another child with whom to renew those dreams.

"We can think about it," he agreed finally.

They reached the entrance to Orlando's apartment building, climbing the steps with more urgency now as the desire they had quelled on the subway returned to the fore. Hurrying inside, they shut the door behind them, enclosing themselves in the privacy and safety of their home. Alain would do as he had said and think about the possibility of a country house—he had to admit the idea still appealed—but he doubted he could ever bring himself to give up their apartment either. Not when it was where they had first made love, had first fallen in love. He had enough set aside for a large down payment on a house, and his salary from l'ANS would more than cover a mortgage without having to draw from Orlando's income at all. They could use that for tools and supplies if they decided to buy a house in need of restoration.

"Penny for your thoughts," Orlando murmured, nuzzling Alain's neck.

"I was just thinking that this apartment will always be special to me, even if we eventually end up getting another place too," Alain explained. "So much has happened here. The first time we kissed, the first time you stood in the sunlight, the first time you truly fed from me. The first time we made love."

"The first time you made love to me," Orlando added with a nod. "I see what you mean about not wanting to let those memories go, but you know they'll stay a part of us even if we live somewhere else."

"I know," Alain agreed. "The rest of what I was thinking was that since you already own this apartment outright, we can probably afford to have a second place without having to sell this one. Marcel pays me pretty well. Certainly well enough to meet a house payment."

"Good to know," Orlando teased. "Otherwise I might think you wanted me for my money."

Alain laughed. "I didn't even know you had money until you mentioned it just now. Hard to want you for something I didn't even know you had."

"I'm not likely to advertise it, given my bad luck in the past," Orlando pointed out. "And I forget about it, most times. I don't do anything. The money's all invested and the dividends are deposited automatically into my bank account. All I do is spend what I need. And I don't need much. Just a roof over my head and blood to drink."

"You've taken care of the roof on your own, but I'll be glad to provide all the blood you want," Alain replied immediately, holding out his wrist.

"That's not how I want it," Orlando insisted, nudging Alain's chin higher so he could reach the stubbled skin of Alain's neck. "I'd much rather bite you here."

"I don't care where you bite me as long as you do," Alain replied breathlessly.

Orlando grinned. "Then we aren't in the right room, because there's no way I'm going to feed without making love to you at the same time."

"Thank God," Alain sighed, leaning into Orlando's embrace.

Orlando led Alain into the bedroom, their lips meeting repeatedly as they moved into the dark room. Orlando reached for the lamp. "I want to see you," he husked as Alain started to undress. He caught the wizard's hands, placing them back on his hips. "I want to do that," the vampire explained.

"Anything you want," Alain promised, leaving his hands where Orlando put them and letting his lover unbutton his shirt slowly, kissing each inch of skin as it was revealed, lingering on the dusky nipples. Alain's back arched into the little nips, but Orlando's fangs stayed well clear of his sensitive flesh.

Alain's hands came up to cradle Orlando's head, tangling in the long, dark strands of the vampire's hair. "You can bite me," he whispered.

"Oh, I will," Orlando promised, "but not yet. I have other things I want to do first, and once I get a taste of your blood, I won't be able to stop."

"I like the sound of that," Alain murmured as Orlando's hands finished unbuttoning his shirt and pushed it off his shoulders.

"I love your chest," Orlando praised as his lips continued their peregrinations. His fingers tugged lightly at the dusting of hair over the strong muscles, enjoying the texture beneath his fingertips.

Alain flushed, a mixture of desire and embarrassment coloring his cheeks, but he accepted the compliment, fully intending to return it at the appropriate time. Then Orlando's lips sucked strongly on the skin below his navel and Alain's train of thought deserted him completely. "Harder," he pleaded.

Orlando dropped to his knees and did as Alain asked, sucking harder until he raised a slight bruise to the surface. As his lips and teeth worked the sensitive skin, his hands attacked the belt, button, and zipper on Alain's trousers, opening them to give him access to his real goal: his lover's cock.

It sprang free as soon as Orlando pushed down Alain's boxers, hard and long and already leaking. Orlando took the entire length in his mouth, feeling it bump the back of his throat as he did. He licked eagerly along the shaft, wanting to give Alain as much pleasure as possible.

Alain's eyes rolled back in his head as he struggled to maintain his balance against the concentrated attack on his senses. His thighs trembled, a signal Orlando caught immediately.

"Lie down," the vampire suggested. "I want you good and wet. You've got some catching up to do."

Alain shook his head as he moved to the bed. "We aren't keeping score," he reminded Orlando. "I won't ever get tired of feeling you pierce me in every way possible, so banish that thought. I want you inside me tonight, just like you were the first time we made love."

"Is that what we're doing tonight?" Orlando teased. "Recreating the first time we made love?"

Alain shook his head. "As precious as that memory is, it isn't complete. You didn't bite me then and I don't want to give up that pleasure tonight."

"Neither do I," Orlando agreed, grateful once again for how willingly Alain accepted every aspect of his lover's vampire nature.

"Come make love to me," Alain beckoned.

Orlando knelt between his lover's spread legs, grinned up at him and returned to lavishing attention on Alain's cock. He had every intention of granting his lover's request—in his own time, at his own pace.

Alain bucked up into the welcoming heat of Orlando's mouth, reveling in how far they had come since that first afternoon together when they had hesitated over every caress. Orlando might linger now, but it was out of desire, not out of fear, an aphrodisiac more powerful than any drug. He gasped as Orlando licked around the tip of his erection, tonguing the foreskin and the leaking slit. He wanted to beg, to plead with his lover to hurry, but no words came out. Only a long, low moan escaped him. Orlando glanced up at him with smiling eyes and proceeded to lick his way to the base of Alain's cock and lower, sucking on the heavy sac, his hand replacing his lips on the hard shaft.

Alain panted harshly as he spread his legs wider, opening himself for whatever Orlando might choose to do. He considered asking Orlando to rim him, but he was not sure how his lover would feel about that request, even if he could make his throat work to give voice to the thought. Then cool fingers slick with lube found his entrance and worked their way inside, stretching him. Alain stored the thought for another time, after he had the chance to broach the subject with his vampire in a less fraught context.

Unerringly, Orlando found Alain's prostate, his fingertips teasing the sensitive bump until Alain was writhing on the bed, babble falling from his lips. He wanted more, wanted his lover's girth stretching him instead, but he could not form that request any more than he could any other. Orlando seemed to know what he needed, though, sliding his fingers free and shunting his cock between Alain's buttocks, teasing him slightly before sheathing himself in the wizard's slick heat.

Alain groaned in hungry desperation, feeling the first connection between them slam into place. Closing his eyes, he let the emotional connection come to the fore as well. Now it lacked only Orlando's fangs. As if on cue, Orlando's lips lowered to his neck, finding the brand and licking across it once before piercing Alain's flesh with his fangs.

"Orlando!"

The desperation in Alain's voice matched the need in his blood, firing a comparable response in Orlando's loins. He forced himself to set a slow, even pace, though, not wanting to rush their lovemaking. It was still too new, too novel, to hurry, however much he could taste Alain's willingness in his blood. His hands stilled Alain's hips, soothing him to the same slow rhythm.

"Please," Alain begged, but Orlando kept his movements slow and languorous.

He joined their bodies in the same way they had joined their lives: totally, completely, and in every way possible. Alain gasped and writhed beneath him, his movements driving Orlando's fangs deeper with each thrust until the vampire thought he might be swallowed up into Alain's flesh, truly one being. He had never known such a deep sense of connection with another being, vampire or mortal, and he knew nothing could ever compare with this. The awareness of Alain's mortality weighed heavily on him, but he pushed it aside, concentrating on the here and now, on reveling in every sensation so that nothing interfered with this moment, with the perfection of this slice of time outside of time. He would carry this memory with him forever, branded into his heart as surely as the imprint of his ring was branded into Alain's neck.

"Please," Alain gasped again, and this time Orlando gave in, his hips pistoning harder, driving them toward their release now, lust spurring them onward. Their bodies fought for release, but it hovered just out of reach.

Breaking the vampire's kiss, Orlando lifted his head so he could stare down into Alain's cerulean gaze. "I love you," he said firmly before sealing his lips over his lover's.

That was the contact they needed, the words, the lover's kiss, enough to send them spiraling into bliss, their release spilling out of them to anoint Alain's sheath and their stomachs. Orlando collapsed atop his wizard, ignoring the stickiness between them as they continued to kiss—softer, slower, more about love than lust now that their bodies were sated. They both knew their souls never would be.

"Every time is even better than the last," Alain murmured, "and yet each time, I think we've found perfection."

Orlando smiled, hiding the bitter pang of impending loss. Alain was a wizard. He would easily live another eighty or ninety years, perhaps more, but that was a blink of the eye for a vampire, and already Orlando dreaded the return to the loneliness he had suffered for so many years. "We're together. For me, that's the definition of perfection."

Alain kissed Orlando, rolling them to the side so they could lie more comfortably. "So, a house in the country," he said after a moment. "Would you really enjoy fixing up an old, tumbledown house just for us?"

"It would be something different," Orlando replied. "I knew a little bit about carpentry before I became a soldier. I've probably forgotten half of it or more by now, but it could be a challenge. Something to keep us busy."

Alain laughed. "You think we'll need something to keep us busy? I'd say we're more likely to need an excuse to get out of all the work Jean and Marcel will find for us to do now that the war's over."

"I thought the war was the work," Orlando countered.

Alain shook his head. "It was, but now we've got a whole new set of challenges ahead as we try to integrate vampires into the rest of society. Not to mention the whole issue of the partnerships and the rest of their effects. We have no idea how far-reaching they'll be, even for partners without an Aveu de Sang. And for the two of us… the possibilities are endless."

If only that were true, Orlando thought bitterly.

"Hey," Alain cajoled when Orlando did not reply the way he had hoped. "We're supposed to be celebrating. We're finally free to live our lives without worrying about Serrier or the war or anything else. We're supposed to be happy."

"I am happy," Orlando insisted resolutely. "Happier than I've ever been. It's just…." He glanced away, unable to meet Alain's eyes, unwilling to put his depressing thoughts into words.

"Nothing will ever separate us," Alain swore silently, guessing the reason for Orlando's silence. "Yes, I'm mortal and nothing can change that, but even death won't take my heart from you. I'll love you forever."

"I'll love you just as long," Orlando swore.

Alain tightened his embrace. "We have years before we have to worry about anything parting us. Rest now. I'll guard your dreams."

Chapter 42

"MESDAMES ET messieurs, it is with much emotion that I stand before you today for the last time as the général of the Milice de Sorcellerie," Marcel said, his voice hoarse as he regarded the press corps he had faced so many times. "As we speak, the Milice is being officially dismantled and its operatives returned to civilian life once again. To those who have served with me these past two years, I say thank you. We owe our survival as a society to your dedication and sacrifice. For those who will be welcoming them back into your offices and your lives, remember what they have gone through and be patient with them. Many of them are wounded in body and spirit. Many of them have suffered great loss. Some of them have also welcomed vampires into their lives, forming partnerships that will extend beyond the Milice and affect them in ways we are only beginning to understand. Those men and women have suffered and sacrificed as well, and they deserve your respect and your open-mindedness. I can't order you to accept them, but I would ask that you give them the same chance you would give any new person of importance in your friends' and colleagues' lives. They have earned that at the very least.

"As I return to private life myself, I begin to feel my age," Marcel continued. "Unlike most of the wizards I commanded during the war, I am not a young man anymore. I've spent the last sixty years in public service to the wizarding community and to France as a whole. I'm tired, mesdames et messieurs. So once the Milice is completely decommissioned, I will be retiring from my other public roles as well. L'ANS will pass into the able hands of a younger generation as we move forward into this new reality where vampires are an acknowledged, valued segment of the magical community and of society as a whole. It gives me great pleasure to introduce to you the new head of l'ANS, whose experience, ingenuity, and dedication will help usher in a new age in the world of magic: Raymond Payet."

As he waited for Raymond to join him, Marcel smothered a surge of impatience. It was barely even noon, and he would have to wait for sundown before he could return to Le Saulnier to continue his conversation from the evening before with Christophe. After today, he would be able to stay as late as the café owner would let them and sleep away the daylight hours in order to be awake again in the evenings. He had worried he would have trouble finding topics of conversation with the old vampire, but their conversation had yet to lag. He hoped it never would.

In the wings, Raymond glanced at Jean for reassurance one last time before stepping onto the dais and joining Marcel at the podium. When the polite applause died down, Raymond focused on the cameras, knowing his true audience was not the journalists assembled in front of him but the people watching at home and the ones who would read about it in the paper the next day. "Thank you, Marcel, for the kind introduction," he began, clearing his throat to be heard more effectively. He and Jean had spent hours preparing for this moment, writing and rewriting his speech, examining every nuance to make sure he said exactly what he wanted to say, nothing more, nothing less.

"Mesdames et messieurs, fellow citizens, I stand before you today greatly humbled by the responsibility placed on my shoulders by one of the greatest wizards, indeed one of the greatest men, alive today," Raymond began. "None of us would be here today to celebrate the end of the war and to look forward to a brighter future had it not been for Marcel Chavinier and the sacrifices he made over the past two years." Hearty applause met his words, bringing a smile to Raymond's face and tears to Marcel's eyes.

When silence returned to the room, Raymond continued. "Today is a new beginning for l'ANS in many different ways. For some years now, l'Association Nationale de Sorcellerie has been synonymous in many minds with wizards. And while we certainly fall within the purview of l'ANS, we represent one small portion of the magical realm. We are doers of magic, calling on an intrinsic ability to create extrinsic effects, but we are hardly the full extent of magical creatures. L'ANS must become more than just a society of wizards. We must become the voice for all magical beings, mortal, immortal, living or undead. We must usher in a new era of equality that acknowledges and celebrates our similarities and our differences.

"Some of you, both here and at home, are asking yourselves right now what you could possibly have in common with some creature of the night, some shapeshifter or faerie or goblin or troll. The answer will vary from person to person, from race to race, but every one of you who has ever married, promising to love your spouse until death do you part, has something in common with one vampire who will have one partner, one lover, one source of blood for as long as that person remains alive. Every one of you who has lost a spouse has something in common with another vampire who buried his Avoué four hundred years ago and still mourns his loss, and with the oldest vampire in Paris who still mourns his Avoué fifteen hundred years later. Every one of you who has held a child you love in your arms has something in common with the werewolves, who celebrate every new birth because they happen so rarely. You may think you have nothing in common with the so-called lesser magical races, but I tell you now: you're wrong. As we move forward, l'ANS has expanded its mission to protect and speak for not only the wizarding community, but the magical community as a whole.

"The alliance that allowed the Milice de Sorcellerie to win the war against Serrier has formally ended, along with the war itself and the Milice, but the need for magic has not disappeared. One of the reasons the alliance was so vital was that it freed wizards to attend again to the necessary task of maintaining the magical equilibrium that allows our world to exist. Imagine our delight then when we discovered that the very making of the alliance contributed far more effectively than anything we wizards could do on our own. The link between vampire and wizard has become more than a military tool. It creates a magical connection in profound, lasting ways that we still do not fully understand. That, too, will be one of the new roles of l'ANS: researching the partnership bonds so that we can use them to their fullest potential and properly prepare any vampire or wizard who wishes to participate for all the repercussions.

"In 1944, we recognized the right of all citizens to vote, regardless of gender, guaranteeing women equal protection under the law. We stand now at another historic moment, having given vampires that same protection. No longer will they be subject to discrimination because of their nature. No longer will they have to hide who they are for fear of being cast out of their homes or having their businesses destroyed. I am not naïve. I know it will take more than just the passing of the equal rights legislation for attitudes to change. However, as the new head of l'ANS, I pledge the full support of the organization—financial, legal, and moral— to seeing that legislation becomes a reality for every vampire, just as we already work tirelessly to address issues related to the wizarding community. Discrimination, in any form, cannot be allowed to exist. We fought a war to keep that very thing from happening. We cannot ignore bigotry from those who do not choose to attempt an overthrow of the government in order to air their grievances.

"As much as we all would like to pretend otherwise, Serrier struck a chord with enough wizards to carry out a rebellion that lasted for two years. While I deplore the methods he used in his attempt to effectuate change, I understand why his propaganda resonated with some wizards. So I say now to those disaffected within society: I welcome dialogue with each and every one of you. The only way we can avoid a repeat of this terrible war is by addressing the underlying reasons behind it. Serrier was a megalomaniac whose madness cost him his life and his reforms. While we are well rid of him, we must be proactive and seek ways to avoid a recurrence, not only of the war, but of the grievances that led to it. Already, I have spoken with the President about revisiting the laws concerning dark magic. Knowledge is never evil. It is how that knowledge is used that determines whether something is good or evil. It is the intent behind a spell that determines whether it is in fact dark magic, not the spell itself.

"Finally, as the new head of l'ANS, I intend to push for an increase in education and outreach services with the intention of avoiding situations like far too many I heard of from wizards who sided with Serrier, where young wizards, teenagers often, were persecuted much as the vampires have been because they were different. Magic is not something to be beaten out of children. Nor is it something to be feared. Rather, it is a gift to be nurtured and trained so that it can be used to the benefit of society. Wizard or vampire, werewolf or faerie, the magical races are a part of this world for a reason. We are a part of this country and it is time everyone recognized that, ourselves included.

"Mesdames et messieurs, thank you for your time and attention. We have a long road ahead of us, but we have taken those first, all important steps. Bonsoir."

The reporters shouted questions after him, but Raymond paid them no attention. He simply walked off the dais, through the wings of the auditorium, and into Jean's waiting arms.

"Whatever the future brings," Jean murmured in Raymond's ear, "I'll always support your position as head of l'ANS. In le Jeu des Cours, in Parlement, within l'ANS, or in the media."

Raymond's joyful laughter echoed off the walls. He had trouble believing how far they had come. Only yesterday, when Marcel had made his announcement to l'ANS, Raymond had received a standing ovation from Alain, Thierry, and the other wizards who had fought with the Milice, a show of support Raymond would not have believed possible a few months ago. And he had the vampires—this vampire—to thank for that. He hooked his arm through Jean's. "Let's go home."

Epilogue

THE ATTENDEES at the funeral began drifting away now that the wizarding rite was complete, Alain's ashes mixing with the soil in his final resting place. Orlando heard voices offering condolences, felt the brush of hands across his shoulders as friends and acquaintances passed by, but he did not move. He had neither eyes nor ears for anything left in this world. Not when Alain was no longer in it.

Silence fell over Père Lachaise finally, the curious and the concerned taking their leave alone or in small groups. He had been surprised at the attendance of many of the foster children he and Alain had sheltered, many of them now elderly themselves, for Alain had lived to an old age, even for a wizard; but as Orlando had always known would happen, the years had taken their toll. Orlando suspected Alain had held on for him far longer than the wizard would have on his own, but nothing could halt the passage of time. Now it remained only to wait for Alain's magic to fade.

"Orlando."

Jean's voice penetrated the fog of grief clouding Orlando's mind, but he did not look up.

"Orlando," Jean repeated, "it's time to go."

Orlando shook his head. "Go ahead if you need to. I know you have responsibilities."

"You need to come inside too," Jean insisted.

"Leave him be, Jean," Sebastien scolded softly. "He's just buried his Avoué. That kind of grief can't be laid to rest in a matter of minutes. We have hours until dawn still, and the night air isn't likely to hurt us."

"But Raymond and Thierry—"

"Are grown men who can decide for themselves if they want to hold vigil with Orlando or not," Raymond interrupted, despite feeling the cold in his old bones. A softly murmured warming spell could take care of that. "Let him grieve, Jean."

Thierry held his silence, his own loss nearly overwhelming, but he forced it aside to focus on his best friend's lover. Alain was gone and nothing would change that, but Orlando was still here and needed his friends more than ever.

The wind picked up, bringing a bittersweet smile to Thierry's face. Alain would never summon a cooling breeze again. The gusts swirled the leaves around the gravestones with a dry crackle, a rush of air circling Orlando's kneeling form. "What's the date?" Orlando asked suddenly.

"October eighteenth," Thierry replied. "Why?"

Orlando did not reply immediately, a soft sob escaping him as tears he could never cry burned his eyes. "It's the anniversary of the night we met," he said finally, voice breaking as he spoke. "I tasted his blood for the first time right here, ninety-six years ago tonight."

"I think he fell in love with you that night," Thierry confided. "I don't know if he ever told you that, but in hindsight, it's as clear as day to me."

Orlando shook his head. "We never talked about it in those terms. He loved me. That's all I needed to know."

They lapsed into silence again for awhile, Orlando's fingers trailing back and forth across the disturbed earth at the foot of the monument l'ANS had erected in Alain's honor. His name was engraved starkly in the dark marble along with the dates of his birth and death. Leaning forward, Orlando traced the letters as well. Alain Magnier. As if the sum of the man's life could be summed up in those two words.

"You were in the seminary, Jean," Orlando said suddenly. "Do you think we damned our souls when we were turned?"

"Of course not," Jean replied immediately, his hand going instinctively to Raymond's back as he sought the comfort of that touch. "Our souls are no more damned by virtue of our nature than any mortal's. We'll answer for our actions just like anyone else, but not for those of our makers in turning us."

"Good," Orlando whispered, fingers digging into the dirt. "Then there's hope for me after all."

"Orlando? What are you planning?"

Finally looking up at his oldest friend, Orlando smiled tremulously. "There's nothing left for me here. I don't have Sebastien's strength. I can't survive hundreds of years of emptiness on the off chance that I might meet someone else and fall in love again. I can't. Alain is the only man I'll ever love." He shook his head when Jean started to interrupt. "Don't tell me I can't be sure of that," he insisted vehemently. "I am sure of it. There wasn't anyone before him and there won't be anyone after. Alain was the air that I breathed and the blood that I drank. He was as much a part of me as any vital organ and without him, I'm only half a man. You'll bury my ashes with his, won't you?"

"Orlando...."

Ignoring Jean's shocked look, Sebastien knelt at Orlando's side, taking his hand gently. "They say time heals all wounds, but it's not true, you know," he agreed. "Some wounds cut too deep to ever be healed. Some bonds go too deep to ever be broken."

"Did you ever think about...?"

"More times than I can count," Sebastien replied immediately.

"Why didn't you?"

"Because before he died, Thibaut made me promise to find another love," Sebastien explained. "I couldn't bring myself to break that promise.

And in my case, he was right. I survived and I found another love, as deep and meaningful as the first. But that was my choice. It doesn't have to be yours." He did not mention that soon he, too, would be facing that inevitable loss, for Thierry was no younger than Alain had been.

"It can't be," Orlando apologized. "I don't want another love. I just want Alain."

"He'll always be alive in your heart," Jean reminded Orlando. "You don't have to do this."

"Yes," Orlando insisted, "I do. I know the magical constraint is gone, but the thought of someone else's blood makes me just as sick now as it did when the Aveu de Sang still bound us. The idea of holding some other body close enough to drink, even impersonally at Sang Froid, makes my flesh crawl. I can't do it, Jean. I won't betray his memory or our love that way. He didn't ask me for the same promise that Thibaut asked for from Sebastien. He knew I couldn't do it. If I were mortal, I'd live out my days waiting for us to be reunited, but I'm not. My days aren't limited by age, so I'll limit them by choice instead. And our souls will find each other and nothing will ever separate us again."

"And if you're wrong?"

"Then I won't suffer for more than a few seconds."

Jean flinched as if struck. "Don't say that."

"Jean, stop," Sebastien chided. "Orlando was man enough to enter an Aveu de Sang. He's man enough to decide how to deal with the consequences. We supported him when people doubted him during the alliance. We owe him our support now."

"Please, Jean," Orlando said softly. "Don't make this any more difficult than it is."

"Difficult? You're asking me to stand by and do nothing as you let yourself be destroyed!"

"No," Orlando said softly, "I'm asking you to hold vigil with me until I can join the man I love for all eternity. I know you don't see it, but be happy for me, Jean. Be happy that I knew a love so strong, so all-consuming that nothing could ever replace it. Be happy that I fell in love with a man I respected as much as I desired. Be happy that I'll finally, truly be at peace."

"Thierry?" Jean appealed to Alain's friend. "You can't tell me Alain would have wanted this."

"Alain wouldn't have asked it, no," Thierry agreed, "but I also know he wouldn't have survived for more than a few days if something had happened to Orlando. Don't you remember what he was like when Orlando went missing during the war?"

"Don't let the last words to pass between you and Orlando be harsh ones," Raymond counseled. "You won't have the chance to make amends later. This is his choice, however hard that is for us. Give him the same respect you always have and abide by his decision."

"Please." Orlando's voice was soft, barely audible over the rustling of the leaves, the wind picking up.

Jean bowed his head in defeat. "I'll stay with you then. You shouldn't have to face the end alone."

"Thank you, Jean."

Jean knelt as well on Orlando's other side, opposite Sebastien, squeezing Orlando's arm in silent support.

The stars wheeled overhead, the hours passing in silent vigil as they waited for dawn. Slowly, the darkness lightened, the harbinger of sunrise.

"I'm scared," Orlando admitted softly as the darkness faded and the sun neared the horizon.

"Say the word and Thierry or Raymond will send you to safety," Jean offered one last time.

Orlando shook his head. "No, this is what I want."

The sun broke free of the horizon. "Good-bye, Jean. Remember me fondly."

Orlando's back arched for a moment, an odd mixture of pain and joy on his face, and then he was gone, his body disintegrating into a pile of ash at Jean's and Sebastien's feet.

Jean collapsed forward onto the ground, unable to bite back his scream of protest. Raymond and Sebastien pulled him into a tight embrace as Thierry buried his hands in the earth next to the pile of ashes. The soil turned, receiving the second offering in less than twelve hours. "Look," he said softly, drawing the attention of the other three men. The marble shimmered, Orlando's name appearing on the stone next to Alain's.

"Did you do that?" Raymond asked.

Thierry shook his head.

The breeze danced around their heads, ruffling their hair. Laughter echoed through their minds, joyous, uninhibited peals of sound.

"I think Alain did."

A Partnership in Blood novel

Perilous
Partnership

By Ariel Tachna

A year after the end of the war that brought them together, Raymond Payet and Jean Bellaiche have found a balance in their relationship: Jean drinks only Raymond's blood; Raymond sleeps only in Jean's bed. The demands of their public roles as president of l'Association Nationale de Sorcellerie and chef de la Cour of the Parisian vampires keep them busy dealing with fallout from the war and the alliance, particularly the not-always-successful partnerships between vampires and wizards.

The foundation of an institute to research and educate wizards and vampires about the implications of the partnership bonds only adds to those responsibilities. When political factions, both vampire and mortal, oppose their leaders' decisions, the stress begins to affect Raymond and Jean's deepening relationship. And when political opposition turns to vandalism and then to violence, they'll have to find a way to reconcile their personal and professional lives before external and internal forces pull them apart.

http://www.dreamspinnerpress.com

Chapter 1

One year later

RAYMOND DUCKED inside his apartment building, cursing the rain that dripped down the back of his neck despite his ensorcelled coat, which was supposed to protect him from the weather. He really needed a coat with a hood.

Either that, or he needed to adjust the wards on his and Jean's apartment to let him displace himself directly inside rather than having to walk through them. He'd been telling himself to do that for over a year, but something always seemed to take precedence. Like convincing the world he didn't have the same megalomaniac tendencies that had possessed Serrier, despite having sided with the dark wizard at the very beginning of the rebellion. He had told Marcel making him head of l'ANS was a mistake, but Marcel had not listened. Raymond was glad of that most days. He enjoyed the work, enjoyed the challenges of addressing all the changes brought about by the alliance and the war and the equal rights legislation. He could have done without the bureaucracy, but he figured it was a part of any job, and at least he had the clout to cut through a lot of it. Not as much as Marcel, but far more than he had expected when he agreed to take the job. It helped that no one knew, even now, exactly what to expect from….

"Jean." The arms around his waist could belong to no other, if only because the wards wouldn't let anyone else through without his express permission. He and Jean had debated that point extensively, but in the end, they'd agreed that making any exception set a precedent for other exceptions, and neither of them could afford to be at risk. Nor did they want people, friend or foe, dropping by at all hours of the day and night. Marcel had maintained a true open-door policy, both at his office and at home, but while Raymond was willing to offer that consideration at work, he had no desire to share the home he and Jean were building with unexpected callers.

"How was your day?" Raymond asked, turning in Jean's embrace. They kept the same hours, having adjusted their schedules to allow both wizards and vampires access to their assistance, but they rarely saw each other for more than a few minutes while they were working unless they scheduled a meeting. The days of spending their entire shift together had ended with the war.

"Long," Jean replied, his lips resting against the side of Raymond's neck, making the wizard hope Jean would ask to feed tonight. It had been three days, and Raymond still missed the intimacy of the near-constant feeding. He knew it had been a product of the situation, not something they could maintain in the long term. That seemed to make no difference to his need, particularly when their schedules kept Jean from feeding every night.

"Mine too," Raymond agreed, arms going around Jean's slender waist, still amazed even after a year at his lover's deceptive appearance. Jean did not look strong enough to hurt a fly, yet Raymond had watched him throw a grown man across the street without straining. He closed his eyes as he breathed in the spicy scent of Jean's cologne, wondering if he dared leave his news until morning. It might not stop Jean from feeding, but it would certainly kill any more romantic thoughts.

Jean sighed, kissing Raymond's neck and lifting his head. "We have a problem."

Raymond echoed his sigh. "I'm guessing it's the same problem that landed on my desk today. Paul Charlot and his partner?"

Jean nodded. "You'd think all our warnings would keep people from forming partnerships unsupervised, but from what Guillemin told me, neither one is happy with the bond."

"Merde," Raymond groaned. "Paul said the same thing. All people need to do is look at Alain and Orlando or Sebastien and Thierry or any of the other partnerships that formed during the war to see there's more to the bond than simply protection from daylight and a boost to the wizard's power."

Jean shrugged. "Vampires see the brand on Alain's neck and look no further than that for an explanation of Orlando's behavior."

"I'll buy that for Orlando and Alain," Raymond allowed, thinking about the instant attraction and almost equally immediate bond between Jean's best friend and Raymond's second-in-command. "The Aveu de Sang puts them in a class by themselves, but Thierry doesn't have a mark. Mathieu doesn't. I don't."

Jean laughed. "You're the president of l'ANS. I'm chef de la Cour. Thierry is a past master at hiding what he feels behind his mask of strategist, and the others aren't nearly as much in the public eye. We see it because we know to look for it and because our ties to the other ex-combatants act as a sort of pass into their confidence. You know what they're feeling without having to be told, and so you see the little signs outsiders miss."

Raymond could see Jean's point. He hardly advertised the fact that he came home every night to the bed and arms of the chef de la Cour. People who knew them realized it, but a wizard who had spent the war anywhere but in Paris might not. Paul, the wizard who had been waiting for him when he arrived at three o'clock that afternoon—he worked from three to one in the morning so he would be available to vampires who were still confined by daylight—had not even been a member of l'ANS during the war, having only come into his magical abilities six months ago. Raymond did not know his partner, Guillemin, to know why the vampire had disregarded all the warnings. Unless the lure of being protected from sunlight by his partner's blood was sufficient to override his common sense. "There's got to be a better way to deal with this."

"There is," Jean reminded him, seeing the concern and frustration on his lover's handsome face. He reached up and smoothed the worry lines from the wizard's forehead, feeling once again the attraction that had little to do with the short dark hair, strong features, and beautiful body and everything to do with the strength of character that lay beneath the surface. "It just keeps taking second place to everything else we're trying to accomplish."

L'Institut Marcel Chavinier. Raymond's dream and the ultimate tribute to his mentor, the man whose brilliance and courage had led to the founding of the alliance and the creation of the partnerships that had won the war and continued to define the lives of so many. "We aren't ready to go forward with it yet."

"Why not?" Jean asked seriously. "What's really holding us back?"

Raymond laughed bitterly. "Time? Money? Curriculum? Faculty? The hundred other things requiring our time?"

Jean nodded his understanding. "I'm not used to being subject to the whims of the Parlement and the rest of the world. I've ruled my own Cour for so long that I'm used to setting my agenda and ignoring everything else. I know it isn't that simple, but we've got two men whose lives have been turned upside down."

"No more or less than ours were a year ago." Raymond had not wanted a partner, much less a lover and had fought the bond between them tooth and nail. Thankfully, he had failed spectacularly.

"No," Jean agreed, "but we were fighting a war, ready to make sacrifices in order to win. For most of us, the resulting partnerships weren't sacrifices at all, but do you really think Adèle wouldn't undo her bond if she could?"

"I know she would," Raymond replied, thinking ruefully of the most heinous case of incompatibility he had witnessed among partners. Paul and Guillemin might not be happy with the far-reaching influences of the bond on their lives, but he doubted it could compare to the kind of misery Adèle and her partner Jude had inflicted on each other before the decommissioning of the Milice de Sorcellerie had allowed her to leave Paris and her partner as well. As far as he knew, they had not seen each other in over a year. The scholar in him wondered if the bond had broken in that time or if it merely lay dormant, waiting for them to be together again. His own need for Jean had in no way lessened, but they lived in constant proximity and Jean fed from him regularly. Even when those feedings did not include making love, they were some of the most intimate moments of Raymond's life. When Jean did make love to him with his body as well as his fangs, nothing else could compare. "Do you think we need to ignore the agenda we've laid out and focus entirely on l'Institut?"

"I think if we don't, we're going to have more and more problems like the one we have now. That isn't fair to our people, yours or mine," Jean clarified. "We've worked hard to establish l'ANS as a voice for wizards, vampires, and other magical creatures alike. We can't afford to lose the faith of our own people, because then we'll have no credibility with anyone else."

Jean's words made sense, a reminder to Raymond that he did not have to navigate the minefield of public life alone. His partner—his lover—was a past master at le jeu des Cours, the subtle vampire game of power and position that governed so much of their interactions with each other. As a chef de la Cour, a leader of the vampires, Jean had lived under constant scrutiny since taking on that role in Paris almost four hundred years earlier. If anyone could help Raymond balance all the demands on his time, it would be Jean. "Then the question is how to explain the change in priorities."

"No, the question is who to leave in charge of other priorities while we focus on l'Institut," Jean corrected. "Alain and Orlando can take over some of the legislative work. Thierry would spell us both into next week if we did that to him, but he can do some of the outreach work you've been doing yourself. He's good with people. Let him take over the education campaign. Fabienne can easily handle the complaints that come in, separating out the ones you need to deal with from the ones anyone in l'ANS can handle. At this point, she probably knows the drill as well as you do."

Raymond had to admit the truth of that statement. His secretary, a paired vampire, had proven herself a genius at organization, handling the bulk of Raymond's correspondence and paperwork with an ease he envied. Being a vampire, she kept him from doing anything that might cause Jean to lose face in le jeu des Cours and helped explain issues relating to vampire culture. Meanwhile, having a partner gave her an equal sensitivity to wizards and their concerns. Her partner spent his working hours with the task force that maintained the equilibrium of the elemental magic. "I could leave Mathieu in charge of the magical balance. He already does all the work. He could make the decisions instead of waiting for me to tell him where to focus."

"That's the spirit," Jean encouraged. "It's getting late. Have you had dinner yet?"

"I had a dinner meeting tonight," Raymond confirmed with a yawn.

"Then it's bedtime," Jean declared. "We'll take tomorrow to look at everything we have going on and decide how to delegate it. By the end of the week, we should be able to devote ourselves completely to l'Institut."

Raymond nodded his agreement. "I need a bath first," he amended. "I couldn't get warm today."

The chill did not bother Jean the way it did mortals, but he was not opposed to having his lover wet and naked.

"I'll join you," he proposed, urging Raymond down the hall into the generous-sized bathroom—generous by Parisian standards, anyway. The white claw foot tub was, like most everything in Jean's apartment, himself included, a remnant of a bygone era, but it was big enough for both men, and the hot water heater was efficient. Jean turned on the taps before turning his attention to his lover, his hands skimming efficiently over Raymond's clothes, buttons and zippers yielding to their expertise. In moments he had his lover naked for his delectation.

Raymond let him, a fact that always warmed Jean's heart, the memory of his partner fighting their bond still vivid in his mind for all that over a year had passed. Raymond's self-mastery was phenomenal, which made the knowledge that he accepted Jean's touch, Jean's bite, all the headier. Jean had not seduced his lover into their relationship, because his lover was proof against such machinations. He was there, in Jean's apartment, Jean's bed, Jean's life, because he had chosen to be. Jean was pretty sure that made him the luckiest man on the planet. His lips lingered on the scar that followed Raymond's spine, a vivid reminder of the past. Raymond would say it was a reminder of his fallibility in falling for Serrier's propaganda at the beginning of the rebellion, l'émeute des Sorciers, as it had come to be called. Jean disagreed, though he knew he would never convince Raymond of his point of view. He saw it instead as a mark of bravery. Despite the scar on his back and all it represented, Raymond had defected, fought against Serrier, and seen him brought low. To Jean's knowledge, only two other wizards alive bore similar marks. The others had met their end in the final battle. As he always did when Jean saw the scar, he traced its length with his tongue. He did not actually expect his saliva to heal that mark as it healed the bites from his feeding, but that did not dissuade him from his ritual. If nothing else, Raymond needed the reminder that Jean did not view the cicatrix as a mark of shame.

Raymond's eyes closed as a gasp escaped his lips, the same reaction he had every time Jean's mouth found the livid line on his back. He kept thinking he would grow accustomed to his lover's insistence on touching his mark of Cain, but even after a year, it still took him aback that anyone would want to lavish attention on his disfigurement. Jean had never hesitated, not from the first time he had seen it, both of them engorged with power from the Piège-Pouvoir they had undertaken to clean up an outburst of wild magic. He shivered as Jean's tongue slid lower, all thought of anything but his lover fleeing in the wake of the hot wet muscle drifting across his buttocks. "I thought we were going to take a bath," he murmured.

"We will," Jean promised, "but I hope that isn't all we're going to do."

Raymond's body reacted predictably, his cock hardening, the rest of him melting with heat. He would have sagged if Jean's hands had not caught him. As it was, his legs trembled as Jean's tongue worked its way into his crease. He leaned forward, bracing his hands on the sink, wondering if this would be the time when Jean's fangs pierced the sensitive skin of his buttocks. He had begged Jean repeatedly to stop protecting him from the feel of his fangs, but the vampire had yet to yield. Jean's lips closed over his entrance, sucking eagerly at his flesh, and Raymond pushed back against him, needing more, deeper, harder. Jean complied as if reading Raymond's mind, his tongue pushing its way inside, hot and agile and driving Raymond wild. His head fell forward onto his hands, little moans escaping his lips. "Jean!"

"In the tub," Jean ordered, pulling back and divesting himself quickly. "Don't worry, I'll take care of you."

Raymond considered begging again, but ultimately he needed a bath—although he was certainly no longer cold! They might as well combine both bath and sex. He stepped into the tub, turning back to watch as Jean's body came the rest of the way into view. Long and slender, he managed to be commanding even when naked, sending a thrill through Raymond as he anticipated giving in to the quietly imposing presence.

Jean joined him in the tub, looming over Raymond's reclining form. Kneeling down so he straddled his lover's hips, he took a moment to stroke his hands down the planes of Raymond's chest, enjoying the way the hard muscles jumped beneath his fingers. When Raymond tipped his head back, Jean leaned down and nipped lightly at the line of the wizard's jaw.

"Please," Raymond whispered.

"You don't have to beg," Jean assured him. "I want it as much as you do."

Raymond doubted that was possible, but protesting gained him nothing. Instead, he let his head fall all the way back against the edge of the tub, offering the full length of his neck for his lover's mark. Jean did not hesitate to accept the offer, his tongue sliding across Raymond's skin before his fangs penetrated, delving deep. Raymond arched up, his body seeking more contact with his lover's.

Jean obliged, bearing down against Raymond's cock, the erotic frottage enough to have both of them moaning. It took only minutes before they were both desperate for release. Jean slipped his hand between their bodies, closing it around both cocks, the additional pressure enough to trigger their mutual climax.

Licking delicately at Raymond's skin, Jean lifted his head and kissed his lover tenderly.

"Did you take enough?" Raymond asked lazily.

"More than enough," Jean assured him. "Let's finish your bath and go to bed. We have a lot to do tomorrow."

Raymond nodded, reaching automatically for the shampoo. He bathed quickly, the lure of lying in bed beside his lover enough to push him past his sex-induced lethargy.

Jean helped him dry off and led him into the bedroom, pushing aside the black brocade curtains that enclosed the four-poster bed. Raymond all but collapsed onto the dark sheets, reaching up and drawing Jean down beside him.

"Sleep well," Jean murmured, giving Raymond a final kiss.

Raymond pulled Jean closer as sleep overtook him, needing the consolation of holding his lover close. Jean moved willingly, watching as the lines of stress and worry slowly faded from Raymond's brow. Smiling, he pressed a light kiss to the corner of his lover's lips and settled in to enjoy the hours spent in his wizard's arms.

Don't miss what happens next in

Covenant in Blood

Sequel to *Alliance in Blood*
Partnership in Blood:
Volume Two

By Ariel Tachna

The wizards and the vampires have forged an alliance based on blood and magic, hoping to turn the tide of the war against the dark wizards. A few wizard-vampire bonds are as successful as Alain Magnier's and Orlando St. Clair's, but some are much less so, leading to arguments, resentment, and outright fights between the allies despite their mutual goals.

Following his best friend Alain's example, Thierry Dumont determinedly forms a partnership with vampire Sebastien Noyer, despite the wizard's discomfort with being so close to a vampire—a man—so soon after his wife's death. But they find that desperation may be the key to forming a covenant that works: Thierry and Sebastien are almost immediately devoted to one another's safety.

With new strength behind it, the Alliance's leaders move to announce its existence to the whole world, hoping to rally support against the dark wizards who threaten to destroy life as they know it. Struggling to find its way in the expanding war, the Alliance discovers that despite its advantages, the partnerships are affecting the balance of magical power in the world, which may be an even bigger threat than the war itself.

The story continues in

Conflict in Blood

Sequel to *Covenant in Blood*
Partnership in Blood:
Volume Three

By Ariel Tachna

As the Alliance wizard-vampire partnerships grow stronger, the dark wizards feel the effects and become increasingly desperate to find enough information to counter them, unaware of the growing strain of the blood-magic bonds on the wizards and vampires alike.

The conflict is spreading. The strife of uncomfortable relationships, both personal and professional, is threatening to tear up the Alliance from the inside, despite the efforts of Alain Magnier and Orlando St. Clair, Thierry Dumont and Sebastien Noyer, and even Raymond Payet and Jean Bellaiche, leader of the Paris vampires, who is fighting to establish a stable covenant with his own partner so he might lead by example.

As the war rages on and heartbreaking casualties mount on both sides, the dark wizards keep searching for clues to understand and counter the strength of the Alliance, while the blood-bound Alliance partners hunt through ancient prejudices and forgotten lore to find an edge that can turn the tide of the war once and for all.

http://www.dreamspinnerpress.com

A Partnership in Blood novel

Reluctant Partnerships

By Ariel Tachna

Thanks to the efforts of Raymond Payet and l'ANS, vampires now have the same legal rights as mortals, and research at l'Institut Marcel Chavinier is focusing on the mysterious partnership bonds between wizards and vampires. But the battle for public opinion rages on. When Detective Adèle Rougier encounters Pascale Auboussu, a shy young woman turned into a vampire against her will, Raymond and Denis Langlois, chef de la Cour nearest the crime, fear a public relations nightmare.

The vampire responsible for Pascale's turning must be brought to justice, but Denis is distracted by an unlikely potential partner—Canadian researcher Martin Delacroix, who is spending a year's sabbatical at l'Institut—and Denis's lingering feelings for his deceased lover prompt him to reject the bond. There's no denying the attraction between them, though, and the allure of companionship is nearly as strong as Denis's grief.

Growing familiarity and yearning for a true mate may induce Adèle and Denis to soften their stances against new partnerships, but Adèle will have to accept a deeper intimacy with Pascale when she has never considered a relationship with a woman, and it will take a near-deadly attack to make Denis admit his most hidden desires. Now he has to hope Martin will be willing to stay.

A Partnership in Blood novel

Lycan Partnership

By Ariel Tachna

By the time the alpha of the Morvan werewolf pack approaches l'Institut Marcel Chavinier for help solving his people's fertility problems, pack numbers have dwindled and the remaining members are desperate. Though the wizards at l'Institut have no experience with werewolves, their lore, or their brand of magic, Raymond agrees to help.

At l'ANS headquarters, Raymond finds Marc Gourlin, a young wizard fascinated with werewolves. Marc agrees to visit the werewolves' home to study their rituals for the source of the problem. But when he arrives, he finds himself distracted by Adenet Silaire, the pack shaman. The attraction between them is powerful, but though Marc suspects he might be Adenet's mate, Adenet rebuffs him. Marc is a man, and Adenet's sense of responsibility will not let him take a male mate when the pack so desperately needs children.

Meanwhile, Jean and Raymond discover the Aveu de Sang allows a vampire's Avoué to calm his inner beast. For Jean and Orlando, this is wonderful news—but it only convinces Thierry how much Sebastien is missing out on because they cannot form an Aveu de Sang. Determined to give his partner everything he can, Thierry sets out to recreate the bond denied them by Sebastien's past.

A Partnership in Blood novel

Partnership Reborn

By Ariel Tachna

All his life, wizard Raphael Tarayaud has dreamed of a vampire—first as a friend, then as a lover. His search for his missing soul mate brings him to the attention of Sebastien Noyer, one of his childhood heroes. While Sebastien isn't his soul mate, he could be the perfect partner for Raphael's best friend Kylian Raffier.

As strange coincidences mount up, Raphael offers his research expertise to try and help Kylian and Sebastien understand what is happening to them, though the more he learns, the less he likes it. But it won't keep him from fighting with everything he has to secure Kylian's future.

When he finally meets Jean Bellaiche, former chef de la Cour and grieving widower, the meeting is disastrous, but Raphael can't let it go. He doesn't stand a chance with Jean—who could compete with the ghost of Raymond Payet?—but nothing can stop him from dreaming.

http://www.dreamspinnerpress.com

ARIEL TACHNA lives outside of Houston with her husband, her daughter and son, and their cat. Before moving there, she traveled all over the world, having fallen in love with both France, where she found her husband, and India, where she dreams of retiring someday. She's bilingual with snippets of four other languages to her credit and is as in love with languages as she is with writing.

Visit Ariel at her website: http://www.arieltachna.com or on Facebook: https://www.facebook.com/ArielTachna, or e-mail her at arieltachna@gmail.com.

THE PATH
ARIEL TACHNA

http://www.dreamspinnerpress.com

Lang Downs Series

ARIEL TACHNA

INHERIT THE SKY

http://www.dreamspinnerpress.com

Lang Downs Series

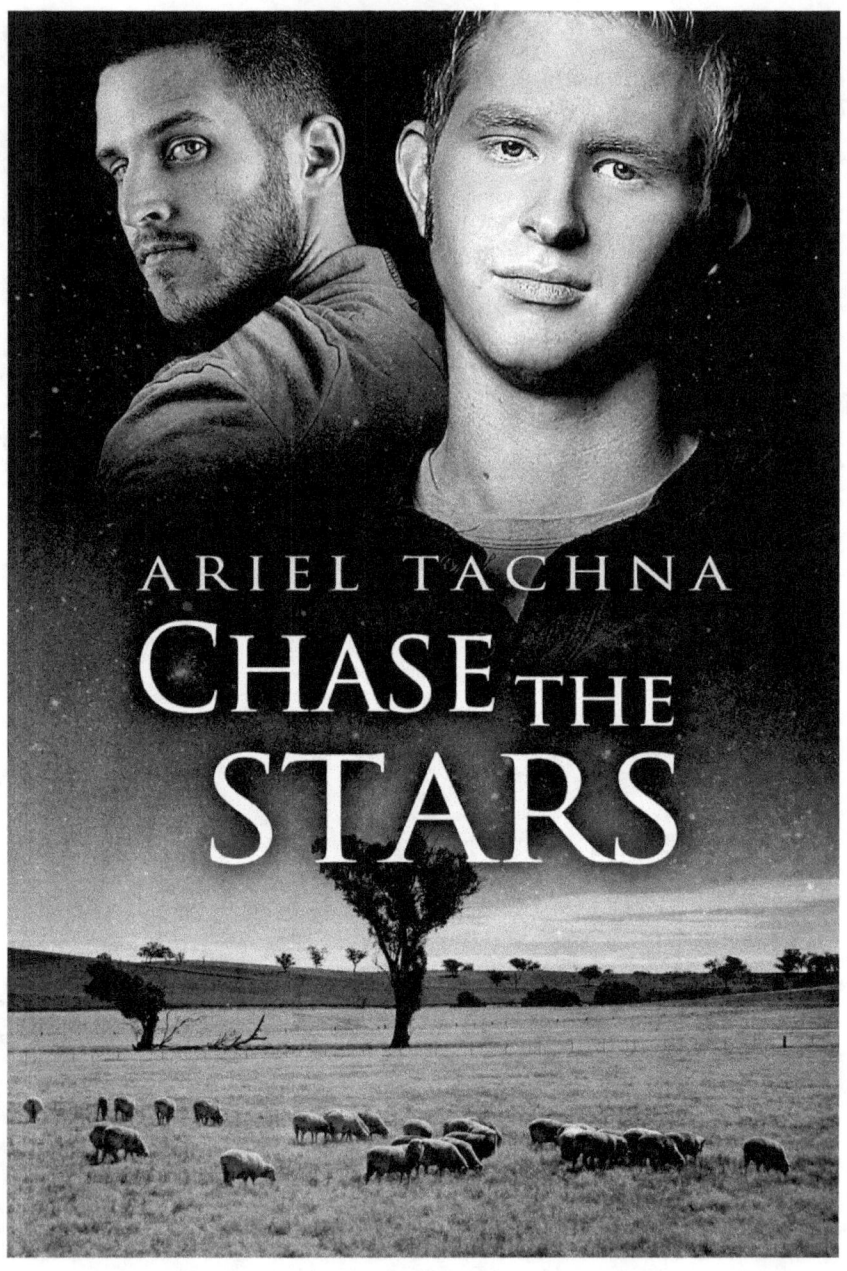

ARIEL TACHNA

CHASE THE
STARS

http://www.dreamspinnerpress.com

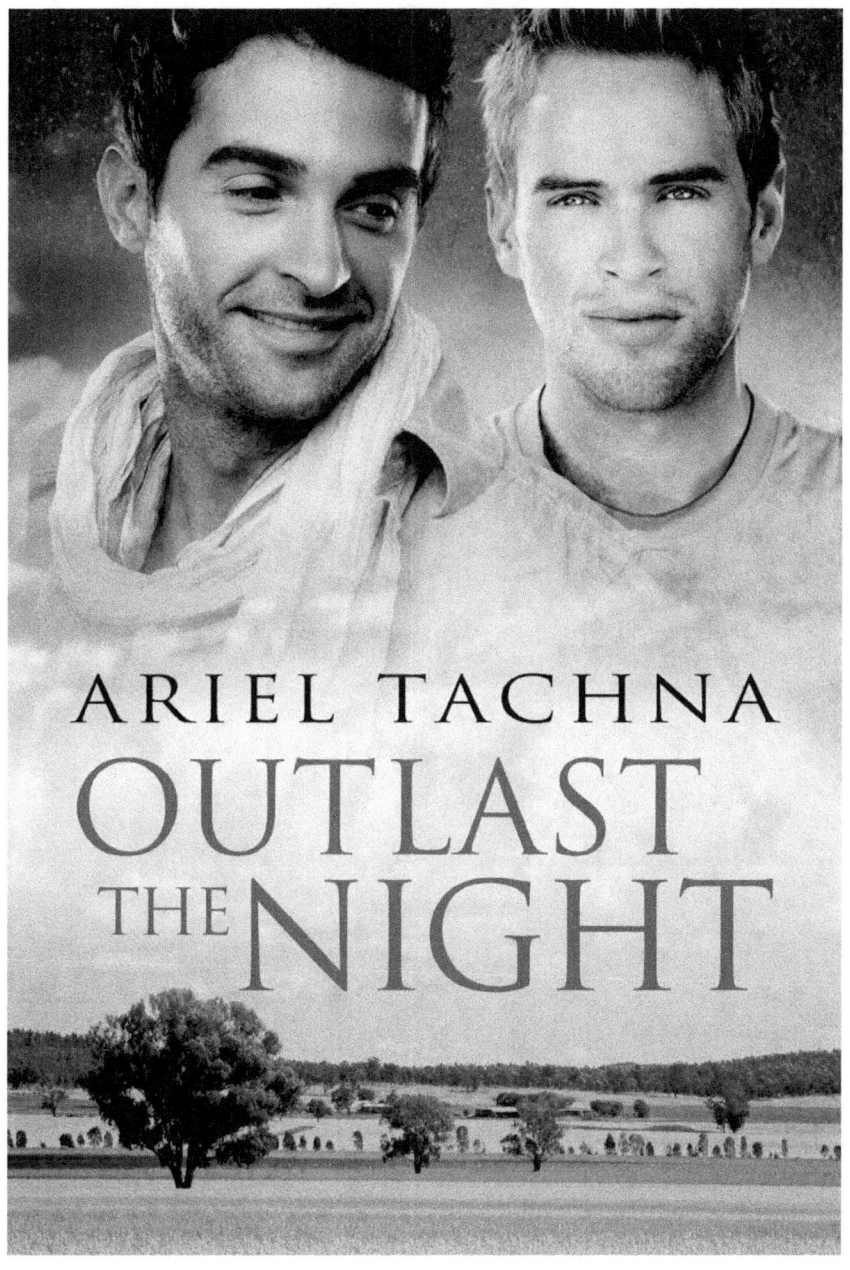

ARIEL TACHNA

OUTLAST
THE NIGHT

http://www.dreamspinnerpress.com

Lang Downs Series

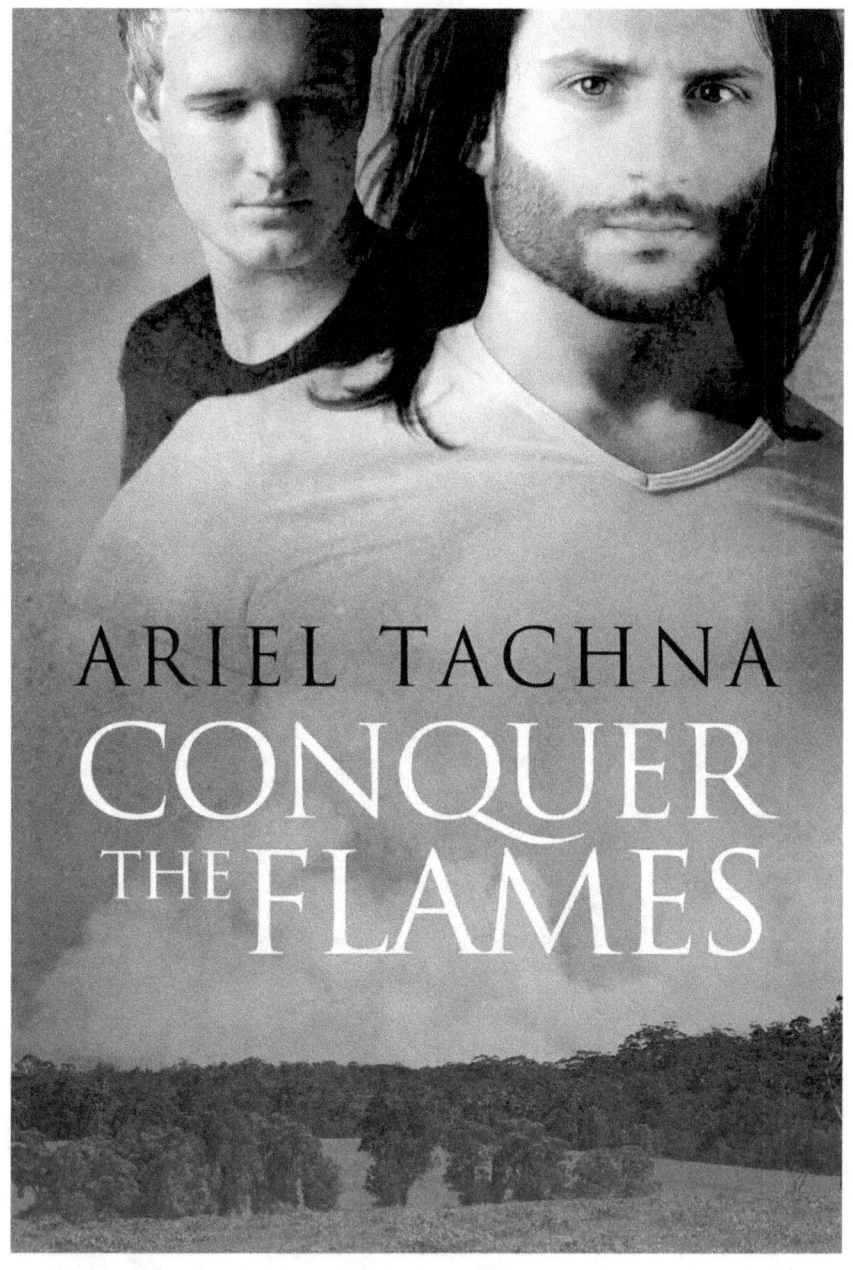

ARIEL TACHNA

CONQUER
THE FLAMES

http://www.dreamspinnerpress.com

Hot Cargo Series

Nicki Bennett and Ariel Tachna

ALL FOR ONE

ARIEL TACHNA

CHÂTEAU
D'ETERNITÉ

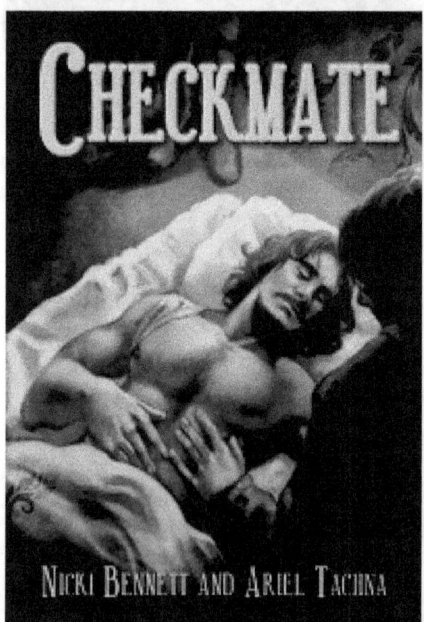

CHECKMATE

Nicki Bennett and Ariel Tachna

ariel tachna
FALLOUT

http://www.dreamspinnerpress.com

http://www.dreamspinnerpress.com

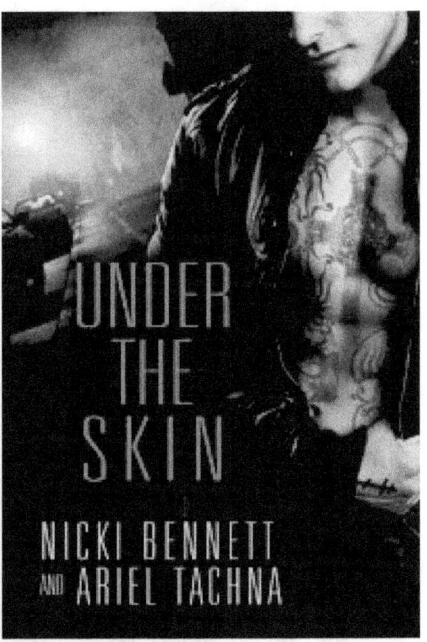

Exploring Limits Series

http://www.dreamspinnerpress.com

Exploring Limits Series

http://www.dreamspinnerpress.com

www.ingramcontent.com/pod-product-compliance
Lightning Source LLC
Chambersburg PA
CBHW070044030726
47506CB00002B/342